NIGHTMARE COUNTRY

NIGHTMARE COUNTRY

Marlys Millhiser

G. P. Putnam's Sons
New York

My thanks to Dr. Dale Howard for his assistance in matters of veterinary medicine, to Ron Sneddon for his patience in explaining the vagaries of light aircraft, to Barbara Steiner for her talents at brain-storming, to Dorothy Sands Beers for her night-blooming cereus, and to Kathleen C. Phillips and Delsa Dee Johnson for using their gifts in helping to prepare the manuscript.

And a special thanks to my family for surviving all those frozen dinners.

For Dorothy Frances Millhiser

Contents

What the sage poets taught by th' heavenly Muse,
Storied of old in high immortal verse
Of dire chimeras and enchanted isles
And rifted rocks whose entrance leads to Hell,—
For such there be, but unbelief is blind.

—John Milton

Chimera—1. A fire-breathing monster represented with the head of a lion, the body of a
goat, and the tail of a serpent. 2. A creation of
the imagination; an impossible and foolish fancy.
3. Biology. An organism, especially a plant,
containing tissues from at least two genetically
distinct parents.

—*The American Heritage Dictionary
of the English Language*

If you can see that the Emperor has no clothes,
science will tell you that it's your eyesight,
religion that the Emperor is not an upstanding
citizen.

—Edward P. Alexander III, *The Key to Life's
Mysteries and the Disharmonies of the Planet*

Prologue

Out of Time

1

Adrian careened through black, through a total absence of light.

She could feel the heating up of her skin, the too rapid shallowness of her breathing, the crush of dread against her chest, the hard prickles in her fingertips as frenzied chemicals called her body to action, rang and buzzed in her ears, threatened upheaval in her stomach.

Even though she knew she'd left that body back on Jerusha's bed.

This was not like the dreaming, the lethargic floating, sinking, surfacing.

And there were "things" in this void with her. Unknown, unseen. She could almost hear them, sensed a whisper of their touch as she hurtled past, and felt sickened at the thought of inevitable collision. Collision with something unbearable. Or something solid enough to shatter what remained of her on impact.

Adrian imagined a scream she had no mouth to utter, imagined it trailing out behind her like a comet in the thick blackness. "Jerusha, please! I don't want to do this experiment. . . ."

No one to hear. Hopeless. Lost. She wanted to die and she wanted to live and she could stand no more. How far she must have traveled from Iron Mountain at this breathless speed.

A wind or air current jerked her suddenly in another direction, a wind that sucked and pulled instead of pushing from behind. Perhaps her body was awaking, drawing her back. Perhaps she was headed home.

The wind turned on her, struck her. Adrian tumbled over and over and down, the wind shrieking by her like it would a diving, crashing airplane. She had only an instant to question how she could hear without ears when light exploded into the darkness. And then colors. Blues and greens shimmered, rushed up at her, blurred, separated, formed shapes, reached for her. . . .

No sensation on impact. Just an abrupt end to her dizzying drop.

This was not home. The blues congealed to ocean, the greens to palm trees. The familiar ingredients of too many dreams. She hovered above clumps of tortured black rock with jags and holes.

An old man knelt among a pile of browned palm fronds, staring in openmouthed astonishment. He wore a khaki-colored shirt-jacket with short sleeves and extra pockets and tabs, like people wore in ancient Tarzan movies. His beard and hair were white and stringy but neatly trimmed, his eyes the color of frost.

A movement at the edge of her consciousness, a sound of human agony or forced breath. Adrian whirled to see a giant in a lacy suit.

"You're an Atlantean," the old man said.

The giant raised his arms. "Primitive in the funnel!"

2

The engineer walked between lines of admiring travelers and stepped into the clean room of the Northern Terminal. Another day, another problem, and all he really wanted was to keep the tiny face of his new granddaughter in mind. He prayed he'd return in time enough to make the preparations for the celebration.

His manager read his thoughts before he'd finished suiting up. "Congratulations. I hope I'm invited to the celebration. But for now," and she reached an arm around his shoulders, "you must concentrate. You're one of the best. I don't know who else to send." She explained the latest in a series of problems tying up the system, gave him a comradely slap on the buttocks as he entered the funnel.

Her demeanor was stern, the problem inscrutable—as most had become recently. "Your father was an implanter and is gone. Revered, honored, but gone before his time. Be careful. Do nothing foolish. You have many details to attend to on your return, with the event of your granddaughter. Just repair whatever-it-is first."

"Just once I wish she'd go out there," he thought in the safety of the shield.

"Sorry about your role in life," his wife would have smugly answered that thought. He tried to concentrate on the problem as the cylinder whirled, but a half-formed dread that all would not go well this trip intruded, and he lifted from the funnel with that mixture of doom and excitement he'd known before. It was the half-knowledge of all whose occupations woo disaster once they are committed to a dangerous mission. The squirmy sensation of regret that it was too late to join the ranks of the safe and the ordinary.

Still, his shock was genuine when the impression of tumbling ceased and he found himself confronted by the old man on the craggy coral beach. And it was some moments before the truth of the situation penetrated his anger, the knowledge that what he'd always known could happen, had.

Visions of loved ones vied with those of colleagues similarly lost to the half-death of time. Now he would discover their fate firsthand, never know his family again. Visions of the Northern Terminal, the respectful glances of those who helped him step into danger when there was a need . . . he'd be only another martyr now to the convenience of others.

"You're an Atlantean." The old man spoke with an unpleasant rasping of voice and movements of mouth showing yellowed teeth, while a foolish jumble of thoughts circled his words.

The prospect of spending eternity with this simple-witted, hairy manbeast overwhelmed the engineer, and a hope that it wasn't too late, that the funnel hadn't closed him out, dissolved even as it formed. He raised his arms and pleaded, "Primitive in the funnel!"

3

The old man's son stood on another beach, and another time, in a cemetery in the sand. Broken pieces of rough-hewn concrete, scattered remnants of plastic flowers, footprints of the living, a salt-scoured picket fence that leaned over the grave of a child.

Thad Alexander had come to Mayan Cay to find his father and had stayed to dream.

> REPORTED MISSING: Edward P. Alexander III, noted adventurer and author, has been reported missing by authorities in the tiny Central American country of Belize, formerly British Honduras. Alexander, the author of many controversial books and articles on . . .

It was one of those "People in the News" things from a wire service and in a newspaper Thad was wadding up to start a fire when the picture of his father caught his eye. An old one off a book jacket. The rest of the article was smeared with animal blood, and he couldn't read it. He hadn't seen the elder Alexander in fourteen years.

Thad squinted against the glitter of sun on sea, had the foolish notion the cemetery was cooking like his brain was cooking, basted in alcohol, stirred by dream. Aromatic spices released in the heat of conch chowder and frying plantain drifted from his father's house to blend with the slimy scent of ocean-born decay.

A man-o'-war bird floated above him on steamy air, wings almost motionless. Its shadow crossed the features of the Virgin Mary on the statue at the head of the grave of Maria Elena Esquivel. The bird's rapier shadow glided over a jagged hole in a sarcophagus, rippled out on the water, where a cross had been cut away in the seaweed.

A dog dug to damp sand in the shade of a tombstone, curled her tawny body into the hole. She stared at him mournfully. He tried to ignore her.

But she felt his pain. It swept over her as he turned toward the house. They almost made contact. She closed her eyes, curled into a tighter ball. She'd never touched thoughts with a human. They were the most guarded of all creatures. The sharp scent of cooking fish cut through her as he slammed the door.

When moonlight softened the sun's heat on the sand and humans slept or laughed and talked in creamy light pools behind windows, the cemetery dog stretched away stiffness and prepared to join others to scavenge fish heads and entrails along the water's edge, tidbits that sea gulls had not already snatched. And scraps left unprotected in backyards and outside hotel kitchens. She shook sand from her coat, perked pointed ears at the yips and snarls of a fight in progress somewhere in the village.

And in the house behind the cemetery, Thad Alexander sank from a fitful sleep into a deep well of dreams. He lay still as death and dreamed of a place he'd never seen when awake—of a ruined mountain pierced by railroad tracks.

I

The Dream Connection

1

The occupants of the Toyota station wagon thought they were never to reach the mountain of Thad Alexander's dream. But Tamara Whelan could see it on the horizon now. She loosened her grip on the wheel and tried to relax the cramp in her back. They'd not met a car since turning off the interstate near Cheyenne. Just treeless hills and telephone wires and fenceposts and power poles rubbed white where cattle had scratched rough hides against them. A windmill etched against unending sky, blades stilled in the torpor of an August afternoon.

Tamara had worried about the frozen foods in the grocery bags, about being stranded with car trouble and no one to ask for help, about the stiff misery of the girl beside her.

Insects in the weeds of roadside ditches made clicking sounds that rattled on wind rushing through open windows, the wind so dry it burned the tissues in their noses, mouths, and throats. Their teeth felt like chalk. Their eyes stung from lack of tears.

A ridge of hills and rock outcropping ahead, as if a giant's fingernail had scratched up a section of the rolling yellow-green and buff prairie. And in the middle, the mountain. Really too low to be called a mountain. Too big for a hill. Ragged, gouged, stained. The color of dead, rusty coffee grounds.

The road dipped to a creek lined with bushes, a bridge, an intersecting road of crushed limestone, and a sign shaped like an arrow. IRON MOUNTAIN.

"We're almost there, Adrian." Tamara turned the station wagon onto crushed limestone. Her daughter didn't bother to answer, but a flush spread over creamy cheeks, fingers clamped over knees as if trying to bruise them. White dust puffed behind the Toyota, rocks pinged against its underbelly.

"At least there's no air pollution out here," Tamara tried again. *Or Seven-Elevens or grocery stores to stock junk food.*

"I'm hungry."

"There's apples in one of the bags in the backseat."

"I don't want apples."

"Now, look, I know this isn't easy, but it's not the end of the world," Tamara said, and then wished she hadn't. Iron Mountain and the settlement at its base, which bore the same name, came into full view. And that's just what it looked like—the end of the world.

She let the Toyota stall and die as it came up to the bridge that recrossed the creek, blocking all traffic because the bridge was one lane. There was no traffic. They sat staring through the glare on the windshield.

"It's fairly isolated, Mrs. Whelan," Mr. Curtis had said, sitting comfortably near his air conditioner in Cheyenne. "But there are only seven students, and the parents aren't demanding. We don't expect you to stay forever. Nobody does. It's a good place to start, gain some experience for your record. Get your feet wet slowly." Mr. Curtis had scratched his scalp with the eraser end of a lead pencil and laughed.

Adrian turned toward her mother, lovely eyes afloat with tears that managed not to drip down her cheeks. "Life isn't fair."

"Oh, baby, this is the only offer I had. And I know how you hate me to repeat the obvious, but we do have to eat. Let's try to make the best of it." *Why do I use the same dumb clichés my mother used?* Tamara coaxed the Toyota into a rumble. *Why am I so tired?*

"If you hadn't left Daddy, we wouldn't be in this mess." Hurt and anger mixed to sound like hate.

"He left me." *How much patience is one parent supposed to have?*

"Daddy wouldn't do that unless you did something awful to him."

"Don't chew on your nails."

"I'm hungry."

Iron Mountain watched as the green Toyota pulled up beside the flagpole at the schoolhouse. The light movement of a curtain here, a shadow hand at a window there. The only sound—a dog barking. The only movement—that of a man in his undershirt bringing a cigarette to his lips. He sat on the low concrete step at his back door. When

Tamara Whelan stepped from her car, he untied the dog and took it into the house.

The quiet now was more empty than peaceful.

The school was an ugly block of formed concrete in a faded mustard color. Its yard and playground were the crushed white limestone of the road leading to Iron Mountain and of its only street. A great mound of the stuff hovered above the school at the rear.

Adrian slouched against a fender. She was taller than her mother. Only the eyes and color and texture of their hair indicated a blood relationship, the hair a soft auburn that curled tightly where it touched perspiring skin. Adrian wore hers long, gathered from the forehead and fastened at the crown with a barrette. Her mother's was short, and it fluffed toward her face.

Tamara stared down an incline at the scattered car bodies lying amidst dried weeds and dulled with a coating of the powdery dust. "Mr. Curtis said there was an apartment here for us."

Two trailer houses connected by a wooden shed supported a monstrous TV antenna. A battered couch leaned against one trailer. In front of it a porcelain bathtub stood on little paw feet. Across the street, a row of four identical triplexes with a gap on the end where there should have been a fifth. All that remained of the latter was a foundation and blackened rubble. The rusty mountain soared behind the lot of them, promising in winter to cut off the sun by three in the afternoon.

"Let's quit and go back to Grandma's."

"Grandma has all she can do to take care of herself and Great-Grandma. We're on our own, and—"

"And we'd better learn to make the best of it," Adrian said in a perfect imitation of her mother's voice.

The street ended just past the school in a metal gate connecting a chain-link fence and a NO TRESPASSING sign. A man in a white shirt and tie, Levi's, and a yellow hard hat stood rolling his sleeves up to his armpits.

Russ Burnham didn't think the women looked like vagrants or hippies. Maybe tourists who got off on the wrong road? Then he caught the tight expression on the smaller one's face. *Oh, shit, not another schoolteacher.* He wanted to turn around and pretend he hadn't seen them, but knew he couldn't get away with it. *Curtis, you son of a bitch!*

"Excuse me, I wonder if you could help us." The smaller woman hurried toward him now, her expression harried and a little frightened, her eyes probing to discover whether he was made of safe or dangerous material. "I'm Tamara Whelan and this is my daughter, Adrian. I'd assumed we were expected, but there doesn't seem to be anyone . . . around."

The Whelans stopped at a safe distance. They were careful people. Both wore the pallor of the East. The daughter was just a kid. A big kid.

"You the new teacher?"

"Yes." Tamara Whelan seemed to relax. "Did Mr. Curtis—?"

"No." He swiped the back of his wrist across the sweat on his forehead and stepped through the gate. "Company provides an apartment. You just have to pay utilities."

Russ nodded toward the brick triplexes with the garish green shingles, blackened around the chimneys from the days when coal was used to heat. He thought of an old family story. A great-great-aunt of his dad's had been torn from her fancy parlor and moved west to a sod hut. She went berserk and killed her baby and herself. A fragile woman, according to family memory.

"Perhaps you'd show it to us, Mr. . . . ." the fragile-looking woman in front of him said.

"Burnham. Russ Burnham." He liked the way sun picked out the copper in their hair. "It's not lush, but better than a sod hut."

"I should hope so. Isn't it unusual for a company to provide housing for a schoolteacher?"

"It's not like we're crowded. B & H is responsible for most of the children here." He led her past the burned-out foundation to the second triplex in the line.

"B & H. That's sugar, isn't it? Mr. Curtis said this was a mining town."

"We mine limestone. Used in the processing of sugar." Why was he always the only one out and about when the teachers showed up? Her next question would be: "Then why is it called Iron Mountain?"

"Why it is it called Iron Mountain if—?"

"Because of the color." *What's Curtis doing sending someone like her out here? Creep's got the brain of a dead gnat.* "But then, he used to be a teacher too."

"What?" Tamara Whelan stopped on the concrete steps up to the chicken-wire fence. "Who?"

"Just talking to myself." *Wait till you've been here awhile, and you'll be doing it.* But he was embarrassed and kicked at the wooden gate. The remaining hinge gave up, and the gate fell into the weeds. He ignored it with a growl. "This one's been altered. Abner Fistler knocked out inner walls. Made three apartments into two. Makes more room for you and Mrs. Fistler. Also gives you three doors instead of two. Made old Kopecky nervous." He stomped up more concrete steps to the porch and tried the front door. Locked.

"Who's old Kopecky?" She probably thought he was crazy. Her daughter had stopped where the gate should have been, not bothering to hide a look of horror. Because of him? Or her new home? Why should he give a damn?

"Last teacher." He walked over to the corner entrance. Locked. A dirty face peered around red brick. Russ grabbed a small arm and pulled it and the body attached into view. "Want you to meet your new teacher. Mrs. Whelan, this is Vinnie Hope."

"Hello, Vinnie." The new teacher smiled uncertainly and took on a whole new look.

"Vinnie, your mom got the key to this place?"

Vinnie snatched a glance at the fat daughter and scurried off through weeds toward the next triplex. Red shorts, tanned stick-legs, tangles in her hair. "Name's Gloria Devine Hope," Russ mumbled for want of something else to say. "That's why we call her Vinnie."

When Deloris Hope arrived with the key, the teacher moved her car across the road and Russ helped them carry in boxes, groceries, luggage, and a stereo. He avoided looking around the place, pushed away memories of the last time he'd entered it, ignored the startled expressions of the Whelans, assumed a brusque attitude to put off questions, and pleaded the excuse of work to get the hell away from there.

A gold brocaded couch and matching armchair sat on a Persian rug in a room with livid aqua walls and grimy ceiling. A small maple dining-room set stood on a floor of chipped institutional-gray tiles. A stove, cupboards, counter, and refrigerator faced into the room from the back wall. A film of chalky dust over all.

Inside cheap metal cupboards and nestled on folded linen cloths—exquisite chinaware, rimmed in gold and decorated with tiny pink and lavender flowers. Goblets of cut crystal, some clear and others shaded in cranberry. Tamara held a delicate teacup in her hand and stared at Deloris. "But I brought my own dishes—"

"Refrigerator's working." Deloris closed the door on an ancient machine with rounded corners. It began to rattle and the floor to vibrate. Faded eyes in a young face looked from the teacup to Tamara and then away. Her blond hair frazzled in that heavily permanented but no-set style, and she looked as if she wore last week's eye makeup. "When you want heat, the thermostat's on the wall by the bathroom door."

"But who furnished this . . . this place?"

"I gotta get back. The baby's got the croupies." Deloris Hope smiled reassuringly and left in a hurry.

That evening, as Tamara selected a linen tablecloth from the maple buffet stuck up against the extra front door, a fire siren ripped the stillness of Iron Mountain for a half-minute and stopped. She and Adrian rushed to the window and pulled aside gritty golden sheers. A screech of tires, a blast of a horn, and four pickup trucks and some cars careened past, laying a cloud of white dust so thick it obliterated the schoolhouse across the road.

"Workers from the mine going home." Tamara wished she could go too. "I didn't think they could all live here."

They dined on fine china and drank from crystal goblets and by candlelight, trying to ignore the horrid barnlike room these treasures inhabited. A thin pretense at celebration. Veal patties, rice with parsley, steamed broccoli, and a tossed salad dressed in lemon juice and herbs.

"What's for dessert?" Adrian's dinner, except for the broccoli, was gone before her mother had finished dishing up.

"Chilled white grapes."

"I'll have ice cream."

"There isn't any. And that broccoli is better warm."

"I know why we're out in this forsaken hole. So you can starve me to death."

"Adrian, the doctor told you if you don't learn to control your weight now, you'll be an obese adult."

"I like being fat."

"No, you don't." The silence grew long and nasty.

"Have you noticed the stains on that wall?" Adrian said finally over the grapes, and pointed to the partition between apartments. "Looks like someone tried to wash off blood and left smears."

"Probably just a moisture stain like we used to get in Columbus."

"What moisture? Bet it hasn't rained here in ten years. My throat's sore from just breathing."

There was no television. Their books were on a train presumably headed for Cheyenne. And none of the mysterious inhabitants of Iron Mountain bothered to pay a call. No hint of sound from the Fistlers on the other side of the stained partition. Tamara thought fondly of the house they'd left in Columbus, and even of their crowded quarters in Iowa City, where they'd lived the last two years with her mother and ancient grandmother while she'd studied to renew a lapsed teaching certificate.

Too tired and dispirited to begin dusting the powdered limestone off everything, they showered and went to bed early. The bathroom had no

tub, only a shower and stool and a cabinet stuffed with gorgeous thick
towels. They had to brush their teeth in the rusting metal sink in the
kitchen.

Tamara crawled into a walnut bedstead that would have brought a
fortune in an antique store. There was just room for it and a matching
dresser and a rocking chair. The dresser's mate was in Adrian's room,
with a valuable iron bedstead. Why would B & H furnish the place so
extravagantly and not spend a penny or so on floors, walls, kitchen, and
bath?

Tamara went to sleep worrying about how they would survive Iron
Mountain even for a school year. But her dreams were of another place,
a place she had never seen. She dreamt of a beach that glistened white
with moonlight, the sand rumpled with footprints. And of a small dog
who crouched in the shadow of a broken block of concrete.

2

Thad Alexander laid scraps of last night's dinner on a stone burial
chamber sunk almost flush with the beach. But the dog waited until he
stooped at the water's edge to rinse his fingers before she crept toward
the food. He remained crouched until the animal had finished. Two
other strays raised noses at the smell of a meal, realized it was already
gone, and went back to sleep.

Thad returned to his father's house, collected fins, snorkel, and mask
and walked in wet sand along the edge of the Caribbean in the shadows
of predawn. There were two hotels on Mayan Cay, one on each side of
the cemetery. He passed the thatched huts of the sleeping Mayapan
Hotel—a yacht and a sport-fishing launch tied up to her dock—and he
was near the end of the village of San Tomas.

Brackish pink traced the sky along the reef. Rows of dead seaweed at
high-water line showed dark against white sand, much of it black and
gooey where the sea had retched man's accidental oil spills and deliber-
ate dumping. It took turpentine to get it off bare feet and forever
marred shoes once attached. A paltry justice.

Thad crawled over the roots of a mangrove tree that fanned out like
fingers to dip into salt water and entered a beach clearing with a shack
on stilts, with chickens running loose.

"Aye, backra, you want boat?" Ramael, the fisherman, sprawled
across wooden steps. "Full of gas. I guide you to special wreck."

The last time Ramael guided him, Thad had taken tanks. When he'd come up from a long dive, Ramael was drunk. They'd run out of gas halfway home.

"I'm just going to snorkel before breakfast. How much for the boat for an hour?"

"One dollar B.H."

The currency printed by the government of Belize was still fondly referred to as "B.H.," for British Honduran, as opposed to the U.S. dollar, and was worth even less. The plump head and shoulders of a young Queen Elizabeth II continued to gaze wistfully from this ex-colony's bills.

Morning sun spread over the clearing, warm and already enervating in steamy air. Thad pushed the old outboard into the water and poled until it was deep enough to lower the motor. Standing and holding the tiller between his legs, he nosed the boat toward the reef line. He drew his T-shirt up over his head, and for the instant his face was covered, the boat swerved. The tiller tried to unbalance him.

When his vision cleared of shirt, a two-masted yacht was moored directly in his path. Although he turned the outboard in plenty of time, shock prickled along the backs of his fingers.

A strip of red at the water line. White hull and superstructure. A strip of blue along the gunwales and outlining portholes. Red life preservers and dinghy. Sails reefed for the night and encased in blue covers. Even a miniature crow's nest. *Ambergris* written in gold across her stern. A man smoking a cigarette stood on her deck.

Thad registered this detail through a fog of reactions. He'd been preoccupied, true, but remembered only an empty sea as far as vision extended before pulling the shirt over his head. The *Ambergris* was simply too large and colorful to be missed. The only explanation was that he'd been so engrossed in thought he'd seen what he expected to see. Yet he could remember thinking of nothing except steering the outboard and removing his T-shirt.

He lined up with the beach and the mangrove tree and began searching for the coral beds he wanted to investigate. He had to backtrack toward the *Ambergris* before he found them, and dropped anchor about forty feet away. The man on the yacht's deck waved. Thad returned the wave, slid into his fins, grabbed mask and snorkel, and slipped over the side, still bothered by his apparent loss of control over his own senses.

He wet down the inside of his mask and paused to watch a slender figure in golden skin and a breath of bikini poise on the *Ambergris'* gunwale and make a clean dive into the water. The man on the deck tossed her a mask and she began to swim and surface-dive minus snorkel or fins. Thad felt his body stirring at the sight.

On the deck of the *Ambergris*, Milt Keller watched his daughter show off her aquatic skills and mused over the sudden appearance of the outboard. He could have sworn he'd been gazing at that very patch of water when the small craft appeared, not arriving along a course from the beach but rather existing or materializing all in an instant.

His daughter's antics drew even closer to the man moving facedown over coral gardens, diving occasionally for a closer look at something on the bottom. Milt was intensely aware of a similar setting and happening, perhaps more than one. But he couldn't place them. Keller had experienced *déjà vu* in his life, but this was different, disturbing, irritating. Like being asked what he'd watched on television the night before and not being able to remember. Or a doctor asking what he'd eaten the day before. . . . Wasn't it yesterday morning Linda'd gone swimming and brought in someone for breakfast? Myrna had made scrambled eggs.

Milt laughed. At least he knew what he'd had for breakfast. And for lunch it was . . . Milt laughed again. Nervously. "Probably fish. Lots of that around these parts."

Pans banged in the galley. He leaned into the hatchway. "Myrna, better put on extra. Linda's swimming in a guest."

"Again?" His wife sounded half-exasperated, half-amused. "Odds it's a male."

"Yeah, but this one's older than usual." Milt was relieved she'd said "again." Curious thing, memory. And aging. But he didn't feel that old. Chalk it up to the good life? Make an appointment for a checkup when he got home? Milt lowered the platform on the stern as the brown head and the silver approached. He reached a hand to help the older man on board and found his hand empty and his clothes wet as both swimmers jumped the gunwale.

"Daddy, this is Thad Alexander." The impish grin of a girl who usually got her way by using surprise tactics. "He hasn't had breakfast either."

"I've already alerted your mother." He shook hands with their guest and looked into eyes colored the gray-white of new ashes. "Milt Keller. Hope Linda gave you the chance to say yes before she hauled you aboard."

"I'm not sure. It all happened so fast." Alexander grinned and caught the towel Linda threw at him before she disappeared down the hatchway. He was as tanned as she, and couldn't have been much over thirty-five.

"Alexander . . . you any relation to the professor on the island?"

"Edward P. III? My dad. And he was no professor."

"Is in my book. Knows more than all those damned eggheads with degrees. Could at least listen to a man before they tar and feather him. I only read his last book. Made sense to me. I mean, hell, he was down here."

As they squeezed around the table, Milt introduced Thad to his wife and son, David, who was civil enough to look up from his *Mad* comic book and smile around a mouthful of braces and scrambled eggs.

"Scrambled eggs again? Didn't we have them yesterday?" Milt filled his coffeecup.

"Did we?" Myrna's forehead puckered in confusion and then cleared. "Oh, well, you always say it's your favorite breakfast. Thad, have some bacon." She never let unimportant things bother her for long.

Thad Alexander's glances were for David now instead of Linda, and the laughter had left his eyes.

"What do you think of the young heir apparent there?" Milt asked.

"Looks like a good boy." Thad looked down at his plate.

"Don't you want to know what he's heir to?" Linda tried to regain some of the attention. "Toilet paper."

"T. P. Maggot's the name," David said, voice lowered in an attempt to sound like Milt. "Toilet paper's the game."

"Oh, honestly." Myrna rolled her eyes. "Can you imagine living with this every day?"

"Daddy's company makes toilet paper," Linda said.

"Companies," Milt corrected her. "And we make other paper products too. But the toilet paper is what pays the bills."

"We live on toilet paper," David said, and then whispered, "Tastes awful."

"God, let's not start the bum-wad jokes. Milt, do something or they'll drive Thad overboard."

"Sorry. Would you believe he's eleven and she just got her B.A. this spring? Tell us about you. Come to dive the Metnál or planning to pick coconuts?"

"I'm looking for my father."

"That shouldn't be hard. Can't go far on Mayan Cay."

"That's what I thought. I made inquiries on the mainland, and I'm going through his things at the house."

"Can't have been gone long. Had a beer with him at the Hotel de Sueños—what, two . . . three days ago? You kids were there. Remember, David, that was the night Roudan played you a game of darts and Linda got sick on Belican?"

"I did not!"

"And he was at that awful party at the Mayapan the night or so before. When you did your T. P. Maggot routine, Milt. And Professor Alexander was wearing his safari outfit."

"And he told me he had a son." Milt was relieved to find his ailing memory returning. "And a grandson in . . . was it Alaska?"

Their guest lowered his toast to the plate. His fingers pushed crumbs into a neat pile. When he looked up, his eyes registered shock. "Are they hiding him somewhere, or is he—?"

"Who's they?"

Some of the color returned to Thad's tan when he inhaled deeply. "Several months ago I read that he was reported missing. I had my own problems and I didn't do anything about it. Then I got a call from his publisher wanting to know what to do with his royalties. With the renewed interest in the Bermuda Triangle, some of his books are back in print. And finally, after a bureaucratic month, I got a letter from the government. Would I please contact the consulate in Belize City? I write, but I hear nothing, so I wind up some affairs in Anchorage and fly to Belize City to find my father presumed dead."

"Can't hide in San Tomas for a day, or even on Mayan Cay. Hell, there's nothing but beach."

"Mr. Keller, he spoke of a son and a grandson in Alaska?"

"Yeah, and just a few days ago. He'd never seen the grandson, and planned to fly up there soon to do just that."

"My son has been dead for over a year." Thad's finger sent a pile of carefully arranged toast crumbs scattering.

Myrna touched his arm. "Maybe the professor didn't want to admit it. Sometimes people can't accept death. Especially a child's. It's too much loss to swallow."

"I've still got Ricky's first baby shoes and his last baseball glove." The roughness marring the voice, the control clamped over the expressions, were intended to save them pain and himself the humiliation of public emotion. But they served only to silence the usual exuberance at the table.

Myrna's hand lingered on Thad's arm. She always let important things bother her.

Milt Keller searched for the right thing to say but couldn't help thinking of how he'd feel if he lost David, and the subject became part of the unspeakable. "Well, there's been some mistake about your father. Hasn't been missing for any months. Couldn't be more than a few days. Somebody's pulling the wool over your eyes, boy."

"Boy" in a broad Texas accent was the last word Thad Alexander heard. It seemed to repeat itself in an echo chamber inside his head. Myrna Keller's warm hand was no longer on his arm. A pressure against his ears.

In the space of a blink, lovely Linda and her family were gone and Thad was sinking underwater, unprepared, not enough air in his lungs. A rubber fin made a lazy descent in front of him.

Thad came up choking, nose and eyes streaming. He swam to the anchored outboard with a strength and speed only terror could produce. Not until he clung to the side of it did he look back.

No *Ambergris* rocked gently inside the reef.

It could not have sunk so swiftly. And if it had, he'd have gone down with it, trapped in the cabin with the Kellers. A lone pelican dove into the water about where he judged the *Ambergris* should have been. Was it possible he'd imagined an entire family? Detail down to the nubby feel of the brown cushions on the bench seats around the table?

Thad pulled himself into Ramael's boat, wanting only to get away from there. But he was still coughing salt water and soon he was vomiting up a breakfast he'd eaten on a red-white-and-blue yacht that didn't exist.

3

Tamara Whelan was awakened just before dawn by a rooster crowing and the bleating of a goat. She vaguely remembered her dreams of a moonlit beach, but the depressing aspect of Iron Mountain hadn't eased with sleep. There was only one help for it. . . .

She slipped into shorts, a loose-fitting blouse, and running shoes. Outside, the dark was fading to light, and the chill on the air surprised her. Following the dull glow of limestone road over the bridge at a slow jog, she shook down all the stiff places in her joints and spine, breathed deeply, watched for uneven ripples in the crushed rock that might turn her ankles, felt intimidated by the lack of other runners on the road. Even in Cheyenne she'd met people running at dawn.

One cranky knee took forever to warm up, but finally all the messages from her body signaled the go-ahead and she straightened her spine, stretched out to the gentle lope that suited her best. Sucking in the clean air, no longer feeling the chill, Tamara concentrated on the gurgles and shwishes of the creek running beside her, the brightening of the sky. She pushed away the traitorous nagging of her mind, which insisted she stop at the first sign of fatigue, knowing it would take a great deal of exertion to make her blood sing above the bleakness of Iron Mountain and to keep her from snapping at Adrian.

Birds awakened in the bushes along the creek. The sun sat on the crest of a hill. The desolate scenery took on the joy of morning. Tamara came to the paved road and turned from the creek, preparing herself for the long upward sweep ahead by thinking of the desertion of Gilbert Whelan. The rage that evoked spurred her to the top without slowing, working its poison out of her system through a patina of sweat.

When the initial shock of Gil's departure had worn off, Tamara began to fall apart, until one of Adrian's teachers pointed out she couldn't do that to her daughter.

Bouts of depression and despair combined with self-loathing made her seek professional counsel. The doctor suggested running, even went running with Tamara. "When you can run this course without stopping to walk in between," she'd said of the impossible, "you will know you can reeducate yourself to support your daughter, that you don't need a man at your side to survive in this world, and that you can be proud of yourself."

Chauffeuring Adrian and her friends, being a Girl Scout leader and secretary of the PTA was no training for this. But one day, after months of trying, Tamara ran the prescribed course without walking.

The rest had hardly been that simple.

Tamara persisted now through the pain of the first fatigue until the surge of a second strength renewed her and her confidence. The sun was warm on her back when she turned around to retrace her steps. She was gasping for air and her legs were threatening revolt when she reached the creek and turned onto crushed limestone. Tamara slowed to walk her tired body in and to cool it off at something like a fourth of a mile from the rusty mountain. It didn't look so hideous under a new sun, looked mysterious and inviting against a clean sky. Now that it wasn't shadowed, she could see patches of grass and weeds on it.

Her breathing and heartbeat returned to normal, new strength replaced the rubbery feeling in her legs. Anticipation of breakfast and the wonder of morning coffee . . . the euphoria after a good run. Iron Mountain was still a dump, but not a sinister one this morning. "Nothing I can't handle."

But back in the apartment, when she tried to fill the coffeepot, there was a great clanking of pipes, a gush of water that slowed to a dripping and then nothing. Poking bread into the toaster, she stared out the window over the sink. Weeds and rubble formed what passed for a backyard, a distance of perhaps twenty feet before the abrupt takeoff of Iron Mountain.

"Nothing I can't handle." She spread margarine on toast with a hint of savagery.

On each end of the duplex a shedlike back porch with wooden steps sagged into the backyard and obstructed the view to either side. In the Whelans' apartment a door off the kitchen led to this porch, where Tamara had already discovered a washer, dryer, and freezer sitting on a concrete floor with a drain.

Splashing water on the same red shorts she'd worn the day before, Vinnie Hope struggled past this enclosure with a pail, and up the wooden steps to the Fistlers' porch.

Tamara was outside waiting for her when she emerged with the pail empty. "Vinnie, we're out of water too. Whom do I see about it?"

"We already sent word up to Russ Burnham. I'll bring you some soon as I feed the chickens and stuff."

Darker brick showed where a third porch had been torn off the middle of the building to make a triplex into a duplex.

"I'd like to meet the Fistlers."

"Only Jerusha lives here, and she's gone. I'm taking care of things."

"Then why carry water into the house?"

"For the plant. Takes lots of water." A shy grin on a pretty but dirty face. Vinnie skipped off.

Roads cut into the side of Iron Mountain. A row of derelict gondola cars rusted on weed-laced tracks near the bottom. And just below them a small goat, jet black with a blaze of white licking up each side like white fire. He sprinted around the fenced yard, tiny hooves meeting beneath him so hard they clicked. A final leap brought him to a standstill on top of a doghouse. Black horizontal pupils in gold-brown irises. Chickens pecked about in another fenced area.

On the other side of the Fistler porch a crumbling sidewalk bordered the building. Two windows here, both densely curtained on the inside with leaves. Elongated leaves with scalloped edges and browned ends. Jerusha Fistler must be a house-plant nut. Tamara stepped closer to peer in at the leaves. They looked thick and waxy and were coated with dust. A faint whooshing sound came from within and then stopped. Through the foliage she could just make out the edge of a bed and a portion of a bare arm lying out of the covers. The whooshing sounded again.

Tamara backed away, embarrassed. Perhaps it had been a roll in the sheet, and not an arm. Sun flashed off a silver propane cylinder at the corner of the house. There were two windows on the front of the apartment, and they too were coated with the long narrow leaves.

"Odd thing to do, grow the same plant in every room," Tamara thought aloud. She looked around to see if anyone had heard, and remembered Russ Burnham talking to himself the day before. But not a soul stirred in Iron Mountain, and she could see it all from where she stood. Sunshine and white dust coated car bodies and weeds, the roofs of two squat clapboard houses across the road by the school, and the double trailer with the gargantuan TV antenna.

Up the road past the gate and the chain-link fence, the company buildings were painted a bright unlikely blue in poor competition with the color of the sky. The aluminum contours of the hopper building towered above water-storage tanks. Its elevator shaft reached diagonally across railroad tracks. And no sound of machinery, of men at work or children at play. If the creek still sang down by the bridge and the birds conversed in the bushes, she couldn't hear them. It was as if sound was swallowed up in so much empty space around and so much cloudless sky above.

"This is no place for the lonely," she said aloud, this time to make sound and to hear it. Tamara slipped into a favorite fantasy, and red bricks and silver propane cylinders blurred in her outer vision. Inner vision focused on a redwood house with a deck, surrounded by pine trees and overlooking a small lake, where Adrian rowed contentedly with a girlfriend. Gil Whelan stood on the deck with her, watching his daughter, the misery in his voice barely suppressed.

"Listen, Tam, give me a chance. I'll make it work. I've admitted the whole thing was a mistake—"

"I'm not sure it was, Gil. Since you left, Adrian and I have discovered we can do very well without you."

"There's someone else."

She checked her earrings and picked up a purse and briefcase off the picnic table. "It's just that I like my freedom. I have responsibilities now, both with Adrian and my career, and I just can't take on any more. That includes you. Stay and have a chat with your daughter. I'm already late to an important meeting."

Tamara had seen a house much like the one in her fantasy in a magazine, the stunning outfit she would have worn that morning in a store window.

The grating screech of monstrous machinery somewhere in the mining area sundered the silence of Iron Mountain and her dream. The red brick and the propane tank snapped into focus. *You'll never be in a position to buy a house like that.* And it would take a lot more than a house to straighten out Adrian. But she felt so good in that dream, so relaxed.

Walking back the way she'd come, Tamara found Vinnie Hope scattering grain in the chicken yard, and the goat butting a wooden fencepost to attract attention. The piquant odor of manure blended with that of earth and sun-scorched vegetation, helped to fill the odd impression of void that seemed to empty Iron Mountain of enough sensations to credit existence. That and the clamor of machinery and the ordinary child doing mundane chores while humming a tune from a TV commercial.

"Vinnie, when will this Jerusha be back?"

"When she wants to be." Vinnie disappeared into the chicken coop.

"But I thought I saw someone inside lying in bed. You sure she's gone, and not sick or something?"

A face appeared at the doorway, partially hidden by stringy curls, the expression less ordinary now, rather too old and knowing. "Don't be like Miss Kopecky. Jerusha don't like snoops."

"Vinnie . . ." But the face was gone, and Tamara waited for the girl to appear with a basket of brown eggs. "I just wanted to be sure she's not lying in there sick and needing help."

"Jerusha can take care of herself. And when she gets back, she'll be hungry." Vinnie held up the basket, which looked like a veteran from last Easter. "And she'll want lots of eggs and peanut butter."

"You *have* checked the bedroom?"

"I've been all over the house since she's gone. She left me in charge."

"Where did she go? Or is that considered snooping?"

"On a search trip. She's a scientist."

What kind of scientist would live in a place like this? "You mean a research trip?"

"Yeah." Vinnie's tone suggested new respect for the teacher. "You know about scientists?"

"Only that they're very hungry when they return from research trips and they like eggs and peanut butter and they raise chickens."

"And goats." Vinnie moved the Easter basket away from the fence, where the little goat was trying to eat it through the wires. His name's Alice."

"Of course." Tamara turned back to the duplex. "I mean . . . why not?"

*   *   *

Adrian awoke in the strange bed, remembering the dream she'd just had of a skinny bird, black with a streak of white along its throat and chest, a long tapering tail. It had glided above her in slow-wheeling silence, seeming never to move spread wings. The wings had a batlike arch about halfway along their incredible length.

She tried to hold on to the musty feeling of sleep, but reality intruded. Thoughts of Iron Mountain seemed to seep through the cracks in the corners of the godawful aqua room. Adrian knew she would die of boredom in a place like this. She would soon know everyone in a community so small. She couldn't for a moment escape to a place where there were strangers who wouldn't mind that she was fat because they wouldn't know her.

Rolling over to face the wall, she pictured a white room and a bed with bars at the sides, bottles with tubes hanging upside down. Herself in the bed, thin, emaciated, cheeks hollow, eyes sunk in dark shadows. "Adrian, hang on, baby. Dad's here. Things are going to be all right now." Gil Whelan leaned over the bars to hold a limp bony hand. He looked up at Adrian's mother on the other side of the bed, his cheeks wet. "Oh, God, Tam, what have we done to her?"

Adrian let herself cry until she heard a door slam. Her mother had probably been out running. Adrian hated to exercise and hated all those superior asses who made such a big deal of doing it. She'd have liked to lie in bed and dream some more, but she was hungry. And breakfast was one of the few times in the day Tamara would let her eat.

Warmed sweet rolls with thick frosting and melting butter, like her grandma made, and foamy hot chocolate would have made Adrian much less depressed, but old goody-two-shoes, small, trim, firm-muscled, old perfect-mother-Whelan would probably serve her an apple and a glass of juice. And a thin slice of birdseed bread, dark and hard, because it was healthy. Adrian wanted to cry some more, but her mother appeared in the doorway.

"Hi, honey. Get dressed and make your bed. I'll fix you some breakfast. And don't flush the toilet. There isn't any water."

Adrian dressed and did not make her bed. The soft-boiled egg, seedy toast, and juice didn't touch bottom. Her stomach still growled when she flopped onto the couch and picked up the book on the coffee table. The only book in the crummy place.

American Heritage Dictionary of the English Language. Not much of a read to help her escape Iron Mountain and make dragging time go away. Bookmarks lodged in various parts of the dictionary, and she absently opened it to the first. It was an F page, and at the bottom of the right-hand margin was a picture of the bird in her dream. But this one had more white on its chest. "Frigate bird, *Fregata minor,*" the caption read. Had the previous tenant marked this page because of the bird, or some other word?

> **Frigate bird.** Any of various tropical sea birds of genus *Fregata*, having long, powerful wings and dark plumage, and characteristically snatching food from other birds in flight. Also called "man-o'-war bird."

"Hey, Mom, do you know anything about frigate birds? I had a dream about one, and there's a bookmark in this . . . Mom?"

Her mother stood with her face and clenched fists against the refrigerator, as if she were going to beat on it. Adrian put down the dictionary and went to her. That niggling anxiety: what does a twelve-year-old do if the one parent present is disabled somehow? "You all right?"

"You could have at least said 'good morning.' "

"I'm sorry." Adrian drew her mother away from the refrigerator and held her. *Why am I always the one who has to be sorry?*

"I can't help this awful place, Adrian. And you treat me like a . . . I'm just doing the best I can."

It was embarrassing to be so much bigger than her mother. *I should be crying on her shoulder. But I'd have to bend over too far.*

"You know I love you," Adrian said. And that was true, even if she found Tamara the most irritating person in the world. "Everything's going to be all right." Adrian wished desperately that that could be true too.

4

Thad Alexander stood in his father's house, tingling where he wasn't numb, the grit of sand between his toes, the *Ambergris* and the Kellers playing like a movie behind his eyes, hunger chewing on a recently emptied stomach. Sea breeze slithered through the slatted windows, warm yet raising chills on his skin. He was sweating, breathing too hard. Fever? Some tropical disease he'd picked up that made him hallucinate? "Bullshit! I was there."

Milt Keller was a balding, good-natured man. Bushy eyebrows. Proud of his family. Slightly absentminded. His daughter, almost too perfect, dark hair, long slender legs, blue eyes . . . or were they hazel? Already the Kellers were fading.

He'd wanted to ask Ramael if he'd seen the *Ambergris*. But the fisherman hadn't been around when Thad returned the outboard.

If his life had not been so bizarre since the shattering of his home, Thad's first reaction would have been to doubt his sanity. Unexplainable things did happen. He had an inkling they always had, but he'd explained them away or ignored them before Ricky's death made him vulnerable. His wife, Molly, had turned to religion. Religion explained everything. Molly'd left him and moved back to San Diego to live with her mother. Molly's mother had all the answers too, and there was no need to question. He hoped they were happy. He wished they'd stop sending him the tracts.

The first story of this house was one room, the kitchen divided from the living room by a waist-high double bookshelf. The inner skeleton of the house's construction was bared, studs and some of the nails exposed. Open joists and beams overhead, all unpainted. The floor—just bare boards of indestructible mahogany from the mainland.

"Good morning, Thaddeus. You want breakfast now?" Rafaela Paz, his father's housekeeper, entered by the screen door. She wore the island uniform for women—two brightly colored pieces of cotton sewn up the sides and ending just above the knees, flat-thonged sandals on her feet.

"Please, and no eggs this morning, huh?" The islanders assumed Yankees ate nothing but eggs or cornflakes for breakfast. "Fix something like you would for Stefano."

Thad stepped out the side door and climbed the exposed stairs to the second floor. Odd arrangement, but practical unless it rained. Rafaela and Stefano Paz's house sat across a courtyard of sand. Both houses were enclosed on all but the cemetery side by the same board fence and shared the same water tank and cistern.

There were two bedrooms upstairs, with a jerry-rigged bathroom tacked onto the back and supported by stilts. Thad showered in a tepid, brackish trickle and could see daylight through the drain at his feet. The sand far below would soak up the water. In Anchorage the whole construction would have spelled poverty. In San Tomas it was sufficient, and sensible on an island where a hurricane wiped the slate clean every twenty years or so and all building began anew. On Mayan Cay, survival was not as hard as it was uncertain.

He brushed away the sour taste of a returned first breakfast and, dizzy with hunger, went downstairs for his second—a tasty mixture of highly seasoned rice and pieces of leftover tortillas fried together. And an orange cut into slices. His plate clean, Thad Alexander leaned back and sipped harsh, invigorating coffee. "Rafaela, have you ever heard of a yacht named *Ambergris?*"

She was at the endless task of sweeping the beach back out the door. The broom paused. She had the face, plump and brown, of one who has seen all but has the strength to remain calm, the patience to remain kind. "You see this boat, Thaddeus?"

"I had breakfast aboard her this morning."

"*Madre mía!*" Rafaela crossed herself and expelled a string of exclamations in Spanish mixed with creole. She started sweeping again.

"You haven't answered my question." But in a way she had. She'd heard of the *Ambergris*. It existed somewhere other than the inside of his head.

"Thaddeus, you talk to Stefano, yes?" It was unlike her to sidestep a question.

Thad stopped the busy broom with his hand. "Why not you?"

"I think Stefano will tell you better." She had to bend her neck way back to look into his face as he stood above her, but she did this without quite meeting his eyes. That was not like her either. "I think this place is not good for you. You should go to your home."

Thad shrugged. "I'll talk to Stefano."

In the cemetery the bitch lay curled in her favorite morning shade. The soggy heat seemed pressurized as he walked next door. Stefano stood between pilings under his house, drawing a line with a thin paintbrush along the wooden model of a fishing trawler.

Placing houses high on pilings was the norm in San Tomas, Thad's father's house more the exception. It served many purposes, but Thad had yet to discover which were originally intended and which had been later perceived as convenient. The obvious one was the hope that a high storm wave would wash under and then recede, leaving the house standing, although any wave worth its salt would surely knock out the pilings and bring down the house.

But it did provide ventilation and the perfect place to dry clothes out of the sun's fading rays and the frequent rains—as his now hung on a nylon rope with those of the Pazes. It also provided storage for canoes and fishing boats and cool shade for work and play.

Stefano Paz had white skin and a military spine, grayed hair and the dignity to carry off the long-sleeved white shirt and dark trousers he always wore. Only his hands showed the effects of tropical sun, his head never outdoors without the incongruous hat—straw, wide at the brim, flat at the crown. Skin color on Mayan Cay, as mixed as the language, ranged from white to black. And hair from black to auburn. But all the eyes were brown. Color had no pecking order here, and no prestige. The only people made fun of were the "backras," those of white skin who cavorted in sun and water until their backs were blistered raw. In the creole-English dialect, "back raw" had become "backra."

"*Buenos días, Señor Paz.*"

"Good morning, Mr. Alexander." Stefano's cultured British made the various slurs of the United States sound uneducated, and it was yet a third language used on the island. He managed to look down his nose at Thad even though he was the shorter of the two. He was as aloof as his wife was endearing. But Thad stepped under the shade of the house, leaned against a piling, and told his story. "Rafaela said I should speak to you."

Heedless of the open paint cans and jar of thinner on the makeshift table before him, Stefano lit a cigarette and kept it between his teeth as he added a red stripe at the trawler's waterline. He kept one eye shut to the smoke crawling up his face and managed to snort derisively around the bobbing cigarette, "Scrambled eggs. . . ."

Stefano Paz put down the brush. "I think, Mr. Alexander, that you should wear a hat when out in the sun."

"What's that supposed to mean?"

"The *Ambergris* vanished two years ago. In a storm."

"Maybe this is a different yacht with the same name."

"Perhaps it is the same *Ambergris* and . . . it just vanished again." The sound of Stefano's laughter bounced fom piling to palm tree and back. Thad was sure it could be heard all over San Tomas.

5

An official from the mainland and the one local policeman, Ramon Carias, had gathered most of Edward P. Alexander's notes and put them in a box, which they handed over to Thad when he arrived on the island. He sat now sorting through them for a mention of the *Ambergris* or the Kellers. They were in no order, and Edward P.'s penmanship was too stylistic to be consistently legible. But it was something to do besides relive the strangest of mornings, or rest and swim and drink —the three great temptations of Mayan Cay.

"Must remember young Ricky's birthday" was scribbled on a list of things to do. Edward P. had never found the time to travel to Anchorage to see his grandson, but a package had always arrived for Rick's birthday, containing some misplaced oddity. A shrunken head when the boy was two, a machete when he was four. Now Ricky was twelve. And would be so always.

Edward P. Alexander III had been an indifferent father, too, dragging Thad and his mother all over the world on his once-famous jaunts. Until Dorothy Alexander, worried about the constant interruption in their child's education, had put her foot down in Anchorage, Alaska. Edward stayed with them long enough to write a book on his adventures in the Klondike and then moved on.

He'd drop in every few years, and when Thad graduated from high school, Edward took him on a trip to the outback of Australia, a sort of sentimental visit to the place where Thad was born—in a tent on an archaeological dig—delivered by his own father.

Thad had seen Edward P. only twice in all the years since. Once at his mother's funeral. And the last time on the day he'd married Molly. Edward's wedding gift to the young couple had been the royalties from his new book, which made a big splash at the reception, where the famous adventurer announced it in his booming voice. After the first year there'd been little in the way of royalties.

The elder Alexander was a showman. He'd caught the people's imagination for a while, been the subject of several early TV documentaries. Scholars put down the theories of a self-educated man who claimed to be an expert on everything, and Thad agreed with them. He considered his father, if not a knowing fraud, at least a genial con man.

He flipped through a three-by-five notebook. "Order new lens cap." "More film." "Write to Pearsons for latest on Mayan hieroglyphs." "Roudan is the key!"

If Thad did find mention of the *Ambergris* or her owners, the note wouldn't make sense. They weren't even dated. Roudan was the key to what?

He picked up another box, containing a manuscript in progress, and took it out to the hammock. The upper story of the house overhung the lower by six feet on the side fronting the beach, and the net hammock was strung between two of the supporting posts set in concrete blocks in the sand. Here Thad had done a great deal of daydreaming, telling himself he was thinking. Now he determined to read his father's words carefully, even attempt to decipher the scribbles in pencil in the margins or between double-spaced type. He'd already skimmed parts of it but hoped a thorough reading would hint at Edward's latest escapade and offer a clue as to what had become of him.

The manuscript consisted of a group of essays, one to a chapter, each relating certain aspects of the places to which Edward had traveled and presumably leading to some central conclusion. And if Thad knew his father, that conclusion would be outlandish. Von Daniken and others had covered similar territory to exhaustion, and he'd have to come up with some new kinky kink to warrant publication.

Thad found himself skimming again. The cenotes in Chichén-Itzá—Mayan ceremonial pools where Edward had dived in a commercial hard-hat suit. Hardships in the unexplored regions of Quintana Roo, where he had lost his way and very nearly his life from starvation and disease. Diving for sunken treasure, for the lost continent of Atlantis. Exploring the famous Blue Hole in the reef off Belize. He'd been imprisoned in Tibet and shipwrecked off Cape Horn.

Next door, Roudan, the bartender and owner of the Hotel de Sueños, laughed in his peculiar high pitch. Thad scratched at the welts left by tiny sand fleas. He was shaded by the porch overhang, but sun drove heavily against a placid sea. He pushed against the house, and the hammock swayed, causing a soft breeze to play across his moist skin. His thumbs left light smudges on the manuscript's margins. Thad dozed . . . and awakened with a thirst that put his father's loony ideas right out of his head. What he needed was a cool Belican. He put away the manuscript and headed for the Hotel de Sueños.

The Mayapan catered to the more affluent, with individual thatched cabanas, a separate bar hut, and a tiny fleet of pleasure craft for deep-sea fishermen or scuba divers. The Hotel de Sueños was locally owned and all of a piece. Bar and dining room on the first floor, double and single rooms on the two remaining floors, with a bathroom at each end of the hallway. It often filled with package tours of schoolteachers from the States, British sailors on R and R, and wandering college students from almost everywhere.

It also had an attic loft with worn-out mattresses on the floor and no bath. This was the stopover home for some on their illegal journey to the Land of Promise. They came from all odd points of South and Central America, spoke various forms of western-hemisphere Spanish, wore crucifixes on slender chains under their shirts, and carried transistor radios that told them of a world they would not have known otherwise because few were able to read. They were already homesick for their families.

Afternoons at the bar of the hotel were more subdued than the evenings, when the men of the village joined the tourists, but for Roudan Perdomo the afternoons were often the most interesting. He could study the tourists and not worry about performing for the locals.

The professor's son came every afternoon to drink Belican. He was as tall as Roudan and as curious behind a quiet, watchful face. But he was not as strong or as clever. Roudan found him intriguing. He already showed the signs of disturbed sleep it had taken his aging father months to reveal. The professor's son came often in the evenings, too, but Roudan had more time to needle him in the afternoons.

"I think what you need is not your father, Meester Alesandro, but a woman," he said now, and watched for signs of worry or at least recognition on a sun-bronzed face born to be pasty white. But the shuttered eyes merely watched him back, reminded Roudan of a dog he'd seen in a picture—a husky with empty eyes that seemed to reflect the light.

Roudan thought of the five men in the loft, weeping over their crucifixes and their memories. Did the professor's son have no memories? "Do you never dream of a woman, Meester Alesandro?"

"Ever hear of the *Ambergris*?" he countered as Roudan slid a brown bottle without label across to him. Beer brewed in a government brewery on the mainland, favored by the locals because of its price and by visitors because Roudan kept it better refrigerated than the Budweiser. Why did people who came here to get warm want their drinks so cold?

"I did hear, backra, of your most interesting breakfast." Roudan turned away, noting the slight quickening in the dulled expression, knowing now just how to twist the knife. He made kissing sounds against the bird cage hanging above the bar, and his parrot clung to the wires so that he could stroke her feathered belly. "You are not the first man invited aboard that ghost ship."

A heat-drugged white couple gravitated from a table in the corner to ask about his Chespita of the flaming colors, and Roudan used their intrusion to irritate the professor's son further. He clapped his hands and whistled, and Chespita sang "Happy Birthday" for the couple.

"Ramael, the fisherman, ate scrambled eggs aboard the *Ambergris* also, Meester Alesandro." Roudan laughed until it hurt the back of his throat as the concrete facade broke into an expression of surprise. He turned away again to the door leading to the dining room, where his assistant still sat at lunch. "Aye, Seferino, come and sing for these nice people, yes?"

Seferino Munoz rose from his meal reluctantly. Three meals a day and the use of a cot in the storeroom behind the kitchen were all the wages he earned at the Hotel de Sueños, and all for the unique privilege of singing for the tourists.

"Sing for us your prison song, mon." Roudan watched Alexander's growing impatience out of the corner of his eye.

Seferino had great dreams of becoming a recording star in the United States and had spent three years in a Mexican prison for trying to cross the border into the land of his dreams without papers. He'd returned home hoping to persuade a U.S. citizen visiting the island to act as his sponsor. But whenever a possible candidate learned that he became completely responsible for any alien under his sponsorship, the offer of help disappeared. Still Seferino dreamed and sang. He sang now a sad song of a young woman brutalized to death in a Mexican prison before her expected child could be born. The white couple looked horrified and then grew misty-eyed.

"And while Ramael, the fisherman, was dining on scrambled eggs," Roudan whispered to the man at the bar while the couple clapped for Seferino and motioned for another round of rum-Cokes, "the *Ambergris* disappeared."

The professor's son grabbed Roudan's wrist and almost made him spill Coke. "When did Ramael eat breakfast on the *Ambergris*? Before the storm or—"

"After she was at the bottom of the sea. The mystery, backra, is where do they get the eggs on the bottom of the sea. Yes?"

In his dreams that night, Thad saw again the rusty mountain. He walked along a chalk-colored road at its base. He knew he was dreaming. He tried hopping, took a few running steps. But the impact of his feet on the road seemed more a remembered response than an actual happening.

He tried to shout and could feel the strain on the muscles of his jaw and neck, yet he made no sound.

But there was sound in the dream. A baby cried in one of the houses to his left, and on the right a door opened and a German shepherd ran out, the tags on his collar jingling. His toenails clicked on the pebbly surface of the road as he crossed in front of Thad to lift a leg on the tire of a Toyota. Nose to the ground, he crossed again to scamper around a blocky concrete building, unaware of the dream walker behind him.

Thad followed to see how much his will could affect his movements. He probably just thought he willed himself to do what his subconscious had already decided he would do anyway.

A flagpole and playground equipment indicated this was a school. A huge mound of crushed rock looked ready to engulf the structure. As the dog brushed past it, a swing creaked and continued to sway after he'd disappeared over an embankment.

Thad pushed at one of the chains of the swing. He thought he felt it against his hand, but couldn't stop the movement or accelerate it. He wandered back across the road. Could he walk through the closed door near the lighted window of the brick building he faced?

He walked up the steps to the porch—clumsily, because he wasn't sure he really felt them beneath him or just thought he did because he could see them and remembered what steps were like. Putting his hands in front of him, expecting a jolt on contacting the door, he started forward and found himself inside the room without having felt the door.

A woman in a terry-cloth robe, with a towel wrapped around her head, stood at the far end of a sparsely furnished room, her ear against a wall as if listening for sound or conversation on the other side. She backed away and ran her fingers along streaks of some kind on the paint. He could hear the faint swish of her robe as she turned.

Thad grimaced, waved his arms to get her attention, but felt himself begin to float away. He had just enough time to notice her preoccupied expression, her obvious ignorance of his presence, before the room and the woman and his awareness disappeared.

6

When water service was restored, Tamara and Adrian cleaned the apartment. They were unable to wash most of the stain from the partition wall.

Then they started on the schoolhouse. Vinnie and Deloris Hope worked with them for a day and lost interest. A Mrs. Hanley, who lived in the clapboard house with the dog, joined them but spent more time gabbing than scrubbing. A plump woman in her sixties who still wore cotton housedresses and changed her apron every day, Mrs. Hanley worried aloud about what they'd do when B & H shut down its operations in Iron Mountain (rumor had it this catastrophe could befall any day) and the state of the world where the "damned Arabs" were allowed to buy up all the land in Wyoming.

Tamara wondered why the Arabs would want it and why the state maintained a school here for so few students, but had to concede a two-and-a-half hour bus ride each way was a lot to ask of young children. She and Mr. Curtis had agreed it would be too much even for Adrian, who'd be the oldest student. At least she'd have full control over the influences on Adrian for a year. They were truly marooned together here. It could tighten their relationship. And without having to pay rent or for any entertainment, she could save most of her meager salary.

The basement of the school had two rooms, one for storage and the other a gymnasium. There were two corresponding classrooms above, with a hall in between. Tamara selected the room used by Miss Ko-pecky the year before, because the other one was coated with more years of grime and its windows looked out on the ugly mountain.

This one had windows on three sides—the ones in back looking directly into the mound of crushed limestone and forever shaded. Adrian stood before the ones at the front of the room, swiping at dust on the books and shelves beneath them. "Mom, you know all that fancy furniture and stuff in our dumpy apartment? It's got to be Miss Kopecky's."

"I'd thought of that too." It was too expensive and personally selected to have been furnished by an impersonal company.

"Then why didn't she take it with her when she left?"

"I've tried to ask Deloris Hope, but she suddenly has to run home to baby whenever I bring it up. I'll have to ask Mrs. Hanley—if I can get a word in edgewise." Tamara realized they were discussing something without arguing. A pleasant lull in the battle. Could she lengthen it? She dropped her gritty rag onto the teacher's desk and leaned back in the chair. A stack of textbooks hid Adrian from view. "Honey, let's take the rest of the day off, pack a picnic lunch, and—"

"Oh . . . gross!"

"What is gross about a picnic? I just thought we might have a—"

"Mother, shut up and come see this." Adrian leaned over a bookcase with her forehead pressed against the window. Tamara joined her.

Across the playground, in front of the attached house trailers, a man bathed in the old-fashioned bathtub that stood on little paw feet. His lips were pursed in a cheerful whistling which they could just hear. Even through panes clouded with dirt, he was amazingly visible.

Sunlight caught brief sparks off water droplets flying from the end of his washcloth. Short dark hair curled to his head and grew all the way down a husky neck. Reaching over the side, he took a tough-bristled toilet-bowl brush, rubbed it across a soap bar, and scrubbed his back.

"God, Mom, stare, why don't you?"

"I just can't believe what I'm seeing. He must be wearing a bathing suit or . . . something."

"No, he's not. I saw him get in."

He pulled the plug and used the brush to clean the sides of the tub while water ran downhill toward the sofa that leaned against a trailer. And then he stood up.

Tamara had hard-boiled some eggs for a casserole but packed them now instead with tomato-and-cucumber sandwiches, carrot and celery sticks, and oranges for a picnic lunch. In less than an hour she was dragging it and her daughter up the creek and away from Iron Mountain, hoping the excursion would take Adrian's mind off the bather. They struggled over hummocky ground in the full glare of the sun, because the short trees and bushes along the creek were too dense. When the stream branched, both rivulets wandered off at a different angle, naked across rolling treeless country.

Tamara chose the branch that led to a rock-strewn hill, expecting to find some shade there, and, without realizing it, slipped into a dream situation in which Adrian became lost in just such a vast place. Gilbert Whelan led a search party, but Tamara went off on her own and found their child where he couldn't, because, as she later told reporters, her mother instinct and basic knowledge of her daughter (which Gil didn't have because of his long separation from her) had told her where to look.

"His name's Augie Mapes. Mrs. Hanley told me."

"What? Who?"

"The faggot in the bathtub."

"Adrian, I want you to forget all about that!" She turned to find the girl sweat-soaked and puffing, her nose and forehead reddening.

"Lock me up in this perverted place. And then not let me talk. Try to tell me what to think or not. I can think whatever I want, and you'd never know." Adrian waited, teeth clenched against the threat of tears.

Tamara felt the cutting edge of panic. It always told her she couldn't cope alone, made her say the wrong things, or kept her from saying the right. "I'm sorry, honey. I want you to be able to talk to me always. It's just that you use certain language to shock me, and it does. Puts me on the defensive." She reached an arm around Adrian's waist. "What else did Mrs. Hanley say about this Augie Mapes?"

"Nothing." Adrian moved off along the creek.

"You see? I try, and you . . . make me feel like a child batterer." Tamara picked up the grocery sack and hurried to catch up. "Your face is getting red. Let me soak some Kleenex in the creek and cool it down."

"Pampering doesn't work anymore." Adrian trudged on.

"I read somewhere that children—I mean young adults—"

"You mean zitzy adolescents."

"That they use foul language to get attention. I must not be giving you enough. I thought maybe we could discuss how I might give more."

"Oh, crap."

They walked on in silence; the hill with the shading rocks seemed to move off ahead of them. When they finally reached it, it was far past lunchtime. Adrian was limping. They had to search out a rock with enough shadow to accommodate two. The juice had heated out of the tomatoes and cucumbers and soaked into the bread so that the sandwiches broke at the touch.

"I can't even make a picnic lunch right," Tamara said with disgust.

Adrian grinned. "Now you sound like me."

But there was ice left in the tea in the thermos, and they managed the sandwiches in soggy lumps and ate everything else she'd brought. After washing hot faces and soaking their feet in the stream, they returned to the shade of the rock to lie with their heads on the grocery sack. They were engulfed in the snappy scent of sage, the buzz of grasshoppers. Drying grasses rustled in the faintest of breezes. They watched a lonely cloud shape and reshape, then split to become two.

"Why do we have to live here?" Adrian asked suddenly.

"Because parents have to support their children."

"You weren't prepared, like you always tell me I should be before I have children."

"Adrian, I was twenty-two when I married, with four years of college, and twenty-three when I had you."

"Then why did you have to go back to school for two years to reprepare to support me, and why did we end up in Iron Mountain?"

Because your father never makes child-support payments. "Because I made the mistake of never practicing my profession. Because I trusted someone else to support us. Don't you ever make that mistake. Don't even think about it."

"There you go, trying to control my thoughts again. Nobody can control somebody else's thinking. Like today on the way here, I couldn't control your daydreaming."

"What are you talking about?"

"You mumble under your breath."

"I do not. Do I? I was just talking to myself." *How can I tell you I was busy heroically saving your life just to show up your father?* "Don't you ever daydream?"

"No."

The next morning Tamara worked up the nerve to visit Mrs. Hanley at the midmorning coffee hour, something that would have been natural in most places but which seemed an affront in this unfriendly settlement.

Agnes Hanley welcomed her with a smile, hot coffee, and sickly bakery sweet rolls that had been in the freezer too long. "You know, this is the first time I've had a visit from the teacher in years." She spread margarine a half-inch thick over the cracked frosting on her roll. Her glasses were the old-fashioned kind with two-toned plastic rims. They looked small and limiting on her large features.

"I would have come sooner, but no one ever visits us, so—"

"Oh, I never go over there. Not since Miss Kopecky died."

"Died? I understood she left. That most of the teachers stayed for a year or two and then moved on because it's so isolated here."

"Miriam Kopecky didn't quite finish out the second school year. The one before, Lomba, stayed one year. 'Course she was Negro and maybe she could live next to Jerusha Fistler and be all right. And Jerusha'd just got here. Jerusha's skin's white, but Kalkasins don't get features like hers."

"Kalkasins?"

"Yeah. White people." Mrs. Hanley wiped her hands on her apron and poured more coffee. "She's not A-rab, but not white neither. I expect you want to know about the people who live here. Well, there's—"

"Wait a minute. Miss Kopecky died? How?"

"In bed. She wasn't young, but she wasn't sick. Had trouble sleeping. Bothered with dreams, you know. Then again, everybody dreams—don't kill 'em. 'Course, like you said, it's isolated here. Me and Fred like it that way. But it's not for everybody. If it was, me and Fred couldn't find a place away from the maddening crowd, could we?" She beamed at this inaccurate literary allusion and opened her mouth to begin again.

Tamara raised her arms above her head. "Wait! Miss Kopecky died in bed? Here? That furniture in our apartment—"

"Hers. Don't feel bad about it. No one claimed it or her body. Must not have had relatives. Anyway, when she came, she threw out what was there. Other people took it in, so it's gone. A regular moving van brought her stuff. Caused lots of excitement."

"What happened to Mr. Fistler?"

"Abner died too."

"In bed?"

"Well, sure. Way most folks go, you know. Had emphysema real bad."

Pausing only to chew rolls and yell out the door at the barking dog chained to the clothesline, Mrs. Hanley rattled on about the inhabitants of Iron Mountain. Tamara was able to filter out only a few details from the welter of disjointed information.

The Hopes, who lived in part of the triplex next to her, were without a father. Deloris, the mother; Vinnie; Bennie, the younger brother; and Ruthie, the baby. Mr. Hope had worked for the company until Ruthie was born and then had deserted. The family stayed on as squatters and lived off welfare. The apartment next to them stood empty, and the

Johnsons occupied the last space in that building. The Baggettes lived in the other clapboard house, and Augie Mapes lived alone in the trailers.

Augie collected junk cars and lived on welfare. Mr. Johnson and Mr. Baggette worked in the mines, and Agnes' husband was the night watchman. Russ Burnham managed the company's operations and lived in one of the blue buildings at the end of the road. The other miners drove in from surrounding ranches or settlements.

So the Hopes supplied two students, the Johnsons one, and the Baggettes two. Two would come from a ranch. That would make the original seven students. Adrian would make it eight and be the oldest. Tamara had a fleeting fantasy of Adrian taking an interest in helping out at the school as a student assistant, blossoming with the new interest and working with her mother instead of against.

"Now, Augie, for eight dollars a month, will let you hook your TV to his antenna. Only channel you can get's Cheyenne, so there's no ghosts from different sets tuned to different programs."

"Does he always bathe outside? In front of a schoolhouse?"

"Absolutely no telling what Augie Mapes will or won't do."

That afternoon Tamara lay down on the bed, in which Miriam Kopecky died, more out of ennui than fatigue. But she slept anyway. A few moments of that luscious tingling as the conscious mind lets go and the body begins to float away. . . .

And she was walking along a narrow street of sand between little wooden houses on stilts. Some white. Others in bright pastels—yellow, green, blue, pink. Some with sand yards enclosed by board fences, lovely flowering bushes and plants growing out of the sand. Clothes hanging to dry under the houses. Poles carrying power lines aloft, looking naked and out-of-place. Footprints in the sand, and dog droppings.

A small black boy, barefoot and in shorts, opened a sagging gate and stepped into the street. She tried to ask him what place this was, but her voice made no sound. He started to walk away, and then turned and ran through her.

Other than surprise, she felt nothing. He disappeared down a side street. A woman swept sand from wooden steps. Her head was capped with tiny pin curls parted so symmetrically that the lines of white scalp between outlined black squares of hair to form a quilt pattern. Tamara could hear the clucking complaint of chickens pecking the earth around an overturned canoe under her house, the slapping of the woman's thonged sandals, and the scratching of her broom as she stepped from one stair to the next. And the unmistakable sound of sea lapping against beach not far away. And a steady thumping, a mechanical background noise . . . and the opening strains of wild rock music, one of Adrian's favorite songs. It introduced a discordant note, throbbed against the buildings to either side and pulsed back against her head, absorbing all the other sounds.

Tamara rose into the air, made helpless swimming motions to keep her balance. She looked down on the woman's pin curls and then on the corrugated-metal roofs of the houses, the gray concrete shell of a roofless building with concrete floor and foot-thick gray partitions. A lean black bird, its wings motionless and as long as her arms, glided by unperturbed at the awful noise and her awkward presence.

The lopsided heads of coconut palms, their fronds parted at the crown and flopping over in all directions. Slashes of violent green jungle. Blue-green glitter of ocean. Improbable white of the beaches. All too intense under the glaring sun, and bulging with the savage pulse of the music.

An inkling that she dreamed. Because this was all impossible if not. But still she fought, panic overriding any direction logic might suggest. She began to tire. The bright scene below dulled to gray and disappeared into a blackness that was even more frightening.

The feel of her weight pressing against Miriam Kopecky's bed brought such a surge of relief that Tamara lay still—almost enjoying the tingles of shock running over her at the sudden cessation of her battle. Sweat under her hair and along the back of her neck made her shiver.

Music from Adrian's stereo glutted the apartment and probably all of Iron Mountain. She'd have to make her daughter turn it down, but for the moment it was comforting just to know the source of the grating noise.

Tamara opened her eyes to Miriam Kopecky's tiny room, and she breathed deeply of the powder-dry air. But she still had the memory impression of tropic air so thick and damp it left a taste on her tongue—the combined taste of sea salt, mixed fragrances of flowering plants, and the overripe greenness of vegetation. Since she'd never been farther south than Kansas, she was impressed at the creativity of her subconscious.

Her imaginary struggles had left her mildly achy, and she stretched. Running her hand through wet hair, she prepared to take on Adrian's love affair with decibels. But her arm fell back on the pillow, and she was drawn into sleep. Against her will. As if she'd been drugged. One moment she was alert and awake, and the next, drifting away again. She fought to waken, but even the music from the stereo began to fade.

The sudden scream of a sea gull. . . . Tamara could smell the sea once more.

7

Several sea gulls screamed, and others kept their bills closed around flapping fish tails or tried to swallow quickly.

The cause of the excitement was a black bird like the one she'd seen before, but larger. Its wingspan must have been seven or eight feet. The gulls scattered at the sight of it, but one luckless victim, tiny in comparison, seemed to vomit from fright in midair. The slimy dinner never reached the water. The black monster caught it without pausing, and floated on to another gull just rising from the water. More sinister than its size, slender shape, and forked tail was the attacking bird's silence in the midst of screaming gulls.

Tamara stood on the beach next to a tall man, who was also watching. He held a hand above his eyes to shield them from the sun. They'd have looked like an ordinary couple if he'd really existed.

She knew she was dreaming now. It would have been intriguing if it weren't so foreign. She had to wake up and get Adrian to turn down the stereo, which Tamara could no longer hear, so she must be very deep in sleep. Fortunate that Jerusha Fistler was away, but still . . .

The man who wasn't real walked off down the beach. She followed, hoping he would do something that would wake her.

The man who wasn't real left footprints and a shadow on the sand. She, who was real, did not.

He bent to pick up a shell, and a white line of skin showed above the rim of his swim trunks, hid again when he straightened. Tamara touched his back, but wasn't sure she felt it or just remembered what a man's back felt like. He obviously felt nothing.

He walked on, and then stopped. She moved in front to look up at him as he stared over her head. It wasn't until she noticed the gloss of skin oils and sweat on his face that she thought she might be overwarm herself. The man was too complete, and at the same time unfamiliar, for the subconscious workings of a dream.

Tamara stepped aside so he wouldn't walk through her as the boy had done, and once more followed him along the beach. It seemed strange to feel in control of her dream. Could she control him? "I command you to stop." Her voice was soundless.

But nothing else was. It was as if her dream was real and she wasn't. Water made a flushing sound as it rolled up onto the beach. Segments of palm fronds shaped like swords clattered against each other in a breeze she couldn't feel.

Ahead of them a tiny house sat on the end of a dock, and beyond that the beach came to a point where trees and their roots grew down into the water. A dugout canoe rounded the point; the man standing in it pushed it along with a pole.

"Ramael!" the man called, and hurried toward the dock to help pull the dugout onto the land beside an outboard with its motor flipped up. He started talking about something called an "ambergris."

Tamara recognized the little building on the end of the dock as an outhouse—a one-holer, by the size of it. A heavy woman rubbed clothes against a washboard under a cabin on stilts and watched the men grimly. A toddler threw a stick, and chickens scattered.

Ramael pointed out to sea, made diving motions, and then spread his arms and shook his head. He was a handsome Latin with pants too tight and his shirttails tied up in front to expose a sleek midriff. He kept calling the other man "Backra."

Tamara had the sensation of too much time passing, and hoped the residents of Iron Mountain hadn't lynched Adrian yet, but when she tried to slap herself awake, there was not enough feeling to provide the needed shock. She attempted to throw herself around on Miriam Kopecky's bed, but merely whirled above the dream sand.

She followed Backra down the beach and through water around the tree roots on the point. He dripped water from the knees down. She made no impression on the water, had no feeling of being wet.

They came to a longer dock, this one painted white, with expensive pleasure boats tied up to it. Identical thatched huts formed a semicircle facing the sea. The well-groomed beach had a long, porched building at the back, and strategically planted palms and flowering bushes.

A group of men sat in deck chairs in the shade. Loud voices in Southern accents. Boisterous laughter. Plastic glasses. One of them waved tentatively at Backra, who merely nodded and looked away, as if shy. Even in a dream she recognized the odd male ritual of the offer of comradeship tinged with challenge. Apparently her companion wasn't up to either.

Statues, crosses, overturned concrete slabs. Tamara followed him through a ruined cemetery, wondering why her imagination would put one on a beach, make it such a wreck. Bizarre, yet familiar from another dream.

Backra entered a house where the porch had no floor. She stood alone outside, staring at a net hammock. She didn't want to be alone. Her hand passed through the door when she tried to open it. That made the dream more of a nightmare.

She put both hands through to the elbow and moved the rest of her through so she could see them.

He was looking down at a round wooden table with thick legs. On it was a plate covered with a paper napkin and three flies. Taking a bottle from an old refrigerator, he uncapped it and sat down to a solitary meal.

She'd always thought that when Gil Whelan ate alone, he'd talk to himself or read. But then, Gil was real.

The dream man emptied the plate and scratched his arms.

Tamara walked through a side door after he'd closed it behind him, and then up an outside staircase, through another door, and into a room with a bed and an open suitcase.

Lying flat on his bed, she rolled around, trying to make herself wake up in the bed in Iron Mountain.

He dropped his swim trunks to the floor and stepped out of them.

"Oh, God, this isn't going to be one of those erotic dreams?" But he didn't hear her, because she couldn't make sound and because he wasn't real.

Tamara jumped off the bed. He just scratched his buttocks and left the room.

"Adrian, please come in here and wake me up!"

With the stereo blaring, she'd be as soundless in Iron Mountain as she was here. But Backra wasn't. She heard the running of a shower. He didn't sing, even whistle. Just the thump of elbows against a wall.

Towel in hand, he returned, making wet footprints on bare wood.

"Mom?"

Tamara jumped at the hand on her shoulder. Backra was clear across the room. Every last inch of him.

"Adrian? Help me wake up. I'm having a nightmare."

"You're already awake or you wouldn't be talking to me."

Backra's bedroom was unpainted, colorless, dim, the light from outside allowed in only in narrow bars through wooden louvers that covered the windows. His light eyes, silvery hair, teeth between parted lips, and the swath of white that had been covered by swim trunks left an imprint on Tamara's brain resembling the negative of a photograph, with light and dark reversed.

Miriam Kopecky's bedroom was dim. Adrian looked more like a shadow than someone in shadow. Wrenched from her dream world to her daughter's, Tamara experienced a sensation of paralysis, while her mind seemed to float without vision, somewhere near the ceiling.

"You've been sacked out all afternoon. I came in twice to see if you were dead." Adrian switched on the light.

The shock of it in her eyes helped Tamara to shove her mind and body back together in time to register Adrian's expression shift from mild concern to anxiety. "You're not sick or anything?"

How old will I be before I can be sick and not feel I've betrayed you? "Just a dream, the longest dream I've ever had."

Dulled and empty, Tamara pulled herself off the bed and into the shower. She thought of Backra. Coffee percolated in the pot when she came into the main room.

"I'm getting dinner tonight." Adrian's look dared her to make fun of the idea.

"Well . . . thank you. That coffee sure smells good. Sleeping in the afternoon always makes my mouth taste like I'd eaten the pillow. Why this sudden interest in cooking?"

"I'm just trying to do something nice. You never question when I do something bad. That you expect. Here." Adrian shoved a cup of half-percolated coffee at her. "Go read the dictionary."

Tamara took her objections to the couch. She would not say that it was only four-thirty and too early for dinner or that Adrian did not know how to cook or that the coffee tasted like hot water with a touch of mud. She picked up the dictionary. "What was the name of that bird you dreamed about?"

"Frigate bird, *Frigater miner* or something. Look under F."

"I think he was in my dream too."

"Big, spooky things. *American Heritage* says they're also called man-o'-war birds because they attack other birds in the air and steal their food."

"That's the one. We must have seen it on TV, and your dream suggested mine."

Dinner was fried eggs, canned pork and beans, canned peaches, peanuts, saltine crackers, and slices of cheddar. Tamara did not mention the calories or the lack of a dark leafy vegetable. "I'll do the dishes, since you made the dinner."

"I'll help." Adrian stared over her mother's head at the stained wall. "You looked so old and . . . tired in there on the bed all afternoon."

"I probably have a few years left." Backra had gray hair, but he didn't look old.

Russ Burnham had called while Tamara slept, to say that Augie had been to Horse Creek, a nearby settlement with a post office, where the mail to Iron Mountain was delivered. He'd left theirs with Russ. They walked up the limestone road after the chalky air had settled from the departing miners.

"Mrs. Hanley says Miss Kopecky is dead," Tamara said. "No one claimed her furniture, and we should use it."

Adrian stopped at the metal gate with the no-trespassing sign and looked over her shoulder. "It's nice stuff. How come none of the poverty types around here latched onto it?"

"Now that you mention it, I wonder too."

They decided to knock on the door of the building with sickly petunias in flowerboxes. One had to work to make the tenacious petunia look that out-of-shape.

Russ invited them in. A portable TV flickered on the counter next to an empty can of Franco-American SpaghettiOs. A loaf of Wonder enriched white bread and a tub of margarine and a can of Coke.

Russ wore his usual white dress shirt and Levi's. He was always polite enough and helpful, yet wary with them. As if closeness would cause the Whelans to become a burden.

Maybe Gil Whelan watched TV while eating alone. But that's the way he'd wanted it. She was surprised to feel a touch of compassion for all men who ate alone.

They left with one letter and a week's worth of advertising circulars and newspapers.

"Nothing from Dad."

"No."

Iron Mountain was dingy with dark. The encampment at its base looked temporary, like something that might heal over, given time.

"There's not going to be anything to do here, Mom."

"How about tomorrow we go into Cheyenne and stock up on groceries for the freezer, buy some paperbacks, and catch a movie?" Tamara pictured the silver-haired Backra riding into Iron Mountain on a horse, looking like a cowboy, and talking like Robert Redford.

Adrian stepped up through weeds to the burned-out foundation.

"Careful. There might be hidden holes or broken glass there."

"Or boogeymen and monsters." Forgetting her concern for her mother's aging state, Adrian stomped across the littered humps that had once been someone's floor. Balancing papers under each arm, she walked the strip of concrete foundation on the other side and then stopped to stare at Jerusha Fistler's vine-covered windows. "Do you ever hear a funny noise over there? Sounds like how Great-Grandma Grace breathes."

"I think it's something mechanical. Probably her refrigerator or—"

"Do you think that's Miss Kopecky's blood on the wall? What they couldn't wash off?"

"Don't be a nit. This place is bad enough without making it scary."

They went around back to say good night to Alice. Adrian was right, if all there was to do in the evening was say good night to a goat. The few inhabitants of Iron Mountain stayed behind lighted windows. Tamara thought of visiting the Hanleys, but he was not as friendly as his wife.

Adrian opened their one letter while Tamara checked the latest grocery ads in the Cheyenne paper. "What's Grandma Louise have to say?"

"The same old glop about her back hurting and having to put Great-Grandma Grace in the nursing home soon and wondering where she'll get the money and baking bread and a new kind of cake recipe and . . ."

Tamara looked up to see her daughter's face redden as she read on silently. "And what?"

"I hate you," Adrian whispered, and water came to her eyes as if she'd been slapped.

Tamara grabbed the letter and scanned her mother's very real worries about her grandmother and money for a nursing home, the details of baking and the neighbor's flower garden, and came to a short paragraph almost thrown in as an afterthought:

> Oh, I talked to Lenore Woodly the other day, and she said her daughter (the one who married the Jarvises' oldest boy, you remember), well, she lives in Columbus and heard that Gil Whelan has remarried. Somebody named Elsie, divorced with two kids. Did you know anything about it? Did he write to Adrian?

8

The moon played light and shadow on the Virgin Mary as she guarded the sleeping Maria Elena Esquivel. Thad stared at the unsteady light of a votive candle, heard the sound of voices from the

Mayapan's compound and the mesmerizing rhythm of the Caribbean retreating, returning, retreating upon the sand. And a tentative whine from the depths of a nearby shadow.

"Sorry, pup, no scraps left tonight." He turned away burdened with guilt. He'd known he shouldn't have started feeding her. But it was as if she talked to him with those wary, limpid eyes. Some night bird shrieked from the bush jungle behind the village of San Tomas. The sea broke white on the reef, sounding distant but appearing nearer in a world washed flat by moonlight.

In the Hotel de Sueños electrical light looked dull and yellow after the moon-dazzle on white coral sand. Roudan Perdomo stood behind the bar, massive and black, a red-and-white cap on his head with "International Harvester" sewn above the bill.

"Ah, the man who dines on the *Ambergris*," he greeted Thad, and broke into a lengthy dialogue in a combination creole-English and Spanish, which sent the local patrons into an uproar of laughter and left the tourists with bewildered looks. Roudan laughed too and pointed at Thad's face. The bartender's speaking voice was a mellow tenor he could use with hypnotic force. But when he laughed, it slipped into a grating soprano that made the listener want to squint his eyes and clamp his teeth shut. The black man's eyes widened until Thad thought the dark iris would swim loose in the yellow-white of the eyeballs.

Thad ignored the challenge and slid onto a solid mahogany stool at the mahogany bar, caught the brown bottle Roudan skimmed along the lacquered surface.

The smells of fishermen, beer, tobacco, onion . . . Thad's face reflected in waves from the bar top. He needed a haircut.

Stefano Paz sat at a table across the room with his two grown sons. No one would have guessed Thad and Stefano had just shared an evening meal. Thad ate dinners with the Pazes in Edward P.'s kitchen, as his father had done, so Rafaela needn't cook twice. But now they sat as if across a gulf. Roudan's was the most popular of the bars, where tourists and islanders mingled. The only islanders in the bar at the Mayapan were those who served behind it.

Roudan slapped open palms on the mahogany bar in time to Seferino Munoz's guitar and the waist-high drum thumped by an island youth, and excited the parrot, whose cage hung next to the Budweiser sign. Always silent unless hanging upside down from the wires of her home, she now upended and began her one song—"Hoppy bur-day to you, hoppy bur-day to you."

Thad tried to visualize his father sitting at the bar in his dramatic sa-

fari suit, probably recounting his adventures to women schoolteachers
or his wild theories to some compatriot like Milt Keller of the *Ambergris*.

Seferino Munoz started in on his hypocrite song, the verses so creole
that only the natives could follow, the chorus so plaintive and clear it
stayed in the visitor's head for days. Something about people who have
it all and want to be your friend. They eat with you and laugh with you
and then go home and don't think about you again, or the way you live.

"Jeeroosha," said Chespita, the parrot, and fixed Thad with a shiny
bead eye as if to ensure that her nonsense be remembered.

"I hypocrite dem," sang Seferino as Thad left the Hotel de Sueños
and walked into the cemetery.

"Hey, turkey?" A man squatted on a sarcophagus near where the little bitch usually lay. "Name's Smith. Bo Smith. B-o —as in Beaure-
gard?" He rose in a clean movement that belied beginning layers of
loose flesh around his middle. "Dixie at the Mayapan said you might be
interested in a dive tomorrow? We need an extra partner. Guides at the
Mayapan're hung up somethin' else on the buddy system. Thought
we'd go down and take a peek at some of the wrecks in the Metnál."

"That's a long way."

"Yeah, well, we thought we'd make a day of it. You know, two-tank
dive, take a lunch and all. We could get in a morning dive, and one in
the afternoon. Hear most of it ain't more'n fifty, sixty feet. Bunch of us
going, but the numbers come out uneven."

The man's stance, his overfamiliarity made Thad bristle. But he had
wanted to dive the Metnál. "I'm not certified."

"Hell, who is? This ain't Florida. Come on over and I'll buy you a
drink." Bo Smith hummed a few bars of "I hypocrite dem" as they
threaded their way through tombstone shadows and the lap of the sea
on the beach kept time with Seferino's high and distant voice.

Floodlights in coconut palms washed the Mayapan's compound free
of moonlight and made it hard on the tourist kids trying to play flashlight tag. The bar was an individual hut with bougainvillea climbing
the walls outside and stuffed sharks the walls inside. A tall woman with
long dark hair and a notebook sat alone in a corner. Her husband too
was to join the "boys from L.A." on the dive. "L.A." stood for lower
Alabama, Smith explained, and introduced Thad to the other "turkeys."
The boys from L.A. took up most of the room and had pulled tables
together for a couple of poker games.

Bermuda shorts, dark socks halfway to the knee, and sandals. Expensive knit shirts. Affable. Competitive. Eyes that laughed and at the
same time held a chilly alertness. They all reminded Thad of younger,

trimmer Milt Kellers. He felt as much an outsider with them as he did with the locals of San Tomas.

"Haven't got the pecking order established yet." Bo Smith nestled in beside Thad with a cozy humor that was beginning to show the liquor. "Just what is it you do, sir?"

"I'm a veterinarian."

"Hey, no shit? Listen up, you turkeys, this man here is a doctor of veterinary medicine."

Dixie Grosswyler, who managed the Mayapan, came in wearing a colorful shapeless thing that reached to the floor. She carried her usual goblet of white wine to ward off drink offers from convivial guests.

"Hey, Miss Dixie, what you drinking there?"

"It's water, can't you see? She's a lapsed fish."

Dixie's smile was tired, her blond Afro a little limp. "Thad, if you're diving with these crazies tomorrow, help the guides keep an eye on them, will you?"

"You worry too much. Besides, I'm the nut who ate scrambled eggs on the *Ambergris*, or hadn't you heard?"

"The Mayapan doesn't need any accidents, Thad."

The cemetery dog whined a soft good night when Thad stepped into his father's house.

"Like hell I'm a veterinarian," he said to the bare-board wall as he prepared for bed. No practice maintained itself for long if the doctor was away. Thad practiced out of an office in his home and performed his surgeries at a nearby clinic. Honald from the clinic was covering for him. And Honald was very good.

Thad could sell the house, split the proceeds with Molly. He could sell his practice, too. With that and savings and what would come to him if his father was proven dead, he could live here and do nothing for a long time, just look forward to his increasingly intriguing dreams.

Later that night Thad dreamed of the same brick building he had before. This time he walked without hesitation through the door. The room was the same; the female in it—different. An overweight girl sat at the table, her eyes and cheeks puffy, a handwritten letter in her hand. She stared over it at some inner torment. Crumpled Kleenex littered the table, and a half-eaten sandwich, so colossal it looked as if she'd emptied the contents of the refrigerator between two slices of bread.

She finally blinked, laid down the letter, and picked up the sandwich. Fresh tears welled as she tipped her head to get her mouth around it. A slice of tomato, smeared with mayonnaise, slipped out the other end.

*　　*　　*

The cemetery dog was not in her usual place the next morning, and Thad walked around the burial ground at the sea's edge looking for her. Finally he laid the breakfast in the sandy hole hollowed out by her body and went back for his father's extra mask and snorkel and the top half of a wet suit. When he came out, two other dogs were fighting over her food. Had something happened to her in the night?

On the dock in front of the Mayapan, Stefano Paz's sons carried air tanks to the dive boat, an open craft with shelf seating rimming the gunwales and wooden boxlike affairs running down the center with holes to hold the tanks safely in place. Everything else was open deck, already littered with masks, fins, wet suits, Styrofoam coolers, picnic hampers, and two watermelons.

"The iceman cometh," said one of the men softly to Bo Smith, and Thad was surprised to find them looking at him.

"Hey, turkey, we got you air. Need anything else?"

"Fins. Tens. Lost mine having breakfast."

"Teach you to eat with frogs. Can you outfit him, Eliseo?"

Both the Pazes were grinning at the breakfast remark. But Thad got his fins, and the boat soon filled. The only woman aboard was the lady with the notebook, introduced to him as Martha Durwent. Her husband, Greg, sat between two of the boys from lower Alabama. She was the only other one who looked out-of-place, so he sat beside her.

Two girls called from the beach, and running and giggling, carried a giant crock covered with aluminum foil. They managed to shove the crock into the hands of the divers before the boat swung away.

Bo lifted a corner of foil and made a face. "Potato salad? In the Caribbean?"

One cooler harvested bottles of beer before the boat got to the reef. Thad thought of all the warnings he'd heard about drinking and diving being more dangerous than drinking and driving. But he'd rarely come across a harder-drinking group than American sport divers on vacation. Maybe Dixie had reason to worry.

The only cigarettes aboard were lit by Martha and the two Pazes.

Aulalio Paz stood at the rear of the boat, his feet to either side of the rudder, a four-foot horizontal pipe about two inches off the floor. His eyes searched out coral landmarks and passages in the shallow lagoon. His brother, Eliseo, worked the engines up front. Barrel-chested men with short legs and protruding, sagging stomachs. The only sign of Stefano in them was their perfect teeth.

Aulalio swayed back and forth as he guided the boat between his ankles. Behind him Mayan Cay looked like a jeweled paradise by Walt Disney. Thad wondered how it looked in a hurricane. Martha Durwent shivered as if she'd heard his thought. She turned toward the surf break-ing on the reef ahead of them. Foam fingers crawling into the lagoon were all that was left of the broken sea.

The dive boat shuddered as it entered a narrow channel, rose to crest the first roller in the real ocean, and swooped down to spill spray across the divers before rising for the next swell.

Martha closed a wet notebook. "I knew I shouldn't have come. But they"—her gesture included all the occupants of the boat—"made it into some kind of challenge between the sexes."

Thad was tired of having to feel sorry for every third woman he met. "What is it you write in there?" He tapped the notebook.

"I'm taking notes for a novel." Her sunglasses tilted as if she expected him to laugh.

"Hey, Doc?" Bo Smith and three beers wove between a watermelon and a pile of diving gear. There was always one in a crowd who took pity on outsiders. Bo handed them each a bottle. "Dixie told us about your daddy? Hope you find him one way or the other. Hell not know-ing." He drew on his beer and then held it away to look at it. "Can't get nothin' cold down here. Sorry about the uh . . . the other, too."

"The other" meaning Ricky. Funny how people could discuss any-thing but that.

"Now, Martha, honey, don't look so glum. We'll bring you up a body for your book."

She was trying to hold the notebook out of the spray and keep the beer from sloshing out of the bottle as the boat dipped and rolled. The others were taking bets on how long the watermelons could tumble from stern to bow before breaking up, lifting their feet off the deck, moving coolers, laughing, shouting.

"These boys do have fun, don't they? You two are going to have fun too, just wait. No fair kicking it there, Abrams. Damn cheat!"

The Pazes just grinned. They'd have some great tales to tell at Rou-dan's tonight. Mayan Cay was out of sight. The little boat was alone on a bright sun-washed sea. But there were clouds on the horizon.

"Dixie tells me that the Metnál is supposed to be Mayan for 'grave-yard.'" Bo nodded solemnly. "Bound to be some bodies for Martha's book."

9

Sun streaks pierced water to illuminate one end of a metal pontoon tube and a giant anchor leaning upright against it, the anchor crusted onto the pontoon by coral growth.

Sounds. The gurgled exhalation of air bubbles from Thad's regulator. The high-pitched but subtle ringing in his ears as the ocean enclosed him with the sounds in his head. A distant roar that could be sea or the air trapped in his ears. Despite the combination of these minor sounds, it seemed a silent, eerie world underwater.

The skin on the inside of his thighs felt the chill change to cold as he and his diving partner, Harry, who owned a "slew" of bakeries, descended toward the wreck on the bottom, the pitch of the sound of their bubbles rising as they sank. Harry was fast on his way to becoming bald, and he kept the few remaining hairs long. They waved in the water like fan coral.

This area of the Metnál had odd-shaped coral heads that soared in mountain cliffs from the ocean floor and broad valleys of sea grass interspersed with barren patches of sand or what resembled piles of volcanic rock, but were instead coral clumps. The Metnál was known for the wrecked ships that littered its coral canyons. Ships of almost every age in history. No one had found the Spanish galleons filled with golden plunder known to be in these waters, but Thad had read recently of salvage crews bringing up pieces of what authorities thought to be a Mayan galley or coastal trader blown off course and out to sea.

What was left of the giant pontoon boat lay in a meadow of sea grass, one end in sun and one in the shadow of a coral cliff.

A blue parrot fish grazed on coral at the edge of a gaping hole in the pontoon. It twined away into the blackness of the hole as they drew closer. Light streaks highlighted waving chartreuse plant blades around the craft, tiny fish darting among them.

Another diver floated down a light streak, and Thad thought of a peculiarly dressed angel descending a shimmery ladder from the skies. And that, for some reason, made him think of the *Ambergris*. Wouldn't it be strange if he came across a sunken yacht by that name somewhere in the Metnál? The skeletal Kellers sitting around the breakfast table?

Wrecked and tangled girders, twisted metal ladders, and coral were about all that connected the two pontoons now. All but an overturned farm tractor, which Thad guessed to be of World War II vintage, had been salvaged. Two of the boys from L.A. were trying to turn a tractor wheel, but it was stuck fast.

Had Edward P. Alexander III been here? The name Metnál alone would lure an adventurer like Edward P.

Maybe it was blood, heredity. Maybe that was what raised the gooseflesh on Edward P. Alexander III's son as he followed his diving buddy along the sunken hulk, feeling the cold draft in the water over the hole in the pontoon, seeing shadow fish flit about in its dark interior. They came to the entrance in the coral canyon at the rear of the wreck, entered it. Thad wondered what it would feel like to die of suffocation. How hard would he struggle? Would he pray?

Fish. Different colors and shapes for different strata. The bottom of this canyon was too deep for the eyes and light to fathom, but Thad had the impression of marine creatures he could not imagine rising to marvel at him, as a strange creature above. At the upper levels he saw the fish he'd seen within the reef. The bright yellow fish with black fins and black puckered "kissing" lips. The fish with markings resembling eyes near their tails that made them appear to swim backward.

An instant of cold as a shadow passed over them, and they looked up to see a huge eagle ray "fly" sinuously overhead with a graceful rippling. The canyon became increasingly populated, but Harry turned, pointed to his dive watch, and gave a thumbs-up sign. Thad followed him back the way they'd come. They'd almost reached the end of the canyon when the current—which was ever trying to drive him against coral walls—lifted him suddenly over Harry, out into the open sea valley, and into a group of barracudas. They seemed as startled as he by the odd slamming noise and the new violence of the current—thrown against him one moment, swimming into him the next. Their slender bodies felt cool and dry against his bare legs, while the jacket of his father's wet suit felt clammy.

Harry-the-baker shot from the canyon as some of the barracudas appeared to be sucked into it lower down. Bizarre. As if there were two currents, one on top of the other and going in opposite directions, the one beneath a powerful undertow that Thad and the fish struggled to keep away from. Coral heads tumbled from canyon rims, expelling debris that looked like dust but was really tiny marine life and trapped air bubbles, much like skyscrapers might crumble in a disaster film. A vibration and a pressure in the water.

Harry's face mask began to fill with blood.

Thad looked around for help but saw only rubber fins and air bubbles heading for the surface. Harry pulled off his mask to let the blood escape. Despite their fearsome reputations, the barracudas seemed not the least incited by the blood streaming from the diver's nose. Thad pulled him to the surface slowly, allowing time for their bubbles to precede them and decompression to take place in their bodies.

"Hell, we'd about decided to come back for you." Hands pulled his buddy away, and others helped him remove his fins and ascend the ladder.

"Harry, stop bleedin', you'll attract every shark in the Metnál."

"Somebody throw a towel around that turkey's face."

They soon had Harry stretched out on the shelf seat, wet towels under the back of his neck and under his nose. Bo and Aulalio Paz were counting heads. Greg Durwent sat down by his wife this time.

"What happened down there?" Martha looked from her husband to Thad. "It sounded like a muffled . . . I don't know. Whump? And the boat shivered."

"Could it a been an underwater explosion of some kind, do you think?" Bo Smith flipped the top off a Styrofoam cooler and withdrew a chicken drumstick.

"Earthquake, maybe?" Don Bodecker, the salesman and youngest of the boys from L.A., stacked used tanks in the container box with holes.

A subdued group. Thoughtful. A few jokes, but more sideways glances to judge the reactions of others, gauge the seriousness of what had happened. Neither Paz had grinned since they'd climbed back into the boat. They glanced often out over the water, at the sky, at each other.

"I never see nothing like that before, mon." Eliseo reached for his pack of cigarettes and then seemed to notice he already had one lit. "You want to go back now?"

"Let us eat and discuss this matter further." Bo Smith heaved the busted watermelons overboard. "We came a long way to dive the Metnál. Let us not be too hasty in leaving these here waters."

Chicken, fresh pineapple, chewy conch salad, some of the awful island bread and more beer. The talk grew jovial. Harry's nose had dried up. Someone threw the crock of potato salad overboard to join the melons. "Goin' to give those fucking fishes the sammynella ole Dixie had planned for us."

"Never did see so many bacca-ruda in one place before, did you?"

Thad stretched out to let the sun soak away the chill of the deep in his bones. The clouds that had been far out on the horizon before their dive had moved in a third of the way across the sky now.

A vote was taken, and only Martha Durwent and the Pazes wanted to go back to Mayan Cay. They didn't count. The sea had gone smooth. Divers draped themselves around the boat to sunbathe and rest while Aulalio guided them to a new spot far from the dangers of the first for an afternoon dive. There was still a wait before they should go down again, and the inevitable pack of cards surfaced.

"Is this still the Metnál?" Martha asked Eliseo.

"Oh, yes, big place, Metnál. All over here."

"What's down there to look at this afternoon?"

"German submarine. Not deep."

"Hey, no shit?"

"All right!"

"You pullin' our legs, boy? What'd a U-boat be doing here? War didn't get down here."

"These were British waters," Thad offered. "And useful for interfering with coastal shipping and trade with the U.S."

"Martha, honey, we are goin' to bring you up a body yet. What'd I tell ya?"

"Just make sure it isn't Greg's." She'd been tight-lipped since she'd lost the vote.

"That am one nervous woman." Bo drew a duffel bag up to Thad's lounging area and sat on it. "Least she gets out here. My wife won't even leave the country. Just stays in her house, raisin' kids and reading her Jesus books all day. And all night."

"Why are women so attracted to religion?" Thad said before he realized he was giving something.

Too late to take it back. Bo picked up on it immediately. "So there's a person inside that walkin' iceberg after all. You got one of 'em too, huh?"

"Had."

"Oh. Well, I think women think they're more helpless than they really are, and they're smart enough to know men aren't very strong, and they figure the Lord'll fill the gap. Don't make me no nevermind. Excepting that over the years a woman'll begin to save all her fire for the Lord. Makes for cold nights."

Bo Smith opened another beer, took a long drag, then lay back to watch the sky. "But hell, I can't complain. Sue Ellen's given me five beautiful children. I just love kids. Wish mine would stay that way. Most of 'em are almost grown and being asses, but then, I got to remember they'll have kids, which means I get grandkids, and like I said, I just love . . . Oh, Jesus, I did it again."

"What?"

"Forgot your problem. Had to go talking kids."

"That's okay, I forgot too." Thad, lying on the shelf seat, looked down into the eyes of the man on the deck below him, and for an instant there was contact. Thad looked away.

"You're gonna be all right, Doc. Time's almost up. One of these days you're gonna start over. I wouldn't want me and mine to go through what you and yours have. But not everybody gets another chance."

Thad felt oddly close to this man, who in many ways represented the macho bigot he despised.

"Your daddy, now—now that we have broached difficult subjects—he would have been interested in what happened to us this morning."

Thad laughed, and every head in the boat turned toward him. "He would have told you that the currents and explosion or whatever we felt was caused by a flying saucer either leaving or entering an underwater space hangar, or that Atlantis is about to rise from beneath the sea. I take it you've read him."

"Couple of his books is all. How do you know it wasn't a flying saucer landing or taking off? If Sue Ellen can believe in what she does on faith 'cause she doesn't have much in the way of facts, why can't your daddy believe in what he does? Probably got more facts than Sue Ellen does. What do you think it was?"

"Earth tremor of some kind."

"Tremors usually mean a quake is coming, don't they?"

"Not always. Odds are we won't have any problems this afternoon."

"Yeah. Probably never know what it was. Things like that irk the hell out of me."

"Make good material for my father's books, though."

"Dopes like me buy 'em to get explanations of the niggling little unexplainables so they'll stop niggling."

Thad wanted to tell Bo Smith about the *Ambergris*. But he didn't.

It was decided that Harry Rothnel, the baker, should not dive that afternoon and risk another nosebleed, and that Aulalio would stay topside with him and Martha. Thad drew Eliseo Paz as his new dive partner.

The divers didn't trade so many jokes this afternoon as they perched on the edge of the boat, their feet in rubber fins on the shelf seat, and one by one threw themselves backward into the sea. The only quip was from Bo, when half the group was in the water. "Keep a sharp eye out for submerged space hangars and flying saucers, you turkeys. And don't forget Martha's body."

"Now, who could forget Martha's body? Bo, you . . ."

Thad hit the water, tank first, and didn't hear the rest. The usual idiosyncrasies at the beginning of a dive—the little shock on impact with the alien medium, the slight hesitation as he was immersed that had no

time to assert itself, the temptation to hold his breath instead of sucking in on the regulator. They'd agreed to stay close this time. Follow
their one guide, Eliseo.

Thad was surprised at how close he was to the bottom, a barren area
compared to that of the morning. The divers were grouping below,
waiting for the rest to arrive. It must have been no more than thirty or
forty feet. What would a sub be doing in so shallow a place?

The others were turning around in circles, nudging each other, shrug-
ging in question-mark pantomime. Perhaps because there were no fish,
nothing crawling along the bottom. As the last divers arrived, the sunlight departed. Even at that depth and in tropical waters, the chill was
instant, clear water took on shadows, became murky.

Eliseo did the turning bit now, as if to get his bearings, and then rose
above them to do it again. Thad sensed a question in Eliseo's posture
too. But Stefano Paz's son finally straightened, regardless of the fact he
was six feet from earth, and arched an arm with the exaggerated
slowness of most rapid movements against water. He'd found a submarine. How do you kill a submarine at thirty feet?

It lay intact, instead of in pieces. Eliseo had to scrape sand from a
patch of it to prove the giant wiener shape on the sea floor was made of
metal. Others scraped. One pounded. The sound, even underwater,
came back hollow. Divers rose away from it, looking down, then at the
man on either side, then down again. Beneath the layer of sand the sub
was surprisingly free of coral encrustation.

Eliseo rose to pivot, search the murky water with his eyes. Landmarks
of some sort may have been destroyed in the turbulence of the morning. The phenomenon might have extended this far. Thad wished he
had an intercom with his diving buddy.

The sub lay on its side, the bare outline of a conning tower shaped
like a giant cigarette lighter under the sand. The ship seemed too small
to hold the lives of men and their equipment within it. Were they still
inside?

Thad recognized the ghoul in himself and turned back to Eliseo. The
guide had gone off alone—exactly what he'd warned everyone else not
to do. He motioned now for the others, and Thad was the first to reach
him. Eliseo swam on, and then stopped, pointing down. Thad could see
nothing but sand, no rocks, no debris, not even a dead fish. As if the
area had been cleaned up for a beach. Eliseo spread his arms out and
then down, shook his head, pointed down once more.

Some of the others wandered away from the sub and angled toward
them.

The sea floor was slightly mounded, the sub lying far off to the side.

Grains of sand trickled down the surface of the mound. Thad had seen
this before, when crabs burrowed to escape detection, but he had never
seen it occur in so many places at once.

What looked like a puff of dust from the center of the mound, some
distance away, and sand particles began to tumble instead of trickle.
The entire ocean floor seemed to tremble so imperceptibly that it took
Thad a moment to realize it was moving.

10

More sand spilled over the sub. It moved slightly, as if being nudged.
Thad was aware of the string of divers making their way toward him, of
sand particles floating in the water instead of settling to the bottom, of
Eliseo's arms waving in the soft, slow rhythm swimmers make underwater when they're trying to stay in one place.

But his consciousness concentrated on the sound and the increasing
pressure against his face that forced his mask into bone, pushed his
nose and jaw back, and drew the blood to his head. This gave him the
feeling of suffocating, even though he still sucked in regular breaths
from his regulator.

Sound filled the water, seemed to be one with the pressure. He
couldn't liken it to anything he'd ever heard before. It wavered, became
steady for a time, and resumed its wavering, a deep grating tone. The
bulge below him became more pronounced. The diameter of the
mound was larger than he'd thought. Dark gray patches appeared between sand ruffles now—shiny, moist-looking.

Approaching divers veered away. Eliseo tapped him on the shoulder,
and the guide's fins rose to join the bubbles oozing from around the
edges of the egg-shaped thing as it protruded more and more from the
ocean floor and grew in size as it did so. It reminded Thad of a sightless
eyeball, mammoth and dead.

He turned to follow Eliseo and the others, abstracted by the thought
that either something had gone radically wrong with the world or he
was in one of those fantastic dreams he'd been having. The location
was not at the base of that ugly mountain, and he'd usually known he
was dreaming before. Perhaps those were only the dreams he remembered. This absorption slowed him enough to allow him a quick glance
over his shoulder, and what he saw turned him around completely.

Thad kicked back into the danger from which everyone else fled.

This was probably just a dream. He'd awaken before things became fatal. If it wasn't, he'd never forgive himself for playing it safe after seeing that diver in trouble.

He considered trying to go through the egg-shaped gray mass still growing beneath him—just to test the dream theory. But he had time to admit he hadn't the nerve. He swam over it, one fin scraping the burgeoning surface. He was on the other side, where he'd seen a diver being pulled into the sand at the rim of the emerging . . . whatever it was, the diver's hands above his head, finned feet already disappearing in a suction of some kind between the sea floor and the rising . . . hulk? Thing? Alive? Machine? His mind balked at "space hangar." Too Edward P. III. Too sensationalized, Devil's Triangle type of crap.

Thad found the diver's air tank, mask, and attached snorkel tumbling down a sand heap, making way for still more of the giant eye. No buoyancy vest, fins. No diver. Thad found the sound and the pressure unbearable, found tears mixing with blood inside his mask and himself rising to the surface, dragging the extra equipment and unable to see through the viscous cloud between his eyes and the mask window.

He screamed at himself to wake up, and was startled when he broke the surface. He couldn't seem to let go of the additional gear, as if it were a lifeline to a lost diver. A tugging sucked at him from beneath, and, finally dropping the other air tank, he paddled blindly away from the thing rising in the water. This was no dream. It was death. Thad was shocked to find it so recognizable.

Would he see Ricky again? Or was there anything of Ricky to see?

A wave, a force, something, propelled him into the air, knocked his mask ajar so he could see again, see the blood escaping on white water near his face as he plunged, defenseless. Drowning.

The regulator wrenched from his mouth, jerking loose teeth that had clamped around rubber tabs. He retreated into his mind. It was not filled with memories on parade to review his life, nor regret at its shortness, nor fear at its end. Merely shock. And anger that this should be happening. Rage.

Thad slammed into something hard. Within that something, the echo of the sound of his impact was the last sound he heard before even his rage gave way to nothing.

"Have we got everybody?"
"Just get us the hell out of here!"
"Can't count heads with everybody flying around so."
"Engine working?"

"Where's Bo?" A woman's voice, next to his ear. She held him from behind. They were both being tossed about on the deck of the boat.

Martha Durwent. He was alive. He couldn't believe it.

"Throw the life preservers out. Maybe somebody'll catch one."

"Where's Bo?" Martha screamed.

"Bo? You on board, Bo?"

"*Madre de Dios . . . clemencia . . . por favor.*"

"Aulalio, get this fuckin' tub moving!"

Thad doubled up in a choking spasm that ripped him from Martha's arms and sent him into the crevice under a shelf seat, where he became lodged but then skidded out again as water washed over the boat. He slid down the deck like the watermelons had done earlier, and into Don Bodecker. The salesman pressed a rough rope into Thad's hands, forced his fingers to clamp around it. "It's tied to a cleat."

One arm of Don's wet suit was ripped almost off and hanging behind, but his exposed flesh looked unharmed.

The bow lunged into the air and a jumble of diving gear and Styrofoam coolers went overboard at the stern. Martha Durwent grabbed his ankle, her wet hair slicked against her head and shoulders. He pulled her up to where she could hang on to the line with him, just as the open boat nose-dived. Thad found himself staring at the giant gray eye. It swelled above an angry ocean and was outlined against the sky.

Clouds twisted in on themselves and then expanded, darkened. Lightning jagged in odd short bursts. Rain added to the swirling wet of the sea. Maybe Thad *had* died.

"I wouldn't be surprised if a flying saucer came out of that big eye over there," he yelled at Martha, and had the urge to giggle, but not the strength. She twisted away from him, and he had to haul her back to the line. "Stay put."

"Greg!"

But Greg Durwent went over the side. Martha turned limp against Thad, and he made the strength to keep them both attached to the rope. They rose again on a gigantic, endless swell, and Thad's stomach seemed to rush to his feet. Martha nearly broke loose from his exhausted grip.

Aulalio Paz slid backward on his stomach, eyes and mouth gaping, finger- and toenails digging into the deck like a startled cat's. He wrapped himself around Martha's legs.

"Grab the line, not her," Thad screamed over the sea's hysteria. "Can't hold you both!"

They were all sliding down the rope, Thad's hands burning, his arm —threaded under Martha's armpits and across her chest—going numb before Aulalio got a hold on the rope and Thad felt the release of his weight. He inched himself and the woman higher up to give the guide more room as the dive boat crested the wave, bucked, and plunged.

The descent was brutal, life preservers flung out to the ends of their rope tethers and high into the air, shining an odd luminous white against the sooty, roiling sky. Aulalio rose too on the end of their line and pounded back into the deck, narrowly missing a corner of the air-tank container.

As they bottomed out in the deep of the trough, Thad could see huddled shapes around the deck but didn't have time to count them before salt water slammed over the side to sting the various scraped areas on his body and threatened once again to drown him.

He had no idea how long this torture lasted, nor exactly when the seas calmed, the sky cleared, and the squall was at an end. But eventually the sun grew hot and his skin sticky with dried salt water.

Men moved about, their wet suits patchy and shredded, blood oozing from scrapes. Dark swellings. One limped, another held an arm tightly with the other hand. Everyone peered over the side. Except Martha Durwent. She sat on the bench seat with her head in her hands. A drying blood trail ran from her hair, down her neck, and across the nipple of an exposed breast.

Other than the few air tanks still in their holes, the boat had emptied of gear. The crowded jumble of food containers, masks, fins—all had washed overboard. Harry-the-baker counted heads.

Thad pulled himself to his knees and then to his feet, stood swaying to look out over a sea still frothy white with grains of sand. No eyeball. No Styrofoam cooler tops floating on the surface. "How many?" he asked Harry.

"Can't keep my wits straight long enough to remember how many we were to begin with. But if I'm counting right, we only lost four," he said with disbelief.

"We're missing Bo, Abrams, Terry, and Martha's husband." Don pulled in a life preserver by its line, as if expecting to find a survivor.

Eliseo tugged open a trapdoor in the deck and crawled into the pit to bail out the water around the engine with a face mask that had hung around his neck through it all. His brother watched dumbly, crossed himself, muttered under his breath.

"Quiet! Listen." Martha looked up, dropping her hands. Everyone else froze. A far-off cry. It could have been a bird. And it could have been human. She stood. "Greg!"

Another faint cry. An answer? Coincidence?

"Could be a sea gull. Don't get your hopes up too high." Harry put his hands to his mouth and shouted, "Over here!"

The answer came back right away, and Thad thought he could even detect the direction.

"That's a man." Don jumped into the pit to help Eliseo. "Sounded like either 'help' or 'here.'"

"So does a gull, if that's what you want it to sound like. Coulda been an echo of my voice."

They called, fiddled with the engine. There were no boats on the horizon; the call must be from a survivor. Martha knelt on the bench seat and gripped the gunwales, staring in the direction of the cries, her body unnaturally stiff but shuddering in spasms paced at about one every thirty seconds.

Thad was surprised there wasn't more evidence of shock. Perhaps there was, and he was too far gone to recognize it. Those not trying to help with the engine sat drooping, staring inward, leaving an outward impression of blankness. Then one would shift or start at Harry's repeated calls and remember to blink strained eyes. The movement would startle the next man into doing the same, and then the next.

Everyone perked up when the engine coughed to life, began to strain with Aulalio's effort to budge a stuck rudder, literally swayed with relief when it moved. But then no one could agree on the direction from which the cries had come. Aulalio headed them in the direction of Martha's pointed finger and let the men argue. They could no longer hear the calls of the probable survivor over the engine, which seemed to be missing on about every other cylinder, but soon saw something bobbing in the water to the port side and eventually made out a man clinging to the lid of an ice chest.

It was the man named Abrams.

Martha's body relaxed, and a certain expression in her eyes died.

The wooden ladders, used by the divers to get back on board, had been lost at sea, and Abrams was too injured to help himself up on the end of a life preserver. So two men jumped in the water and helped him on board with a life preserver ringing his chest and another his legs. He groaned only once. Thad ran his hands gently down Abrams' torso.

"Got a drink of water, Doc?"

"Sorry, we don't have anything."

"Great," Abrams whispered, and passed out.

Thad calculated that almost every rib in the man's body was broken. He bent close to Aulalio's ear. "We've got some serious injuries here."

He saw broken toes and fingers, ribs, at least one broken arm, and some head cuts he didn't like. "You've got to get us back fast."

"Can't." Aulalio burst into a mixture of Spanish and creole, from which Thad thought he extracted the information that the guide didn't know the way.

"But how did you know how to get us here?" Now Thad remembered that neither Paz had referred to chart or compass. There was no land in sight from which to sight a course. No stars. These men went out to sea almost every day during the high tourist season and always came back.

Aulalio shouted something to his brother, and Eliseo scanned the horizon, making a complete circle, shielded his eyes to take direction from the sun. He looked confused, shrugged, and then raised a tentative finger. Aulalio shrugged an answer and headed the boat that way. The Pazes were scraped and bumped and bruised too. And uneasy.

"How *do* you know how to get around on the open ocean without something to guide you?"

"I jus' know. Metnál's big but very shallow some places. I can see coral or wrecks, and I know—but now I'm switched around."

Not that the guide's confusion mattered greatly, because the engine stalled, sputtered, spit, and quit. Eliseo was unable to restart it.

Carl Abrams died as they watched. He opened his eyes with a surprised expression and then just stayed that way.

Someone suggested they try to resuscitate him. Thad vetoed the plan. "He's all broken up inside. Must be lots of internal bleeding."

"The rest of us'll probably die too," Martha said indifferently.

"Eliseo, just what was that thing that came up out of the water?" Don Bodecker asked.

"I never see anything like that before, mon." His right hand came up to his chest for the pack of cigarettes he always kept in a shirt pocket there. They were gone. So was the pocket.

"How often do you come out here?"

"This place, only second time. You see wrecks better when they're not all covered by coral. More and more hear about Metnál and ask to go here, so we look for new wrecks. But this never happens before."

"You know, I miss Bo already?" Harry Rothnel said, as if it fit right into the pattern of the conversation. "He'd have us all cracking jokes about dyin'." The long hairs that were supposed to be trying to cover his bald spot were wisping down in his face instead.

Thad looked past him to where a shadow spread across the water. It was huge and moving rapidly toward the dive boat.

11

Jerusha Fistler returned to Iron Mountain. The mystery to Tamara was how she'd managed to leave it.

It was the morning after they'd received her mother's letter, and Tamara looked out to see a tall stick of a woman leaning on Vinnie Hope as they descended the wooden stairs of Jerusha's utility porch and slowly made their way to Alice's pen. The excited goat went through his entire repertoire of antics. The woman stretched her arms to the sun, and Tamara thought she could see the very bone and tendon under the taut skin. She hurried out to get a better look at this creature and to offer help. Her neighbor appeared frail enough to fall.

"Here's the new teacher." Vinnie patted Jerusha's bottom in warning.

Jerusha wore a cheap nylon robe of yellow, her hair a bush of black matted curls. She turned with one hand on the girl's shoulder and the other on a fence post.

"I'm Tamara Whelan. My daughter and I . . ." Tamara almost felt an impact at the intense interest Jerusha Fistler directed toward her, and was stunned at the youthfulness of the ravaged face. Jerusha's stiff movements had led her to expect an aging person. The bony body and sunken eyes reminded Tamara of pictures she'd seen of walking skeletons at Auschwitz.

"Are you ill?" she said stupidly, knowing she was too late to hide her shock.

Jerusha smiled, and her teeth were enormous in the skeletal face. "Oh, I'm going to be fine." Her voice was surprisingly strong, low and melodic. "Just stayed a little too long, didn't I, Vinnie? Should have knowed better, ummmm?"

"Vinnie said you were on a research trip."

"It got so interesting I forgot to eat and everything." There was an unfamiliar lilt to her speech that turned up the edges of words so each one seemed to ask a question. It wasn't Southern, but similar.

"Where did you go to do your research, and what is it you study?" Tamara didn't believe a word of this.

"Alice, you've grown so, baby." Jerusha turned awkwardly to the goat. "You know, he wasn't *this* high when I left?"

"When did you get back?"

"Vinnie, I believe I'd like some more eggs. Have you had your breakfast yet, Mrs. Whelan?"

"Tamara."

"Why don't we get to know each other while we eat, Tamara?"

Tamara would have eaten twice for a chance to see what lay on the other side of the stained partition. She suspected this woman's "trip" was related more to drug or alcohol abuse than to scientific research.

Jerusha's living-room/kitchen was stuffy with damp and meager light. Tamara stood blinded after the sunshine. The whooshing sounded louder here, and as soon as her eyes adjusted, they rested on the largest vaporizer she'd ever seen. Plastic ribbed hoses sprouted from it, aimed in different directions and hanging from strings nailed to the ceiling. Mist puffed from the end of each hose with every "whoosh." Water burbled in a giant glass jar.

The dimness was caused by the covering of waxy-leaved plants at the windows. But it proved to be one plant—a vine growing up a pole out of a floor pot and then along the ceiling, where it was tied by thread to nails. It formed a leafy cornice all around the room and dropped down to catch the light and bunch up at every window. There were corners cut out of the bedroom doors so it could grow into these rooms without being affected by the position of the door.

". . . nosy," Vinnie whispered to Jerusha, who was breaking eggs with shaky hands. "Just like Miss Kopecky."

Jerusha's grin full of teeth was even more grotesque in the dim light. "That plant is my very first experiment, Tamara. It's called the night-blooming cereus. It won't grow in such a dry place, so I keep wetness in the air for it."

Hence the stain on the other side of the wall.

"Still, it blooms only once a year here. Pour us coffee, please?"

They ate scrambled eggs seasoned with onion, tomato, and herbs off thin plastic plates—discolored with use. Vinnie watched the older women suspiciously, and Tamara sensed her irritation at having to share Jerusha.

"What do you do for a living, Jerusha?" Tamara asked, aware of how rude it sounded.

"Oh, there is some widow's pension from Abner's company, and some welfare. I do not need much."

Especially with your own little unpaid slave. Tamara watched Vinnie pour soap into the dishpan. But she had to admit the furnishings here were spare enough, and Jerusha's biggest bill was probably electricity to run the vaporizer.

"And is your husban' dead too, Tamara?"

That question, asked with the cheerful lilt, brought back the night before, the letter, and the signs of a nocturnal eating binge still on the table. She'd managed to block it all out for a while.

"No, I'm divorced." And Gilbert Whelan remarried a woman with two children. *That's how he goes about finding himself?*

"I am sorry if my question upset you, Tamara," the skeleton face said. Even Jerusha Fistler's laughter was low and melodic—almost tuneful. It mixed with Vinnie's higher giggle as Tamara hurried across the backyard to the door of her own utility porch.

Vague terrors added up from all her mother's warnings, plus all the things the world told Adrian and refused to tell her, had seemed like a big black block sneaking closer with every day.

News of her father's remarriage had pushed the block into sight and dropped it on her. The weight made it difficult for her to fill her lungs deeply. And if her breathing sounded like sighing, it was only a fight for oxygen. The block enveloped her and extended for miles around. Every movement, every gesture, seemed to be slower yet take extra effort, as if she lived underwater.

"My problem is with your mother, not with you," her daddy had said. "You'll always be my little girl."

Now he had two new kids, and Adrian's body had not stayed little. She'd grown too big and fat to love, to be worth even a letter of explanation. An end to all the daydreams of a reconciliation.

Adrian slipped out the front door at the sound of her mother's approach to the back. Her sandals flapped under her heels, the white grit worked its way between her damp skin and the sole. Adrian walked up the chalk road until she came abreast of the burned-out foundation, where insects clicked to each other in the weeds and the world smelled hot already.

She roamed the ghost rooms, wishing some of the dangers her mother warned were lurking here would make themselves known—prove fatal. She hated herself as much as her father did. It would be a relief not to have to live with Adrian Louise Whelan anymore.

Her mother came out to check on her and then went back into the house. Adrian picked up a wedge of glass, roughly triangular. It wasn't blackened like much of the glass around and had taken on a tinge of that lavender color glass assumes when exposed long to the sun.

The little brat, Vinnie Hope, unfolded a webbed lawn chair on the porch of the Fistler apartment and led out the thinnest woman Adrian had ever seen. Her legs looked like sticks, and Adrian was amazed to see them bend as the woman settled in the chair and turned her face to the sun.

"Aye, woman-child, come please and talk to me," the stick woman called.

Vinnie crawled up on the stone-and-brick parapet rimming the porch and looked at Adrian. "She means you, stupid."

"Now, Vinnie, you must not speak in that way to my new neighbor," the woman said as Adrian shuffled reluctantly over to the porch and stopped on the steps. "Please, come on up and sit. I am Jerusha, and the girl-child here tells me you are Adrian."

Adrian thought the woman must be dying, the way the bones and teeth stuck out of her face. That thought gave Jerusha more authority than the average stranger, and Adrian obediently walked up onto the porch and leaned against the shady side of the parapet.

"Oh, such lovely eyes." Jerusha's eyes hid in the shadows of their sockets. "And so sad. It makes me want to cry." She didn't sound like she wanted to cry. Her voice moved along as if she were singing. "What makes such beautiful eyes so sad, I wonder."

Adrian felt tears coming, and looked down at the glass in her hand. She scraped the sharp edge lightly across the inside of her wrist and left a white line on her skin. She looked up to see Jerusha staring at the glass and then at Adrian's face.

"Such lovely skin and hair. How lucky you are to have these things."

"Yah, but she's fat," Vinnie said.

"Oh, fat, what does that matter? It can be gotten rid of—fat. But there is no place in the whole world you can go for skin and hair so fine as that."

Vinnie looked at Adrian as if she'd never seen her before. "Really?"

"Yes. And, Adrian, you must be careful." She nodded toward the ruin next door. "There is much glass and nails over there."

"How did it burn?" Adrian didn't care, but she felt she ought to say something.

"Oh, that was my second experiment," Jerusha said wistfully.

"You mean you burned it down?"

But Jerusha Fistler just closed her eyes as if going to sleep. Adrian wrinkled her nose rudely at Vinnie, walked quietly off the porch and around the duplex. She could feel the loose flesh on her thighs wobble, hear her fat legs slap together beneath her shorts. Only somebody as ugly as the woman back on the porch could find anything beautiful in Adrian Whelan.

"And you like anybody who'll scratch you, huh, boy?" She ran her fingernails between Alice's little horns, and the goat playfully lipped her leg through the fence.

She slipped behind the chickenhouse and peeked around the corner.

No sign of movement or of anyone watching from the Whelan side of the building. Adrian made a dash to the rusted gondola cars and checked again. She ran bent over along the tracks until she was far enough around Iron Mountain to be hidden from the settlement below, and began to climb—sweating, puffing, the piece of glass still in her hand, salty tears on her lips.

Adrian walked around a rock outcropping and stopped in front of a hole with old boards across it—some of which had fallen in. She stood swaying with the heat and exertion, hunger and thirst. Carefully she bent to pick up a rock and tossed it into the hole. She listened a long time before it hit.

She looked from the piece of glass to the hole. Excitement and fear tingled in her stomach, drained the last bit of moisture from her throat. Adrian relaxed a little, and that increased the swaying motion.

If she could let herself just fall into that hole . . . Adrian clenched her teeth and eyes shut, felt the glass cut into her hand as she forgot and clenched that too.

"Hey! Jerusha said to tell you not to do anything silly!"

The shout came from behind and jerked Adrian out of her trance so suddenly her foot slipped. She slid over the edge of the hole and flung her arms out.

One hand hit something. She grabbed it, reaching with the other hand to hold it, and hung on. Icy air surrounded her bare legs. Her screams echoed around and around the hole.

Vinnie Hope's face leaned over between Adrian and the sky. Her lips moved, yet Adrian could hear nothing but her own voice. Vinnie pointed down and then to one side. Her mouth looked like she was yelling now.

Whatever Adrian was holding on to moved and shook, and dirt fell into her face. She screamed harder and looked down. There was a broad shelf with grass growing on it about six inches from her knees. The noise stopped in her throat.

"Why don't you just stand on that ledge and crawl out, retard?"

Adrian hiccuped, brought first one leg and then the other up onto the ledge, and let go of the board. When she straightened, her head and shoulders were aboveground. She had to tighten herself to keep from wetting her pants.

"Jerusha said not to let you do anything silly, and now I know what she meant."

Adrian looked down to find the shelf covered more area than the entrance to the deep hole did. She pulled herself out and sat cross-legged next to Vinnie, and listened to her heart.

"If you're such a grown-up 'woman-child' like Jerusha said, then how come you cry for your mommy?" Vinnie said with a sneer. "You were yelling, 'Mommy, Mommy, Mommy.'"

"Oh, shut up, baby." Adrian couldn't even try to die without making a fool of herself.

"Maybe that's why." Vinnie stared at Adrian's crotch. "Does it hurt?"

"What?" She looked down to see the slow spread of menstrual blood staining her shorts. Adrian stretched out with her head on her arms and sobbed long shuddering spasms against the rusty soil of Iron Mountain.

Tamara watched her daughter sneak up the side of the mountain from the kitchen window and saw Vinnie follow. Probably some attempt at revenge, a strategy to hurt or frighten Tamara because she alone was responsible for the divorce, Gil's remarriage, Adrian's weight, and probably World War III when it arrived. She sighed and walked over to the schoolhouse to work on lesson plans. There must be some reason why people wanted to have children.

When she returned to the apartment for a late lunch, Adrian was in the shower. All the emotional strain had left Tamara with a headache, so she took a couple of aspirin and lay down on Miriam Kopecky's bed, setting an alarm to be sure she wouldn't sleep the day away.

She was immediately glad she had, because as she began to drift off, she felt the familiar pull and knew she was in for one of those dreams. Perhaps she'd see the man called Backra again. Anything would be a pleasant change from the present state of her life. She smelled the sea first and then heard it.

Tamara stood in that incredible graveyard on the beach next to a statue of the Virgin, who held her arms out as if blessing the white sarcophagus on which she stood. The engraved inscription filled with dirt read: MARIA ELENA ESQUIVEL. EN SAGRADA MEMORIA DE MI HIJA.

Footprints rumpled the sand, and a stretch of long patterns resembling the skeleton of an endless leaf. Clouds dimmed the light. People rushed about in excitement farther down the beach. Three fair-skinned children—two boys and a girl—knelt to peer under one of the shaggy thatched huts lining that end of the cemetery. These cabins stood a few feet up off the beach on wooden pilings.

"Oh, gross."

"I feel sorry for it," the little girl said. "Can't we help it?"

"Yeah, shoot it."

Just then a man emerged from the crowd around the dock. He wore the remnants of a rubberized suit like divers wear on top, and tattered swim trunks below. His legs were scratched and bruised between streaks of dried blood. As he drew closer, she could see his nose was swollen, his eyes blank and staring. He was the Backra of that other dream.

For a moment he seemed to be looking at her, almost recognizing her as he turned from the sea to angle toward his house. But the little girl spoke to him, and he blinked back the blankness.

"Hey, mister? Can you help this poor dog?"

A piercing whine sounded from under the thatched cabin, and Backra turned to kneel beside the children. Then he lay flat, grunting as if the movement hurt him. Sliding back on his stomach, he withdrew a limp dog and stumbled to his knees and then to his feet.

The buzzing of her alarm clock descended from the clouds as Tamara watched the wreck of the once-beautiful Backra stagger toward the house with the net hammock, cradling the dog in his arms.

12

The dead man on the bottom of the boat still looked surprised, but Thad felt himself incapable of any more. He pointed listlessly past Harry to the engulfing shadow almost upon them.

Some had seen it and watched without speaking. Others turned now that the light was getting funny, shielded their eyes to see what was happening to the sun.

"Listen," Don said, and Thad noticed the quiet, the fading away of the sounds of the sea against the boat. The world turned yellow.

The water under the shadow appeared higher than that under the boat. The quiet intensified. Martha Durwent's lips moved as if she spoke, but no sound came to Thad. A wave of darkness instead of ocean swept the boat into the air with the heaving motion of a carnival ride gone berserk.

Thad had some cornball ideas of their being sucked up into a giant spacecraft to be examined by alien beings and taken off somewhere and reported as another missing victim of unexplainable happenings like those missing in the Bermuda Triangle. Except this wasn't the Bermuda Triangle. This was the Metnál. And those unexplainable happenings were all explainable if the facts could be known. There was a perfectly logical explanation for the giant eyeball. Just because he didn't know what it was didn't mean one didn't exist.

The ends of his hair rose up off his head. He grabbed the edge of the shelf seat to keep from floating. His legs floated out in front of him anyway, and on air, not on water. But there was no air to breathe. Still his body drifted upward, moored to the boat and reality only by his hold on the seat. The blackness was so intense that when he closed his eyes it seemed lighter.

Some military experiment that was top-secret, and this luckless group happened on it just when it was being tested. This and the eyeball were all part of the same experiment.

This was nightmare country, an extended dream which came from reading all that glop his father wrote.

He had been going slowly insane on Mayan Cay, or even since Ricky died, and he hadn't known it, and now the crazed part of his brain was in full control and he was hallucinating with a vengeance.

But the physical part of Thad Alexander needed air, so desperately writhing muscles forced his body back to the seat and his brain drifted toward blankness. He felt another body against his leg as the agony of suffocation twisted him in convulsive shapes, and his hands tore from their hold on the seat.

He floated into someone in the dark, and held on, still floating slow-motion-wise, until he bumped against another person and that sent him off in yet a different direction. He thought fleetingly of movies of astronauts floating weightless in space labs, and then he sank helplessly and was flung, jackknifed, over the edge of the boat. The slap of the gunwales into his midsection forced an intake of breath which he was shocked to find available, but the air was filled with salt spray and it burned and he gagged.

Dark yellow light spread over the world. Someone took hold of his ankles and yanked him into the boat. The light continued to brighten, and the boat settled back into the water. The water seemed to lower.

They'd lost Abrams' body, and Aulalio Paz. Eliseo hung over the side, alternately calling for his brother and vomiting. The remaining air tanks were gone, sucked up out of their holes.

Martha and Don-the-salesman huddled together on the floor of the boat. He sobbed against her shoulder and she patted his hair, murmured automatic comfort, and stared beyond him.

Thad had dull pains in more places than he could monitor. Even the teeth hurt that had been loosened when his regulator was ripped from his mouth. But each breath answered with air seemed a joy. He drew in all he could and held on to it as long as possible.

He'd never seen so many weather changes on one patch of ocean in one afternoon. Now a fog bank rolled in their direction, shoving cool misty air ahead of it.

Thad's conscious mind still scanned possible reasons for all the impossible events of the afternoon, his lungs still gratified themselves with gulping breaths while he watched what was at first a shadow and then a solid form pull away from the mist—a two-masted yacht, sails reefed and skimming choppy water under engine power.

Thad smiled and reopened a cut on his lip. It was the *Ambergris*, of course. Perhaps the Kellers would know what was going on. Men waved and shouted, and Thad joined them. The *Ambergris* headed straight for them.

There were two worlds existing side by side that couldn't see each other (normally at least). The *Ambergris* belonged to one now, and Mayan Cay and everything else Thad knew belonged to the other. That afternoon the dive boat had passed into the *Ambergris*' world. Thad nodded thoughtfully. That made sense.

But the yacht that pulled up alongside didn't have blue gunwales and red life preservers and dinghy. They were all dark maroon. And the man who threw them a line wasn't Milt Keller or even young David. Two others joined him, and they weren't Milt either. The three faces above him looked shocked as they stared into the dive boat.

One shimmied down a rope, and the others began throwing things to him. Women appeared at the rail to help, and soon Thad was wrapped in a blanket, drinking water and then hot coffee laced with brandy. The yacht was the *Golden Goose*, a rented boat out of Roatan, with three couples from the U.S. aboard. Two of the men were medical doctors.

That was the nice thing about people doctors, Thad mused. They had the money to travel, and you met them almost anywhere. And they always carried a few things more than just booze and cash in case of an emergency.

While the *Golden Goose* towed them, both doctors and one of the wives worked in the dive boat. The wife passed him a cheese sandwich, and the mere act of eating gave Thad enormous pleasure. The brandy eased the aches in his body. One M.D. cleaned Martha Durwent's head wound while the other applied a makeshift splint to someone's swollen arm.

When one of their rescuers pulled deck splinters from his shoulder, Thad asked, "Did they send you from Mayan Cay to look for us?"

"No, but that's where we were headed when we saw a . . . tidal wave, or some kind of wave, and your boat being tossed around in it. How could that wave just subside like that?"

"Didn't it get dark suddenly where you were?"

"It was like a solar eclipse. But none are scheduled."

"I thought maybe the whole thing was a secret military experiment."
Thad didn't go into the wilder theories that had occurred to him.

The other M.D. joined them. "From what I can gather, they've lost
five of their number, and one guy keeps babbling about a mammoth
egg coming up out of the water." Both M.D.'s looked to Thad for explanation.

"I thought it looked more like an eyeball, but it was egg-shaped."

"Could there have been a submarine surfacing in this area?"

"It was too big for that."

"From the perspective of a boat this size, a submarine's going to look
pretty big."

"But it came up out of the sand on the bottom. It was buried under
a mound or hill. We were diving and saw it."

The people doctors exchanged classic glances, and one patted Thad's
knee.

Eliseo squinted at the sky. "What is the time, please?"

"Don't worry, we'll get you in before this weather front hits."

"I've got one-thirty," one of the wives said.

"That can't be." Harry grabbed an M.D.'s wrist. "They started their
second dive about one, remember, Martha? We looked."

"Yes, and everything couldn't have happened in just a half-hour."

But all three watches from the *Golden Goose* agreed that it was
within five minutes of one-thirty. There were two dive watches on
board that were still unbroken and running. Both of them read exactly
4:32.

The survivors had an entire afternoon to live over again.

The fog bank had lifted, but clouds hung low on every horizon as
they cleared the reef off Mayan Cay. The yacht must have radioed
ahead, because most of San Tomas had gathered in front of the Mayapan by the time they docked.

The island policeman—Ramon Carias—Dixie Grosswyler, and four of
the hotel staff were on the end of the dock with a couple of stretchers.

"Who are the five? What happened? Eliseo? Thad?" Dixie stood
brittle-straight, her eyes searching the boat. "Oh, not Aulalio? And Bo?
Not Bo—what happened, for God's sake?"

But people crowded them apart, and the M.D.'s insisted on seeing
about a plane to evacuate three of the survivors to the mainland and
then to Miami. Except for monthly visits of two government nurses,
there was no medical care on the island, and the hospital on the mainland wasn't much better.

Ignoring questions and offers of help, Thad threaded his way through
the press of bodies and headed for his father's house. A haze of exhaus-

tion mingled with the growing cloudiness to dim his vision, and the figure of the woman in his dream—the one who'd worn her hair wrapped in a towel and listened at a stained wall—stood beside the statue of the Virgin. But now she wore blue jeans, and her hair was reddish-brown and fluffy.

"Hey, mister? Can you help this poor dog?" A little girl with big tears looked at him beseechingly, and the dream woman vanished.

A piercing whine sounded from beneath the cabana, and Thad lay flat, to peer into the shadows. A few plumbing pipes, some rotting coconut husks, lizard tracks, and the little cemetery bitch.

She lay limp but still breathing, no longer straining. Placenta sac, its end partially chewed open, but dried to a leaden gray and covered by flies, outlined the shape of the stillborn within. He covered it with sand and felt her belly. Still swollen with pups. And he'd thought her new figure had been because of his feeding.

She opened one eye, fear of him dulled by the stoic acceptance of death. But when he slid his hands under her and lifted her out, she jerked her head in an attempt to snap at him, and then fell back.

Thad Alexander and the cemetery dog eyed each other with mutual distrust. She lay on the oilcloth-covered table and he sat on a wooden chair beside her, uncorking a bottle of cheap local rum. "You know, five people died out in that ocean today? Now, why don't you get busy and whelp those pups so they don't die too? And you with them."

He gulped straight from the bottle, and his eyes swam. The thought "resignation" or "giving up" leaped into his mind.

"No, my lady, you are not. Dr. Alexander is just as tired as you are." He reached into a cupboard for a bottle of Valium and crushed three of the ten-milligram tablets into a pale-blue powder and mixed it with water. "But what the hell, I got two afternoons in one day. Might as well keep busy."

He tilted her nose back and pulled out her cheek, spooned the liquid slowly between her cheek and gum so she couldn't panic and inhale it. She tried to nip him, and some of the medicine trickled between her teeth and down her throat. He worked the rest through clamped teeth by teasing the cheek against them.

Thad held her to the table until her renewed struggles ceased. He took another swig of rum and selected a kitchen knife and sharpened it against the stone doorstep his father had found somewhere.

Fatigue and rum and the mind-chill of his other afternoon left him almost as groggy as she looked. Her eyes followed him, expecting the worst. Thad concentrated on what needed doing now so he couldn't dwell on what had happened before. But the thought that Bo Smith hadn't lived to enjoy his hoped-for grandchildren overtook him as he pulled down the ropes that held the hammock. He thought again of how the man had reached out to him on the dive boat. When he stepped back into the house, she hadn't moved but she was panting heavily.

Thad put a pan of water on to boil and went up to his room for a sheet, a pillowcase, some handkerchiefs, his travel mending kit and razor. When he returned, the dog was almost to the edge of the table, had lost control and urinated. Her eyes rolled. She drooled.

He cleaned up the mess with some of Rafaela's rags and placed her on the folded sheet.

"First Ricky, then Bo. Probably old Edward P. III, too. But not you, my lady." He threw the sharpened knife, a needle, and the little scissors from the mending kit into the boiling water to cook, and strips of thread into a bowl of rum to soak.

"I may be completely helpless when it comes to the giants of the deep"—he took a long swig from the bottle—"and I may be getting more anesthetized than the patient . . ."

He cut a rough hole out of the crease of the folded pillowcase with another kitchen knife. When he unfolded it, there was a vertical oblong hole in the center. He stuffed it in another bowl of rum. "And I'm probably losing my mind. . . .

"And we're likely to have a real mess when it comes to tying off." He tapped the inside corner of one of her eyes, pinched the webbing between two toes for pain response, and decided she was sufficiently sedated. "Because we don't have any forceps and because the surgeon's getting a tish blurry. . . ."

He tied each of her feet with a piece of rope, turned her onto her back, and tied the ropes taut to the table legs, leaving her spreadeagled and trembling, helpless and dozy but not out.

He lathered her from umbilicus to vulva with soap and shaved her belly, thinking—not for the first time—how obscene this all could look to a bystander, and feeling almost like a violator as he splashed her with rum, wrung the rum out of the pillowcase, and draped it over her. Only the area of the incision remained visible through the hole—and her head and roped feet on the ends. "Let us just pray that we do not run out of rum."

Bringing everything he needed to a chair next to the table, he opened another bottle, scrubbed his hands, and wondered what some of his colleagues in Alaska would think of this whole thing. Thad took the hot knife from the pan on the chair and tossed it back and forth between his hands to cool it. He swore at the burning.

She jerked slightly but didn't cry out as he cut into her just below the umbilicus to well down in the groin. His hands felt naked reaching inside her bare-handed without the protection of rubber gloves. He pulled out one horn of the uterus and laid it on the drape next to the incision. It looked like a fat sausage with thin purple-gray skin. Three distinct lumps with corresponding greenish bands indicated the number of pups in this horn.

She whimpered softly.

Thad began to describe to her the horrors of his other afternoon, punctuated by occasional pulls on the rum. He slit the wall of the uterus at its lower end and milked a pup down and out, ripped open the sac, and kneaded the tiny body. When it did not respond, he shook it. Again no response. He laid it aside and milked down the next, mopping the oozing incision with a handkerchief dipped in rum. And all the while babbling on about giant eyeballs and little eclipses that could neutralize gravity.

The babbling grew louder and more animated, and was for his own benefit, not the patient's. He could revive none of the pups in the right horn, so he pulled out the left, where two bands remained, and looked up to see Dixie Grosswyler standing in the doorway, her face pale and her eyes wide with horror.

One of the M.D.'s from the *Golden Goose* slid in behind her, the one with the stringy legs and caved-in chest of the dedicated runner. He had a fashionable mustache and pointed beard. He took in the scene with one glance, and his lips smiled reassuringly. But his eyes turned wary.

Thad looked at the bloody knife in his hand, at the shreds of his father's wet suit that hung between and around swollen abrasions and scabbing cuts, at the little dog roped to the table next to a bottle of rum. He noticed for the first time that it was getting harder to see around his nose. A sudden sober embarrassment swept over him.

"We came to see if you . . . needed anything," Dixie said blankly.

"Get out of my surgery."

"What kind of surgery are you performing?" The M.D. took a few steps toward him, keeping watch on the knife.

"He *is* a veterinarian, Dr. Morrison," Dixie said uncertainly. "But, Thad, you haven't even cleaned up your own wounds. You know you can't do that in this climate."

"A C-section?" Dr. Morrison looked interested in spite of himself.

"That was the original idea," Thad said defensively. "But I think I'll do a hysterectomy while I'm in here. Pups are dead, and she doesn't need this."

"Why, it's just one of the village dogs." Dixie's horror had not altogether abated. "She's still awake."

To humor him, they agreed to assist, and with another set of hands to serve as forceps when it came time to pinch off the blood supply and with Dixie on mop-up, Thad soon had the uterus and ovaries removed, blood vessels tied off, the bitch's belly sewn up with simple interrupted sutures and splashed down with rum.

Dixie and the M.D. sent him to shower while they cleaned up, and then they went to work on him.

"I have known shock to cause people to do weird things"—Dr. Morrison looked at Thad curiously and prodded the swelling on the bridge of his nose—"but you are one for the books."

13

Russ Burnham took the Whelans into Cheyenne in his pickup when their trunks arrived. The outing was such a welcome change, even Adrian livened up. They stopped for dinner before coming home, and Tamara asked Russ, "Do you think Jerusha Fistler is on some kind of drug?"

"Don't know where she'd get it."

"She came back from her 'trip' so emaciated. And she doesn't have a car. Have you ever seen her coming or going?"

"She hops a ride now and then with one of the men from the mine or Augie. I think she comes in for groceries with Deloris Hope. They both get food stamps." He watched his knife and fork carefully.

"But when she's supposed to be gone, how do you know she isn't just holed up in her apartment and going on a binge?"

Russ speared the piece of steak with an upside-down fork, slipped it into his cheek, and pointed his knife at her. "I don't know nothing about Jerusha Fistler. What she does or where she goes."

He wore his hair in a flat-top. Tamara hadn't seen that haircut in years. A streak of pale skin just below the hairline showed the shading of the hard hat he was rarely without. He looked from her to Adrian. "I make a point of staying out of her way. I suggest you two do likewise."

He normally seemed stuffy and withdrawn, but then a spurt of humor would crinkle up the corners of his eyes and he was almost handsome. The open manner in which he watched women walk by their booth and the way he would forget himself and speak his thoughts gave him an air of uncomplicated honesty.

" 'Course, it was probably nothing to do with Abner's going . . ." He crunched down into gristle and blinked when he realized he'd said it aloud.

"Abner Fistler? Mrs. Hanley said he died of emphysema."

"He'd been a miner all his life and smoked a couple of packs a day. Lungs were in awful shape." Russ's eyes slid away.

"How old a man was he?"

"Abner? Oh, must've been sixty-three anyway. Company pensioned him off early because of his health."

"But Jerusha can't be thirty yet."

"Yeah, he was a lot older." Russ refused to answer any more questions about the Fistlers.

Tamara tried a new tack. "Mrs. Hanley says that B & H might close down Iron Mountain."

"Wish they would, and transfer me someplace else." He talked then in a choppy, no-nonsense tone about himself. His family lived in Kearney, Nebraska. He had never married because he didn't approve of and didn't think he could handle divorce.

That night Tamara dreamed Backra was in Iron Mountain and wore pajama bottoms and a strip of tape across his nose that shimmered white like his teeth against tanned skin.

She dreamed she was asleep, and awoke to find him standing beside the bed, his chest and arms still covered with scrapes and bruises. Tamara'd had several ongoing dreams in her life, nightmares. But they had not been consistent, and they'd been repetitive. This one unfolded new aspects each time, and she always knew she was dreaming.

Now she dreamed she lay very still while he touched her hair. She couldn't feel his touch, but things stirred elsewhere and reminded her of how long she'd been without a lover.

She spent a delicious moment tracing the muscle in his upper chest, the sandy mat of hair that formed a T—the bar stretched above his breasts and the tail extended down to his navel. Then she drew back the covers and stood, her motions slow, fittingly dreamlike because her body seemed so languid.

Backra looked stunned. And then amused.

"Why are you so beat-up?" Tamara's lips said, but her voice made no sound. "Have you been in a fight?"

"Fight?" His voice was silent too. "You are not real," he mouthed, and grinned. Then he made a grab for her.

Tamara didn't bother to sidestep his arms as they passed through her. Wasn't that just like a man? *It's my dream, but he thinks he's the one who's real.*

She glanced down at the bed. Her body still slept in it.

Panic rose with mute cries, and she lunged at the bed, horrified by the thought that she might not be able to get back. She awoke sweating and dry-mouthed—Backra gone, herself back together, her heart thumping.

Tamara had worked hard to exorcise her other self, who wanted to share life's joys and problems with another, to be dependent, to lean, to be held. But now she knew regret at not having felt Backra's arms. And that made her feel silly. And old.

The next evening, Augie Mapes appeared on the doorstep to invite Tamara and Adrian over to watch television. Images of him standing up in his outdoor bathtub flashed repeatedly on the retina of her mind, and she wondered if the same thing was happening to her daughter.

Adrian had been disappearing for long periods and being sullen and uncommunicative. She wanted to go, and Tamara accepted, hoping to lighten their boredom and find a way to cajole Augie into putting his bathtub inside during the school year.

They threaded their way among car bodies and other questionable humps in the weeds to the door of one of the house trailers.

"It is certainly nice of you ladies to join a lonely old man for an evening of telly-vision in his humble abode," his voice said, but his eyes turned to Tamara and said: *Call you and raise you three.*

The interior had been gutted and rebuilt into one large living room with a kitchenette and bar at one end. The wall of the trailer had been cut away where it attached to the shedlike building that connected the mobile homes, and in the shed stood the largest television Tamara had ever seen. It faced the cushions and couch-lined walls of the living room.

"Awesome," Adrian pronounced it, and settled into a bean-bag chair.

The bean-bag chair and studded stools at the bar were black plastic. Various low tables and the cupboards were brown. Refrigerator, stove, and sink were white. Everything else—walls, carpet, curtains, couches, cushions, pillows, tile in the kitchen-bar—was powder blue.

Tamara stifled a giggle as Augie handed her a can of beer and Adrian a soda. He switched on the TV by a remote control built into the arm of a corner couch and set to making popcorn.

"You must be a real TV fan . . . all this for one channel."

"KYCU selects shows from two networks for my entertainment pleasure."

"Welfare must pay pretty well."

"Oh, enough to keep skin and bones together. But I have to admit inflation's eating into my life-style."

"How is it you qualify?" She resented this strong healthy man living so contentedly off tax money while she struggled to make a subsistence living for herself and her child and then had to *pay* taxes.

"I suffer from a mental and emotional illness that prevents me from securing and holding down employment to support my meager needs, and I must rely upon the kindness of our good government for the—"

"I don't suppose it would be any use asking you to stop taking baths—"

"Ma'am? You would deprive me of my constitutional right to cleanse the filth fom this poor body just because I number among the poverty-stricken?" He stretched his magnificent loins suggestively, and Tamara was glad Adrian had become immersed in an old Cousteau special.

"No, but do you have to do it out in front of a schoolhouse?"

He merely crossed his arms and glowered at the TV screen.

That screen was too large to convey a clear picture. The colors were bright but not sharp, tended to melt together at the edges and give everything a liquid aura—even the scenes on shipboard or land. Given this and the blending of the aqua waves of the Caribbean with the powder blue of the room, Tamara felt drawn into the watery world of Jacques Cousteau, felt herself among the cavorting fish and blacksuited divers.

Backra'd worn part of such a suit, but it had been in ribbons.

A man-o'-war bird glided over and around a white beach, never seeming to move spread wings, a streak of white along its throat and chest, as silent as a dream. And Tamara could smell the sea salt on humid air, the excretions of thickly growing plant life.

"That's the bird of my dream," Adrian said as if in a trance, "and everything's just like that. . . ."

Augie Mapes stared at the girl in the bean-bag chair and at Tamara, all the challenge and teasing gone from his manner, replaced by an expression Tamara couldn't read. "Don't let her dreams carry your daughter away, Miss Schoolteacher," he warned.

14

Thad and his patient slept for about eighteen hours. He'd insisted she lie on a blanket on the floor of his room.

"These village dogs aren't housebroken, and she's probably got fleas, ticks, worms, and everything else," Dixie had protested.

The dog felt weak and sick and helpless and expected to die. She was sore but not in intense pain. She was troubled by a deep longing she couldn't put a name to, had the feeling she'd forgotten something urgent she'd planned to do before she ceased to be.

So she was surprised to awake occasionally and find herself still inside the wooden structure and the man still asleep on the raised platform across the room. The lizard on the far wall sent the thought that surely she must die soon, and then its tongue flicked out to catch a fly and it forgot about her.

Once she awoke to bands of moonlight striping the floor and a shimmery figure rising up from the man who still lay as he had.

Thad dreamed he walked on railroad tracks running along a shelf on the mountain's side. The moon shadowed the group of buildings below, and he recognized the school he'd seen in another dream. Thad placed the dream woman's house directly beneath him. Rough rock and weeds pressed unfelt against his bare feet as he moved down to it. He was surprised to find himself dreaming that he wore pajamas, which he knew he actually was.

The German shepherd he'd seen on another night was sniffing and digging around a little shed, and Thad could hear the mutter of nervous chickens. This time the dog saw him too, froze for a moment, gave a startled yip, and tore off between houses.

Thad moved through the back door as easily as he had the front, and realized he could just as well have walked through the wall. He was in a sort of utility porch. A very dark one. But, as befitted a dream, he had no trouble seeing. The main room was uninhabited. He found her bedroom.

The dream woman looked to be in a very deep sleep; the covers over her chest seemed not to move. He reached down to touch the fluff of her hair, and pondered the liberties one was allowed in a dream. But his fingertips had no sensation of touching her.

The tiny room had one window. The closet door stood half-open, and her shoes were a jumble on the floor. An open book spread face-down on the night table, its spine aglow with the luminance shed by the digits on her alarm clock.

The woman in the bed smiled languidly, making a gesture to pull back the covers, but they remained in place. In a slow liquid motion she rose through them and stood before him, her smile part quizzical, part invitation. At least one of her did. The other still lay under the covers.

Shadows hinted at some interesting shapes beneath the gauzy night-gown. She spoke to him soundlessly, as if to tease, and he thought her lips and tiny even teeth formed the word "fight" on the end of what-ever she said. He repeated the word but found his voice silent too.

"You are not real," he said slowly so she could read his lips. And as that was the case, he dared to discover more about the shadows beneath her gown. Although she didn't move away, his arms filled with nothing.

The bridge of his nose shot aches into his cheeks and brought tears to his eyes, one shoulder pained deep in the joint, and surface scrapes burned everywhere. His head pounded with the receding effects of the rum, and he awoke to bars of moonlight and the little cemetery bitch asleep on the floor. He staggered into the bathroom to swallow some as-pirin, certain he'd never get to sleep again.

The next he knew, Thad was putting up a basketball hoop above the garage door and Ricky was trying to hold the ladder and hand him nails at the same time. Thad reached down to take a nail and noticed how the smooth boy cheek was losing the extra flesh of childhood, the bones firming to take on the lines of the Alexander face. Odd that this boy would grow to look like Edward P., the grandfather he'd still not met.

Molly came around the corner of the garage, honey-colored hair curv-ing smoothly toward her face. The dimple in her cheek deepened. "Thad, I realize you have great expectations for Ricky, but don't you think that's a little high?"

"High? It's regulation height. He's going to be tall, Molly. That's al-ready where they are at school."

"I still think you're jumping the gun a little. Come on, baby, Mommy'll warm your bottle."

"Bottle!" Thad turned with the hammer still poised against the back-board, to see his wife pick up a drooling baby, fit him comfortably over a hip, and carry him toward the front door. One pudgy leg shaped itself perfectly down the curve of her buttock, one fat little arm waved "bye-bye" to Thad.

He clamped sore loosened teeth together and tried to shout "No!" between them. It came out sounding more like a growl, and his eyes

shot open to unpainted rafters and the whimper of the cemetery dog as
she struggled to her feet. His heart tried to pound through the top of
his skull when he sat up too fast. Dizziness whirled him around inside
his head.

Thad carried the dog down the outside stairway, ringing her muzzle
with the circle of one hand. When he set her down, she swayed and
then squatted, giving tiny yips as she voided in the sand.

She tried to stagger off, but he scooped her up and carried her into
the house, where Rafaela stood at the stove stirring something that
smelled delicious. Thad remembered he'd had no food since the cheese
sandwich he'd eaten while the *Golden Goose* towed in the dive boat.

"You should be with your family. I can take care of myself for—"

"The living must eat, Thaddeus. The angels look after my Aulalio
now. And I look after you." She eyed the dog with something less than
enthusiasm but made no protest as he placed the animal in the corner
and put a bowl of water beside her. "He is with his brother and sister,
my Aulalio, and has much hoppiness."

Thad downed a tumbler of papaya-and-pineapple juice and poured
himself another. It barely mollified the rage of his rum-induced thirst.
"I didn't know you'd lost children before."

"A wave comes that sweeps them out to sea, and they are no more."

Thad thought the sea that provided so bountifully in food and climate for this paradise did, nevertheless, exact quite a toll. Rafaela set a
plate before him of rice and pieces of barracuda and tomatoes and
herbs, all fried together with a side of black beans and another of
doughy tortillas just right for scooping the solids and sopping the juices.

"How old were they when you . . . lost them?"

"Marina she had six *años* and little Marcos had four years. The sea
took many children and the old ones and the sick. And many of the
dead." She gestured toward the graveyard outside. "But the sea can
have only the body to keep. *Las almas* . . . the souls, God takes to
heem."

"She has all the answers too," Thad said to the little dog when the
housekeeper had left. "Somehow her answers don't explain what happened out there yesterday, though, do they, My Lady of the Rum-
Soaked Belly?"

She'd lapped water when she thought he wasn't looking. Now her
chin settled on her paws. Her eyelids drooped but snapped open again
whenever he moved.

He finished a cup of the thick sweet coffee, slipped upstairs to dress.
The sky was cloudy and the sea gray. For the first time since he'd
come to the Cay, Thad put on long pants and a sweatshirt. He picked

up the blanket the dog had used in the night. When he covered her with it, she stirred but didn't waken.

Taking down the box with his father's manuscript, selecting certain books from the bookshelf, and hunting up the shoe box full of bits and pieces and his father's notes to himself, Thad placed them all on the table, boiled himself another cup of coffee, and set to work. His father's desk top was too small to contain all this material.

That evening, when Rafaela came to cook dinner, he had to pile everything on the floor so she and Stefano could sit and eat with him. Steamed lobster and crabmeat, breadfruit, and candy-coated sea grapes.

Stefano sat in his usual superior silence. One would never guess he'd just lost the third of his four children. He glanced at the dog in the corner and then at Thad, as if he'd expected as much from a stupid Yankee. When he left, Thad knew he would go to sit at Roudan's as always. But this time with only one son.

He fed the dinner scraps to his patient, the first food she'd accepted that day. Not every dog was lucky enough to recuperate from surgery on lobster and crab.

When he was alone again, he arranged the books and papers back on the table. Closing all the slats in the windows against the chill, he could still hear the crashing of the sea on the coral reef, talk and laughter at Roudan's bar, even Chespita, the parrot. It had never ceased to amaze Thad how life could go on so normally, no matter how recent the calamity.

He'd been working for several hours under the dim light of the one unshielded bulb that hung above the table when he heard a knock at the door over the thrashing the wind was giving nearby palm fronds. Harry Rothnel, the man who owned a "slew" of bakeries, stood outside cradling four bottles of Belican, the dark so thick behind him Thad could barely make out the gravestones and the sea beyond.

"Have a beer and chat, Doc?" Harry's eyes looked chiseled out in shadow. Of the various scars that were visible, the one running from his chin and down his neck was definitely the kind he'd wear for life. But the few long hairs that had hung in his face the last time Thad had seen him were once more swept neatly back over the bald spot.

"Sure, why not?" Thad didn't know if he was ready to talk to a fellow survivor yet, but he couldn't ignore the plea in Harry's voice. "Thought all the boys from lower Alabama that are left would have headed for safer waters by now."

"Couple of us stayed behind to . . . mediate with the authorities and families back home and . . ." Harry shrugged and handed Thad two of the Belicans. "You know, there might still be word on the others.

Could of been another boat out there we didn't see that picked somebody up, and word hasn't got back yet."

"After yesterday, I wouldn't swear to anything's being impossible."

"Heard about the dog," Harry said as the little bitch left her corner and walked fairly steadily to the darkness under the couch. "Boy, the dogs down here sure know how to slink, don't they?"

"I suppose the surgery yesterday is the talk of the island."

"Well, you were upset. We all were. A crazy vet carving on a stray dog's a lot easier to talk about than . . ."

"Two afternoons in one day?"

"Yeah, and that . . . thing that came up out of the water."

Thad pushed aside his work again so they could sit at the table.

"I just can't believe ol' Bo's really gone. The others maybe, but not Bo. He was so alive and tough. You'd have to work overtime to kill a guy like that." Harry looked at the window that was slatted shut, at the corner where the dog had been, at the table—obviously making an effort to keep his eyes dry. "And poor Sue Ellen trying to ride herd on that bunch of hell-raisers of theirs."

He emptied the bottle and rolled it around in his hand, staring at it but not seeing it. "'Course, they ain't going to hurt financially. That's one thing. Ol' Bo was worth bucks."

"Doing what?"

"Owned a string of fast-food joints. Used to kid him about bein' the hamburger king of Alabama." He lost the battle of the tears, and they streamed down his cheeks. "Shit!"

Thad decided it took someone from the deep South to give that word the proper inflection. "Martha gone home yet?"

"Won't budge. Dixie keeps trying to get her on a plane for the States, but she's still waiting for her Greg—like she expects him to walk on the waters or something."

"Like you waiting for Bo?"

"Yeah, I guess. Did you know Martha pulled you into the boat almost single-handed? We all thought you was dead, and we were busy just hanging on. She wouldn't give up, and it was either help drag you in or lose her over the side. Saved your life's what she did."

Thad regretted the few impatient thoughts he'd had of Martha Durwent. "I've been going through my Dad's writings and research, hoping he had a lead on all this. Haven't been able to put anything coherent together yet."

"Beats cuttin' up dogs. Think something happened to him like what happened to the others?"

"Maybe. But no one's come up with any boats missing with him."

"The Metnál isn't in the Bermuda Triangle, is it?"

"Most of these writers place it east and slightly north of here. One of them charts the western edge as far as the tip of Yucatán, which is probably something like three, four hundred miles north of the Metnál. But there are stories of people and craft missing, time getting all mixed up, and people and navigational instruments getting confused in the Triangle—similar to what we experienced."

"So what else did you dredge up, even if it isn't coherent?"

Thad scanned his notepad. "This is going to sound dumb."

"Hell, I was out there, man, you don't get any dumber than what happened."

"Okay . . . uh, some people, including my father, believe man didn't descend from the ape but had a high level of civilization before the Mediterranean cultures developed. It was lost or destroyed or just died, and the Phoenicians and Greeks and Egyptians and Mayans, et cetera, were merely tiny outposts of survival for a dying culture. Everything we know now was known better tens of thousands of years ago and is just being rediscovered."

"Horseshit. Man, you sure don't read your Bible. That's where the truth is at. There's just no question. And what's all this got to do with the thing in the water out there?"

"Nothing, as far as I can see—I think it's all hogwash, and for different reasons. But my father thought there are some hidden vestiges of this civilization in the form of machines left that still work or get out of control. Why these machines didn't oxidize and turn to dust like everything else that old, he didn't explain. But he claims to have seen one of these things himself."

"Where?"

"That he doesn't say. Or if he does, I haven't found it."

Harry Rothnel stared at Thad with a full measure of pity, looked away as if embarrassed, and then said very quietly, "Your dog's peeing on the floor, Doc."

15

Tamara drove across dry rolling plain toward Cheyenne, morning sun in her eyes, edginess playing along her nerve ends because she'd not had time for her run and because she'd left Adrian alone.

Three full days of teachers' meetings before the start of school the next week. But Adrian was twelve. She'd had jobs in Iowa City taking care of other people's children. *So stop fretting, Mother.*

There was little in the way of fattening food in the apartment, no stores to buy any. She'd be happy with her stereo and books. Adrian had been ignoring her whenever possible anyway, so Tamara's absence shouldn't increase her loneliness.

Tamara slowed the Toyota to watch a small band of antelope leap the fence on one side of the ditch, cross the road, and bound over the opposite fence. Their pronged horns reminded her of old-fashioned can openers. They had strawberry-brown coats, white bellies, and streaks at the throat.

The creatures brought a sense of proportion to her day. Tamara could use some time away from Adrian and the shoddy settlement where every problem loomed so large because there was nothing else to think about. She straightened her spine and began to look forward to a day of intelligent adult company, not that of crazies like Augie and Jerusha. She was a professional now, and about to take part in professional meetings. Tamara hummed to the tune of tires on asphalt.

Coming back that evening, her stomach growled with hunger and with anger at all the coffee she'd downed to keep awake. Her bladder shot warning pains at her groin. Her tailbone ached with too much sitting, and her shoulders drooped with fatigue. Tamara'd had no idea boredom could be so tiring.

"The total waste of a whole day!" she said to a windshield aglare this time with the setting sun.

As the ugly mountain came in sight and her stomach, bladder, and aching head all demanded immediate attention, Tamara understood why her working-women friends used to say they wished they had a wife. It would have been wonderful to come home now to dinner prepared, to put her feet up afterward and read the paper while someone else did the dishes, to shower and go to bed early in order to build up the stamina to endure another day like this one.

Adrian stood at the sink when Tamara entered the apartment and dashed for the bathroom. It wasn't until she stepped out that she registered the smell of cooking food and an elegantly set table. Adrian was tossing a salad in Miriam Kopecky's silver salad bowl and had lit candles. The oven door stood open, and the fragrance of roasting beef forced Tamara to swallow squirting saliva.

"I didn't know how to make gravy," Adrian said matter-of-factly, "so I baked the potatoes and we can have them with margarine."

"But how did you know how to do the rest? That roast was frozen . . ."

"Jerusha told me how to thaw it and when to put stuff in the oven." Adrian took out a covered dish of string beans and tomatoes. "Sit down."

The next day Tamara returned to find the leftover roast chopped up in a delicious casserole with rice and vegetables. And the stereo playing softly!

Jerusha didn't like too much noise. Jerusha had helped Adrian think of something to do with the leftover roast.

"Honey, you don't hang around Jerusha's apartment all day, do you?"

"No. Jerusha has to rest a lot. Vinnie and I took a walk today, but her snotty brother tagged along and spoiled it. The Baggette kids came home from their grandma's today. They're nerds. Larry Johnson comes home this weekend. He went on a fishing trip with his uncle. Jerusha's chickens got out, and we had to round them up before the Hanleys' dog got to 'em. We helped Vinnie's mom wash the baby."

Tamara was pleased at the reversal in Adrian's behavior, her interest in someone other than herself—but uneasy at the suddenness of it.

By Friday evening when she staggered in carrying stacks of forms, questionnaires, outlines, and plans, she was too dispirited to care. And too grateful for the creamed-egg-and-noodle dish Adrian put before her to comment on their recent cholesterol intake or the fact that the fresh eggs had come from Jerusha's hen house.

The next afternoon there was a cloud in the sky. Tamara left Adrian with her nose in a book and went out to see it. It was not a large cloud and it obviously didn't plan to do anything, but it did break up the tedious consistency of blue sky. She remembered ironically of having prayed for a break in the rain in Columbus and for the sun to shine. Any change in this changeless place was worth remarking.

Tamara wandered up the road to the company fence and along it until it ended at the base of the mountain. A track with old gondola cars and weeds growing between the ties lay along an embankment, and she followed it into no-trespassing territory.

Some stockpiles of limestone nudged up against the mountain and looked like giant snowbanks next to its iron-stained sides. The mining operation's buildings spread around the mountain's curve and formed a separate town, larger than the one down the road near the school. Metal sheds, obviously in use, sat next to wooden shacks with their roofs fallen in. An ancient outhouse leaned away from a rail siding as if blowing in the windy wake of a motionless ore car loaded with rock.

A shack with a flat tar-paper roof still had glass in its windows, antique glass—murky, dirty. And a once-painted door with a porcelain doorknob and an elaborate bronze knocker that belonged to other years and richer doors and merely thudded when she dropped it against the striker. She could see a wooden table just below the window and a spider making hairlike tracks in the dust across a patch of sunlit surface.

"There's some history there you're looking at," a voice said behind her, and she swung around to find Russ Burnham in pin-striped coveralls and a hard hat with padded metal earmuffs swung back out of the way. "Used to be the chemist's shack."

"I . . . probably shouldn't be here."

"Used to check samples of the rock that came out of the mine every day." The corners of his eyes crinkled and his ears stuck out below the helmet. "Up until a few years ago, used to run an average of ninety-seven, ninety-eight percent. Purest anywhere in the country."

He slapped heavy gloves against his leg, and white dust flew. His workshoes were white to the laces, as if he'd been walking through powdered sugar. "Yeah, been producing since 1905. Used to use horses to pull wooden cars out of the mine. Company'd send men down to Denver, Larimer Street. Hire drunks out of the gutter, bring 'em up, put 'em to work. Nobody sober wanted to come out here. Made for some pretty rowdy times and some pretty tall tales."

"Russ, I know the sign says not to come up here, but I was curious—"

" 'Course we're more mechanized now, don't need many men. Still hell trying to find and keep those we do, though." He pointed to a sagging shed next to a snow fence. "That used to be the magazine, held explosives. Mostly ammonium nitrate. See those big doors? That's the three-hundred-foot portal. Three hundred feet from the top of the mountain. That part of the mountain's almost hollow after years of mining, and that portal's sealed off. One good earthquake, and that whole baby'd cave in."

Tamara laughed and threw up her arms. "All right. All right, you're hired. I'll bring my students up for a guided tour."

"I only guide teachers." The eye crinkles disappeared. "If you're going to teach in a company town, you ought to know something about it. Curiosity's been known to kill more than cats."

He snorted and spit into the weeds. "Now, come around here and look down." He led her to the curve in the mountainside, where the ground fell away sharply. "You can't see it from here, but down there's the six-hundred-foot portal, where we're working now."

"Aren't you afraid the hollowed-out top half will cave in on the tunnels and miners below?"

"Yeah, but like I said, it'd take a earthquake. Which has never been known to happen here. 'Course I don't imagine the Indians and buffalo kept much in the way of records. I think the company'll shut down here soon. Cheaper to surface-mine limestone. And the purity's giving out."

"It's odd to have the bowels of the mountain so white and the outside so rusty-colored."

"Unusual land formation, all right. There're a few others like it. Those big buildings at the other end of the tracks down there are the crusher, where all the noise comes from, and the screening plant. Back up on this level here, that foundation used to be the hotel for single miners and that great heap of boards behind it was the old icehouse."

"Hey, boss?" A man with a light on his helmet strode up the road from the lower level. "She's back down there again. Says she's checkin' on our progress. What the hell's that supposed to mean?"

"I don't know, but just get her out, by force if you have to. You know the insurance won't—"

"No way, man, I ain't messin' with that."

"I'll be down in a minute." Russ Burnham sighed and then stared at Tamara for the longest time while the other man waited impatiently. "I sure wish you'd just chuck it in, leave this place, go back East, anything."

16

Thad stood next to Dixie Grosswyler at the Mass for the Dead Padre Roudales celebrated for Aulalio Paz. Padre Roudales flew in every three weeks to administer to the needs of the citizens of San Tomas.

The women of San Tomas still covered their heads in church, even though the church didn't cover their heads. The gray concrete shell had no roof and no seats. Sun flooded from above, drying puddles left by the rain the night before. Lacy scarves and the priest's vestments fluttered in the sea breeze. Palm trees spread a moving shadow benediction over the celebration for Aulalio.

A bird screeched from the jungle as if being murdered, and two silent frigate birds wheeled overhead, so narrow of wing and lean of body they barely left a shadow on the church and the people gathered below. The sky-roof was too blue, the palms' greenness suspect. The murmur of believers blended perfectly with the surf against the barrier reef. The world appeared lullingly normal.

After hours of poring through his father's junky literature, Thad decided the surfacing-submarine theory sounded better and better. He said as much to Harry when they left the open-topped services.

"Oh, Doc, I liked the other one." Harry turned to Dixie as they walked down the beach. "You see, we are just the leftovers of a once-advanced people who were destroyed or died off, now we are just rediscovering knowledge that's been around since before God and even before the earth was formed, and this huge egg that came up out of the Metnál and almost sank our boat is a machine from those old times before there was anything, and it's going berserk 'cause there's no one around to run it anymore."

"Well, you've seen the egg, you should know." Dixie forced a laugh. "Rafaela will be busy, Thad, come eat with us."

He followed them through the compound and across the veranda to a dining room where guests served themselves at a buffet and sat at long tables from which fans in the ceiling kept the flies moving.

"Had any reservations canceled yet?"

"No, but we will when news of this gets out." Dixie rested her elbows on the table and brushed frizzy curls off her forehead. "Thad, what really happened out there? You've had time to recover your senses."

He chewed a piece of gristly conch and buttered a slice of bread. "Rafaela's chowder is so much better than this. You should get the recipe."

"I have to know. There's a British naval officer coming in. He's booked a cabana and wants to talk to anyone 'familiar with the disturbance in the Metnál.' We can't tell him a big egg—"

"How about a gray eyeball?"

"That's even worse. Thad, I've got a business to run. I can't have stories like this—"

"Five people died out there."

"And more will. If this gets too crazy, every nut in the U.S. and Europe will want to dive the Metnál."

"And rent cabanas and buy booze in the bar hut."

"I thought you were a friend."

"All right, how about it was a submarine? Might be tough to convince a British naval officer that there's a submarine twice the size of the *Titanic* that can lie buried under the sea floor, but—"

"We have to make up some kind of crazy story that can be believed. The whole tourist industry of this area could be ruined. And the people of Belize can't afford to lose any money-making industry. Have you seen the slums of Belize City?"

"I bounced off it like I was a gnat—but it could have been metal. I remember an echo inside it when I hit."

"I had an uncle who went on vacation to Mexico and said he saw a flying saucer." Dixie still hadn't touched her food. "When the Mexican authorities wouldn't look into it, he raised hell with the American authorities, got furious with any family or friends who suggested it was something else and maybe he'd been mistaken. Ended up losing his job, wife left him, got a drinking problem—the whole bit. All because of that one little thing."

"Five dead people are not 'one little thing.'"

The helicopter had impersonal bug-eye glass windows wrapped around its front. They shed back the sunlight like the dark glasses on a highway patrolman. Jungle grasses spread away at the edge of the landing strip, palms tossed frantic heads as if a hurricane were upon them, and Dixie's long skirt flattened against her legs as the squat machine pulled up its nose and lowered itself onto Mayan Cay.

A door slid open far enough to emit a tank, but one man jumped to the ground—red-haired, chubby, dressed as a tourist, but with the indefinable stamp of the British Navy.

Belize had achieved its independence somewhat reluctantly. It remained under the protection of the Queen because Guatemala claimed the tiny country that blocked her coastline and wasn't above sending troops down the Belize River or planes over the airport at Belize City. So a small portion of her Majesty's dwindling fleet was stationed in these coastal waters and six British Harriers at her main airport.

A disembodied arm handed down a suitcase to the new arrival. Dixie waved as he turned from the dark-olive helicopter and walked briskly toward the jeep, bent low under the still-whirling blades. Dixie usually sent one of the boys to the airstrip to meet guests, but this trip she'd decided to make herself.

"Miss Grosswyler? Geoffrey Hindsly here. Splendid of you to meet me. I've heard nothing but good news about the Mayapan."

"I hope you won't be disappointed, Mr. Hindsly—or is it lieutenant or captain or . . . I'm afraid I don't know your rank." She slid behind the wheel, and he came around to sit beside her.

"Let's forget all about that, shall we? I'm looking forward to a small vacation. The other matter we discussed by radio is just a by-the-bye, so to speak." Geoffrey Hindsly would never make a decent liar. "You might tell me something of the people I'll be meeting, though. The ones we discussed this morning? Might make matters move more quickly. Get this little business over with so I can enjoy myself, what?" His smile was expectant, his eyes studied her closely.

"Mr. Hindsly, the government of Belize has yet to get off its collective butt to begin an investigation—except to interview survivors before they flew back to the States. The press won't be here for two hours, but the British Navy has a sudden interest in this 'little business' in which four of my guests and one employee lost their lives and others were injured, by-the-bye, so to speak."

"Well, yes, won't be good for business, will it? Then again, it might be very good. In any instance, it will have some effect, won't it?" He settled back, glanced pointedly at the ignition key.

"What's up? I mean, God, the press is coming."

"We've sidelined a bit of that, I think. Some of the Mayan Airlines planes have been pressed into duty elsewhere. May interfere with the arrival and departure of your guests. Inconvenience shouldn't last long. Uh . . . shall we go?"

"Not until you tell me what's happening."

He withdrew a pouch with pipe and tobacco, made a great display of filling it and tamping. "Miss Grosswyler, her Majesty's Navy does have some interest in what happens in these waters. You must know that."

"I know that two years ago a yacht anchored inside the reef off this island disappeared with a family of four aboard."

"We can't be responsible for every boat lost at sea." He lit the pipe and squinted at the windshield, his manner chilling perceptibly.

"Some months ago an American living on the island just disappeared."

"Edward P. Alexander, the writer. Yes, I'd heard. But one need not make a mystery of every death or disappearance. Accidents do happen. And not just here."

"And her Majesty's Navy shows little interest in them," she yelled over the departing helicopter.

"You must admit the stories of the people involved in the Metnál incident were indeed strange."

"You've talked to them?" There went her plans to keep things rational.

"All but those that are still here."

"Mr. Hindsly, I don't care if your rank is admiral. You've come to question my guests and interrogate me about them. Before I cooperate with you or move this jeep one inch, I want to know why."

"It's all rather embarrassing, actually." And indeed his face reddened to almost match his hair, but in anger at her persistence, Dixie thought, instead of embarrassment.

She had still to decide if his David Niven/Terry Thomas act was real or feigned. "What is embarrassing, Mr. Hindsly?"

"One had hoped, you see, that it had merely been misplaced on paper. That it would turn up before the press got after it, but we can't seem to raise it by radio. News may be going out on the wires even now."

"Misplaced what?"

"See here, couldn't we discuss this over a whiskey somewhere? I'm afraid I'm fairly done in by all this."

"Misplaced what, Mr. Hindsly?"

"It seems we've lost a vessel. In the vicinity of the Metnál." He'd let his pipe go out, and made a face when he tried to draw on it. "Possibly about the time your guests had their accident."

"What kind of vessel, Mr. Hindsly?"

"A destroyer, Miss Grosswyler."

Interim

Between Time

It was an almost automatic thing for Edward P. Alexander III to be walking along assuming his mind was concentrating on his journey and to discover instead that it was reworking an awkward sentence he'd written earlier in the day: "*The bane of science, like that of religion, is not that which it explains but all that which it ignores.*" No. Too many "thats." How about: ". . . *rather that which it ignores*"? He was still stuck with the excess "that." Edward was on his way to a point of craggy coral at the very tip of one end of the island.

Although from the air the island looked to be ringed by sandy, passable beaches, Edward had found that in fact walking around it could be a messy business—sucking mud one minute, the need to wade in the sea shallows the next. He feared Rafaela would have a fuss washing his clothes again.

He arrived at last, camera and film dry, and set to reconstructing the blind he'd built several days before but which had fallen over—merely a batch of palm fronds stacked in such a way as to provide shade, hide his rather large form, and offer a suitable hole through which to poke a camera lens.

He settled into it thankfully, aware of his age after the long walk, and took a pull on his canteen. He'd come to photograph an iguana. They often crawled up onto the craggy dead coral on the other side of his blind to soak in the sun, and he needed an especially good one now for a book jacket he wished to propose to his publishers.

This book would surely set the world on fire and some of his scholarly detractors on their asses. Now that he'd pieced everything together, it was almost luridly simple, and he couldn't fathom why someone smarter than he hadn't figured it out long ago. Perhaps one had to adventure without preconception and yet seek with determination in order to relate all these mysteries of existence. And then of course it helped to have come across the machine.

There were still some loose ends. The most baffling one, Edward thought, as he took the luncheon from his rucksack, was how did they manage to get fresh eggs on the *Ambergris*? He unwrapped the tortilla rolled around a mixture of seasoned black-bean paste and stringy strips of chicken. If Ramael did actually breakfast aboard the yacht a year after her disappearance, how, then, did the Kellers renew their egg supply? Or were they the same eggs they'd eaten the morning of their disappearance?

But once consumed, that would be impossible, wouldn't it?

He finished his lunch, wondering what had become of the iguanas, and adjusted his tripod, put a 500-millimeter lens with an ultraviolet filter on his Nikon, and stuck it through a hole in the blind large enough to allow for proper movement. He ought to get a fine shot of any creature at this end of the point. He'd barely settled himself in for a long wait when he heard a splash and the clicking of many long toenails on a hard surface. An iguana, looking every bit a tiny dinosaur, reared its warty face above a coral peak and then drew its body up onto a flat resting place with a flap of its tail. The ridge of spines along his back glistened wet with sea water. He settled his belly on the warmed coral shelf with what Edward imagined to be a "humph."

Iguanas numbered among Edward's favorite creatures, good enough reason to have one on the jacket of his book. Besides, the iguana represented a hint of mystery, of other worlds and other ages.

Bending low to the viewfinder, Edward saw another iguana pull itself into view as he adjusted his aging vision to that of the Nikon F2A, heard a "whumping" sound that sent little stabbing pains through his ears and impacted with a pressure that caught at his breath.

It startled him, so he sat up and the blind collapsed around him.

The iguanas appeared disturbed also. One pushed up on his forelegs and flailed his tongue at the air. The other lashed his tail about as if looking for a fight.

And no wonder. A man stood before them, as though he'd risen from the sea all in an instant. But he wasn't wet. He wore a one-piece suit of a color somewhere between that of a ripe peach and the flesh tones of a ruddy Caucasian. It was made of a lacy material, yet opaque, and fit him like skin, outlining every hump, bump, roll of rib and muscle. It had no visible points or lines of fastening for zipper, button, or even Velcro. His skin tone was a tad lighter in shade than that of Rafaela Paz. His face showed not one wrinkle, pouch, or blemish. His hair was cut short and curled tightly in a dark shade of auburn. He showed no expression and reminded Edward P. of a retouched photograph.

The man was the finest specimen in both looks and form that Alexander had ever encountered. Edward, who in his youth and when standing at perfect attention had measured six feet and four inches, judged this apparition to be well over seven feet.

The old adventurer, rarely taken for lack of words, found himself speechless before this amazing entity while a nasty gas bubble racked its way through a kink in his lower intestine. The two iguanas swiveled a hasty retreat into the Caribbean.

There was little of the unexpected Edward had not either experienced, imagined, or read of in his lengthy lifetime, and he waited for some reaction within himself to offer a clue as to what life expected of him now. Fear might be healthy, his mind suggested, but his being waited, as if separated from logic until understanding offered a glimmer of itself.

"Ohhhhh!" said the creature without blinking or moving his mouth or one muscle in his beautiful face.

Edward P. sat back on his heels, and the Nikon F2A toppled facefirst in the sand onto its ultraviolet filter. He was still waiting for fear when understanding presented itself unannounced. And vindication. "You're an Atlantean."

The stranger widened his eyes, which were an indeterminate shade of dark, as though he'd heard, but his response was to raise open palms to the sky and shout, "Primitive in the funnel!"

He did this without moving his lips or the smooth skin of his throat. He stared back and forth across the heavens as if expecting an answer.

Edward P. looked up, half-expecting a crash of thunder, but saw nothing more than a man-o'-war bird lazing on air above them. Not even a cloud.

The man walked to a high and relatively smooth stonelike outcropping of coral and sat. Neither his suit nor his skin wrinkled with his fluid movements. The slight hunch of his shoulders, the clasp of his hands, suggested dejection. His face showed no expression. He ignored Edward altogether, and looked skyward once more. "Help! I'm caught."

The man-o'-war bird hesitated in its flight, lowered its slender head. Edward had never seen one do that before. It swooped very low, circled twice, and wheeled out over the bush jungle of the island's interior, leaving them alone.

Edward's ankles and legs pained him, and he stood finally, marveling that fear still hadn't arrived, but uneasy about that. Fear had saved him more than once. He tried to think of something to say, but again his tongue surprised him. He reached into his rucksack for his other canteen, which contained something stronger than water. *He must be from Atlantis. How else can he be so magical? Speak without words.*

"You are merely receiving my thoughts in such manner or 'words' as you can perceive them, primitive." The man answered Edward's thoughts much as one would speak to an animal. If one could speak to an animal. "You and the fowl that just left us."

Edward took a swig of rum and tried to decide if this guy was human or just unusual. "But I am a man like you, not a fowl."

"In your state, there is little difference." He rubbed a chin that looked too smooth to have ever grown a beard. "What does it matter? We are doomed."

Edward P. turned his back on the man to see if he could still hear the motionless mouth. Mental telepathy? Or was this all just a dream?

"I knew the malfunction was in this century, and I told them where it was within twenty-five years."

Edward turned around. This guy not only wasn't talking with his mouth, he wasn't even looking at Edward, and still Edward could hear him.

"Amstrack said the terminals had to be located in inaccessible places." The apparition was obviously talking to himself. "He pointed out the geological changes in landmasses with the fall and rise of continents and oceans. What he didn't predict was the mental energies of primitives, the interference of their rudimentary power systems. You savages play with energy waves as if they had no force."

"You are not from Atlantis." Edward P. capped the rum canteen. He felt his vindication slip away.

"I know nothing of Atlantis." The perfect man stood. "I can't believe we ever looked like you creatures."

"I'm old but still human."

"I suspect I'm older by far than you. But that makes no more difference now than the fact I've a new granddaughter I'll never see again. Just your ugly bearded face forever. Not that you could understand my plight."

"You, sir, are probably nothing more than a bad dream generated by Rafaela's excellent but heavy black beans and Belize's questionable rum. I am an author." Edward P. Alexander III straightened an imperfect, aging spine that had climbed mountains in Tibet and curled under fever in the jungles of Quintana Roo. "I'm an adventurer. I was once on the Jack Paar show. I have been interviewed by the best. Criticized by the worst. Until a short time ago I had a grandson. And I resent your attitude."

"You've organized into formal families, have you?" He walked around the tumbled blind of browning palm fronds and almost stepped on the extended 500-millimeter lens. "My survivors are all female, thank God."

"Why thank God for females?" Edward, still expecting to wake up at any moment (*no more black beans, Rafaela*), slipped in behind the stranger to retrieve his Nikon F2A. "I've a son, had a grandson, and am damned well pleased—"

"In a matriarchy, females are a blessing."

"You consider us so primitive and you still have a god?"

"Even in your day she was a necessary evil, right?" The mouth finally opened, smiled perfect teeth. But it had remained closed while the words came out.

They'd been following each other in a circle around the fallen blind. Edward P. stopped, and that brought the giant up against his back. Edward sensed the revulsion of the other man, but when he turned, could read nothing in the blank face. "Who are you? And why a matriarchy? This is my dream, and I may be getting old, but if the men look like you, I'd surely love to see the gals."

"The women took over after the destruction." The apparition turned away from Edward. "I am a time engineer and I come from your future."

"And God's a woman?"

"She's the creator, isn't she? Tell me, old man, for the sake of curiosity, when some fool created the combustion engine"—there was almost the hint of a crease in the smooth forehead now—"did she know it would take the planet's atmosphere two centuries to recover?"

"It was a man did that," Edward P. said. "If you really are from the future, your ignorance of history is shocking. Even for a dream."

"History is not my specialty. And this is no dream." He sat again, and again allowed a dejected hunch to his magnificent shoulders, and Edward P. quite literally felt his sadness. "We are doomed to relive this moment throughout time, never remembering that we've met and talked before, because we are between time. At least that's the theory. As in death, no one's ever returned from this no-man's-land to inform us for sure."

"What's a time engineer, and how can we be between time?"

"Enough, old man. Give me some peace to mourn my losses." The engineer's hopelessness overwhelmed Edward suddenly, bore down on him so that he had to sit at the man's feet. Those feet were covered by the same material as his suit, with no hardened sole for support.

II

The Witch of Iron Mountain

17

Russ Burnham stood in the entrance to the lower six-hundred-foot portal of Iron Mountain, the great wooden doors opened flat against the walls. A line of overhead lights extended back into dimness and disappeared, unable to hold away the darkness of the hollow mountain for long. The rails below shone dully under the lights and narrowed in the distance. Then they too disappeared.

The smell of dirt and damp the sun never purged from his pores, that went to bed with him at night, hung unmoving on the air. Sandstone walls left by the miners between broad passageways gouged of their limestone were thinner than the tunnels they separated at this level. Instead of walls, the level above had only pillars remaining to hold up the mountain. It was like a vast and empty ballroom.

This main entrance below was a good twelve feet wide and ten high. B & H and Russ sent the men ever deeper into Iron Mountain in search of the rock for making milk-of-lime, used in the purification process at all the company's plants in Colorado and Nebraska. Tons of sugar beets were grown in these states each year.

But B & H had just opened a surface mine nearer Cheyenne, where rock was extracted by a contractor with machines instead of skilled miners. Less remote and cheaper to operate, the new mine would soon spell the end of this one. Reclamation laws of the state of Wyoming would require the portals be filled with concrete, the company buildings demolished. Only the prairie winds and the pocket gophers would be left to listen to the whispered tales of the old-timers.

Russ Burnham shook himself and took a deep breath. The closing of this place would be a relief. He'd been here too long. It was just that sometimes Iron Mountain took hold of him—its history, its people. He'd miss the old-timers.

"Here she comes," Saul Baggette, his underground manager, said behind him. "I'm going to take a leak."

Saul's boots crunched off in the other direction as the sound of footsteps approached ahead. Where would she and the other squatters go when Iron Mountain closed?

Jerusha Fistler was a witch. Russ couldn't have described how he knew this. Not that he was sure what one was or that he believed in such things. He just believed in Jerusha Fistler. And although he'd never discussed it with any of them, he knew the other men did too. Life in Iron Mountain had become comfortable for Russ only because it had become familiar. He did not enjoy change. But getting this woman out of his life was one change he looked forward to.

The beam of her flashlight probed out toward Russ and the mine entrance. Her footsteps slow and careful, she emerged from the darkness behind it. The print dress hung on her loosely; shadows deepened the hollows in her face. But he was amazed at how quickly she was adding weight, how recovered in strength she seemed. The first time he'd seen her this way, he'd decided she was dying of cancer.

"Mrs. Fistler, you know company rules about nonemployees in the mine. And you also know—"

"Oh, I know, Russel Burnham, that we are getting closer. I can feel it, the strength and power just flowing out of the middle of this mountain like a river." She walked on by him as she spoke, her big eyes and big teeth sparkling at him.

"I keep telling you," he shouted after her, "there's nothing inside this mountain but rock! Do you hear me? Rock!"

The crusher started up at the other end of the tracks, and its screeching grind drowned him out. Jerusha turned onto the path up to the old level without looking back.

"Goddamn-son-of-a-bitchin'-biscuit-full-of . . ." Russ kicked the side of the tunnel with the iron-reinforced toe of his work boot and then socked it with his fist, felt the pain cut into his anger as the rock cut into his knuckles, saw his underground manager slip into the mine entrance through eyes teared over by rage.

"Hey, boss, you don't think there's anything to what she's always talking about? I mean, there's all them old stories and—"

"There is nothing inside this mountain but what you have seen. You got that?" They were shouting over the noise of the crusher.

"Yeah, well, the guys thought they might of heard something—"

"Baggette, do you know what it is that I am going to hit next?"

"Uh . . . yeah. See ya." Saul Baggette switched on the light on his helmet and disappeared down the tunnel.

Russ walked out into daylight, and the earth beneath his feet shuddered with the crusher's thunder as it chewed the bowels of Iron Mountain. He'd recommend Baggette and Johnson, the aboveground manager, to the company for transfer when operations closed down here. The rest would be on their own. He took the path Jerusha had taken, but slowly, so as not to catch up with her, stopping at the little ledge on which he'd found the other teacher, Miriam Kopecky, walking in her sleep one night.

There had always been stories about the mine, and that was not unusual. Miners were a superstitious lot. Russ was the only one who would sleep on the company compound. Most refused to live free in the company town below, would rather commute from Horse Creek or even Cheyenne. And not since the days the company imported every able body by rail, miner or not, had the mine worked full shift. Night or day made no difference inside the mountain, but B & H couldn't get enough men to run more than one shift a day. Even so, things had not been so bad until old Abner Fistler brought home a wife less than half his age.

Russ kicked a pebble down the incline and stared into space. Not that he hadn't seen the ghosts before that, or had trouble getting workers. But since then, life had become decidedly more complicated, and Russ preferred simplicity.

Abner Fistler had come to him on Russ's first year on the job, complaining of not being able to sleep. He was trembly and coughing a lot, and Russ decided it wouldn't be long before B & H would have to pension him off. Headquarters and the insurance companies demanded there be a night watchman on patrol around the grounds even in so remote an area, and particularly since the mine and crusher shut down at night. Russ took Abner out of the tunnels and made him watchman, thinking he might sleep better during the day.

This had seemed to work quite well for a while, but then Abner took to drinking and talking about the pretty young thing he was going to marry. And one day he cashed in all his savings bonds, borrowed money from everyone he knew—including Russ—and left to get married. He was back in two weeks with Jerusha. She did not look, talk, or act like anyone from Horse Creek or Cheyenne, the only two places Abner ever went. Rumor had it she must have come from Denver, where odd people were reportedly abundant. Jerusha simply ignored the question whenever asked.

Flexing his sore fist, Russ tramped up the rest of the path that was a shortcut from the curving road connecting the two levels. Since Abner's death, Russ had dreamed more than once that the old man had joined Iron Mountain's ghosts.

He honked, snorted, and spit into the weeds, his eyes searching the buildings and ruins of the upper level. He couldn't see Abner's wife, and he fervently hoped that she'd gone on home.

The next Monday was the first day of school in the mustard-colored schoolhouse in the company town. Tamara stood at the cloudy window and watched her new students through fly spatters as they circled each other on the playground. There were Vinnie and Bennie Hope (he was an inveterate sniffer), Will and Nate Baggette, Larry Johnson, and Adrian from Iron Mountain. And Rene and Mike Nygard from a nearby ranch.

Tamara would have liked to escape the dusty room and go out in the sun too, but she had a series of preliminary forms to fill out on each student and had to study Miss Kopecky's files. Much of this kind of thing would have to be done on noon hours and recesses so she could prepare lessons in the evenings. She stooped to pick up a paper that had fallen off Vinnie's desk. A spidery hand had scrawled "Gloria Devine Hope" across the top, and page numbers for tomorrow's assignments below. In the margin, she'd doodled a line drawing that reminded Tamara of the topside of a palm tree—like those she'd seen in one of her dreams when she'd risen above them into the sky with the frigate birds. And below that Vinnie had sketched that marking that had been in the sand of the dream cemetery in front of Backra's house. The one that looked like a leaf skeleton, with the long central vein and evenly spaced ribs extending diagonally from each side *ad infinitum*, as though the leaf had no beginning and no end.

Putting the paper down firmly, she went to her desk. She was seeing these dreams in too much of her waking life. If this continued, they might interfere with her work, and Tamara needed a good record her first year if she hoped to make teaching a career and support herself and her daughter.

Miriam Kopecky's files on the school's students were complete through the winter quarter and blank for anything beyond the last year's spring break. Did this indicate the time of her death? Tamara was startled to find the improvement in Vinnie's test scores over the last quarter recorded. And in every subject. Previously an indifferent scholar, Gloria Devine Hope must have knuckled down last winter.

Larry Johnson had been quick in math and anything smacking of the scientific throughout his schooling, but in the last recorded quarter, he too had shown a surprising improvement in other subjects.

Curious now, Tamara leafed through the folders and found the scores were close to identical. They were all A's and B's or the letter representing that grade level's equivalent in jargon. As if Miss Kopecky had filled out report cards by marking the same thing in every box she came to. All except for Bennie Hope, who went from failing to the equivalent of a C in reading.

"Well, that's one way to speed up the paperwork," Tamara said to the clock above the door, the hands of which never moved. As far as she was concerned, Bennie Hope was still a failure at reading. In the back of Rene Nygard's folder, slipped in as if by mistake, Tamara found a partial letter in Miss Kopecky's small, precise, and blocky handwriting. It was merely dated "Friday":

> Dearest Bea,
>
> Remember my telling you of the young widow in the apartment next to mine and of the odd experiments? I'm beginning to think she might be on to something. She claims the mountain itself or something inside it is responsible for the disquieting happenings I've encountered here. She says some people are more sensitive to whatever it is than others, and that she can help me. You know I've always had an interest in the occult.
>
> I think you're right in that it was a mistake to stay another year. As I get older, I find I need more sleep, and all this has made me so weary I'm not sure whether I'm being reasonable or, as you suggest, taken in by others. I'm going to try an experiment over spring break. I can think of little else right now. Perhaps I'll wait to finish this missive until afterward, so I can tell you all about it.

The mountain, something inside it? Tamara crossed the hall to the unused classroom and stared at the rusty slope out the window. What kind of rubbish did Jerusha Fistler feed poor old Miss Kopecky?

"Besides being nosy," she asked Vinnie after classes had resumed and the others worked on tomorrow's assignments, "what was Miss Kopecky like?"

"Tall. Skinny." Vinnie stuck the eraser end of a pencil in her ear, twisted it, pulled it out, and flicked a piece of ear wax onto her history book. "She always wore dresses, even when it was cold. And she had glasses with the little half-circle at the bottom."

"Was her hair gray?"

"Yeah, with lots of curls. And she had pretty scarves she'd put around her neck and pin them to her dress with a different pin every day. The pins were pretty and gave you something to look at when she talked boring."

"That sounds like a good idea. Maybe I'll have to get some jewelry. Did you like Miss Kopecky as a teacher, Vinnie?"

"No."

That night Tamara drank too much coffee while she worked on lessons and daydreamed about Gil's new wife after she (Tamara) was a highly successful professional person. In her fantasies the exact occupation in which she would miraculously make her mark was never spelled out, but it apparently had nothing to do with education. In this one she walked down a city street on Backra's arm, aware of how elegant a couple they made, and who should they run into but Gil and his new wife. Elsie was short and frumpy and fat and chewed gum incessantly. Gil had gone to pot and looked an unhappy man.

Once in bed, Tamara embroidered on this fantasy, and it and the coffee kept her awake late into the night. She heard Adrian get up, and heavy footfalls pass her door. Tamara rolled over, wishing she could dream of Backra tonight, beginning to feel drowsy at last, when she realized Adrian hadn't returned. "Adrian? Are you sick or something, honey? Adrian?"

The silence in the house was almost noisy. And just when she might have fallen asleep. . . . Tamara grabbed her robe and headed for the bathroom. The light was on, but the room was empty. She checked Adrian's room. Empty. So was the barnlike main room. Alarm began to overcome irritation.

The door to the utility porch stood open, but when Tamara switched on the light, this room too was empty of Adrian. Two layers of door led from the porch to the wooden stairs outside. The screen was shut, but the heavy winterized door inside was not. Tamara stepped out onto the top step in her bare feet. The chill on the night air held a promise of first frost. "Adrian?"

The moon was not full, but it was high enough to illuminate the figure moving past Alice's pen and then the hen house, to give it a ghostly corona as it glided up the mountain to the first row of rusty tracks.

"Adrian!"

But Adrian didn't turn at her mother's voice, or even pause.

18

Tamara stubbed a toe when she raced back into the house for her shoes and a coat and shoes for Adrian. She was outside, crossing the yard in a limping, hopping run seconds later, but Adrian had disappeared.

Remembering Miss Kopecky's troubles with sleeping, she wondered if there was something contagious about that apartment. And the funny gliding manner in which Adrian had been moving made her think the girl was sleepwalking. She'd known Adrian to do that only once, several days after she'd been told her parents planned to separate. She'd glided into the guest room, where her father slept, and just stood like a zombie.

Tamara started up the mountain in Adrian's path. Her real worry was that if her daughter was sleepwalking she might fall into one of the exploratory holes Russ Burnham had warned them of.

Searching the shadows around the ore cars on the first level of tracks, she hurried on into the company's no-trespassing area and stopped. On her right, Russ's blue house and sick petunias slept under a glaring yard light. To her left the hillside rose in shadows. Another yard light stood in the center of the buildings on this level. Yet another over by the main-rail siding lighted the loading area and tall hopper building. But there were many shades of darkness in between, and Tamara studied these for a sign of movement. She didn't know if Adrian had headed up the side of Iron Mountain or was now wandering among the company buildings, some of the older ones threatening to collapse at any moment.

Tamara had expected to overtake her easily, had been alarmed but not really frightened until now, when it looked as if the night and this unlikely place had swallowed up her child. Who could well be helpless if sleepwalking, or confused and frightened if awake.

"Adrian?" She cupped her hands around her mouth, tried to make her voice carry, stretched out the name. No crickets chirped in the chilling grasses. No pebbles loosened by Adrian's bare feet trickled tellingly down the mountainside. Only the low groan of a wind that had begun as a breeze several days before and had not let up since, and the whir of it through dead and stiffening weeds. The creak of a loosened board on some tumbledown building.

Tamara shivered because she could see her breath on the air even in the darkness and because instinct spread cold fire through her middle at the thought of her child in danger.

She moved deeper among the company buildings but glanced up at the mountain at every chance, walked carefully among shadows that looked like puddles on the ground. The smells of motor oil and dust. The sneezy tang of tiny weed spores afloat on the wind. A shadow moved around a corner of light and disappeared with the sound of footsteps.

"Oh, thank God. Adrian!"

Tamara lurched around the same corner and grabbed a dark shoulder before she realized it was too large to be Adrian's. The shoulder seemed to leap away from her as she leaped back, and the figure whirled to shine a flashlight in her face. She glimpsed the double barrels of a shotgun rising to aim at her chest. Tamara fell, with a jolt to her rear that made her bite her tongue. The flashlight blurred through smarting tears.

"Mrs. Whelan?" Fred Hanley said with relief. "What're you doing up here this time of night?"

"I forgot about you being the night watchman. I didn't mean to startle you, but Adrian's out walking in her sleep and I—"

"What?" He lowered the light and the weapon, helped her to stand. She'd also forgotten about his hearing difficulty. "Adrian's out sleepwalking. I saw her come this way," she yelled slowly. Her tongue was bleeding.

Fred reached up to adjust the mechanisms in both bows of his eyeglasses. Then he cupped a hand behind each ear, and she could hear the wind beep in his hearing aids. She explained again.

"Sleepwalkin', you say?" He shook his head and stepped out to an open area, looked from side to side. He was a stocky man, all torso, with short, bowed legs. "Sure hope she don't bother them ghosts any."

"I'm more worried that she'll fall into a hole or cause an old building or wall to fall on her or something," Tamara said. "I'm afraid I don't believe in ghosts, Mr. Hanley."

"Me neither. Don't make a point of botherin' them, just the same." He was bareheaded and wore an ancient sport coat over a flannel shirt and blue jeans. He handed her his flashlight. "You take everything on this side of that center track there and up the hill a ways, and I'll take the other side and the lower level. And, Mrs. Whelan, I'd appreciate it if from now on you could keep her at home at night, where she belongs."

Tamara bit off a reply as to exactly where Fred Hanley could stick his opinions on Adrian's nocturnal movements and took off for her prescribed area, trying to carry Adrian's coat and shoes while using the flashlight and keeping her wraparound robe closed.

The night watchman's remarks about ghosts had seemed stupid when she was standing near him and practically under a yard light. But now, off by herself, skirting a roofless, windowless building—where things scratched and scurried under a rotting floor and a chilly wind whistled through cracks and around corners—ghosts did not seem so out-of-place.

If she hadn't gone back for the coat and shoes, she'd probably have kept Adrian in sight and this late-night escapade wouldn't have been necessary. Then again, with her own feet so tender, she'd have been no use on the spiny weeds and cold rocky soil. And as long as she had to go back for her own shoes, it didn't take that much longer to grab something for Adrian. Still, she had to admit this was one of her split-second decisions that had turned out wrong. It wasn't the first.

She walked around a wooden ore car rotting on its side, shining the light into its shadow. She'd read of sleepwalkers curling up in improbable places and waking later, not knowing where they were or how they'd gotten there. Aiming the flashlight's beam at some huddled bushes whose leaves were beginning to show a frost coating that shimmered back from the bottom of a ravine, Tamara glimpsed motion out of the corner of her eye and swiveled her head to look in that direction before she could sweep the flashlight around to aim at it.

There was nothing there, either before her light reached the area or after. A leveled heap of boards extending over a fairly vast area, which Russ had told her was once an icehouse. But nothing above it existed to make the movement she'd seen.

The moon was a funny shape, not half of it showing, and what did looked like a shallow bowl, slightly tipped. Its light was undependable, she decided, making the heavens dark and menacing and causing her to see nonexistent things below. And yet, for a few seconds, she carried the memory image of a human form—a man with dark, possibly red, shirt or jacket and loose trousers and a tannish-colored hat with a narrow brim and rounded crown. The image had been taking long, purposeful strides. It looked straight ahead, as if unaware of her.

Tamara knew this figure was a manifestation of the hour, the darkness, and the superstitions of others at play on her imagination. But she was reminded of Miss Kopecky's reference to "disquieting happenings."

She moved on slowly now, trying not to see anything but what lay directly in front of her, dreading that she might see more. Every rustling sound or creak of old wood startled her, every shadow held a threat. The skin on her arms prickled at each pore with anticipation of the approach of something sudden and unknown.

It was times such as this she sorely missed Gilbert Whelan.

Finally she crossed between the chemist's shack and the old magazine and started up the side of the hollow mountain, calling out for Adrian at intervals, sweeping the beam of the flashlight from side to side, sweating with nervousness while her teeth chattered with the cold. The mountain loomed shadowed and one-dimensional, moonlight glancing off the edges of things—the side of a boulder or the ends of a frosted weed stalk.

The thing for which her nerve endings had waited dropped suddenly from a pool of darkness above with the sound of thumping air, like an umbrella being rapidly and repeatedly opened and shut. She sank to the earth as a large bird, all dark but for its eyes, beak, and extended talons, swept over her. It grazed the ground a few feet away and rose into the air once more with a small squealing rodent in its claws.

"Dumb silly ass," she called herself aloud, but in a whisper, gathered the things she'd carried, and stood. How could she expect to cope alone in this world, when the mere suggestion of the supernatural (and Fred Hanley was no expert on that or anything) could put her in such an exaggerated state?

She pulled her robe tightly around her, arranged the shoes and the coat and the flashlight so she could proceed, and looked up to see Backra standing next to an outcrop of rock ahead of and above her.

He seemed to glow faintly, and he was nude.

Tamara was too startled to blink. She froze in the teetering position of being about to take a step, her balance off center.

Backra returned her stare with one of thoughtful consideration, as if trying to determine how to approach her. The wind that pulled at the opening in her robe and tossed her hair did not touch his silver head.

He took a step forward. She couldn't move.

This was her dream Backra. Perhaps she and Adrian were safe asleep in their beds and Tamara was dreaming all this. She'd never seen this man when she was awake before. Or was he really one of Fred's ghosts, haunting Iron Mountain and what she'd thought to be dreams? Perhaps he'd haunted Miriam Kopecky. Perhaps he'd frightened her so, she'd died of it. Perhaps he appeared before her now in the nude as an enticement to lure her inside the mountain. Maybe he was the thing in the mountain Jerusha had told Miss Kopecky about. She could still see the scars on his body from the horrible battle he'd fought with something. Maybe it had been an angel. Maybe Backra was the devil himself.

Tamara had grown fond of him as a dream, and felt an angry disappointment at the thought he might mean her harm. "Where is Adrian? Do you have my daughter?"

She threw the flashlight at him. It went through his rib cage and broke on the rocky soil behind. He turned to look at it and then back at her. His lips moving in soundless words, Backra walked toward her, his hands in front of him with palms up, as if in plea.

A short scream, suddenly cut off. It sounded as if it came from the lower level of the six-hundred-foot portal. Adrian.

Tamara picked up the skirt of her robe and ran down the slope. She turned once, to see the glowing Backra fade and then vanish.

Adrian walked down a street of sand, trying not to trip on the icy rails of the track cutting through its center. Darkened houses sat on stilts to either side of her. A rangy cat spit and raced through a gap in a board fence. She came to an intersection of sand streets and a lone streetlight that hung from a utility pole bristling with wires. Similar poles lined the street on either side, but without streetlights.

Some feeling she couldn't put a name to drew her toward the end of the street marked ahead by floodlights and a chain-link fence, an open gate. She could smell blossoming flowers over the strong salt smell of the sea, hear dogs yipping and growling down the next side street.

A paved area with weeds growing in its seams stretched out on the other side of the gate, large enough for a parking lot, but there were no vehicles. Only some lengths of rusty chain, two oil drums, and a rubber tire. And a concrete-block building with giant metal doors standing open to the night. Light streamed through the doors, and so did the repetitive sounds of machinery, a low thumping. All the utility wires from the street behind her converged on this building.

"Public Service Company of dreamland?" Adrian tried to walk through the gate, but hit her forehead and nose against something that hadn't been there a moment before. Darkness fell over her head like a cloak. She reached out to feel a barrier that wouldn't yield to her touch. Adrian fought to get back to the light and the gentleness of the dream place. She pounded on the barrier and stopped at a crunching sound behind her, a hand on her shoulder. Adrian screamed. The hand clamped over her mouth.

"Quiet, now. You'll rile up the ghosts and we'll all be in trouble."

Mr. Hanley wrapped his jacket around her. "Let's go find your mother."

He led her along some railroad tracks that had rough cindery shoulders. She was unable to reconcile what had just been to what was. She was outside in the cold in pajamas and bare feet. The tracks were like those in her dream, but there was no soft sand here, no power plant. It was like dreaming she was urinating in a toilet, only to awaken while in the act and realize she was wetting her bed. The awful dislocation and shock were the same. What was old Mr. Hanley doing in her dream? Where was her mother? "Did something happen to my mom?"

"She's out looking for you. You been sleepwalkin', girlie." He led her up a steep path to a more lighted area, and Mr. Burnham came hobbling toward them with his shirttail out and his boots unlaced.

"What the hell's going on?" He squinted at Adrian. "Oh, no, not again? Fred, tell me she wasn't—"

"Sleepwalkin'. Yep. Just like the other one. You know who Agnes says is causing this, don't you? Maybe she's right."

Russ stared at her like she was a thing. "Her feet are bleeding."

"Couldn't carry her. Must weigh a ton. Glad I caught her when I did, though. She was trying to get in the lower portal. Pounding on the door." Mr. Hanley talked about her as if she wasn't standing right there. Why did people do that? Because she was a kid or because she was fat? "Her mother's around here somewheres looking for her."

As if waiting for that cue, Tamara Whelan rushed out of a nearby shadow in her robe. All windblown and beautiful.

She looked like she'd seen a ghost.

19

After she'd settled Adrian back in her bed, Tamara had dropped off to sleep, only to dream of Backra. It seemed a night full of activity instead of rest. Miriam Kopecky had complained of being tired too.

That last dream of Backra haunted Tamara through the next day. It was as if he'd set out to hurt her asleep or awake. *If you start believing he's real, you're in for a long stay at a mental hospital.* She'd found him standing on the end of a dock, still naked. Just staring at the night. With the sea sloshing against the pilings and rocking the boats tied alongside.

He looked entranced. When he blinked, it was with the barest of flutters. Tamara could see nothing but dark water, a pale line of white breakers in the distance, and a moon tipped more than it had been in Iron Mountain. A strong breeze off the water blew his hair about now and left hers still.

The sound of sandals flopping on wood, and Tamara turned to see a woman walk under one of the lights along the dock. She wore a long dress, her head topped with tight curls that needed brushing up.

Backra suddenly noticed Tamara. He spoke rapidly, soundlessly, raising his arms again in that strange palms-upward gesture.

"Thad? Who are you talking to? And what are you doing out stark naked?" The woman wrapped a towel around him, tucked it in at the waist. "Not all my guests can handle this kind of thing, fella, and none of the locals. Thad?"

Backra, or Thad, still looked at Tamara and appeared unaware of the woman in the droopy Afro.

"Hey, zombie, this is old Dixie talking. Where are you? Jesus, you're not asleep?" She shook his arm, and he blinked, his body jerked.

"What are you doing in my dream?" he said thickly and in a voice Tamara could hear. It was a deep, raspy voice that held a timbre and a whisper at the same time. She hadn't heard it since he'd spoken to the man named Ramael many dreams ago.

Why could she not hear him before but could hear him now? Because he'd been wakened? Was the man in her dreams dreaming too? She'd heard Dixie. But Dixie had heard him when Tamara hadn't.

"Dream?" Dixie put her hands to either side of her head in a helpless gesture. "Everybody in this place dreams. At least the rest of us don't go around without clothes on."

Thad looked down at himself and shivered.

"I provided the towel. First thing I could grab. If you're going to walk in your sleep, better wear pajamas to bed."

"You mean I walked all the way out here?"

"And who knows where else? Could have walked all over the village. . . . I just remembered something. There was a rumor that Stefano caught your dad out sleepwalking. You don't think he walked off into the jungle? If he did, we'd never find his body. Full of sinkholes in there."

Tamara followed them down the dock, jealous of the possessiveness with which Dixie took her dream man's arm.

"Do you ever dream about a funny-looking mountain? Half mined out?" Thad asked her.

"You know, I have. And just tonight. Maybe there's something in the air around here, but one of the biggest topics at the breakfast table is some guest's weird dream. I get so sick of it, sometimes I sneak off to the kitchen to eat."

They were all three passing the end thatched hut now and entering the unlikely cemetery. Tamara realized she was hearing that low pulsating background noise again. She'd visited this dream place so much that it had become like the crusher in Iron Mountain, a sound she heard too often to listen to.

Thad rubbed his arms and hunched his shoulders.

"Isn't it funny you weren't cold till you woke up?" Dixie put her arm around him. "I don't remember so much talk of dreaming when I first came to Mayan Cay. Maybe I wasn't looking for it. I didn't have so many."

"Hey, My Lady of the Rum Belly, how were the pickin's tonight?"

The dog Tamara had seen before in her dreams walked along the waterline but stopped at Backra's voice, then stared straight at Tamara. It gave a yip and did a running slink off down the beach.

Tamara was furious at the way Dixie, the pop-eyed female, had herself tucked under Backra's arm so it would have been awkward for him not to put the arm around her. They reached the door of his house, and Thad hesitated, then looked down at Dixie with a smile.

Tamara followed them right through the door and into his one-room first floor. She could see before he switched on the light. Leaning against the wall by the door was a slab of rock with markings cut into it. How dare this Dixie person intrude this way. Tamara stomped through a bookcase, across the sitting-room area, and almost out the opposite wall, stopping just short of a desk with a covered typewriter and piles of papers and books. A shelf on the wall next to it held an assortment of seashells, and another some masks made of coconut husks.

While Thad went upstairs to change out of his towel, Dixie splashed liquor and what smelled like pineapple juice into glasses.

"We have something that's a bit more of a problem than dreams right now, Thad," Dixie said when he'd returned in robe and pajama bottoms.

He'd even combed his hair. Tamara felt superfluous.

"The Royal Navy lost a destroyer in the Metnál the same day as you had your little disaster. There's no keeping the lid on this thing now."

Nothing prevented Tamara from going out to roam the cemetery, scare the dogs, leave these two to their romantic interlude. But a streak of perversity made her follow them up the outside staircase. She wished she hadn't. Hadn't seen them on the bed, the arch of his lean, muscled body. . . .

"Adrian's asleep," Larry Johnson announced, standing before her desk and pointing to where Adrian sat with her head on her arms.

"Let her be, Larry. She was up so much in the night."

"Must be nice," he muttered, "having your mother for the teacher."

Tamara chided herself for daydreaming during school hours and called Bennie Hope up to read his lesson. Later, when each student was busy and Adrian had awakened, Tamara searched a wall map of the world for Mayan Cay.

By the end of the week she'd still not found it, but Friday morning when she entered the classroom, she noticed someone had taken a black felt-tip marker and made a circle. It enclosed an area in the Caribbean Sea off the coast of the tiny country of Belize. An island, a microscopic dot with tiny lettering beside it, "Mayan Cay."

Her throat went dry. The place of her dream existed. She'd never even heard of Belize. Dreams came from one's own mind. How could her mind cough up something she hadn't put in it? None of her students would admit to making that circle. Tamara suspected Vinnie Hope, who drew coconut palms and leaf markings on the margins of her papers and who was a special friend of Jerusha Fistler.

Friday night Adrian had a job helping Vinnie baby-sit with Bennie and baby Ruthie so Deloris could go out. "Vinnie knows how to take care of the baby all right, but I don't think Bennie'll mind her," Deloris explained.

That left Tamara free to accept a last-minute invitation from Russ Burnham to go out to dinner. She needed to get away from Iron Mountain, and she intended to make Russ do some serious talking about what went on in this place.

She almost split her skirt climbing up into the cab of Russ's pickup. He wore clean jeans, cowboy boots and hat, and a leather jacket with fringe hanging from the sleeves. She felt overdressed.

As they pulled off the limestone road onto the asphalt and began up the curving hill, another pickup passed them with blaring horn. "Augie Mapes and Deloris," Russ said. "Going the same place we are."

"Why didn't we all go together, then? Save on gas."

"Four in a pickup's kind of crowded."

"We could have taken my Toyota."

Russ stared at her until he had to look to his steering, as if he expected her to laugh at her own joke. When she didn't, he rolled down the window and spit into the wind. "Jeez."

They were to dine in Horse Creek, and she was anxious to see it. Horse Creek, Iron Mountain, and Cheyenne seemed to be the whole world to these people. But all she saw was a rambling knotty-pine building on the outskirts with flashing beer signs and a trout dangling from a neon line. The parking lot was full of shiny pickup trucks. "I . . . uh, suppose the Toyota might have been just a little out-of-place here, huh?"

Russ looked at her as if she was an alien, and helped her down from his truck much as cowboys in movies used to help ladies off horses. The distance to the ground was similar.

There was no lobby or entryway. One entered the main room directly from the parking lot. The strong smell of beer mixed deliciously with that of hot charcoal. Rows of booths, three aisles deep, ringed all but one side of an enormous dance floor with a jukebox discharging twangy music. The open end of the room held a bar that must have been forty feet long, complete with foot rail and spittoons.

Dim smoky light, blended conversations, laughter, silverware clanking against thick plates, and the mournful lady in the jukebox complaining of an errant lover. "All this place needs is a couple of drunken cowboys swinging at each other over a girl."

"More like a truck driver and a doped-out hippie." Russ led her up one aisle and down another until he found a vacant booth.

Catsup, A-1, and Worcestershire bottles and a plastic-covered menu already graced the table. Paper place mats showed the shape, major highways, and points of interest of the state of Wyoming. The menu offered steaks. In every size imaginable, as long as one liked them large. And hamburgers.

Tamara wondered why not a neon bull on the roof instead of a trout, and when a waitress in a short black dress and a tall blond hairdo appeared, she ordered the smallest T-bone offered. Russ delighted her by ordering a whiskey with a beer chaser. She hoped booze would loosen this taciturn man's tongue, and she asked after what might be available in a glass of wine.

"Comes in red, white, and pink," the waitress declared with a straight face, and stared at the open rafters.

"Uh . . . red, please."

"Dago juice," Russ pronounced when it came in a giant goblet that would have done justice to Henry VIII. After the first few sips, Tamara grew used to the vinegar and her eyes stopped watering.

More people filled the dance floor now, and the music switched from a slow clincher to a hopping slide. Tamara picked out three distinct groups, those who dressed cowboy fashion, in the nonfashions of the old counterculture, or like businessmen. All with their counterparts among the women, who wore everything from sequined blue jeans to one outfit that looked like a nightgown made of flour sacks.

The small T-bone was enormous and the best she'd ever eaten. She managed half of it and planned to take the rest home for Adrian.

Russ drank whiskey with his dinner too and worried aloud about a new limestone strip mine B & H had opened up. "What'll the people in Iron Mountain do when the company closes it down?"

"Have you been notified of the closing?" She'd be out of a job.

"No, but word's bound to come through soon. It's in the air."

"That's not all that's in the air at Iron Mountain, is it? I mean, Fred Hanley's ghosts and everything."

Russ had speared a stack of at least eight french-fried potatoes on the prongs of his fork and had the whole business halfway to his mouth while his eyes ran appreciatively over the extra-tight-fitting Levi's of a young thing walking in the other direction. When his attention reverted to Tamara, he repeated "Fred Hanley's ghosts" in the manner of one not listening to a conversation but hearing a key phrase anyway.

"Fred worried that Adrian's sleepwalking might upset the ghosts."

The thick-glassed wine goblet she'd thought held enough to last the weekend was mysteriously empty, and he signaled the waitress to bring another, and a whiskey for him. "Lonely job . . . night . . . people see things . . . superstitious." He finally noticed the fork full of french fries and stuffed them into his mouth.

"That won't work, Russ. I saw a couple of them myself that night, and it was my little . . . it was my daughter sleepwalking up there."

Augie danced by their booth, wrapped around Deloris Hope. She was about half his size. He winked at Tamara.

"You saw the ghosts?" Russ said when he'd chewed and swallowed enough of the potatoes to talk through what remained.

"I saw two. How many are there? One had a red shirt, tan baggy trousers, and a tan bowler. He—"

"Walks like a lumberjack. Must have a five-foot stride, that guy."

"You've seen him too?"

"Out by the old ice barn."

"Well, who is he? Why's he there? It's not all that common a thing to have happen. You're the supervisor."

"What am I supposed to do?" He pushed his plate away and fished a toothpick from his pocket. "Sprinkle holy water on a bunch of dead boards? I'm a mine manager."

"Have you seen the naked one too?" She gave him a rather complete description of Backra that made Russ redden and fidget.

"He's a new one on me. Deosn't fit in with most of the old-timers floating around."

"Old-timers . . . miners?"

"Yeah, there's stories come down through the years of a man just disappearing now and then, never found. Probably got drunk and fell down an old exploratory shaft. Or lost out in a fight and got dumped down one in the night."

"Tell me some of the stories."

"Oh, just crazy stuff. People seeing things. Those drunks were seeing things on Larimer Street long before the company ever got ahold of them."

"How can you say it's all crazy stuff when you've seen things too?"

"I don't have to believe what I see, do I?" Russ stood and held out his hand. "Let's dance."

"Not until you tell me how Miriam Kopecky died."

"Suicide." He pulled her out of the booth none too gently. "Now, are you happy?"

20

"Went to bed for a week and never got up." Russel Burnham shook his head sadly. Things were getting serious all around at the Stage Stop Inn—that was the name printed on the paper napkins. Lights dimmer, music slower, voices mellower. Dancers melted into one another.

Augie Mapes stood in the classic cowboy pose with his back to the bar, beer in hand, elbows resting on the bar top and one boot heel hooked over the foot rail. Lazy eyes explored the cornucopia of shapes on the dance floor.

"Dehydration and starvation, the doctor said. And a refrigerator full of food in the next room. But she wouldn't get up and go get it. Wasn't even cold yet. Damnedest thing I ever shaw."

Tamara had finally gotten Russ to start talking, and now she couldn't get him to stop. "Told everybody she was going to relatives over spring break. Home in bed the whole time."

"I know, damnedest thing you ever shaw."

"I heard of skin and bones before, but you never seen anything till you seen someone's just gone to bed for a week and don't get up to eat."

Augie floated over to lead her onto the dance floor, and Russ went on mumbling and shaking his head. "Sad drunk, ain't he? Gets this way every Friday night. Nobody sees him till Monday morning."

"I saw him last Saturday, and you don't look so sober yourself."

"I get this way every night. Not such a shock to the system."

"On taxpayers' money."

"You wait till the winter wind blows across the prairie all day and all night and howls like a murdered banshee, Miss Schoolteacher. You wait till all them coyotes start howling along with it, and maybe right under your bedroom window, and you'll want a few spirits in you to ward off the spirits of the night that roam the mountain and—"

"Have you seen the ghosts too, Augie?"

"No. They don't like television."

She did not feel like running the next day.

"Do you know what Jerusha does when she goes away on her trips?" Tamara asked Adrian later, when the girl returned from a visit to the next apartment. It was becoming impossible to keep her away from there.

Adrian was helping to fold clothes still warm from the dryer, and she paused but didn't look up. "Sure. She does research."

"What kind of research?"

Adrian shrugged. "How should I know?"

"What were you doing over there all morning?"

"Watching cartoons on TV."

"Don't you think you're a little old to be watching the Saturday-morning cartoons?"

As their hands met in the middle of the clothes basket, Adrian met her eyes. "I'm always either having thoughts too old for me or too young. You don't know what you want, do you?"

"Honey, Miss Kopecky died here in this apartment in bed. She died of starvation, with all kinds of food in that refrigerator. Jerusha comes back from her trips looking half-starved. Which is not her natural condition, if you'll notice how quickly she's filling out now."

"Are you trying to say Jerusha had something to do with Miss Kopecky's dying?"

"I don't know the connection, but I think there is one, and I don't like you spending so much time over there."

"You just can't stand it that I've found a friend here, can you? That I like being with Jerusha. You want to own me all the time."

"Can't I be your friend?"

"Just be my mom," Adrian said with a hint of desperation, and buried her head in Tamara's lap.

"All them old stories." Mrs. Hanley rolled her eyes behind the little cat-eye glasses. She was doing up her dinner dishes, having sent Fred to his night duties at the mine. "You heard about the strip mine opening? Don't know where we'll go. Not much call for a deaf miner, or watchman either. They'll have to give us six months' notice. Wouldn't be fair not to." The fear in Agnes Hanley's voice sounded deeply ingrained, as if this woman had never known economic security. Was that fear to become a permanent part of Tamara's life?

"About those old stories of Iron Mountain . . ."

"Oh, we heard about them before we ever came here. 'That sounds like the place for us, Agnes,' Fred says to me. 'Man could work his way up to be something at a place where it's hard to get men to go. Maybe even mine manager.'" Agnes laughed. "You know how it is when you're young and don't know nothing. Anything's possible."

"Yeah, I know." Like her own daydream of becoming some kind of successful professional. She'd have had to start fifteen years ago. Tamara felt the approach of a heavy depression. "You don't believe there's anything strange about Iron Mountain?"

"Didn't say that."

"Your husband told me there were ghosts up at the mine."

"They don't hurt nobody. Just poor lost souls got stuck here somehow. Mostly the old-timers. Fred says he's seen Abner up there some nights."

"Abner Fistler? Did he die of starvation like Miss Kopecky?"

"Just the opposite. Sick in bed and eatin' off a tray's what I heard. Choked on some food when he got a coughing spell. But them apartments never been lucky. That's why we built this. Figured if we ever left, company'd buy us out. Now, the Baggettes, they—"

"Mrs. Hanley, about the dreams everyone seems—"

"Ain't so bad here. They're worse closer in to the mountain where you are. Folks used to say when we first came that people slept better before they got electricity out here. Which wasn't till the thirties. My daughter claims she don't have half the dreams she used to when she was a kid here, and don't remember the ones she does. Could just be 'cause she's got a job and family now and more on her mind." She poured coffee for them both and let a whining German shepherd in the back door. "Dumb dog doesn't want to go out at night anymore. If he does, he wants right back in again."

"I don't understand you people. You see ghosts, dream, sleepwalk, and everybody pretends it's all normal."

"Now, Mrs. Whelan, you're old enough to have noticed that people can get used to most anything if it comes on slow enough. Look at the cities, where they take murder, rape, stealing, like it was regular. Much rather live out here with a few ghosts and dreams. 'Course, if you ask me, things have speeded up some since Jerusha Fistler moved here. She don't belong to the place, neither. Maybe she's enough of an irritator she stirs things up."

The wind was chilly when Tamara crossed the limestone road. As usual after a chat with Agnes, she felt frustrated and defeated. Perhaps Fred Hanley's hearing problem was a blessing.

Miriam Kopecky's golden sheers were pulled across the window, but Tamara saw the shadows of two people behind them as she stepped up onto the porch. Inside, Jerusha Fistler stood with a coat over one arm, both hands clutching the back of a chair. The air seemed charged.

With the plumping of face and figure, Jerusha was turning into a remarkably beautiful woman, and oddly made more so now by a look of fury that caused Tamara to flinch. All the laughter and mockery were gone.

"Deloris Hope tells me," Jerusha said slowly and as if biting down on rage, "that Russel Burnham is planning to close the six-hundred-foot portal, block it up with cement like the three-hundred-foot portal."

"Not Russ. It's the company. B & H has opened a new strip mine, and it's easier and cheaper to mine. Russ expects to get word any day of the closing of Iron Mountain. Mrs. Hanley thinks the company will give us six months' notice. But we'll all have to leave here when—"

"They can't do this." Dark hair, pale skin, bright red lips and nails, dangling earrings, tight-fitting flowered dress, stiletto heels held on by the thinnest straps. Did she have a date on Saturday night?

"I'm afraid they can. Can I get you a cup of coffee or . . . were you going out?" Tamara hoped it was the latter.

"Deloris and I were going to the Stage Stop. I felt like dancing," she said vaguely. "How can they do this? The mine has been here since 1905. Won't the government stop them?"

"I don't think the government has any authority in this matter. The company leases the land and pays to keep the mine open. If the mine no longer pays a return and there's another source of limestone, there'd be no reason for them to continue at Iron Mountain."

"But I cannot leave here."

"Russ says a Wyoming reclamation law would make them raze the buildings. Everybody'd have to move."

"Raze?"

"Tear them down, level them. I assume so that they wouldn't become dangerous eyesores." Would that mean future generations would never see a ghost town?

Jerusha sat in the chair and let her coat drop to the floor. "I do not feel like dancing now."

For some minutes she stared inward, her eyes unfocused, and ignored Tamara's comments and questions. Finally she picked up her coat and rose in one graceful movement, focusing on Tamara. Her glance moved to Adrian. "I see that I mus' hurry up my plans."

21

Hoarfrost made weed stalks and pods, tree limbs and leaves look like ghostly lace against the darkness before dawn. Tamara ran away from Iron Mountain, cold air burning in her lungs, warm breath steaming on the air. The prairie wind ran with her, pushed her from behind, whispered at her side. It made cold things crack and creak in protest.

But on the way back, the prairie wind was in her face, made her eyes water and nose run. It tried to hold her away. The sun was behind her, and the hoarfrost shimmered and fell to the wind. The mountain was bright with splashes of red and yellow and the white of remaining frost patches. The sky behind it swirled with clouds. Jagged streaks of clear sky separated the clouds and radiated out like lightning flashes, almost too symmetrically to be natural. Dried leaves clacked and clattered on the cottonwoods along the creek, and the creek ran very low.

Tamara was tired on her return, but not sated. She walked into the backyard and Alice leaped in delight, clicked his tiny hooves together, butted the fence, and baaed a greeting. She pulled some weeds and stuck them through the wire for him to nibble. "Are all goats as happy as you?"

His little devil face with the dark slits in the yellow eyes surrounded by black and topped with horns should have looked evil, but she'd grown so fond of Alice, even his goat smell seemed pleasant. "It's after a run, and I still feel as jumpy as you act. Think I'll climb that mountain. Pick you some more weeds when I come down, okay?"

Alice's objections followed her up the side of Iron Mountain. The funny cloud patterns were not as obvious from here. She wondered if they meant snow. And she wondered what she and Adrian would do if the mine closed. Perhaps Mr. Curtis would have to find her something in Cheyenne for what was left of her contract and the school year.

Several times as it hairpinned up the mountain, she crossed a dirt track that had once been a road. The body of an ancient roadster with scraps of cloth or canvas still clinging to it lay off to the side. The foundation of a cabin filled with rotting boards. A gully cluttered with empty cans, their color a uniform rust. Some miner's dump? Could those all be pork-and-bean cans? Two leaning fence posts. Some barbed wire. A leather strap that looked like it might have belonged to a horse. And holes everywhere, some hidden by weeds and rocks. Others filled with debris.

As she neared the top, piles of crushed limestone below stood out like sugar and the prairie stretched in gentle rolls to every horizon. There were some ranch buildings, dots of cattle, and a ribbed windmill to her right—probably where Mike and Rene Nygard lived. The road to Cheyenne shot straight toward the eastern sky and the one to Horse Creek angled off to her left.

Tamara didn't know what she'd expected to see from the top of the mountain, but she hadn't expected to feel so alone and small. Of course, with the morning and a rested mind she didn't see danger and conspiracy in everything. There would be an element of the unusual and coincidental in a place with so few inhabitants. And people had dreams and claimed to see ghosts in places other than Iron Mountain. Still, she was uneasy.

That intuition was at work, the one most women supposedly put their faith in, and it told her something dreadful was about to happen. She'd had these intuitive warnings before, and they'd been invariably wrong. When something did happen, she was taken as much by surprise as anyone.

Perhaps it was just that emergency resources were so far away. Something comforting in having police and fire departments and hospitals close to hand. Perhaps it was just that Tamara felt Jerusha was in some way responsible for the death of Miriam Kopecky and probably Abner. And she didn't know how to keep Adrian away from Jerusha. It could even be that Tamara, too, sensed something evil inside this mountain.

She started down, idly tracing the outlines of the awful-yellow school when she should have been watching her step. She was even higher than Augie Mapes's television antenna. What possible harm could Jerusha do Adrian? Certainly not starve her to death. Adrian would have to be tied to the bed to keep her out of the refrigerator.

If someone like Jerusha had tied Miss Kopecky into her bed and untied her just before Russ found her . . . But any kind of binding would have left marks on the skin. Someone would have heard her cries for help. Unless she'd been drugged. The Hanleys' dog ran up and down along its clothesline tether, barking wildly. Tamara pitched forward onto her face and chest as something caught her toe. She slid downward toward a yawning hole along with a bunch of rubble she'd knocked loose in her fall.

She grabbed the root of a gnarled bush that grew in groves low to the ground. When her feet swung around past her, she rolled over and dug in the heels of her running shoes. The hole was an uneven diameter of perhaps five feet, fairly open. She could see into it only partially.

Tamara waited. Her nose and chin felt scraped, burned. Her frightened nervous system struggled to recover some sense of equilibrium. Still she waited for the sound of the debris, which had tumbled into the hole just before she almost had, to hit bottom . . . knowing that if she hadn't heard it by now she wouldn't, but not ready to accept that fact.

The twinge of a stretched muscle in her armpit. Her wrist threatened to separate. She reached for another root with the other hand and pushed sideways with her heels. A loosened rock bounced off a neighbor and cleared the edge of the hole. Again no sound of its landing.

Her escape route brought her to the side of the opening and would have been less difficult had she not felt trembly and ill. She peered over the edge. And heard a rumbling sound, muffled. And felt cold damp air streaming from its depths. Probably some kind of ventilation system used in the mine. But the three-hundred-foot portal was closed. Could this come all the way from the lower shafts?

Retying her shoelaces to be sure they wouldn't trip her up, Tamara determined to walk carefully back down. On no condition would Adrian be allowed on the mountain again. Russ Burnham and B & H simply had to put a grating or something over this hole. She couldn't imagine how such a dangerous condition had been allowed to exist.

The muffled rumbling grew fainter, and she turned to listen. A woman with tightly curled gray hair rose up on the air stream coming out of the hole. A pink velour robe covered a nightgown with gathers at the wrists and throat. Tall. Rather gaunt. Lips beginning to wrinkle with age. She stared through Tamara as if sightless. Tamara could see through her, too. It was Sunday morning. Broad daylight.

Boulders, bushes, weeds, clouds—all showed clearly through the gray curls, the pink velour robe. The woman turned and walked on air through the very shrub that Tamara had clung to a moment before. Then she evaporated.

Tamara's screams hung in the wind and chased her down the mountain. For all her careful intent, she flung herself along the most direct route to safety, ankles twisting, detouring for obstacles only at the last minute. She wasn't aware of when her screams stopped, but when she reached the gondola cars and rusted metal tracks above Alice's pen, all she could hear was the wind and her heart.

Even from here she could see over the duplex's roof to the school, the Hanleys', Augie's trailers. Most of the settlement. A normal early-morning scene for Sunday. No one peering out a window or running across a yard to investigate screams on the mountain. Because they didn't want to get involved? Because they were used to odd happenings here and no longer paid attention? Whatever the reason, people minded their own business altogether too well in this place. Would anyone have investigated Miss Kopecky's calls for help from her bed if she'd made them?

Still breathing hard, Tamara walked thoughtfully into the backyard. Not even Alice appeared to notice anything abnormal. Perhaps the wind had blown her screams away and no one had heard them. Perhaps Adrian should return to Iowa City and live with her grandmother until Tamara was transferred to a different school. Adrian still slept when Tamara showered and began preparing breakfast.

Augie Mapes arrived to take their order for a Sunday paper before they'd finished it. He was on his way to Horse Creek for some, and he too acted as if this were a perfectly normal Sunday morning.

Tamara explained the scratches on her face were due to a fall on the mountain and warned Adrian that it was a dangerous place. Then she called Russ Burnham and told him of her near-disaster on the mountain.

"No ventilation holes on top there. And I told you about the dangerous holes all over that hill and to stay off it."

"Russ, I heard machinery rumbling from clear down in the mine."

"No machinery running. It's Sunday. Nobody in there to run any. Wouldn't hear it that far up anyway. Hell, we're working six hundred feet."

"I demand you investigate, and today."

"Oh, shit. Anything else?"

"Was Miriam Kopecky wearing a heavy pink robe and a long white nightgown gathered at the neck and wrists when you found her dead?"

A long pause. Finally an exhalation, and his voice dropped an octave. "Augie tell you?"

"I saw her this morning. By that hole you're going to barricade."

"She's on the mountain too? Christ, what next?"

Tamara put a roast in the oven and cored some apples for baking. When the papers came, she and Adrian stretched out on the Persian rug in a patch of sun to read. The pork soon began to splatter. It all seemed natural and cozy, made it hard to believe in the bizarre events of the morning. So many unusual things had occurred, maybe she was merely getting used to them, as Mrs. Hanley predicted. She hadn't even asked Russ or Augie why they hadn't heard her screams.

Regardless of the morning, Tamara planned to spend some long idle hours with the thick paper. Iron Mountain, Wyoming, had swallowed her up, and she'd lost touch with the rest of the world.

They read contentedly until Tamara rose to add carrots, potatoes, and onions to the roast. The apartment took on the sweet, tangy aroma of roasting pork and cinnamon apples. Adrian's stomach gurgled. Tamara had begun to feel listless and stiff from too much relaxing when, in a world-news section, she came across an item toward the bottom of a page:

BRITISH DESTROYER
RUMORED MISSING
IN CARIBBEAN

Belize City: Undisclosed sources here today report that a British naval vessel has been lost in the waters off the coast of the tiny Central American nation of Belize, formerly known as British Honduras. HMS *Gloucestershire*, a guided-missile destroyer, which normally carries a complement of 230 men, was known to have been on maneuvers in the area. The 410-foot, 3,500-ton vessel is believed to be armed with missiles, long-range guns, and to be carrying a helicopter. The *Gloucestershire* was last sighted in an area of sea known as the Metnál, an extensive region notorious for its many coral reefs and shipwrecks.

Although officials refuse to comment on the incident, a massive sea and air search is reportedly under way, with the cooperation of the U.S. Navy operating out of Florida and Guantánamo.

The Metnál has long been believed by some to be too far west to come into the range of the controversial Bermuda Triangle. Others believe it forms a western corner of the supposed Triangle, where such disappearances are touted as being more common than elsewhere.

When an official at the Admiralty Office in Lon-

don was asked to comment on the possible similarity
to Triangle disappearances, he answered with a brief
"Rubbish!"

"If you want to eat, you'll have to get dressed, lazybones," Tamara said, and rose to set the table, pour the milk, find the horseradish.

In her dream, the Dixie woman had told Backra of a missing British destroyer. Mayan Cay was in the Caribbean off the coast of Belize. What connection could that place have with this one? Why did she dream that Backra dreamed of Iron Mountain? It all made no sense. But apparently HMS *Gloucestershire* had really disappeared, and she'd dreamed of it before she could have known it.

A gust of wind swirled around the duplex and buzzed in the weather stripping.

If the British destroyer was real, did that mean Backra was real?

22

Alice was gone. Tamara looked out the window and noticed the empty pen, realized she hadn't heard his bleating in the last few days. Adrian said that Jerusha simply wouldn't say.

Every time she looked out in the backyard now, Tamara felt as if she'd let down a friend. How she'd become so involved with a goat, she didn't know. But then, life had come to make less and less sense the longer she lived in Iron Mountain. Finally she stomped over to Jerusha's. Jerusha raised thin perfect eyebrows and Tamara felt instantly silly. Alice was, after all, the other woman's goat.

"I sold him."

"Sold Alice? How could you? To whom? You never go anywhere."

The vaporizer chugged steam into the room. The night-blooming cereus seemed to have grown more leaves to crowd the light from the windows. The sun had gone down behind Iron Mountain. Jerusha sat at the table under a hanging fixture with a metal shade that spread the light in a circular pool below. The apartment was overwarm.

"I will miss Alice too," she said sadly. "But time is running out, isn't it, Tamara?"

"Running out for what? And if you miss Alice, why'd you sell him?"

Jerusha rose and began sponging off leaves on the cereus. She was tall enough that by standing on tiptoe and stretching she could reach the highest leaves. "My one experiment that did not fail," she crooned.

"Jerusha, Alice wasn't an experiment too? One that did fail?" *And Miriam Kopecky? And your husband, Abner?*

"Look, Tamara, see this?" Jerusha fondled a cone-shaped bud about two inches long with traces of white and pink at its end. "This will bloom one night soon. And so will this one, and this, all together. Just one night, and I will have a party and you will come, and Adrian. On the night the cereus blooms." Jerusha turned, a flush on her cheeks that wasn't makeup, a swath of steam from the vaporizer swirling around her chest, disembodying her head.

"I'm sending Adrian back to Iowa City to live with my mother, Jerusha Fistler. I know you're up to something. I don't want my daughter around here. Around you."

"I'm not going," Adrian said. "I won't get in the car to be taken to the train, plane, or bus. What are you going to do? I'm bigger than you."

"I'm your mother, legally responsible for you, and you'll do—"

"No. I lost Daddy. I'm not going to lose you and Jerusha too. You're all I got left."

Tamara wasn't the first parent to have a child larger than herself. She couldn't force Adrian physically. If she couldn't maneuver her in some other way, what could she do? She could hardly call in the police. Nothing illegal in disobeying a parent. What did other parents do? If she could no longer control Adrian, she couldn't protect her.

"Honey, I'm worried that you're in danger here. You've always been my first concern, you know that."

Adrian slammed her bedroom door in Tamara's face and turned up the volume on her bedside radio.

In Columbus, Ohio, Gilbert Whelan pulled his car into the narrow space left beside his wife's in the basement parking under their condo apartment. He was glad to see she was home from work, and hoped she'd started dinner. He had the day-end lag that only a martini and dinner could ease. Elsie's kids had better behave themselves tonight. He was too strung out to make even a pretense of patience.

The smell of something warm and meaty met him at the door. A brisk fire in the fireplace. Rain drove against the windows. Her kids in the den with the television on low. Gil Whelan hung up his coat and leafed through the mail. Thank God for women who could cope.

"Hey, I'm home." He peered around the corner into the hall-

way-kitchen, where Elsie stood mixing his martini, the telephone cra-
dled in her neck. Tall, thin . . . the flash of costume jewelry and nail
polish as she worked. Wrinkles in her pantsuit from sitting at a recep-
tionist's desk all day.

"Just a minute. Here he is now." Elsie handed him the drink first
and took the receiver in both hands, covering the mouthpiece. "Your
ex," she whispered, and cocked an eyebrow.

"X? Who . . . ? Oh, ex." He took a good gulp of gin before he took
the phone. All the rapidly relaxing muscles along his spinal column
tensed up again. "Hello . . . Tam? I've been meaning to write to
Adrian about—"

"We heard about your remarriage. Never mind that. I need your
help." The memories that flooded over him at the sound of her voice—
most tinged with guilt or anger or both. His stomach was knotting now.

"Look, we're both working and can barely make ends meet here. I'll
send something when I can."

"Gil, I want you to take Adrian for a few months. She won't go to
her grandmother's, and I thought she might come to you if you were to
ask."

"Hey, she should be with her mother, you know that. You got cus-
tody. Besides, she'd be lonesome here. There's nobody around. Elsie's
got two we have to send to nursery school while she works. I'm in real
estate now and gone lots of evenings. Business is bad, Tam. And there's
no room. She'd have to sleep on the couch. That's no life for a girl."

"God, don't you care about anything? She's your child."

"Don't start that shit again. Of course I care."

There'd been an odd laid-back tone to her voice, but now desperation
cut through. "I'm worried that Adrian's life is in danger here."

"How could her life be in danger? She's only ten years old. Who'd—?"

"She's twelve now, Gil, going on thirteen. She's about five-feet-eight
and at least forty pounds overweight."

"Jesus, how'd you let that happen?"

"Gil, I'm trying very hard not to lose my temper, because I'm so desperate for Adrian—"

"Let's not start the goddamned martyr routine again."

"There's a woman next door—we live in a tiny dump called Iron
Mountain, Wyoming, now—and this woman named Jerusha is, I'm sure,
responsible for a number of deaths around here."

"Wyoming? I thought you were living with your mother."

"She can't afford to keep us. I'm teaching here. This woman may be
after Adrian too. She has an enormous influence over her, and I—"

"Go to the police, then."

"I don't have any proof. But we can't take a chance with our daughter's life."

We and *our.* Couldn't she see those words would make him see red? "What's this woman do, put razor blades in their Halloween candy?"

"She . . . it's very hard to explain . . . but she does these experiments and people dream and sleepwalk and sometimes they just don't get up at all and they die. I've already caught Adrian sleepwalking out on the mountain, and then the dead people or . . . well, their essence or something comes back like a . . . ah . . . ghost. Oh, I know how unreal this must sound, but, Gil—"

"You can say that again. Look, Tam, I just got home from work. Bad day. Tired. Haven't had dinner yet. And frankly, I can't handle this right now. Tell you what, give me your number and I'll call you back tonight after I've had time to get my head straight. Okay?" When he had the number, he added, "Oh . . . and, Tam . . . Thanks for not crying."

Gil hung up before she could start in again, and looked at his empty glass. He didn't remember drinking any of its contents. She could even take the joy out of a martini.

"Pretty tough on her, weren't you?" Elsie reached around him for some napkins.

"Just the sound of her voice and all this resentment comes up my throat. When am I ever going to get that woman out of my life?"

"This is the first time I've known her to contact you since we met. She doesn't hound you like Jeff does me."

"She wants Adrian to come live with us."

"No way. Not unless you hire some help. I've got too much to handle now."

"I know. But it sounds like Tam's really botched things good this time. The kid's gotten all fat and they're living in Boondocks, Wyoming, someplace and seeing ghosts. Maybe she's not responsible enough to raise Adrian. What do I do, Elsie? She claims the kid's life is in danger."

Brian and Donny came screeching through the kitchen on their way to the dining-room table. He wished he could take the two of them and Tamara and send them all to Mars.

"Maybe you'd better go out there and see for yourself, if you're going to worry." Elsie followed the boys into the next room and left him staring at the refrigerator door.

"I haven't seen Adrian in two years," he said to the refrigerator. Total panic gripped his midsection. "What would I say to her?"

Gil Whelan called his ex-wife back after dinner to reassure her that she was just being overimaginative and that if she would just relax, everything would be all right.

23

Thad Backra, he became in Tamara's fantasy. He wore a white turtleneck and dark blazer. Fluffy silver hair swept back off a tanned face, ash-gray eyes looking cold and unimpressed as she introduced him to Gil Whelan at a party. A possessive arm around her waist swept her away as soon as possibly polite. "How'd you ever come to marry a guy like that?" he said in that low raspy voice Gil wasn't meant to overhear but did.

"Mom, Larry took my pencil."

"Careful, Johnson." Mike Nygard snickered. "Adrian might fall on you."

"That's enough." Tamara saw she'd doodled in red pencil down the margin of Nate Baggette's spelling paper. Profiles of Backra, the pattern of the long leaf skeleton, even a fair representation of one of those thatched huts. She shredded it, threw it in the basket, and entered a perfect score for Nate in her grade book.

After Rene's private social-studies lesson, Tamara stood at the back of the room, hoping thus to keep herself awake and monitor Larry Johnson's shenanigans at the same time. She'd been too tired to run the last few days. Running would give her more energy if she'd get up when the alarm went off instead of rolling over for another hour's rest. And she hadn't been eating properly, merely munching on whatever was the least hassle instead of planning and preparing nutritious meals. All of this sapped her natural good health, energy, and will. She'd stop this erratic behavior.

The wooden flooring trembled almost imperceptibly beneath her feet. Outside the window at her elbow, grains of crushed limestone slithered down the huge pile behind the school and out of sight below, long after the vibration had ceased. Earth tremor?

Her students appeared to have noticed nothing. Tamara slipped across the hall to look out the windows of the unused classroom. She could see no change in the mountain or the settlement at its base.

*　　*　　*

Russ Burnham was on his way down the path to the lower level and headed for the crusher when he felt it too. At first he wasn't sure it wasn't just the surprise surfacing of his long-buried dread of a quake under that mountain, with men he knew and liked inside it. But Darrell Johnson came running out of the crusher building and then Russ knew. He was down the path and on the tracks in time to meet Darrell at the portal doors. They grabbed battery-operated lanterns stored at the mouth of the mine.

"Don't see any dust, leastways."

"Slow and easy. Eyes open and no shouting," Russ told him, and they started in, looking carefully for piles of rubble or signs of slippage. It wasn't long before they met Saul Baggette and another miner supporting a man between them.

"Winn. Just got knocked on the head," Saul said. "Rest are coming."

"Get him on out. Talk to you outside." When Russ had counted the men passing him and assured himself the mine was empty, he joined the others at the portal doors. Winn Davidson sat with his head in his hands, elbows propped on his knees. Russ put him in the company pickup with Johnson and sent them off to Cheyenne and a doctor. He listened patiently to each man, then ordered them home for the day. Pulling the portal doors closed, he locked them and took Saul Baggette to his house.

He sat Saul down at the table and poured them each a whiskey. "Okay, now, I want the truth. Nothing else. Nothing you wouldn't have seen before Abner's widow started filling everybody's heads with her motherfuckin' stories. But I want everything you did see."

Saul rubbed his forehead, and dirt balled up in the tracks of his fingers. "The damage isn't bad if nothing more comes down. Like I told you, the trouble's in that one wall we couldn't seem to drill. And, like the guys said, we finally got a bore hole through—all of a sudden, because it was hollow on the other side and the wall came down, part of it on Winn. And we barely got him out of the way before the whole damned shaft caved in at the end there."

"Hollow on the other side . . ."

"We thought we'd gotten turned around somehow and bored through into one of our own tunnels."

"And before the cave-in, you saw this thing too?"

"Yeah. It was kind of gray and chrome-looking and—"

"How is it you were all working the same tunnel?"

"We weren't, but Winn and Charlie came to get me when they got a hole through, and the men with me came too. You know the trouble we been having there, and then . . . well, we all been stickin' fairly close because of the noises."

"Noises."

"I tried to tell you the other day, but you wouldn't listen. And don't ask me to describe 'em, 'cause they're like nothing I ever heard."

"Make a stab at it."

"Something like machinery running, maybe. I couldn't tell you what kind if you paid me. Anyway, it was louder after we got the bore hole through. And it was a lot louder when the wall came down."

"And you saw something gray." Russ poured his underground manager another shot. "You personally."

"Yeah. It had a shape embedded in it, and—"

"Shape of what?"

"Person maybe. Big rounded one. I don't know. But there was glass or plastic or something . . . a see-through film around it."

"And you saw all that in the seconds before the cave-in and while frantically trying to dig Winn out of a jam?"

Saul slammed his glass down with a splash of amber. "Shit, Burnham, I'm not trying to make this up to—"

"Okay, okay. I just have to get it all straight, sort out the truth from the excitement. Nobody's calling anybody a liar. We'll let things settle good, and you and me'll go in in the morning and scout before letting the men work the tunnels."

Tamara didn't keep her promise to prepare a nutritious meal that evening, but went to bed on canned soup, crackers, and an awful pudding mixture Adrian had concocted in sugar-starved desperation. Too exhausted to care and certainly to dream, she gave herself up to Miriam Kopecky's expensive mattress before she'd completed grading papers and filling out the preliminary questionnaire of the National Education Council on Learning Disabilities and Modular Systems Planning. Sleep came quickly and deep, and if there were dreams in the first part of the night, they spun into view and around and back into her memory bank without a lasting impression.

But later, every time Bennie Hope would sniff, Tamara brought a ruler down on his head until it became almost rhythmical—sniff-slap, sniff-slap—and Larry Johnson laughed and cheered her on, and Vinnie cried. And Tamara felt the cruelty in what she was doing but couldn't stop. And even worse was the sensation of glee in finally repaying the child for hours of nerve-rasping sniffles. Her guilt over this last was so heavy she found herself reeling under its weight as she followed Backra down the sand street. He glided like Adrian had on the mountain. He wore only pajama pants.

A series of ugly scabs still marred one shoulder, but when he stopped and turned to stare at something she couldn't see, she noticed the swelling on the bridge of his nose had receded and his profile was once more clean and smooth in the moonlight.

They passed darkened houses, a side street, a cat on a board fence that arched and spit and ran away, a shuttered storefront with cases of empty Coke bottles stacked waist-high along one wall. Backra turned at the next corner and again at the next, so he was going back the way he'd come. He stepped into a doorless, roofless structure made of concrete. By the arches on the window holes Tamara guessed it to be a church under construction, but there was no building mess or scaffolding about.

A scurrying, a succession of ruffs and growls and then yips and barks. She turned to see what looked like a miniature dinosaur with shortened legs, perhaps the ugliest creature she'd ever seen. Shivers tingled over her skin as the creature, who did not look built for such speed, ran-slithered across the floor. He was green, over three feet long, and with a ridge of spines along his back. He had wartlike bumps all over his face and inch-long toenails that clicked on the concrete. His tail and hindquarters swiveled from side to side as he ran. And close behind him, in a scramble of feet and fur, came a pack of canines, perhaps four or five, who skidded to a wide-eyed and squealing halt at the sight of Tamara. They turned and left the green creature to make good his escape out the opposite door hole, across the beach, and over the edge of a dike or breakwater of some sort.

The commotion made Backra stop and turn. He looked past her, again at something she couldn't see. And a dark mass she'd taken for a shadow became instead a kneeling woman with a black shawl draped over her head. She stared openmouthed at Tamara as she rose to her feet and crossed herself. Tamara was surprised that someone other than a dog or Backra could see her. There seemed to be a progression in her dreams. At first she wasn't visible to anyone, but recently more and more of the dream island's occupants could see her. Were dreams really meaningful, as some people claimed? Were these dreams trying to tell her something by way of this progression?

The woman backed carefully toward the door hole that led to the beach. "Thaddeus, come with me. You must wake and get away from this place. An evil one is here." Her whisper trembled, and her eyes never left Tamara. "Thaddeus, please, this is Rafaela. We must . . ." The woman in black was out the door and gone.

Backra had taken no notice of her, and now wandered back toward the hole he'd entered by and out into the sand street once more. Tamara followed. In this place of green monsters, he alone seemed safe and familiar. She kept close behind him now, fearing that strange creatures lurked in every shadow, beneath every house. Her dream senses sharpened, making her aware of the background throbbing she always heard here but rarely listened to, and the constant sounds of the sea.

They came to a tall chain-link fence. The throbbing sound came from a lighted building behind it. Backra seemed confused by the fence. As if he could feel it but not see it. A gate stood open not ten feet to his right, but he moved to his left instead, feeling along the fence as he went. When he came to the corner, he started off into the jungle.

"Don't go in there barefoot! Dammit, Tamara, this is just a dream." But she hurried in after him, worried about what could happen to a sleepwalker here. That woman with the pop eyes had spoken of sinkholes.

He floated through shadows and out into moonlight again, unaware of the plant life clawing at his pajama pants, the debris fallen from the tangle of palms and low trees that might harbor poisonous insects. The air here was filled less with the brine smell of the sea and heavier with the odors of blossom, fruit, vegetable rot, and damp. It smelled as she imagined a snake would, and she wouldn't have been surprised to see all sorts of green demons with spines along their backs.

White splotches at intervals in and out of shadows, and a long vine that connected ground to tree, tree to palm, branch to branch. It twisted back on itself and then continued. Tamara knew what it was even before she stepped closer to look. Thick waxy leaves, elongated. Here, bristlelike hairs on the end of each, instead of the brown ends like those in Jerusha Fistler's apartment. Huge white blossoms gave off a sickly scent like that of rotting pineapples and lemons and a hint of gardenia. They reminded her of pictures of exotic orchids. But she knew this to be the night-blooming cereus.

Backra had been stopped by a wall of vines and other vegetation. He stood motionless, staring at it. A vine above his head moved, lowered part of itself as if to get a better look at the sleeping man. As it did so, it unwrapped for at least the five feet Tamara could see. It had an eye that shone back at the moon and a forked tongue that swept the air before it. The snake lowered onto Backra's naked shoulders, and Tamara lunged forward to pull him away, but she struck something hard. Her feet slid out from under her, and she fell backward, to sprawl on something icy. Her breath was knocked from her lungs, and her senses spun.

The sudden cold scared her, and her breath returned with a gasp. Places hurt around her body. Bright lights swirled in front of her eyes. She wondered if the snake would get her before she froze to death. The cold air was crisp and dry, the smells now were of earth, metal, and frost. The colored lights swirled away, the white ones fell thick and wet on her skin and soaked into her nightgown.

Through the snowflakes, Tamara could just make out the huge doors to Iron Mountain's six-hundred-foot portal looming above her in the darkness. She lay spread-eagled across the tracks in front of them.

Interim

Time and Again

Ralph Weicherding was a reporter for a UPI bureau based in Guatemala City but responsible for all of Central America and most of the Caribbean. He heard the news from a contact while on a stopover in Belmopan, the capital of Belize, and was on the next flight to the coast, certain that the contact must have been mistaken. No one could keep a lid on that kind of story for hours, let alone days. But if there was such a story, Ralph was determined to get to it before his counterpart from Reuters. The lack of real news in this region was enough to make a grown reporter cry.

He arrived in Belize City only to find all planes at Mayan Airlines either conscripted as search planes or mysteriously grounded. No flights to the cays allowed. Delayed but undaunted, Ralph Weicherding took passage on the daily supply boat to Mayan Cay. The engines ground ominously and the crew had to shout to be heard over them. Coral heads broke the water in places. Stretches of coral banks that extended close to the surface darkened huge patches of sea. Then they'd enter an area that was clear and deep. They were about an hour out of San Tomas when the supply boat jerked and nosed into a wave no one had apparently expected. Ralph had been dozing, and was awakened by the captain's shouts, followed by a cold drenching as water cascaded over the deck.

"Aye, what's your name again?" The captain was from the U.S. and sounded like a New York City taxi driver.

"Weicherding, Ralph." He picked himself up out of a puddle.

"Come over here and see this, Weicherdink." The captain yanked Ralph around the wheelhouse, where his crew lined the rail. About two hundred feet away was a gleaming white ship.

Even the gun turrets were white. And the towers topped with complicated radar devices. And a helicopter on her rear deck that several sailors seemed to be working on or preparing for flight. The only colors were the black letters on her side—Do6—and the flags she flew. The top one was the red-and-white crisscross on blue of the Union Jack.

"Bit much for these waters, isn't she?" Ralph asked.

"Get Belize City," the captain ordered through the wheelhouse window. "Only one destroyer that size ever been around here. That's the *Gloucestershire*."

"I heard she was lost."

"Don't look lost now. In a clear channel. Ought to make it in with no trouble. Where in hell's she been?" He waved back at a seaman on the destroyer's deck. "And how'd she get right here so quick?"

Heavy static from the wheelhouse and a "whumping" sound that flashed across the water and hit them with the impact of a shock wave. Ralph felt sharp pains in his ears and a momentary pressure against his chest that stopped his breath.

HMS *Gloucestershire* was gone, more as if she'd never been than as if she'd vanished. No disappearing in the gradual sense. The destroyer just wasn't. The men on the supply boat stood silent, staring at empty water, holding on as the boat pitched. The static from the wheelhouse silenced too, and then:

"Belize City, here," said a very English voice. "We read you, *Bella Donna*. Over."

"Tell 'em never mind," the captain yelled, and slid his back down the exterior wall of the wheelhouse until he hunkered, lips puckered, eyes darting with the rapidity of the thoughts in his head.

Ralph knew how he felt. Whatever was happening here, it was too unbelievable to make news. If the bureau chief decided to send it out at all, some of the newspapers might use it—put it on their back pages maybe. He doubted any of the TV networks would touch it. Only the kooks would pick up on it.

Too much hard stuff like terrorism, revolution, hostage-taking, impending war, energy crisis. That's where the stories were. With all the American tourists that came to the Caribbean, he thought just one good hostage story wouldn't be asking too much. But this . . .

Ralph Weicherding sighed and sat next to where the captain of the *Bella Donna* hunkered. "I had a dream once," Ralph said, "where the Reverend Jim Jones rose from the dead and started a whole new suicide colony right here in Belize. Down between Placentia Point and Monkey River Town. My territory."

"Talked to a 'Naivee' over a beer and darts couple o' weeks ago in Mingo's Bar," the captain answered. "Said the British put something as big as the *Gloucestershire* down here to show Cuba their support for the U.S. in the Caribbean. Kind of a deal with Washington. Don't know if he knew what he was talking about. She ain't been here hardly a month."

"Why'd you radio Belize City and not just hail the *Gloucestershire*?"

"Hell, I wouldn't know what to say to something that big . . . and clean. One good whiff of this garbage scow and she'd probably blow us out of the water. Keep the world clean for Englishmen or something. You say you're a reporter?"

"Yeah. But this is one story I don't know how I'm going to file."

"See those tanks over there?" The captain gestured toward a row of crates containing scuba tanks. "Them's for the Mayapan Hotel. Classiest place in San Tomas. Lost most of its rental gear in an accident out here somewheres. Same day as that destroyer turned up missing. One of the guides and a bunch of divers didn't come back."

"I was on my way to Mayan Cay to interview some of the survivors."

"Most of 'em have been sent back to the States and some of 'em to hospitals. Now, the stories they had to tell before they left, about how this accident happened, are something else. Something you ain't going to believe, and neither am I. We'd even be embarrassed to repeat 'em. Now, you heard any news reports about them stories?"

"Lid's been put on the whole thing."

"Nothing to keep those divers from talking when they get home. And most of 'em are home."

"They can talk all they want to, but if nobody listens, they—"

"Exactly." The captain of the *Bella Donna* began to whistle significantly. He walked past the excited crewmen, who were still discussing the freakish phenomenon, and nonchalantly peed over the side into the clear blue waters of the Caribbean Sea.

Ralph headed up the beach for the Mayapan, his clothes stiff and scratchy from his salt-water bath on the *Bella Donna*.

A tall bronzed man in swim trunks crept among toppled headstones and tumbled concrete coffins. Three other men stood poised on the far side of the cemetery, spread out at even distances as if to catch whatever the first man flushed.

"I say, you don't plan to cut her up again, do you?" said the man with a British accent and a dead pipe.

"There she is, Doc. To your right." This was the balding man in the middle, who had a glass in his hand. An angry scar ran from his chin down his neck and under his shirt. "Watch out, Bodecker, here she comes."

Ralph Weicherding was beginning to wonder if he should pull a camera out of his gear bag when the man called Bodecker, who was on the end closest to the water, gave a yell like an attacking Comanche and leaped into the air.

"I got her. She's mine!" Beer spewed from the bottle in his hand as he landed on his chest and stomach in the sand and a little tan dog dodged the fingertips of his other hand. One of those village mongrels Ralph saw all over Latin America, this one was plumper than most. It had its ears laid back and wore a look of hysterical terror. Whoever said animal faces were incapable of expression had never seen one so small being chased by four big drunks.

Because of heat and hunger, these dogs were usually sluggish, but this one scampered, dashed, dodged, and swerved like a seasoned football player. Suddenly it broke and headed straight for Ralph, the bronzed guy in the swim trunks right behind. Ralph dropped his bags, and before the panicked animal realized its mistake, he had it by a front leg, and before it could bite him, its pursuer had a hand ringing its muzzle.

"Orderlies!" the pursuer yelled to the others and to Ralph, "Thanks." There were scabs and scars on his arms and chest, yellowing bruises. It took the two of them to hold the struggling dog until the others got there. They released it to the three helpers, and it still almost got away.

"What'd you do, Doc, grease her?"

"God damn, Doc, you're gonna pick every last flea off me."

"You did promise, Mr. Alexander, to discuss the matter I mentioned if I helped you catch this . . . this creature."

Mr. Alexander swept them all a formal bow, so low Ralph could see abrasions on his back too. When he came up, he held a pair of tiny scissors like the ones Ralph carried in his suitcase to cut thread if he had to sew on a button. Alexander held them high, and they returned the sun's rays. His smile was too wide and rather abandoned.

"Hey, you're not really going to cut that dog?" Ralph asked. "That's kind of . . . sick, isn't it?"

"Belly up, and hold her still," Alexander ordered his orderlies, and snipped and tugged out tiny threads in the lower end of the dog's stomach.

Bodecker grinned at Ralph and winked. "Stitches. She's the Doc's patient, you know."

They flipped the animal over, and she leaped from their grasp before they could set her down. She was away across the beach like a tan streak.

"If you're smart, you'll hide in the jungle for a coupla years," the balding man yelled after her. "This man's crazy."

The crazy man blew on the end of the tiny scissors. He looked very smug.

"You, Doc, are basically a nurturer," Bodecker said with that serious authority that can be brought off only by the inebriated. "You just think you're a cold asshole."

III

Something in the Air

24

Dixie Grosswyler had become more aware of her dreams since she'd come to Mayan Cay, but had only lately begun to find them disturbing, interfering with her rest, becoming almost more real than her daytime world.

She'd been married and divorced twice before she was thirty. The last husband had moved her down here so they could manage the Mayapan. Two years later he took off with a lovely guest and divorced Dixie by mail. She'd stayed on, managing the hotel for a Florida-based company, determined to make enough money to return to Texas and live in a state of financial independence.

Dixie would play around with men, but never again would she trust one. She earned an annual salary plus a commission for every increment of profit. The Mayapan ran full for about four months—when it was cold and nasty in the States. The occupancy rate was hit-and-miss the rest of the year. Her nest egg wasn't keeping up with inflation.

She dreamed now of walking along a scarred hillside she'd dreamt of before, and falling into a hole like Alice descending to Wonderland. Instead of finding a fantastical new world, she'd found a labyrinth of dark tunnels, and the harder she looked for a way out, the more panicky she became, and grew claustrophobic to the point of fearing she'd suffocate.

Dixie woke, surprised to find her bed unrumpled after the agony of her struggles and herself unable to stay in the enclosure even of familiar walls with the memory of them. She slipped on sandals and a shapeless muumuu and hurried through the office and out to the veranda. She sucked in night air and shivered with reaction rather than chill. Spits of adrenaline still set fire to her nerve endings.

Folding her arms against her middle, she paced the veranda from end to end, her sandals crunching coral sand that had encroached on black-and-white squares of paving tile. Lizards scuttled behind potted plants. The moon wasn't half-full and sat low in the sky. Night shadow darkened all but a faintly luminous sea.

Dixie leaned against a supporting post and hugged herself tighter. She had to get more sleep. Every night this happened it made her increasingly nervous and depressed. And that was bad for business.

The form of an obviously naked man glided along the water's edge, outlined by the subtle light of the water. Dixie blinked. Only two men of that height on the island, Thad Alexander and Roudan Perdomo. This man was white.

My God, what's he up to now? Grabbing a beach towel left on a lounge chair, Dixie rushed toward the dock. He'd reached the end of it and stood looking out over the water. Then he turned sideways, raised his arms, and spoke silently to the air, as if rehearsing for a play and pretending a fellow actor was at hand.

"Thad? Who are you talking to? And what are you doing out stark naked?" She wrapped the towel around him and tucked it in at the waist. "Not all my guests can handle this kind of thing, fella, and none of the locals. Thad?"

He just stared into space as if there was someone there. His eyes twitched like a dog's would when dreaming. But Thad's eyes were open.

"Hey, zombie, this is old Dixie talking. Where are you? Jesus, you're not asleep?" She shook his arm, and he jerked. His skin felt hot.

"What are you doing in my dream?" His voice was thick with sleep.

"Dream? Everybody in this place dreams. At least the rest of us don't go around without clothes on."

Dreams were more often a topic of conversation on Mayan Cay than anywhere else she'd lived. She did remember hearing of Stefano catching Thad's dad out sleepwalking, and she told him of it, guiding him down the dock. He was wobbly, and she wondered if it had been a mistake to wake him so suddenly. They talked of dreams as they walked along the beach, and he began to shiver. His skin felt chilled now under her hand.

"Isn't it funny you weren't cold till you woke up?" She put an arm around him. "I don't remember so much talk of dreaming when I first came to Mayan Cay. Maybe I wasn't looking for it. I didn't have so many myself."

"Hey, My Lady of the Rum Belly, how were the pickin's tonight?"

The little bitch Thad had performed drunken surgery on approached along the beach but stopped at his voice. It gave a startled yip and ran off.

"That's gratitude. After all you've done." Dixie realized she was jealous of the dog.

"Far as she's concerned, all I've done is cause her pain."

"You really like animals, huh? I mean, besides the fact they provide you with a living?"

"That animal is a fellow creature who has gotten the short end of the stick in this world."

"You know, you were almost sane when you came to this island?" They'd reached the door of Edward P. Alexander III's house. Dixie snuggled closer to his son. "Offer another fellow creature a drink?"

It was too dark to see his expression, but his hesitation revealed they both knew what she was asking for. He relaxed against her, and a light line opened in his face as he smiled. "Sure, why not?"

Later, Dixie wondered who he was pretending she was as their hands explored the other's body and she felt the rough and healing places from his day of horror on the Metnál. Perhaps he thought of the ex-Mrs. Thad Alexander.

No matter. Dixie knew he'd be a part of her fantasy life for a long time, even if he never touched her again.

25

With the sutures removed from his patient, Thad consented to talk to Geoffrey Hindsly. He told him of the *Ambergris* and his father's crazy notions about ancient machinery running amok. He didn't expect Hindsly to believe any of it.

The next day he went out with Eliseo, Don Bodecker, and the Englishman to set a marker buoy where the "thing" had risen above the water. Harry refused to go. No one bothered Martha with the plan. All they had to do was to locate the submarine and they'd know they were in the right place. The U. S. Navy would fly in a group of specialists—oceanographers—to investigate the waters marked by the buoy.

Don Bodecker was grim. And sober for the first time Thad could remember since what they all referred to now as the "accident." Their wet suits ruined, both he and Thad wore T-shirts and blue jeans.

"This really isn't necessary." But Hindsly gazed curiously over the side of the dive boat, a smaller version of the one in the accident. "The experts will be here shortly and surely can discover more than you."

He'd impressed them with the credentials of the luminaries about to descend on the Metnál. A geologist would take samples of any volcanic rock found in the area. A chemical oceanographer would check for unusual chemical properties or imbalances in the water—acidity perhaps— or the ozone content. An ichthyologist and biologist would check out the fish, live coral, and plant life. Every conceivable aspect of the mystery would be probed by those with the knowledge to solve it.

"We have our own ghosts to lay." Don adjusted his air tank, popped his regulator. The muscles and veins in his neck stood out in ridges. "I know you're scared shitless, Doc. How come you don't show it?"

"I was just thinking the same thing about you."

Don's answering grin showed only in his eyes.

Hindsly seemed to have acquired a new crop of freckles every time Thad looked at him. His pipe successfully lit, the buoy bouncing on gentle waves, he leaned back and stretched his legs out before him. He swiveled to peer again over the side into the waters of the strange stories. "If what you tell me is true, I shouldn't think you'd want to go in. Eliseo here seems to be the only man of sense among you."

Eliseo chain-smoked and stared out over the Metnál with an expression half-vacant, half-sad. "I don't want to stay long in this place, yes?"

"Member ol' Bo teasing about Martha Durwent's body? Those were the last words he ever said. Wonder if we'd've laughed if we'd known." Don pulled down his mask, stuck his regulator in his mouth, and went over backward. Thad did the same, wondering if terror would strike again and those were to be the car salesman's last words.

Tourist brochures listed these waters as running between 80 and 84 degrees year round. But the sudden contact with sun-warmed skin made an icy first impression. Or was it the chill of memory? A momentary fluttering of his heart as it was shocked into changing gears.

The sun was weakened by a lace-thin layer of cloud. The water alternately brightened and darkened around him. They'd anchored closer to the sub than before. What had been a mound some distance from it was now a depression. A grouper swam over to investigate him, then nosed off with no show of concern or hurry—just the usual glum grouper expression. There'd been no fish here before.

An old maxim among divers was that if the fish suddenly clear out of an area, the diver would be wise to head for the surface. Why hadn't they thought of that maxim last time? A school of skinny silvery fish darted about overhead as if catching live, moving food too small for Thad to see. Don hung over the shallow crater that had been a mound, his fins treading slowly, his head connected to the light pool of the surface by a string of bubbles. His clothes clung in ripples to his muscled body.

Thad kicked his way to where (guessing by the location of the sub) he'd seen the diver sucked into the sand. Finding nothing, he circled the rim of the crater. No bodies of the lost, no gear washed from the dive boat, no coral growth, rocks, seaweed, or grass. Only fine white sand that floated through his fingers and hung on the water before drifting back into the crater. Was there some current here that kept the ocean floor so clean? Or did the monstrosity emerge at intervals? Such upheaval would wipe away normal growth. Would only sand tumble back into the crater when it submerged?

Don scraped and scooped at the center of the crater as if trying to find a trace of the thing. Thad moved farther beyond the perimeter, looking for signs of debris shoved off to the sides. The thing had been so big he'd have to go a ways. Why wouldn't the debris have tumbled back in and filled up the crater?

Not everyone had the opportunity to reexamine a nightmare. Perhaps a nightmare laid to rest was like a ghost. It no longer haunted. Perhaps the giant eyeball was a vehicle of some kind that rose up and out of the water, causing a partial eclipse of the sun as it rose heavenward, with some kind of antigravity device that had caught up the dive boat and the water beneath it. But he couldn't see how that would explain the disappearance of ships or the fact that time had been altered to give the victims another afternoon.

Could there be any connection to the fact that people on Mayan Cay dreamed a lot? No. That was probably something in the air or some unknown component in the food or water. Thad thought grimly of how his views of what constituted the ridiculous had altered since his first visit to the Metnál.

And then on a roughly elliptical course from the submarine—as if the crater were now the pupil of a vast eye and the submarine lay in the eye's inner corner and he was at the outer corner—he found what he looked for. Normal debris on the ocean floor. No living coral, but dead fish, a mucky-looking rock, uneven contours in the sand. Knowing the shape he was looking for now, he could follow the outline of it back to the center of the eye, where Don still scooped away. Sand formed a cloud around him, some of it rising toward the surface with his bubbles.

Thad kicked over to him, and the car salesman held up both hands like a surgeon waiting to be gloved after scrubbing up. A coating of sand grains stuck to his hands and halfway to his elbows. Thad sank a fin, ankle, and part of a calf into the hole his companion had made in the center of the pupil-depression. He could feel sand clamp onto his skin under the blue jeans and above his fin.

When he withdrew his foot, he reached down, to feel the sand clinging to the denim of his jeans transfer to his hand and continue to cling, much like strands of hair charged with static electricity try to bond with any nearby object. Kneeling to dig with Don, he too found hands and arms encrusted with the clingy sand. But as the surface sands slipped into the space left by the charged grains beneath, they could make little headway. On their way up, the clinging sand dropped away, and by the time they climbed into the boat, it was gone. Eliseo pulled in the ladder and started for home before they could remove their tanks.

Don tried to explain the sticky sand to Hindsly through the spray, engine noise, and clapping of the boat bottom against water as they took the low swells too rapidly. "So I figure it's gone now. Just left behind a depression and some electrically charged sand. And I think it took Bo with it."

"Where is it that you think whatever-it-was has gone, then?" Hindsly asked through teeth clamped tightly around his pipe as they all sat in the bow to keep it down, and had to hold with both hands to stay on the seat.

"I think it went into space, where it came from, but from now on I'm claiming I don't have any idea or that maybe it was a Russian experiment or something. Not good for the reputation to go around seeing things from outer space."

That afternoon, as Thad walked toward the Hotel de Sueños, Roudan came out onto the porch. He seemed to be listening. Even My Lady turned her head from side to side.

Roudan raised his eyebrows as if he could understand Thad's thoughts like Thad often picked up on My Lady's. "You don't hear what is missing, Backra? Try for once to come out of your head and listen."

"I'm getting tired of your riddles, Perdomo." Thad decided he was also tired of this man's intimidation. He stepped up onto the porch and passed Roudan before he stopped. The sound My Lady and Roudan had heard for years and Thad for weeks was no longer there. "The generator."

Roudan smiled beautiful teeth. "Makes for warm Belican, Mr. Alesandro."

Old Stefano came out from under his house and looked at the air around him as though there was something in it he could see, and then over at Roudan. As if some verbal agreement had been reached, Roudan went to meet Stefano halfway across the cemetery, and they walked off in stride between houses.

In the dim interior, Seferino Munoz stood behind the bar. The man who'd caught My Lady, Ralph Weicherding, was the only customer. "Dr. Alexander, I was looking to get a chance to talk to you. Let me buy you a drink. What'll it be?"

"A Belican. You another investigator?"

"Press."

"You're not going to believe any of the stuff that's been happening."

"Probably can't use it, but I can sure as hell believe it. Saw the *Gloucestershire* on the way here. Appeared out of nowhere, and poof— went right back where it came from." He described seeing the destroyer along with the crew of the supply boat. Thad told him about the *Ambergris*.

"Do you think unlikely things are happening all over the world all of a sudden?" Thad asked him. "Or is it just us?"

"Haven't heard about anything like this anywhere else."

"Yeah, but who's going to hear about here?"

They discussed the impossible matter-of-factly, as though they'd always known such and were used to it, until Rafaela came to get Thad for dinner. She scolded him all the way across the cemetery and into the house.

"A big man such as you must have his food in him, Thaddeus, not that Belican poison." What really made her angry, he suspected, was that she hadn't been able to find Stefano at all and that she was sure food was already spoiling in the refrigerator and there looked to be no light to mend by this evening and what was she to do? Even entertainment at San Tomas' one movie house required electric power. Electricity was a fairly recent innovation on Mayan Cay, but it hadn't taken the people long to forget how life was lived without it.

"I think Stefano and Roudan went off to see if they could fix the generator."

"Ayah, they don't know anything of that. Eliseo, now, can do good with motor things, but not Stefano."

The electricity was still not on by morning, which meant no water. Thad wandered around San Tomas and noted the people with buckets lined up at the few backyard hand pumps that hadn't been converted when electricity befell the island. There were no wells on the Cay, but rainwater was collected and channeled into underground cisterns.

Between the beach-side police station—which was so tiny the one officer of the law sat inside and talked to everyone through the window like a sidewalk vendor—and the half-finished church was a paved basketball court with concrete benches surrounding it. On the back of each bench was the name of the donor—usually a businessman—just the last names lettered in fading paint. "Grosswyler" looked strange right next to "Perdomo."

Without really thinking, Thad leaped into the air and slam-dunked an imaginary ball through a hoop with broken strands for a net. Then he slid his hands into his pants pockets and turned away from the court, willing himself to put aside the picture of Ricky's last basketball game. It had been Ricky's last game of any kind.

He hadn't done too badly, either, for a gangly kid who was all feet and was meant to grow into a big man. Thad, Molly, Ricky, and a teammate had gone out for hamburgers afterward. Ricky complained about pains in his legs. They all thought it was just because of the strenuous game. Sometime in the night he threw up the hamburgers and complained about a headache. Kids vomit for the least reason, and that act alone could cause a headache. No fever. He'd be better by morning. Kids are tough. By morning Ricky couldn't walk. Thad had to carry him to the car and then into the hospital. By noon Richard Edward Alexander was dead.

The impossible had happened then, too. And it was every bit as horrible.

An autopsy along with blood samples taken before death proved Ricky was missing an important antibody in his blood. Sooner or later Ricky would have come in contact with a strep germ and been unable to fight off the infection, the doctors said. It was a miracle that it hadn't happened sooner. Ricky had rarely been ill, had an enormous appetite, was active and bright. And growing faster than most of his friends. There'd been no warning of that disaster, either.

Thad stared at his feet. He held his breath and squinted at the toes of his shoes until he made himself see the dream woman with the fluffy auburn hair instead of the stilled face against the satin sheen of a casket's lining.

26

Geoffrey Hindsly perched on the edge of a low dresser, a plastic glass in his hand. He leaned forward like a captain about to brief his squad.

"I've asked you all here this afternoon to give you the information the team of oceanographers gleaned from the Metnál."

Thad sat on the rushlike matting that covered the floor of Hindsly's cabana and leaned against one of the twin beds. Don Bodecker sat next to him, while Dixie and Martha Durwent lounged on the bed at their backs. Eliseo Paz and Harry Rothnel sat on the other bed. And the reporter, Weicherding, stood in the doorway as if, once he got the scoop, there could be a battery of telephones in San Tomas to run to and rush in the story. Geoffrey had poured them each a Scotch on arrival, and Eliseo looked as if he'd like to find a potted plant to dump his into.

"You were all involved in some way and have every right to be informed of at least what can be known at this time."

The room was close, jammed with too many people, too much tension. And it wasn't easy to work up tension in the lazy tropics. Still Hindsly rattled on his excuses for telling them what he'd called them them there to tell them. The bathroom door stood open about two feet from Thad's foot, and he traced the mud-termite tunnel up the pipe that brought cold water to the sink.

"God damn, get to it, will ya?" Don helped himself to more of the Englishman's Scotch. "Worse than a whole convention of Baptist preachers."

"What? Oh, yes, yes, of course." Geoffrey reached behind him for some papers he'd been sitting on. "Now, this shouldn't take long, all very simple actually. Let me see here . . . Yes, here it is. Now, the sand sticking to your hands the other day could not have been electrically charged, as you suggested, Mr. Bodecker, because water is a conductor, and particularly salt water, and any such charges or whatever would have dissipated throughout the medium."

"So what was it?"

"No one knows, but the scientists did find evidence of this odd phenomenon on their dives as well, and have taken samples back to laboratories for further study. Also, Mr. Alexander, your concern for the barrenness of that particular spot—actually, there are vast regions in all the world's oceans that are desertlike, compared to the colorful coral gardens tourists tend to visit. And even within the Metnál, not every last foot is covered with coral banks, as illustrated by the fact that there are great channels all the way through it that allow the passage of heavy shipping, you see. So that's no real mystery there, is it?" He pointed his pipe stem at Thad.

"How about her Majesty's ship *Gloucestershire?*" Ralph Weicherding asked from the doorway.

"She has been listed as presumed sunk, lost at sea with all hands on board, until any further evidence proves otherwise. All ships of the County class and similar construction and design, which add up to only three or four, are being called into the yards for a full structural investigation. They're fairly new, you know."

Don threw back his head to rest on the bed, narrowly missing Martha's kneecap, and brayed at the ceiling. "Just another damn recall!"

"Well, it really is the only logical procedure, isn't it?" Hindsly turned back to Thad. "Further, on the matter of sparse coral growth in the area, there were certain chemical imbalances in the water that might well have discouraged coral growth."

"Why wouldn't the chemicals just 'dissipate in the medium' like the electrical charges?"

"Ummn, good point. Afraid I don't know. See if I can scare up someone who does, though, what? Now, for the cause of the tragic mishap that has brought us all here. Over half the survivors of that trip mentioned the presence of great quantities of sand in the water directly afterward. That phenomenon invariably occurs after earthquakes that have disturbed the ocean floor. And you all reported having experienced something like a shock wave in the morning. So severe, in fact, that your nose, Mr. Rothnel, began to bleed. The oceanographic team submits that was a tremor, preparatory to the earthquake which was to follow that afternoon."

"Any seismic records of a quake in the Caribbean that day?" Harry asked quietly. One didn't come to own a "slew" of bakeries by being stupid.

"None that I know of. But that matter is still under investigation. The team, remember, just left Belize early this morning. I'm merely giving you the preliminary findings because I thought after all the strain it would be unfair to let you wait. Another factor leading to the verdict of an earthquake, by-the-bye, is the Moho or Mohorovicic discontinuity—which I don't fully understand but which apparently is a dividing line between the earth's protective crust and whatever is beneath it, or some such thing. The Moho off the east coast of Central America is suspected of being very near the surface, making it an ideal spot for subterranean activity."

"How about the egg?" Don asked.

"Eyeball," Thad corrected the car salesman.

"The humongous silver thing," Harry compromised.

"Yes, well, they postulate that too can be explained by the earthquake theory. Since so many wrecked ships litter the area—"

"And just why is that?" Martha spoke up for the first time. She sounded sullen and unconvinced.

"Because, Mrs. Durwent"—Geoffrey Hindsly sounded gentle and condescending—"there are so many coral banks about for shipping to snag against and sink. There's no mystery as to why the Metnál is known as a graveyard for ships, nor has there ever been."

He paused to relight his pipe, and the sweet smell added thickness to the close air. "But to get on with what I was saying, the gray or silver object variously described here could have been the metal hull of a ship —long wrecked and abandoned and perhaps partially buried—pushed to the surface by the force of the earthquake. It is unlikely, but conceivable, and would account for most of the events experienced by the passengers of the diving boat."

"Except for the size," Thad said.

"The size, yes. Well, that might be explained by the fact that in the extreme danger and horror of the turbulence, the object appeared larger than it was, merely because of the understandably shocked condition of those viewing it, as is not unusual in a case such as this. None of the witnesses' accounts have agreed on exact size or shape. Or color, for that matter."

Eliseo decided to drink the Scotch after all, made a face, and cleared his throat. "So if this wreck comes up as you say, mon, then where does it go?"

"That, I'm afraid, is still a mystery. One suggestion is that it sank into a crevasse opened by the quake in the ocean floor. The crevasse then might have closed up again—no more wreck. Which I realize is a fair-size crevasse and sounds a bit farfetched, but you must admit not nearly as farfetched as what you've all been thinking." The freckles on his forehead scrunched together in a look meant to denote significance.

"How about the big wave?"

"I'll give you that tidal waves formed by earthquakes start sooner and don't manifest themselves greatly till they come against land, but it is possible that the beginning of a small, localized tidal wave started and was foiled among coral banks some distance away and returned or swept back to provide that particular experience for you. Little is really known about them at their point of origin, you know. The total blocking out of sunlight is still a mystery also. The sense of a lack of gravity could have been caused by the sudden dropping of the boat off the wave."

"Happened *before* the water went down," Thad insisted.

"If it were totally dark, you'd have no way of knowing, really. Remember, science is not meant to provide answers for which there is no proof. But it is indefatigable, and given time, can probably explain most everything. And now that this has been taken proper care of, for the moment at least"—Geoffrey Hindsly set down his glass and stood, in an obvious gesture of dismissal—"I propose to begin my vacation, which is long overdue I might add. What say, Eliseo, is it too late in the day for a spot of fishing, do you think?"

When all but Eliseo and Hindsly stood outside in the Mayapan's compound, Martha said, "Am I imagining things or were we just treated to a first-class snow-job?"

"Didn't really explain a damn thing, but it sure did sound good." Harry Rothnel straightened his shoulders and stretched his hands toward the palm fronds and coconuts above them. "I feel better already."

"How about you, Doc?" Don scratched at thick curls and squinted at the sun. "Think we been had?"

"No, I think it was a very straightforward, unbiased, and logical explanation based on a professional study of the evidence at hand, on sound scientific principles, and on knowledge of natural laws inherent in this universe. And if I hadn't been in that little 'tragic mishap' myself, I'd buy it. In fact, I'm thinking of doing so anyway, because I want to feel better, like Harry."

Thad pushed against his father's house, and the net hammock swayed gently. He closed his eyes on the sun glancing off the sea. It was time to make plans. It had been for some time. But it was so easy to let time slip away on Mayan Cay, to relax into lethargy.

His plans for himself and the future had all been oriented around his family and his practice. Now only the practice was left, and the old plans and dreams no longer related. His goals had once been to save enough to put his son through college, maybe have another child, pay off the house, perhaps start his own clinic, have enough to retire comfortably with Molly, do some traveling. Dull but comfortable goals. They'd already begun to seem a little too dull and comfortable before his family was torn from him. But after, he'd have given anything to get those goals back.

He lifted the letter again but didn't read it, just looked at it—notice from the lawyer that his divorce from Molly was final. Thirty-seven years old, and no ties except to a house and a practice, both of which could be disposed of. He could be a veterinarian anywhere. Or something else. Thirty-seven years old, and he didn't know what he wanted to do. Middle-aged adolescence. . . .

Thad Alexander was suddenly skiing down an endless slope in Switzerland with the dream woman. Then they were sipping wine in front of a blazing fire, sitting close, talking. Thad didn't feel like an outsider.

That night he found himself wandering through a dark tunnel, and he knew he was dreaming. He had been here before. He was inside the ruined mountain. He felt the presence of others gliding past, wandering aimlessly as he did, like spirits he couldn't quite see. Could almost hear their vague whisperings. Could almost feel the rush of air as they passed, apparently unable to see him either in the dim passageways.

Thad wandered a long time, contentedly. There was something here he was meant to find. The passageways were a maze, and he was lost before he started, but knowing he only dreamed, this didn't matter.

Then Rafaela's voice spoke to him out of the dark, sounding like an eerie echo in this hollow mountain. "Thaddeus, come with me. You must wake and get away from this place. An evil one is here. Thaddeus, please, this is Rafaela. We must . . ."

The voice seemed to come from everywhere. He moved off into a side tunnel, but he didn't find Rafaela. Again he felt drawn in a certain direction, and moved toward it, curious as to what was to be revealed to him. Perhaps his goal in life lay before him, where it had been hidden from his conscious mind and would now become apparent in a dream, as was often done in the Bible. Suddenly there was a barrier in front of him—invisible—but his senses warned him just in time. He put his hands out to the cool touch of a series of diamond shapes. Odd that they should feel so firm and still be invisible. Could this be what he was meant to find?

As he couldn't pass through the barrier, Thad walked along it, trying to discover what it was by its size. A vast screen or door? To what? It suddenly either came to an end or opened for him to pass through, and the passages continued, one leading off another in no logical pattern.

Thad sensed the thing for which he looked beckoned him on and guided him along the right corridors. He could feel excitement in the air around him, knew he was growing closer to his destination. Those other wanderers who barely escaped his vision seemed agitated and brushed against him, their movements tugging at his pajama pants.

The tunnel curved, and there was light ahead. Dull. Metallic. A portion of the rock wall had fallen away, to lie piled on the floor. Above it, about shoulder height, was a jagged crack from which the light shone. That light blinked and then began a gradual flickering that picked up speed as a shiny object on the other side of the wall began to spin even more rapidly, and with a whirring sound that reminded Thad of a cold wind singing through snow-laced pine boughs.

The smell of lemon intruded on the cave smell of damp and dirt. It grew into a heavier scent that suggested the cloy of gardenia with something spicy added, and finally matured to the pervasiveness of rotting fruit and vegetation.

Jungle. Thad stood barefoot, facing a wall of jungle vine, his heart thudding with the shock of waking to something so opposite from that which he'd just been living. Part of the vine was wrapped around his shoulders as if it had reached out to thread him into the wall.

Something prickly crawled with agonizing slowness across his instep, and the skin half-way to his knee prickled an answer. There was a damp squishiness beneath the heel of his other foot.

Thad shuddered but couldn't move as the vine along his shoulders stirred and began to slither. It coiled back on itself until an end emerged from the endless vine with white blossoms that carried the sweetly sickening scent. The vine lowered the head of a snake. His stomach lurched.

He told himself this was just another fellow creature and there was nothing to fear, but his complete disorientation made self-suggestion useless. The snake appeared to notice that this bulky object was capable of movement too, and some strength. It lifted itself back up onto the vine, writhing away into it until snake and vine had become one.

Thad swallowed back the reaction forcing its way up his throat, and looked about him. He had no idea which way led to San Tomas. He stood there imagining hundreds of tiny biting insects attacking his skin, and listened for the sound of the generator to guide him. Instead, he heard the whirring that had reminded him of wind singing through a winter forest. The sound in his dream. It came from the other side of the wall of vine.

His vision had been better in the unlighted tunnels of his dream than it was in the moon and shadow reality of the jungle. And the stench of the orchidlike blossoms was overwhelming. But he stepped in closer to the vine and peered through it. He saw patches of things. Of light and of dark. Of a stone building on stepped rises coated with vines and jungle plants. And of Roudan Perdomo wearing his International Harvester hat.

Whatever lowered itself on him this time was harder than a snake and made his stomach lurch more violently.

27

Thad awoke to the throb of the island's generator. He sat leaning up against the chain-link fence surrounding the power plant, dried mud and vomit crusted on torn pajama pants. He leaned his head back against the fence and quickly changed his mind. A good portion of his skull was tender and began shooting dartlike pains toward his left eye.

"Aye, backra, you wanna leetle rum?" A bottle waved in front of his face and then withdrew. "No, maybe you haf too much already, huh? Sleepin' in the street. Mon, I dun even do that." Ramael, the fisherman, squatted down in front of him. His eyes traveled over the embarrassing mess Thad had become. "You wan' help, backra?"

Thad pulled himself up by the fence and then ran a hand over it. Cool metal diamond shapes like the barrier in his dream. He pushed past the fisherman and headed down the street toward the sea. Staggering along a silent beach until he came to the cemetery, he turned in to the water and walked almost until the end of the cross cut into the seaweed before it was deep enough to swim. The first glimmerings of dawn silhouetted the line of white surf breaking on the reef when he splashed out of the water and onto the cemetery beach, naked and cleansed.

My Lady growled low and showed him her teeth.

"Goddamn world," Thad snarled at the Virgin Mary, and trudged to his father's house.

Thad told no one of his sleepwalking dream or of the attack on him. He made flight reservations on Sahsa Airlines for New Orleans, filled out forms to liquidate his father's bank account, and began sorting through Edward P.'s belongings, deciding what to ship to Anchorage and what to give away to the islanders. He would sign the house over to Lourdes Paz just before he left so that she and the children could be next door to Rafaela. The shed they lived in wasn't large enough even without Aulalio. His longing grew for the crisp, energizing air of his home, the snappy pace of life there, the satisfying flavor of red meat, the relationships with his patients and their owners.

But he had to reschedule his time of departure because the one bank in all of San Tomas, the Bank of Nova Scotia, held an extreme version of bankers' hours. It was open only on Tuesdays. And there was more paperwork to satisfy the government of Belize before Edward P.'s funds and property could be released to Thad. It would be another three weeks, at least, before all was in order.

He kept a wary eye on Roudan Perdomo and on Stefano Paz. If Roudan had been in front of him, chances were that it had been Stefano who'd hit him from behind. They seemed to wander off toward the generating plant together often. For all he knew, they had some kind of a still in the jungle. Whatever it was, he didn't care. He was leaving Mayan Cay forever. He was no hero type who had to solve every mystery that came his way.

He had another strange dream, but awoke to find himself in bed this time, which was fortunate, because he was out of pajamas and had taken to sleeping in the buff again. He'd also taken to carousing far into the night with the boys from L.A. so that he wouldn't dream, and then sleeping just as far into the day and dreaming anyway.

In this one he found himself in the dream woman's apartment and didn't have to walk through doors. She was there with the heavyset girl, and he listened passively as they argued about going to some party. He watched the dream woman a little sadly, as if saying good-bye to her. She was really having a problem with this girl he assumed to be her daughter, but he could sense the deep ties between them even though they warred, sparred, parried. Even though they existed only in his dreams. Once he left Mayan Cay, Thad hoped never to dream again.

He made a day trip to the U.S. consulate in Belize City to enlist help in expediting matters with Belmopan. Martha Durwent's son, Greg junior, arrived to take his mother home. Thad threw a good-bye party for her, Geoffrey Hindsly, and Ralph Weicherding, who were also leaving the next day. It didn't seem to Thad the party had been over for more than a few hours when he was awakened by a pounding on the door leading to the outer staircase.

He grabbed a pair of pants and opened the door to a chilly fog and Harry Rothnel. Harry wore a straw tourist hat with a Budweiser hat band, a jacket, and long pants.

"Need help, Doc. Bodecker's gone. Walked off in his sleep. He's been doing it a lot lately, but we've always found him before he got far."

Thad finished dressing and joined Harry in the cemetery. The fog coming off the sea was almost rain. The tilted tombstones and tumbled sarcophagi looked drippy and eerie. My Lady looked miserable. He couldn't see the water, but its lapping sounded louder on the mist, and the surf out on the reef roared even though there was no wind on shore. With sight limited and sound magnified, they searched carefully around the buildings of the Mayapan. The echo chamber under the long dock warned of the build-up of heavy seas rolling in to shore even in the lagoon.

"Don's been havin' this same dream over and over, about wandering around in a bunch of tunnels," Harry said as they walked past the wooden fence that divided the Pazes' and Edward P.'s portion of sand from the sand street that led directly into the village. "You won't believe this, but I had the same dream not too long ago . . . Where you going, Doc?"

"I think I may know where to find him." Thad led his companion through a sleeping San Tomas to the power plant. The gate was closed, and all they could see through the chain links was mist. He followed the fence to its end, remembering again the barrier in his dream. When he reached the corner, he headed past it for the jungle behind San Tomas.

"Oh, Doc, hey, I don't think we better go in there. Roudan says it's full ah snakes and sinkholes. Don'd have no reason to go in there."

"Reason's not what's guiding him now. Look, there's even a path." It wasn't a very good one, strewn with all sorts of deadfall from the bushy trees and the coconut palms. There had once been a coconut plantation on Mayan Cay, and though not native to the island, the palm had taken over beach and jungle interior alike in the years since its introduction.

The morning fog was thinner here back off the beach, and wisps and strings of it floated from tree branches and palm fronds like gray Spanish moss. It dripped onto their shoes and pants legs from tall grasses and broad-leaved weeds along the trail.

"We should be looking on the streets of the village and in people's backyards or along the shore—not in here." But Harry stayed close behind him. Small hermit crabs lugged their appropriated shell homes across dried coconut husks and flattened weed stalks in an effort to get out of their way. "You may be the best damn doggy gynecologist on all of Mayan Cay, turkey, but you are one hell of a people finder. Now, ah came to you for help . . ."

The trail soon ended, or rather diverged off in several tangents.

"Leave it to a goddamn Yankee. If we are not already lost, we are going to be soon. Now, will you please tell me just why we are here to begin with?"

Thad didn't know if these "trails" had been worn by foot travel or water drainage. But he chose the widest and continued on, telling Harry about his own sleepwalking experience. "And I'd been having that same dream about the tunnels, and I think I walked in here. Maybe there's something in here that attracts dreaming minds."

"You know, I've been to Grand Cayman, Haiti, San Salvador, Roatán—all pretty exotic places—but I don't ever remember a place as weird as this one, even disregarding humongous silver things that—"

"Shhh, listen!"

The sound of a man sobbing somewhere ahead, and then a shout of outrage and pain.

"Take back everything I said. That's ol' Bodecker, all right. Biggest baby you ever saw," Harry said disgustedly, and stepped into a puddle that gave way clear to his knee.

Thad reached a hand to help him out, and hurried in the direction of the sobbing, leaving Harry to limp, curse, and squelch along behind. Don Bodecker stood in front of the vine wall in a pair of Jockey shorts. One side of him was mud-splattered. He turned slowly, eyes wide, rubbing his hands up and down his bare arms.

"Thank God," he mumbled when he saw Thad, and rushed to meet him, enveloping him in a suffocating bear hug. "Jesus, Doc, how'd I get here? And where's 'here'?"

"Now I've seen everything." Harry appeared on the trail. "Donald Bodecker, you unhand that man. Have you no shame? And you in your underpants!"

Don let go of Thad and rushed to embrace Harry.

"This boy needs help bad." Harry patted his friend's shoulder and explained to Don that he'd been sleepwalking again. They put Thad's jacket over his arms and tied Harry's around his waist.

"I want you two to do me a favor," Thad said. "I want you to go with me to the other side of that vine and see what's there."

They followed him reluctantly as he looked for a passage through the vine wall. The blossoms were closed up now, and their opulent fragrance had pleasantly diminished.

"Keep your eyes open, Bodecker. Last time Doc was here, somebody hit him over the head," Harry said, and picked up a stick.

They found an opening along the trunk of a palm where the vine had been hacked away by a machete. The raised tangle of growth on the other side looked more like a steep hill than a little building on raised steps, as Thad had thought when he'd seen the place at night and in pieces through a veil of vines and blossoms. There were even trees growing over the top of it.

"If you're expectin' some kind of ancient machinery left over from thousands of years before Christ," Harry said dryly, "this don't look like it."

Thad moved around to the left of the hill. The fog had lifted into the sky, and now it came back down as rain. They were soaked in seconds. "I didn't know there were any hills on the island." Thad had to shout over the clatter of rain on jungle leaves. "From the air it all looks flat."

"Probably 'cause of the trees on top. Maybe the green flattens out everything. Come on, Doc, let's get out of here. Ol' Don's chilled."

Don was sitting on an oblong slab of moss-coated rock. Thad ran his hands over it, and even through the rain-slippery moss and the water cascading over his fingers, he could feel the ridges of ancient writing. Every possible inch was filled with hieroglyphs. A section of one end had broken off, and one of the two pieces was missing. Thad had a hunch that the missing piece now lay up against a wall in his father's house. He guessed this to be a stela, lying on its side, and probably Mayan.

"So what?" Harry said when Thad made a point of this. "Probably not called Mayan Cay for nothing."

The rain came down in sheets as they made a bumbling threesome trying to stay on the trail. But eventually they emerged from the jungle near the power plant. Few people were out in the weather to see Don running through the streets in his odd outfit.

It rained on into the afternoon. The surf crashed against the reef, and waves lapped up into the cemetery, leaving foam on the sarcophagi. My Lady crept into a dry spot under the overhang of the bathroom jerry-rigged onto the second story, and Thad pretended not to notice.

"Are there any ruins, Mayan ruins, on the island, Rafaela?"

"A few old broken things is all. Not important."

Several of his father's books on Mayans implied that they were a mainland culture only, and with no more than small boats to ply trade within sight of the coast. He hunted again for that clipping his father had saved about the discovery of what was believed to have been a coral-encrusted segment of a Mayan galley in the Metnál. He went back to the chapter in his father's manuscript that discussed the Maya, but found no clue to any on the island. Edward P. merely made his usual diatribe against established scientific fact. In this case he pooh-poohed archaeological claims that the great pyramids and road systems of Chichén Itzá, Copán, Tikal, and others had been built by a race who had yet to discover the wheel or make use of draft animals.

"We are expected to believe," wrote Edward P. Alexander III, "that blocks of stone weighing up to twenty tons were quarried, hauled, and dragged into place in ever-higher piles of pyramid by conscripted peasants using the lever, ropes, pulleys, and a succession of rolling logs à la Cecil B. De Mille. One would think that the rolling logs alone might suggest the wheel to a race already well versed in astronomy, mathematics, and using a calendar superior to our own. But no, apparently there were so many disposable peasants about, one had no need to invent.

"And why raise these monstrous monoliths anyway? The professional archaeologist will tell us, as he will anything else he can't explain otherwise, that these huge stone works most certainly had something to do with religion. Is he not merely explaining something ancient and magnificent in the light of our own primitive culture?"

Thad researched while the rain poured and surf pounded. But about midafternoon the weather departed, the sun arrived, and Mayan Cay steamed. It was like being suddenly tossed into a teakettle. He put down the papers, notes, and books and walked over to the Hotel de Sueños for a cool Belican. He told himself he was really investigating Roudan.

Rafaela had to hunt him up again for dinner, and Thad accused Stefano of hitting him over the head. Stefano Paz scooped some of his dinner onto a tortilla and looked superior. "This island, Mr. Alexander, has not been good for your head since you came. Do not blame me for what happens in the *cabeza*."

"Stefano!" Rafaela spooned more black beans and rice onto his plate, and he answered her with a torrent that held a lot of the word "*loco*," and Thad caught many "*padres*" as well. He assumed this all meant that he was to be considered as crazy as his father.

A packet arrived finally, containing the finalized paperwork on that part of his father's estate which was in the country of Belize. Thad confirmed his airline reservation and set to packing in earnest.

He was eating a late, solitary lunch and glancing over some of the bills Edward P. had not paid before vanishing, when the screen door leading to the cemetery burst open and the woman from his dream walked into the room.

She stood with lips parted and eyes unblinking as the blood drained from her face. Shadows darkened the skin beneath those eyes. She was solid. Real. Breathing, but with difficulty. She put a hand out to the refrigerator to steady herself. Still she stared at him without speaking.

Thad, too, was shocked into silence, but so many questions ran through his mind, they would have formed an incomprehensible glut on his tongue had he tried to ask them. Instead he stood and walked over to her, a sense of unreality making his breathing shallow and too rapid. He reached out to touch her face, half-expecting her to vanish.

"Oh, God, where is she?" the dream woman whispered. She began to cry and to beat against Thad's chest with her fists.

Interim

Lost Lifetime

The engineer wanted only to be left alone with his sorrow, but the old man's curiosity could not be curbed, and angering him created only pain for them both. "Do control your anger, primitive. I'm very sensitive to strong emotion."

"Name's Edward," the old man snapped. "Quit calling me primitive. You have a name?"

"Herald." Herald knew he would question too if he were this Edward. The creature's unrestrained brain waves wielded an astonishing force. He searched for the simplest manner of speaking to this curiosity, in order to gain himself some peace.

But a sense of his own lost life interfered, and despair at missing the youth of his granddaughter. Her mother and grandmother would name her at the celebration. Now he would never know that name.

"And you use these terminals and the funnel thing merely for travel?"

"And for transporting goods." Herald recognized the decay of the flesh-eater in the man's perspiration. He'd encountered a similar odor on visits to preservations ringing the human cities of his own world, where beast-predator and victim roamed freely, killed and consumed one another at will or at need. What need had a human to consume flesh?

"Flesh is matter," Herald attempted to explain, "and the brain is energy. When traveling at the speed of time, therefore, they must be separated and transported individually. The mind is intelligent energy that automatically stores its own code, keeps itself in a form of . . . altogether, let's say, while transporting."

"You sound like a cross between a scientist and a computer programmer."

"Matter in any form, including that of the body," Herald continued patiently, "must be coded at the terminal of departure, and the receiving terminal then translates from the received signal to reassemble the matter."

"How do you get the mind back into the body once you've got the person where he's going? And why doesn't the body die when separated from the mind?"

"The mind naturally reunites with its body at the end of the funnel, just as a dreaming mind returns to its body upon awakening or rising from a deep level of sleep to a lighter one."

"Are you responsible for all the dreaming that goes on around here?" Edward drank from an oddly shaped metal flask, and Herald could smell spirits.

"All creatures dream, Edward. They always have."

"Well, your machines sound like material for a nightmare to me. What if mind and body don't arrive at the same time?"

"Eventually the body dies. The mind continues to search for it."

IV

Night of the Blooming Cereus

28

Russ Burnham didn't wait for his underground manager before entering the six-hundred-foot portal the morning after the cave-in. He'd had trouble sleeping the night before, and one of the things he thought about while lying awake was that if he was ever going to get to the bottom of the disturbing mysteries of Iron Mountain, he'd have to go in there alone without the influence of Jerusha Fistler's stories working on Saul Baggette.

By morning he was convinced that he would see nothing but a cave-in. Fears of the night always look silly in the morning sunshine, and after scrambling himself a couple of eggs he walked down to the mine entrance alone. Some of last night's meat still stuck in his teeth, and he worried it with a toothpick as he followed his lantern light down the tracks toward the core of Iron Mountain.

Russ could see no sign of further slippage or debris about. The soles of his work boots crunched on the grit along the tracks, sending hollow echoes off to return from all directions. If a guy didn't know better, he'd think other boots paced his along the side tunnels. Russ knew better.

The sound of water plinking into a puddle somewhere close. Nothing unusual. If strange things did happen in this world, and Lord knew they appeared to, they didn't happen to people strong and stubborn enough to ignore them. Only when the levelheaded were in a weakened state did creepy things dare to bother them. He didn't feel any power flowing like a river from this mountain, as old Jerusha claimed she did. Nor did he hear any machinery running like Saul Baggette had. Russ didn't hear anything but the echo of himself moving through an empty mine. . . .

And the gentle brushing sound of air. Almost a sigh. Not quite a whistle. Like a breeze moving through dried weeds. Higher-pitched than a whisper. Russ Burnham stopped, flashed the lantern around, and wished to hell he'd never seen all those scary movies when he was a kid. "Son-of-a-bucket full of high-grade monkey tits, Burnham," he chided himself, and walked on. "Talk yourself into being scared, why don't you?"

An electric ore car sat waiting and empty at the end of the tracks. Russ continued on, deeper into the mountain. There was a light coming from somewhere ahead.

Russ stopped again. He bit down so hard the toothpick between his teeth snapped in two. He turned off his lantern to be sure. It was a dim light. But it was there. It was possible that one of the men leaving in such a hurry the day before had left a lighted lantern behind and its battery wasn't dead yet. Not likely, but possible.

He moved toward the light at the end of the tunnel. There was rock down in several places here, and a good pile of rubble at the end. But no lanterns left behind. Just a shovel leaning against a wall. No dust on the scant air. Things seemed stabilized and would have seemed normal if not for the dull light coming from a fair-sized crack in the wall above a jumble of rock and dirt. And if not for the funny airy hum coming from the same direction. Russ spit out the broken toothpick and wiped his mouth on his jacket cuff.

He crawled over the pile of rubble to peer through the crack, and saw what looked to be a lighted room with a large metal object in its center. The object was encased in glass or clear plastic. And it was shiny, just like his underground manager had said.

Now, who would bring something like that inside the mountain, and how? The air seemed fresher up next to the crack than it was back away from it. Could there be an entrance to the center of the mountain that he didn't know about? He stuck his hand into the crack and accidentally knocked some dirt out on the other side. Russ reached for the shovel and poked carefully along the opening, watching for signs of a more general cave-in.

"B & H leases this mountain," he fought it out with his good sense. The crack widened. The roof didn't fall in on him. "And I am the company's representative here."

He had a hole big enough to crawl through, and still the roof hadn't caved in. "It is my duty to investigate anything funny going on concerning the company's interests in Iron Mountain."

He set down the shovel, turned off his lantern. There was plenty of light without it now. He stared at the hole, and before his good sense could talk him out of it, Russel Burnham made a dive for the opening.

The floor on the other side was lower, and the limestone here looked cut, laid, and polished. He worked his feet through and righted himself in a tumble of panic, half-expecting someone or something to rush him. But the room was empty. Just Russ and the large metal object. There were steps leading up to it. Although there was plenty of light below, the ceiling was lost in darkness. The air was cold, faintly fresh. The cave smell of the tunnels was gone. A different smell here. He couldn't place it.

Keeping his back to the wall, he circled the metal object in the center of the room. There was absolutely nothing else in there with them. When he reached the hole he'd made, he put a hand up into it for reassurance, but kept an eye cocked at the thing on top of the steps.

That sound like rushing air was coming either from the thing or from something on the ceiling Russ couldn't see. He could always go back and get Johnson, he decided. Now, Darrell Johnson was levelheaded enough, stolid, dependable, unimaginative.

"I oughta go back and get Darrell," he said even as he moved toward the center of the room.

He put his foot up on the first step. Nothing happened. The thing did look like a machine of some kind. And there was an indentation in it like Baggette reported. It could fit a human body of almost any shape, it was so nebulous. But that didn't mean that's what it was meant to do. Russ took another step, and a section of the see-through casing (too clear for plastic, too thin for glass) parted noiselessly along a crack, which hadn't been there before, to make an opening about the size of a high doorway.

"Holy shit!" And Russ was off the stairs and back to the hole to the tunnels practically before he'd had a chance to think about it.

The doorway remained. What could the damn thing be for, anyway? He circled the room again, inched his way back toward the steps. He couldn't see anything on them to activate the opening of the shield or whatever it was. He stepped onto the second step again to see if the doorway would close, but nothing happened. The third and last step brought no change either.

The doorway lurked before Russ like a trap. "I ain't that dumb."

Someone came in here regularly to dust, that was certain. The place was surgically clean except for the pile of dirt he'd knocked in while making the hole larger.

This setup must be for some kind of criminal purpose. But what, he couldn't imagine. He pulled out his pocketknife and tossed it through the opening. It lay unharmed on the shiny aluminumlike floor of the machine.

Russ watched his pocketknife for a while and then threw in his helmet. Again nothing reacted. He put his hand into the opening, and when he was able to withdraw it without mishap, he tossed in his jacket. He knew he was playing with fire, but he couldn't help it. He was able to hook the jacket around the helmet and pull them out.

He knelt in the doorway and leaned into the machine, expecting it to try to close up on him, trap him. Like he used a good lure to trap animals on the family farm in Nebraska. He could remember a few getting caught, with the trapdoor snapping shut on their middles.

The knife was situated so that Russ had to crawl forward to reach it, and only his feet and ankles were outside the doorway. Why put a trap in the center of a mountain where nobody came? He grabbed the knife and stood so suddenly that he forgot and brought his feet inside rather than backing out and onto them. Panic took his breath away when he realized what he'd done.

But the doorway remained open for him to pass through. No hole opened in the floor to swallow him up, no blade dropped from above to pin him. None of the worries that came upon him in that instant of panic materialized. He walked out and down the steps unscathed.

Shivering from the coating of sudden sweat that had sprung out everywhere in reaction to his crazy fantasies, Russ groaned a halfhearted chuckle. He'd never claimed to possess great intelligence.

His hand was still in his pocket, replacing the rescued knife, and he was over halfway to the hole that led to the tunnels, with his back to the machine for the first time since he'd entered the room, when the machine made a noise. The light on the wall in front of him blinked. He turned, to see the cylindrical metal object revolving slowly inside its clear casing. It would have been a perfect cylinder if not for the curved-in place.

It revolved more rapidly and the light flickered instead of blinked, and Russ watched his jacket billow toward it, felt something tugging at his helmet, and watched it fly through the doorway and attach itself to the indented place in the cylinder. His short hair stood up and bent in the same direction.

All his commands to his body to run for the escape hole went unheeded as Russ was sucked across the room, up the steps, and into the swirling cylinder, along with the dirt he'd knocked into the room. He was barely able to turn so that his back pressed into the depression that could have been meant to fit a human body. The pressure flattened him into it, increased as the spinning speeded up.

The whirring sound revved itself into a scream. The hole to the tunnels stretched into a black band that appeared to circle the room. The only other time Russ had been too shocked and overcome to swear at himself was when he'd been in an automobile accident. The suddenness and complete loss of control over his environment had been the same. He'd expected to die then, as he did now. He melted into the cylinder, his body feeling like jelly, and the cylinder spun so fast on screaming air that it no longer seemed like movement, and against all reason, he could see the circular room. Russ felt amazingly comfortable, lulled and floating.

Russ floated over a wooden building, the size of a small warehouse, with a tar-paper roof. It had an attached dock area next to a set of railroad tracks, and a man in tan pants with only red long underwear above hoisted a block of ice over his shoulder with giant tongs and walked down some steps. The old-timer with the five-foot stride. A white horse, spotted, with heavy legs and matted mane, pulled a wagon out of the three-hundred-foot portal and along the tracks to the old crusher building Russ had seen only in pictures. The wagon was loaded with limestone. The man on the wagon seat lifted his hat to the man with the ice. Neither of them paid any attention to Russ.

"Malfunction, malfunction," a calm voice repeated mechanically in his head. "Malfunction, mal—"

"Primitive in the funnel," another voice said, and Russ was spinning with the cylinder once more. "Full body . . ." and there followed a series of word sounds that meant nothing to Russ.

The room turned a deep green. Russ glimpsed a gorgeous blue sea and a beach of white through a veil of leaves. Except for the slight movement of the leaves, it looked like a postcard picture.

29

Jerusha Fistler sent word by way of Vinnie that the cereus would bloom that night and everyone was to bring a hot dish and come to a potluck dinner party to last until all the blossoms had opened. The Whelans were having breakfast when Vinnie dropped her little bomb and then rushed off to tell others.

"Will we have time to make something after school?" Adrian carried her cereal bowl to the sink. "Want me to get some stuff out of the freezer?"

"No, because we aren't going. There's no reason why we have to jump every time that woman—" Tamara pretended to choke on her coffee to hide her shock. Her fantasy life was getting out of control. She thought she saw Backra standing by the gold brocaded couch.

"But it'll be fun. I haven't been to a party in years."

"Adrian, I resent your constant refusal to listen to me. I'm not trying to be unreasonable, but I am responsible for—"

"Well, you are unreasonable. The whole town's going to be there. All the kids who live here. Jerusha says there's some long folding tables in one of the empty apartments she's going to clean up and put in her place. All of Iron Mountain will be having a party next door, and—"

"I don't trust that woman. She's up to something. A lot of people feel that way about her, and I doubt there'll be many there."

"I'm going, Mom, with or without you." Adrian looked pensive and then turned to walk past where Backra had stood. He had vanished.

The children were still out on the playground before school started, when Saul Baggette walked into the classroom. He was Will and Nate's dad and he and his wife had become a little more friendly since school started. Saul was young, bearded, with the sad deep-set eyes of a poet and the solid body of a workingman.

"We was just wondering if you might have seen Russ around . . . last night maybe? Or this morning? Fred didn't see him when he went off duty, and I wasn't supposed to let the men in the mine until me and him checked out a cave-in. Thought maybe he'd said something to you or . . ."

"Saul, I haven't seen him to speak to in several days." There was apparently some talk around concerning the mine manager and the schoolteacher on their off-duty hours.

"Not like him to go off without leaving a message. But his pickup's gone. We don't know whether to send the men on home or . . ."

"He could have gone into Cheyenne and been delayed."

"Yeah, I guess . . . Well, thanks." But he hesitated at the door. "It's just that the lower portal doors're unlocked, and I saw Russ lock 'em myself yesterday."

"What if he went in to check on the cave-in and got in trouble?" But then, why would his pickup be gone? "Have you asked Augie if—?"

"Augie's gone too. But his pickup's still here. Thought maybe he went with Russ." Saul shrugged and reached for the door. "Suppose we'll see you at the party tonight," he said somewhat reluctantly, and left.

Tamara was surprised the Baggettes were going to Jerusha's party. She'd never known them to exchange visits before. Over the lunch recess she went out onto the playground to enjoy some sun and saw the miners' vehicles pass the school. Darrell Johnson, Larry's father, walked down the road carrying his metal lunch pail.

"No sign of Russ yet?"

"Naw. Sent the men on home. Just not like him to . . ."

"Has anyone checked inside the mountain?"

"Me and Saul just got done doing that. Called. Took us hours. Searched every last tunnel." Darrell Johnson's eyes slid away from hers.

"Do you think you should report him missing to the county sheriff?"

"Already called the company office in Cheyenne. Might just be stuck with a broke truck someplace. If he don't show up by the time of the party, I'll call somebody. See ya tonight." He walked off. So the Johnsons were going too. If enough people went, Jerusha couldn't very well do anything.

By the end of the school day, and after listening to her students' excitement about the party, Tamara relented and helped Adrian concoct a hamburger-and-macaroni casserole.

"I do love you," she said wearily as they worked side by side.

"I love you too, Mom. More than anybody. That's why . . . Just remember that, no matter what, okay?"

"No matter *what* what? Adrian, you're not getting involved in Jerusha's experiments or anything?"

"I meant, no matter . . . no matter what I say when I mouth off and say mean things."

"Oh, honey, I understand." They hugged each other. "Actually, we're doing better in this awful place than I thought we would." But when Tamara tried to turn back to the casserole, her daughter clung to her so tightly she couldn't move.

The main room in Jerusha's part of the duplex was filled with two long folding tables covered with cheap paper tablecloths. In the center of each, a dried-weed arrangement and candles stuck in old wine bottles. Balloons hung from streamers that were already wilting in the false, vaporized-induced climate. And everybody was there. Everybody except Russ Burnham. Even baby Ruthie squealed and drooled in a much-used playpen in the corner.

But to Tamara the most pervasive impression was that made by the vine. Its luxuriant growth was out-of-place in the dingy room and the dry climate in winter. And the scent of the white buds sprouting on it overcame that of the food she and the other women were arranging buffet-style on Jerusha's kitchen table, of the beer and assorted booze being sloshed and served by the sink, and even of Deloris Hope's perfume. The sickly, exotic scent of overripe fruit and gardenia and lemon made her see again the snake coil about Thad Backra's shoulders, and she drew in her breath with a shudder.

"You cold?" Agnes Hanley pushed her glasses up farther on a sweaty nose. "I think she keeps this place hotter than Haiteez."

"Just thinking of something that made me shiver." Tamara lowered her voice. "I'm surprised to see you and Fred here."

"Didn't want to come, but Vinnie said if we didn't, we'd be the only ones in town not here. Everybody always talks about the ones that aren't around, you know. Fred'll eat and then go on up to work. Where's Russ?"

"No one's seen him all day."

"Truck's out front. Figured he was back."

"Here, try one. They're delicious!" Deloris Hope handed Tamara a glass with what turned out to be a pineapple-coconut-rum drink, and she thought of the Dixie woman fixing one like it for Backra when he went upstairs to slip into something more comfortable and to comb his hair, and she realized she was thinking of her dream-fantasy again. It worried her that she couldn't seem to forget about it. That every little thing reminded her of it. She was obviously losing touch with reality.

The children served themselves first and sat together at one end of the table to insult each other. Tamara filled her plate and sat next to Nancy Baggette. "When did Russ get back, do you know?"

"No, but his truck's out in the road. We thought he'd be in here. He's probably up to his house washing up." Nancy wore Levi's, heavy hiking boots, and her hair in one long fat braid that hung down the back of her sweatshirt. She leaned over and whispered, "How'd she get you to come?"

"Oh, Adrian didn't want to miss a party."

"Told us if we didn't come, we'd be the only ones not here. Can you imagine throwing a party for a house plant?"

Jerusha had provided drinks, coffee, a fruit salad, and a cloying bakery cake. All the hot dishes were a variation of either hamburger or tuna. Tamara could remember other neighborhood potlucks, in what seemed now like another life, that would look like a rich man's banquet compared to this. She wondered if Adrian remembered too. But Adrian's eyes followed Jerusha, who was refilling coffee cups and freshening drinks. She didn't notice the other children giggling as Larry Johnson shook pepper into her strawberry pop.

Nancy Baggette was into things like sewing and crafts and canning.

She grew the only vegetable garden in Iron Mountain. It was organic, and she let her chickens run in it to eat the grasshoppers that would have otherwise eaten the garden. Tamara rarely saw her or Helen Johnson except to wave to when they got into or out of their cars.

Jerusha kept the liquor flowing after everyone had eaten, and the group began to thaw. Oddly, these few people who lived so closely in this isolated spot didn't seem to have much in common or to feel particularly comfortable with each other. The room was overwarm, and the beer and iced rum drinks disappeared faster than the coffee.

The buds on the night-blooming cereus had been large and fat when the party started, but they'd been gradually opening unnoticed. What had seemed white with a pinkish tinge became salmon-colored tendrils separating to release thick snow-white petals. Long white hairs with yellow fuzzy ends poked out of the opening horns, and the giant blossoms grew still bigger as the petals stretched and parted.

When Tamara looked directly at a blossom, she could see no movement, but after she looked away and back again later, the flower would have opened further and have changed position. Their odor grew heavier, took on the oppressiveness of incense. The heat, the steamy, crowded room, the alcohol and heavy food, and the jungle smell of the vine combined with the scent of the blossoms to produce a druglike languor on those at the tables.

A cold prairie wind was rearranging the dusting of dry snow outside and swirling around the mountain to whistle in the weatherstripping and to rattle the windows in their frames. It seemed to be off in some other world and have no reality inside.

"Vinnie"—Jerusha licked her index finger and poked at cake crumbs on the table—"you did tell Russel Burnham about our party?"

"Couldn't. He wasn't home." Vinnie yawned.

"Not all day?" Jerusha looked beautiful with candlelight flickering across smooth skin. But she did not look pleased. "Perhaps you, Mr. Hanley, could tell him when you go up to work."

"What? Oh. Yeah, guess I'm late." Fred Hanley, who'd been reluctant to come, seemed reluctant to leave now, or maybe it was just the drugged atmosphere. A refreshing draft from that other world swept into the room before Fred closed the door after him, and the talk perked up for a few minutes.

"What's his truck doing out front if he ain't back yet?" Darrell Johnson stretched and blinked.

"Augie and I took it into Cheyenne to buy things for the party," Jerusha said. "Augie's truck wouldn't start this morning."

"Where do you get off, taking the boss's truck, Mapes?" Saul Baggette had both elbows on the table, and his shoulders hunched.

"Keys were in it. He's got the company truck, and he's borrowed mine before." Augie'd been strangely quiet until now.

"You are saying that Russel has been gone all day?" Jerusha asked.

"Nobody's seen him." Saul looked at Darrell and then away. "Thought he'd gone off in his truck."

Jerusha parted the vine at the window over the sink to look out at the night and Iron Mountain.

"You'd better report this to somebody." One blossom near Tamara resembled a sea anemone as its pale-salmon tentacles were flung out to make room for expanding petals. Another, which was at a different angle, looked like a ragged tutu.

"Yeah, I suppose," one manager finally answered her.

"He's old enough to take care of himself," the other one said. Both wiped sweat from their foreheads with their napkins.

Jerusha turned from the window, her white shift dress so out of season but making her the only comfortable-looking person in the group. In the dim light, the white of her dress and the white splashes of blossom seemed to unite the woman and the plant. "Have you looked inside the mountain?"

"Yeah, he ain't in there. Nothing's in there. Not even a cave-in."

"We must of looked in the wrong tunnel," Darrell said.

"No, we didn't. I know where it was. And now it isn't."

Little Ruthie had fallen asleep in the playpen. The nippled bottle had slipped from her mouth. Talk subsided, and it grew quiet. A balloon near the ceiling burst. No one even jumped.

Bennie Hope sniffled. Agnes Hanley got up and poured herself another drink. A series of yipping sounds like old-style Hollywood Indians used to make, and then drawn-out wailing howls, came from somewhere on the mountain. They seemed to move closer to the back porch. Other voices joined the wailing in a ragged tempo, and the wind moaned an accompaniment.

"My God, the ghosts!" Tamara came out of her lethargy with a start and began a rush for Adrian. "Jerusha's raised the ghosts."

Somebody snickered. Augie grabbed her. "This teacher lady's spooked." He laughed and held her tight when she tried to push away. "I'll protect you, teacher lady. Settle down, now."

"Way to go, Augie." The sound of clapping hands and cheers. The chuckles multiplied, became laughter.

" 'Nother schoolmarm bites the dust."

"Suppose that's what killed the last one?"

Tamara could hear them, but couldn't see past an enveloping Augie. "Adrian!" Didn't anyone else hear the ghosts?

She kicked Augie repeatedly, as hard and fast as she could make her leaden feet move. He put her down and backed away, looking surprised and sleepy. She made a dash for Adrian, but stopped short when the back door burst open.

Tamara's screaming filled the crowded room and her head.

30

Russ Burnham stood in the doorway, blinking as if the light bothered his eyes.

Tamara's screams turned to coughing and then to barely audible squeals that happened every time she exhaled. She had no more control over them than she'd had over Augie Mapes. The room came back into focus. Adrian hadn't moved, and was apparently asleep. Bennie Hope had crawled into the playpen and slept with his baby sister. The rest of the children looked half-asleep or dazed.

"What time is it?" Russ's voice broke.

"We're having a party," Jerusha said, as if everything were normal. "I will fix you a drink."

"It's close to midnight."

"Where you been all day, boss? We had to send the men home."

"Mrs. Whelan thought the coyotes was ghosts," Larry Johnson said in the tone and with the sly grin he usually reserved for Adrian.

Russ stood in the open door to the utility porch and stared into the room without appearing to see it.

"Want some food?" Jerusha handed him a glass. "I can heat it up."

"Just had breakfast a couple hours ago. What day is it?"

"Thursday. Been that way all day." Darrell guided his boss into the room and closed the door on the fresh air.

Russ downed a tumbler full of rum and pineapple and coconut and handed it back to Jerusha. She mixed him another. "Where have you been, Russel Burnham?"

"In the mountain." He walked with a funny wobbly motion to the nearest free space on a bench and sat. "Thursday."

"What's wrong with Adrian?" Tamara said suddenly.

"She's just sleeping, worrywart." Jerusha put a hand on Adrian's back. "Still breathing, Mama."

"Went into the mine this morning, early." Russ emptied half of the refilled tumbler. "Came out a couple hours later and it was night."

Jerusha dribbled long fingers across his crew cut. "And what did you see, Russ Burnham? In the mountain."

"Saw the old-timers alive." He drained the glass and handed it to her over his shoulder.

"Careful with those drinks." But Tamara's voice didn't cut through the stuffy, tropical air to reach him.

"Saw a whole city of white and blue plaster, right here at Iron Mountain, and people in funny clothes lined up at the six-hundred-foot portal. Some of them saw my shadow. They pointed to it and talked English and another language all mixed together, without moving their mouths." He still didn't seem to see the room, the awful party, the danger breaking out everywhere.

Tamara tried again to warn him through the humidity and heavy scent. Only Agnes Hanley heard her. And Agnes just patted her hand. She'd taken off the little cat-eye glasses and set them on the table. Her eyes looked smaller and pinched around the edges, like Miss Kopecky's lips. Everyone had stopped talking and stared sleepily at Russ. The coyotes no longer howled out back. The vaporizer "whooshed" more steam into the room, and Tamara expected to see it hanging in clouds near the ceiling soon.

"Me and Darrell went in looking for you when you didn't show up this morning. You couldn't of been in there. You'd of heard us calling."

"You know that cave-in site? Well, you were right." Russ ate a few bites of the cake Jerusha set before him, pushed it away, and reached for his drink. "There's a round room behind that wall, with a machine in it. Didn't you see the hole I made to get in?"

"No hole, no cave-in. Like it'd all been put back together. Like it never happened." Saul looked pointedly at Darrell Johnson. "And I knew just where it should've been."

"Can't be. I made a hole big enough to crawl through."

"Dammit, Burnham, I know where it was!" The underground manager jumped to his feet.

Nancy Baggette took hold of her husband's arm. "Sit down, Saul. Being as overdramatic as the schoolteacher."

"Way I figure it, the mob is using that thing in the mountain to transport drugs up here from South America."

"Why South America, Russel?" Jerusha opened another bottle of rum.

"Because that's where the motherfucker sent me by mistake. 'Least there was lots of palm trees and ocean and stuff."

"Mayan Cay," Tamara said, hearing the wonder in her voice.

"You dream about Mayan Cay too?" Nancy Baggette turned around from the other table and stared at Tamara.

"Way I see it, the mob can go back and forth on that machine without having to go through the metal detectors at airports and can carry their guns with 'em this way." Russ nodded at his own logic.

"Ain't that the place Jerusha tried to send us in our heads?" Agnes asked Tamara. "At the last party, when somebody fell against a table, knocked over the candles and all. And burned the place down."

"I didn't live here then." She was surprised to find a drink in her hand and to realize she'd been sipping it.

"Oh, yeah. Augie, wasn't that the place at the last party, where—?"

"Sure sounds like it. Lucky nobody was killed."

"Jerusha and Abner used to live next door before the fire," Agnes explained.

"I dream about that Mayan place," Will Baggette offered. "All the time. It's an island."

"You do?" His mother looked startled to find him still in the room. "How come you never told me?"

"You never asked."

"Where's Adrian?" Tamara set down her glass and pointed to the place where her daughter had slept at the table. "Jerusha made her into a ghost like she did Miriam Kopecky!"

"Oh, God, here she goes again."

"I don't know about you, but I'm going home before the fire starts this time." Darrell Johnson went into Jerusha's bedroom and returned with his coat and those of his wife and son. Helen gathered the place settings she'd brought for her family and found her casserole dish.

"Thanks for the party. Nice plant," Darrell said with little conviction, and pushed a sleepy family out the door ahead of him.

Nancy Baggette tried to get Saul to leave too. When he wouldn't, she took her boys and left without him.

"Be home as soon as I convince old Russ here that his hole's gone," he yelled after her.

"I think there is only one way to prove it," Jerusha said. "And that is to move the party to the mountain."

"Company policy don't allow civilians in the mine. Insurance company—"

"Russel . . ." Jerusha took hold of his shoulders, turned him to face her, and said in her cheerful lilt, "If you refuse me this, I will do it anyway, and I will make your life very miserable."

Tamara lost track of some time, because the next thing she knew,

Augie was carrying the folded playpen, Deloris held Ruthie and pushed Bennie. She said she'd be back for Vinnie and had no intention of going into the mountain. Then Tamara stood in Jerusha's bedroom, where the vine was even thicker, the blossoms bigger, and the scent deadening. Adrian slept under Jerusha's coverlet, and Vinnie slept beside her.

"Don't they look cute and innocent when they sleep?" Tamara's tongue was too swollen to get around the *th*'s properly. "I really don't drink like this very often."

"Fresh air'll do us both good." Agnes Hanley helped her into a coat sleeve. "Adrian'll be all right till we get back."

"I can't leave her here with Jerusha. Jerusha's evil, bad person."

"She's going with us into the mountain to find Russ's hole, remember? She won't be here to do anything." Agnes and Tamara were suddenly helping each other down the wooden steps of the utility porch, and Tamara took thankful bites of the cold fresh air.

Jerusha walked ahead between Russ and Saul, linked them with her arms, and made them walk slower so the other two could catch up.

Saul Baggette stumbled suddenly and went down, taking Jerusha with him and forcing Russ to his knees. There was much good-natured cursing and insults.

"Some night watchman you got, Burnham. Hasn't even come to see what all the commotion's about."

"Probably having coffee in the guard shack with his ear aids off."

"How come he never brings the dog up, Agnes? Thought that's what he bought him for."

"Dog won't go past the school no more. Gettin' so's he won't even go out to pee-pee if I don't give him a kick. Damn dog."

They stumbled through shadows and guided each other over rough places in the path down to the giant doors of the six-hundred-foot portal. Russ opened them with a flourish and then handed out helmets and lanterns.

"Company policy," he told Tamara, placed a helmet on her head and a kiss on the end of her nose.

Five pairs of shoes crunching along the tracks echoed and magnified to make them sound like an army. Lanterns, held haphazardly, danced on walls and ceiling and ground, and cast deformed shadow shapes.

Russ and his underground manager argued over several turnings, but Russ finally found the lantern he'd left outside the round room with the machine in it. "And here's the shovel I used."

"How'd you get out with no lantern?"

"One minute I was in South America and the next I was outside on the mountain behind Jerusha's house. Heard the party and headed for people." Both men ran their lanterns over the end of the tunnel. "Well, I'll be pussy-whipped."

"Told you. It's clean." Saul set his lantern down and tried pounding on the wall and pushing at it, till his face turned red.

"Yeah, too clean." Russ struck at it repeatedly with the shovel, then put his ear up against it.

"Who do you suppose put things all back together?"

"The mob. What I can't figure is how come we never see them coming and going."

"Mob of what?" Jerusha asked Tamara.

"Criminals."

Jerusha flattened herself against the wall at the end of the tunnel.

"Hear anything?" Agnes sat down hard on the ground with a grunt of surprise. She looked at her lantern as if she'd forgotten she'd carried it in with her.

"I can feel it. I can feel the power of Russel's machine stronger than I've ever known it." The melody in Jerusha's voice slid into rapture. "Tamara, are you thinking of Adrian?"

"Ummmm?" Tamara leaned against a cold, dank-smelling wall and thought more of falling asleep. "Adrian?"

"Yes, your daughter. You do love her, don't you? So much that you can feel her now?"

"I love my Fred," Agnes said matter-of-factly, and listed far to port. "Most of the time."

"Tamara, come over by me and think of Adrian." Jerusha's eyes were dark and compelling, her voice soothing. "Stand right here and let's think of Adrian together. Adrian."

"Adrian." Tamara found her back pressed against the end of the tunnel.

"Fred," Agnes insisted.

"Don't you feel the power?" Jerusha asked them.

"I feel it," Saul said.

Tamara blinked as Agnes and the floor trembled.

"Holy . . . me too. Come on!" Russ pulled Agnes to her feet and started down the tunnel with her. Agnes' helmet had fallen off, and it jumped around as if it were alive. The mountain shivered. Pieces of dirt and rock clunked and pinged on Tamara's helmet. Saul grabbed her arm, and Jerusha's.

The young widow pulled away. "No, not when I am so close."

"Follow Russ. I'll get her. Hurry!"

But Tamara, woozy as she was, knew he'd need help with Jerusha

Fistler. Rocks exploded from a corner as part of the roof came down. One hit Jerusha on the back and head and literally pushed her at her rescuers. They each grabbed an arm and dragged the woman along the tunnel, leaving her lantern behind, choking on dust, sobering with every running step on and in a pitching earth.

Tamara made a squeaking noise every time something hit her body. She expected to die momentarily, to be crushed, suffocated. And now she could think of her daughter with no trouble. She couldn't die because of Adrian, but she was about to anyway. All that mining of a mountain since 1905 to hollow it out so that it could come down on her now. Why hadn't she turned the car around and driven away that first day she'd seen it, as Adrian had wanted her to?

Tamara lost her lantern, and they were guided only by Saul's. She continued to help drag the deadweight of the woman she hated. Someone in her head said, "Malfunction. Do not enter. Macrordial systems repairing. Do not enter funnel. Repeat, do not—"

But Tamara drowned it out screaming, "Adrian!"

31

Russ deposited Agnes on the tracks outside of the portal and raced back in to help the others. He was sweat-cold sober. Clouds of dust came at him up the tunnel as if moved by a giant fan. The ground jumped up to jar his legs whenever he stepped down, much as he would expect it to do in an earthquake. Tracks buckled, ties splintered. Just before the line of overhead lights went out, he saw them straggling toward him, two dragging the third between them.

And then, instantly, Russ was outside with Agnes—not sure how. The three others were with him—all dark shadows, one of them unconscious. The earth stilled. Russ looked up, expecting to see the mountain diminished, caved in upon itself. Although sandstone dust still puffed along its moonlit side, the mountain remained the same.

"Did you hear a voice like God or somebody telling you not to go into the tunnels?" Saul asked.

"I thought it said 'funnel,'" Russ said. "It was the same voice I heard in that round room, and it wasn't any god. He would've known we were in there already and trying to get out."

"Then just how did we get out?" the teacher asked.

Russ didn't have an answer. He helped Baggette get the limp Jerusha up to the first level, where some of the older buildings had tumbled. Dust on the air here too, but the yard lights were still on. He wondered where Fred Hanley was. Even if his night watchman hadn't heard anything, he would have felt the disturbance beneath his feet. The concrete plug in the three-hundred-foot portal had buckled. A pile of debris spilled out the opening, to sprawl for yards. Russ couldn't understand what was holding the mountain up.

Darrell and Augie came running toward them as they reached Russ's house. They'd loaded all the women and children they could find into the back of a pickup and had Saul's wife drive out onto the prairie and away from the mountain.

"I've called Gridley from the office in Cheyenne, and the sheriff," Darrell said.

"Adrian . . . ?" the schoolteacher asked in a dazed voice. "Is Adrian in the truck?"

"Ain't she with you?" Augie looked over the bedraggled group. "When Deloris went back for Vinnie, she said Adrian was gone, and we checked at your place."

"I knew it. Where is she?" Tamara Whelan pummeled the unconscious woman Russ and Saul held between them. "I knew it!"

Russ had Augie take Jerusha into Cheyenne in Russ's truck. How was he going to explain the presence of civilians in the tunnels to his supervisors? This probably meant the end of his future with B & H.

He, Darrell, and Agnes helped Tamara look for her daughter. If she sleepwalked that mountain tonight, the kid was in real danger. They searched all the buildings in the settlement first. There were noticeable cracks in the walls of all the homes next to the mountain. But the Hanleys' house across the road seemed barely touched, and Augie's TV antenna still rose straight and true into the sky.

The huge pile of crushed limestone behind the school had slid into it, almost encased the back of it. Russ insisted they stay together while searching there, and feared the structure could give way any second. Then they hunted through the company buildings. No trace of either Adrian Whelan or Fred Hanley. Russ wouldn't let anyone on the mountain to look.

They took the Hanleys' dog and old sedan and left Iron Mountain to join the truck on the prairie and await the authorities. Russ had an arm around Tamara Whelan. She cried softly against him and drifted into an exhausted sleep.

Help arrived, including Al Gridley from the home office. Russ, Gridley, and half the sheriff's office went back into Iron Mountain, while the residents were moved into Cheyenne to temporary quarters at F. E. Warren Air Force Base.

"We were about to close this mine anyway," Al Gridley said as they stood before the tumble of rock sprawling from the three-hundred-foot portal.

Just what is holding this mountain up? "Yeah, folks here've been dreading that for a while. Heard about the open pit."

"Russ"—Al placed a comforting hand on Russ's shoulder, and that's when Russ realized how frightened he must look—"I just put through a recommendation to send you to Eagle, Colorado. It's a lot quarry and not much mine, but with your experience in limestone, we weren't going to forget you."

"Whole damn thing should've caved in by now. Wait till you hear from the widow Fistler."

"Huh? Hey, you'll like Colorado, Russ. 'Course Eagle is a going concern, and you'd only be assistant. But you'd be next in line, and things do happen to managers."

"They sure do. Thanks, Al." They shook hands. Russ wanted to recommend Saul and Darrell but figured his word wouldn't be worth a slag dump once Al heard of the party. Let him hear it elsewhere. Honor was for thieves. Russ had more important things to consider now. "Two people of this little community are missing. One's a kid, the other a deaf old man. Want to help me search?"

"Sure, Russ." Another slap on the back.

More men arrived to help, and they spread out among buildings and along the prairie. Russ left the reporters who came with them to Al Gridley and started up the mountain. Two deputies who met him on their way down said they hadn't seen anything and worried that the missing could have fallen into one of the bottomless holes. Russ went on alone, passing the body of an old roadster rotting in the weeds, traces of an old roadbed. He continued to the top, puffing with effects of the excesses of the night before and lack of sleep.

He searched along the upper ridges of Iron Mountain for the hole Tamara Whelan had found, but couldn't find any that far up. Using her apartment roof as a rough guide, he zigzagged partway down until he found a hole that fit the description. He took off a glove and held a hand over it, but with the constant wind it was difficult to tell if there was a special movement of air coming from the opening. Kneeling beside it on the downhill rim, he leaned over as far as he dared. The air was damper here, and there was a low, muffled rumble that wasn't wind. And a smell he'd never be able to describe, that wasn't limestone dust or the dankness of tunnels.

It was one he would always associate with the blue-and-white city that had encased Iron Mountain, diminished it to the proportions of an anthill. But he knew something now that he'd never admit. That city was of a time other than his own. And he doubted even the mob had the means to eject people instantly and unharmed from the tunnels, as he had been twice. And the second time, those tunnels had been collapsing around him. He tossed rocks down the hole. He could hear none of them land.

Too nervous to swear, Russ turned and walked rapidly downhill. Someone had somehow managed to shore up the inside of this mountain without showing themselves. And they left at least one vent hole into the heart of the mountain. No sheriff or Al Gridley would believe any of this. So if anybody mentioned it, it wasn't going to be Russel Burnham.

Newspaper headlines talked of the cave-in and the fact that "Night Watchman Disappears with Twelve-year-old Girl!" intimating Fred Hanley had abducted the adolescent Adrian for foul purposes.

"Fred ain't had no interest in sex for fifteen years," Agnes replied to the charge, and the newspaper gleefully reported that too. Some official declared the earth stabilized, and the residents were allowed to move back into their homes temporarily until they relocated. B & H was closing Iron Mountain.

"Hope my daughter'll take me in," Agnes Hanley had worried to Russ. "Without Fred, I don't have nothing. All those years of work, and I don't have nothing." Because Fred had not yet retired from the company, his wife was not entitled to the "widow's portion" of his pension. He'd been with B & H for over thirty years.

Jerusha Fistler was judged to be in a coma and put on a life-support system. Russ convinced the others to uphold the story that they'd all chased Jerusha, who'd had too much to drink at the party, trying to get her out of the mountain, and had rescued her when the tunnels caved in—which wasn't too far from the truth and would help Russ keep his job. And all the men who'd worked the mine could vouch that she'd been known to enter it regardless of repeated warnings. If Jerusha revived from her coma, she'd tell of Russ's mistake in practically inviting the party into the tunnels. She was the vengeful type. But if she didn't revive, they'd never know the whole story. Russ believed only Jerusha Fistler had any idea of what was going on inside the mountain.

The Cheyenne school system closed the school permanently. It was considered unsafe, with the giant slide of crushed rock that appeared about to eat the mustard-colored cinder-block building. Parents were expected to relocate their children near other schools as soon as possible.

Tamara Whelan sat in her daughter's bedroom and refused to come out.

Agnes finally came to get Russ. He was packing company papers and office equipment and didn't know what he could do to help. The teacher had just closed herself in. But he went along with Agnes. Privately, Russ had decided the big kid had gone sleepwalking on the mountain and fallen into a hole. Probably never be found. That didn't sound like something that would happen to Fred, though.

After trying to talk her out of Adrian's bedroom individually, they stormed in together prepared to pick her up bodily and move her out. But a change that hardened her expression stopped them.

"Backra," she said with a snap of her fingers, and stood of her own accord. They had to step aside to let her pass.

32

"You'll have to excuse me." Tamara busied herself in the kitchen. "I haven't eaten in a long time."

When Agnes and Russ tried to leave, she insisted they stay, and soon had everyone arranged around Miriam Kopecky's coffee table with sandwiches and coffee. At first she ate steadily, staring through the wall over Russ's head. Finally she said, around a tumbler of milk, "He was even here that morning. I don't know why it didn't occur to me till now."

"Who was here?" Russ looked uneasily at Agnes Hanley.

"Backra. He and Jerusha . . . somehow have done this thing between them. We've got to make her talk. Adrian, and maybe Fred too, Agnes, could be somewhere—"

"Called the hospital this morning," Russ said. "She's still unconscious. Look, I gotta—"

"Sit down, Russ, or I'll tell the sheriff and B & H just how it came to pass that Adrian was left alone that night in Jerusha Fistler's bedroom," the teacher said sweetly.

Russ sat down and reached for another sandwich. He liked her better frail. "Who is Backra, and what—?"

"Thad Backra, Thaddeus, tall, gray-haired man I've never met who lives on an island I've never visited."

"He the one lives next to that sand cemetery?" Agnes asked.

"So you do dream of Mayan Cay?"

"More lately than I ever used to. Them big black birds fly in circles over the tombstones, and the place's all wrecked. Remember that first party, Russ, when Jerusha and Abner lived in the next place over and she had us think of that island?"

"I was in Cheyenne. Didn't get back till the fire." But he knew the island, had visited it in dreams as well as by way of the machine in the mountain. He was amazed anyone else knew of it.

"You've had a few dreams about Mayan Cay too, haven't you Russ?" Tamara read his expression. "Odd we should all dream of the same place so often, since none of us have been there. What happened, Agnes, at the first party?"

"Well, it was kind of like the one you went to. We all ate and then got sloshed, but she didn't have that creepy plant. Got us all to think about the same thing, like one was a coconut, and she stood by these candles with her eyes shut, like a witch in a movie. I thought coconut so hard, I saw one on the table in front of her. But it kind of faded away. All some kind of game, she told us. Then she shows us a picture of this plant, like the one she's got now. I don't remember it, but the next day she claimed our 'experiment' had made a cutting of it appear on the table, and she'd rescued it from the fire. Big fuss. Made poor Abner go buy her a vaporizer. Folks kind of stayed away from her after that. Thought she was crazy. Till Miss Kopecky came, she—"

"Agnes, remember Jerusha asking us at the end of the tunnel to think about Adrian?" Tamara Whelan's skin was pale, veins feathered blue at her temples. Her hands trembled as she held her coffee cup. But the small lithe body had folded itself into Miriam Kopecky's armchair, Indian fashion, as supplely as a child's. She was a pretty woman even under stress.

Agnes Hanley shook her head. Her troubles showed too in shadows around the eyes and in the nervous clasping and unclasping of her hands. "Hate to admit it, but I don't remember too much of any of that."

"I do," Russ said. "She put you against the wall and kept repeating 'Adrian,' and Agnes kept saying 'Fred' instead."

"And both Fred and Adrian are missing. And it was the same way she got people to think of the night-blooming cereus," Tamara said.

"But it's not missing. It came, not went. 'Materialized,' Jerusha said, but she's always been nuttier than a fruitcake."

"And she was interested in the mine, and Russ's room with the machine, and . . . somehow these things are all connected." Tamara set down her cup wearily. "I just can't think how."

"Maybe she sent Fred and your girl someplace and brought the plant here the same way," Agnes said. "Don't make much sense, though."

"I've seen the night-blooming cereus on Mayan Cay, and Backra on Iron Mountain."

The last thing Russ wanted was to get further involved with these mysteries, so he was surprised to hear himself saying, "There's some connection between this island and Iron Mountain. I don't think those two are still alive, but we might find out what happened if we knew where this Mayan Cay was. Maybe we could call down there on the phone, sound 'em out."

"I know where it is, and I think we should go there, not just call." The frail schoolteacher sat up straight and spoke with a strong, take-charge tone. "You, Agnes, because you might discover something about what's happened to Fred. You could sell either your car or Fred's truck for air fare, and we'll sell Miriam Kopecky's antiques for money for the trip too." Tamara turned to Russ in a way he'd been expecting but dreading. "You should come with us, because you have some time off with pay between jobs and because there are some mysteries which, if not explained, can haunt even you, Russel Burnham, for the rest of your days."

It snowed the night before Tamara left Iron Mountain, and in the morning she pulled the Toyota over to the side of the road and stepped out to look back. In its coating of clean white, the mountain stood pristine and tall against a sky of snapping blue. It appeared to have dressed up to celebrate her departure, to have shed all those sinister qualities that had shadowed her life for months. Those months seemed like years.

Did she leave her daughter's body in a hole on the surface of that mountain? Had her baby died in lonely, painful agony? Terror? Would she roam the mountain now, like Miss Kopecky?

Augie Mapes hammered on the shack he was building for his generator. The clack of the hammer cut across to her sharply on the cold air, and his red-plaid mackinaw looked like a flare against snow and new wood.

Augie intended to invoke some form of squatter's rights to the land on which his trailers and collection of junk vehicles sat and which was part of the parcel B & H had leased from the federal government for three-quarters of a century. He planned to dig a well and install his own generator. Russ didn't think he'd get away with it, but if Tamara knew Augie and the mess he'd cause hosts of government paper-shufflers, it would be years before he'd be forced to move, even if his squatter's rights were denied.

He'd soon be alone with the mountain and its ghosts. Deloris Hope and her children had already moved into low-income housing in Cheyenne. Saul Baggette had found a job with an oil-drilling company in Casper. B & H would transfer Darrell Johnson to Colorado with Russ. Agnes Hanley had given Fred's German shepherd to Augie, and Augie planned to move Jerusha's chickens to his "lot" if she didn't wake up.

When Tamara and Agnes had driven Fred's pickup into Cheyenne to sell Miriam Kopecky's antiques, they'd stopped to see Jerusha in De Paul Hospital. And "see" was about all they could do. Jerusha lay thin and pale but not yet skeletal, kept alive with tubes and wires. Tamara had pulled the plug on the vaporizer in Jerusha's apartment, left the night-blooming cereus to wither and dry, turn brown, and die. She'd have loved to do the same to Jerusha Fistler.

Laramie County School District One had offered to transfer Tamara to a school in Cheyenne to assist in a class with "special needs." But she had to look for Adrian. Which meant she broke the contract, and that would go on her record.

Tamara turned now and crawled back into the Toyota, where Agnes Hanley sat crying quietly, and drove away from Iron Mountain.

Interim

Moment in Time

Adrian careened through black, through a total absence of light. She could feel the heating up of her skin, the too-rapid shallowness of her breathing, as frenzied chemicals called her body to action. Even though she knew she'd left that body back on Jerusha's bed.

This was not like the dreaming had been. And there were "things" in this void with her. Unknown, unseen. She could almost hear them, sensed a whisper of their touch as she hurtled past and felt sickened at the thought of inevitable collision.

Adrian imagined a scream she had no mouth to utter, imagined it trailing out behind her like a comet in the thick blackness.

A wind or air current jerked her suddenly in another direction, a wind that sucked and pulled instead of pushing from behind. Perhaps her body was awaking, drawing her back. The wind turned on her, struck her. Adrian tumbled over and over and down, the wind shrieking by her like it would a diving, crashing plane. Light exploded into the darkness. And then colors. Blues and greens shimmered, reached for her. . . . No sensation on impact. Just an abrupt end to her dizzying drop.

The blues congealed to ocean, the greens to palm trees. The familiar ingredients of too many dreams. She hovered above clumps of tortured black rock with jags and holes.

An old man knelt among a pile of browned palm fronds, staring past her openmouthed. He wore a khaki-colored shirt-jacket with short sleeves and extra tabs, like people wore in ancient Tarzan movies. His beard and hair were white and stringy but neatly trimmed, his eyes the color of frost.

A movement at the edge of her consciousness, a sound of human agony or forced breath. Adrian whirled to see a giant in a lacy suit.

"You're an Atlantean," the old man said.

The giant raised his arms. "Primitive in the funnel!"

He startled Adrian so she almost spiraled off the beach. The next she knew, they were following each other around in circles, apparently unaware of her. Adrian tried to hear what they were saying, but it became work just to keep from drifting off.

She'd never felt this disembodied in her dreams, this bewildered, had always been able to see herself as whole. But since that peculiar current of air had caught her and tumbled her to this place, she'd had no sensation of body at all, not even the remembered response of the amputee, as though she'd lost all contact with the solid part of her.

And as her fright grew intolerable, it bounced her about. That frightened her more, and the fear fed upon itself until colors spun, melted, merged, and she whirled. Nothing to grab on to to stop, nothing to grab with.

She catapulted away from the beach and the human shapes below. Would she disintegrate? Fly off into pieces of thought that couldn't recombine to form Adrian Whelan?

What had Jerusha said? "Just relax, let your body sleep and your mind wander, and the fat will melt away without pain, because you won't need food. And, oh, woman-child, when you wake, you'll have a body to match your beautiful hair and eyes. And your mother will be so proud."

At the thought of Tamara, Adrian's whirlwind ascent slowed and she began to drop.

Jerusha had said nothing about her becoming separated from that body, traveling around alone and half-complete. Something had gone wrong with the experiment. That realization sent her spinning up once more with a sort of screaming panic that had a sound of its own. A sound as out of control as her motion.

Mom? Mommy! Again, a lessening of the bedlam of this nightmare. She fought to form a vision of the thought of her mother, a comforting image, and to hold on to it as she settled back onto the beach.

Now the giant sat on a rock with the old man at his feet. "We have perhaps repeated this conversation many times before, old Edward, and we are certainly doomed to repeat this moment many times again." He said this without moving his lips. "Because we have slipped between time."

"Help! Please, help me." Adrian tried to keep quiet thoughts smoothed over the desperate ones to hold herself together. She would have given anything to have her own misshapen flesh back to shield her from the rawness of this experience, and for a tantalizing second she saw it form beneath her—the colors of her blue jeans and blouse, slightly transparent but with unclothed forearms and hands extending from the blouse's sleeves. But all vanished with her excitement over the sight, and she spiraled.

Adrian concentrated on her mother, tried to remember what her daddy had looked like the last time she'd seen him, tried to relax—found herself hovering behind the giant's left shoulder. The old man stared right through her. He kept asking the giant about God and time and nutty stuff. And she could feel the giant's deep sadness pushing through the fancy lacework of his clothes. Adrian longed again for her own body to shield her from the pain of it, and blue jeans and blouse formed beneath her.

"Who's that?" the old man asked the giant, but looked straight at Adrian. "One of your angels?"

"Help me," Adrian pleaded, and watched the chimera of herself disappear.

V

Chimera

33

When Tamara stepped off the Sahsa jet that had flown her to Belize City from New Orleans, she realized just how foolish had been her hopes of finding Adrian alive anywhere, or even finding news of her in a place like this. The near-certainty that her daughter was not hopelessly lost, which had sustained her until now, weakened in the sudden on-slaught of blinding sunlight, soaking heat, and humidity.

"Feels just like Jerusha's apartment." Agnes Hanley removed her sweater and added it to the coat over her arm. "Really think I'll find my Fred . . . here?"

Tamara swallowed back a disappointment so intense it stuck half-way down and made her cough. She stumbled on the ramp stairs that led to the concrete runway, and a stewardess—Latin, beautiful, cool-looking—reached up to guide her last few steps.

Sweat tickled down between her breasts. It had been snowing when their plane left Cheyenne the night before. It had been snowing when they left Denver at four that morning.

"Belize International Airport, *Bienvenidos a Belice*" was emblazoned in blue across a building of white concrete block about the size of a small-town high school, with a tiny control tower where there might have been an old-fashioned bell tower. One runway. A huge military-drab helicopter approached over nearby jungle. A white man in tennis shoes and khaki shorts jogged along the runway. Antiaircraft guns sat surrounded by dun-colored sandbags covered with camouflage netting.

"Looks like a military base," Russ said as they waited under a hot sun outside the approach to the customs area and in a line of heavy-jowled

North Americans of retirement age. A small dark plane screamed down the runway and rose into the air like a helicopter. Five more followed it at staged intervals. "Fighters. Fixed-wing. Vertical takeoff."

The weaponry everywhere around them seemed incongruous with the smiling black faces of the young airport personnel and the lilting, laughing tone of speech that had already haunted Tamara for months.

"You suppose Jerusha came from here?" Agnes asked.

"But she's not black." Russ looked out of his element in this alien place.

"Not Kalkasin neither."

No passport was required to enter Belize, just proof of citizenship, and they passed through customs and out to a waiting taxi for a hair-raising ride along a narrow jungle-shrouded road and then through foot and bike traffic to an even smaller airport. Here they crowded into a propeller-driven Mayan Airline plane which held a pilot and nine passengers.

Tamara sat next to the pilot, a Yankee who wore a leather flight jacket and a white scarf. He looked like Robert Wagner without the Pan-Cake makeup and told them that if they really wanted to see Belize they should visit Belize City sometime. Tourists were generally shunted around it and out to the cays. "You'd see the real Central America and some of the most incredible slums this side of Calcutta."

When they were over the Metnál, he pointed out dark shapes under the water that he claimed were wrecked ships encrusted with coral. The water was a true sea-green today, and so clear she could see the ocean floor, trace the shapes of coral banks and mounds from the air. Tamara wondered how the *Gloucestershire* could have sunk from view.

Her dreaming of the *Gloucestershire*'s disappearance did form a link between this exotic place and barren Iron Mountain. Possibly a link to Adrian? "Accepting the loss of a child," she'd overheard a sheriff's deputy tell Russ, "is just near to impossible for some women." Was that all it was? Had she given Agnes Hanley false hope?

Behind her Agnes said, "I never been anywhere before. I never saw anything like this except on TV. Never knew it was really this beautiful. . . ." She droned on in astonishment to her hapless seatmate. Perhaps both she and Tamara would begin to face their mourning here.

An island appeared off one wingtip, its center a swamp of muddy water and long-rooted bushes. The pilot told her it was uninhabited. After a stretch of empty sea—another island, long and narrow, its beaches cutting a dazzling line between the green of the sea and the dark of inland jungle. Tamara imagined the taste-smell of sea salt and a fragrance mixed of flowers and the overripe greenness of vegetation.

The memory impression of her dreams. Her heart speeded up even before the pilot announced, "Mayan Cay," and circled above the lopsided heads of coconut palms, their fronds parted at the crown and flopping over in all directions.

The plane lined up with the shortest, narrowest runway imaginable. And at the end of the runway, a settlement—one of its larger buildings a direct target ahead of them as they touched down. On either side, palm trees hemmed them in. They stopped just short of the swath of sand that separated the runway from the building—two-story, with children all dressed alike sitting on outside staircases and with lettering above the second-story balcony overhang that could be seen only from the air but which Tamara's startled eyes had registered, *"Escuela de San Tomas."*

"*'Escuela'* means 'school,' right?" She realized she'd grabbed the pilot's knee. "They built it at the end of a runway?"

"Sort of like we'd put a housing development there, back in the States, or a shopping center."

"Well . . . you certainly earn your white scarf."

"Just remember, whatever you think of the way things are done here," and he patted her hand, "these people think all backras are crazy."

"Backra? You know him?"

"That's what they call all Anglos."

A jeep from the hotel carried them and their luggage along a narrow street of sand between wooden houses sitting on stilts. Some white. Others in bright pastels—yellow, green, blue, pink. Some with sand yards enclosed by solid-board fences, lovely flowering bushes and plants growing directly out of the sand. Clothes hanging to dry under the houses. Poles carrying power lines aloft, looking naked and out-of-place. Footprints in the sand, and dog droppings. Theirs the only vehicle in sight.

"Holy gonads," Russ whispered reverently. He recognized this street too.

"I think I'm scared." Agnes' eyes widened to fill her glasses.

The sagging gate from which a little boy had stepped and then run through Tamara's dream body. The house where a woman had been sweeping the stairs, her hair in even pin curls, her thonged sandals slapping as she moved from one step to the next. The storefront on a corner that she and Backra had passed when he sleepwalked to a roofless church. Its shutters stood open now, and racks of canned goods and packages of potato chips and candy bars were set out for sale. Cases of empty Coke bottles still lined one outside wall.

She could see the ocean and the beach in patches at the other end of side streets. This street ended with a familiar thatched hut, and the jeep pulled into a courtyard of beach between it and a two-story building, its veranda paved in black and white tiles.

The Dixie woman walked up to the jeep. "Welcome to the Mayapan, folks. My name's Dixie, and your cabanas are . . ." She stared at Russ and then from Agnes to Tamara, the same way they were staring at her. "Have you been here before?"

Tamara's mouth was too dry to allow for speech. But she and Agnes were soon ensconced in a hut with a thatched peak in the roof, with its own bath, porch with patio chairs, twin beds, and a rush matting on the floor. Expensively primitive. Tamara figured that in two months she'd have spent every cent she had in the world.

"Never thought I'd sleep in a little grass shack," Agnes said as Tamara slipped into shorts and a sleeveless top and still felt damp. Her hands looked ten years younger as her dry skin drank in the moisture on the air.

The windows were a series of wooden louvers with a screen outside and adjustable to take advantage of the ocean breeze. Agnes played with the louvers on the back window and then bent to squint through them. "Come take a look," she said in a choked whisper.

Tamara was shorter than Agnes and didn't have to bend to look out at the graveyard in the sand directly behind their cabana, the tumbled concrete coffins and farther down the statue of the Virgin Mary blessing the bones of Maria Elena Esquivel.

"That'll be his house, then." Agnes pointed to the farthest of two houses at the back of the cemetery. "The one with the hammock."

"Yes." Tamara turned and walked to the door on rubber legs.

"Want me to come with you?"

"No, Agnes, not this time."

Russ Burnham stood outside, talking to two men sprawled across lounges and brown enough to have been here awhile. She shook her head and walked away when he made a gesture to include her. She was aware of her winter-white legs and the patch on her nose that was beginning to redden. *God, Tamara, how can you even think of such meaningless things at a time like this?*

An older man in a straw hat stood in the sea, his pants legs rolled to the thigh and shirt sleeves rolled above the elbow. With a long knife he cut seaweed and threw it away from him. For a moment their eyes met and held. Then he flung the green weeds in his hand and bent back to his task. He was white. His sneer was Latin. Different, say, than that of the pilot, who definitely had an Anglo sneer. *Hell, Tamara, they're both just men looking at a woman. A sneer's a sneer.*

Three dogs in this dreadful burial ground—two together, one alone, all of a similar tan color. Small, short-haired mongrels with sad, suspicious eyes. They looked like the kind that would yap and bark, but remained quiet as she approached, backing off just far enough to make a leisurely getaway if they had to.

The one off by itself was fatter and spryer than the others, its look more intelligent. Tamara thought of her daughter again, fat and healthy but unacceptable—she pushed the pain of Adrian away with a grunt, stared at the Virgin Mary and ran her fingers over the dirty letters. EN SAGRADA MEMORIA DE MI HIJA, in sacred memory of my daughter. . . .

Tamara turned to face the house with the hammock, felt the eyes of the man in the water. The little lone dog in front of her curled a lip and began a backward slink at her approach. Its silence was more unnerving than her awareness of the man cutting seaweed. As if this creature could not make sound. Guardians of the dead, perhaps, had no voice, because the dead cannot hear.

Tamara worried she might be sick on the clean sand, under the ponderous sun and the black ugly bird circling above—huge, silent, intent.

You're just afraid to face him. What kind of a mother are you? Poor Agnes probably watched her between wooden louvers. Tamara was small, but she wasn't helpless. She'd seen that fact register in Russ Burnham's eyes and was still trying to digest its import.

The treacherous thought that not everyone had the opportunity to confront a fantasy . . . She hoped he wasn't home. She hoped he was different from the man in her dream. She hoped she could go through with this.

The frayed ends of loose strings in the net hammock on the porch trembled on a breeze from the sea in time to the trembling in her. But her hand was steady as it reached for the screen door. She could remember walking through it without opening it in her dreams. She didn't knock now, but barged in before she had time to think it over.

Everything here, too, was as she remembered. Backra sat at the round table with the oilcloth, eating and looking at some papers. He set down a fork filled with food and stared at her. His suntan was even deeper than she'd dreamed it, and made the light metal-colored eyes and hair seem to glow in the shuttered room.

Blood thundered in Tamara's head. She ordered herself to stomp over to him and demand to know what he'd done to Adrian, but she froze, balancing with one hand against his refrigerator, realizing how stupid she must look, and wondering why he didn't look more sinister. He just looked stunned.

Backra opened his mouth to speak but shrugged instead, pushed back his chair, and stood. He came to stand over her, and still she couldn't move. His fingers felt hot on her cheek when he touched her. He drew them away, stared at them and then at her.

She'd been screaming at him inside her head, but when her repeated words finally found voice, they came out as a whisper: "Oh, God, where is she?"

And then she was pounding on him and sobbing childishly. "You have her. I know you have her somewhere. Give her back to me. Please!"

He held her away and lifted her to look into his eyes. Suspicion replaced the shock on his face. "Where do you come from?" he said in that familiar raspy voice, but as if he expected the answer to be Mars.

"Iron Mountain." Tamara, who'd never fainted in her life and didn't believe in it, felt herself going and began gulping in air to ward it off.

"Iron Mountain. Does it have railroad tracks and tunnels?"

"Yes. Please give her back to me." She started slipping through his hands and toward the floor; the buzzing in her ears threatened to snap something in her brain. She was suddenly on one of the hard kitchen chairs, her head pressed down between her knees, staring at pieces of sand dotting the unpainted boards of the floor between her running shoes.

"All right now?" His voice was cold, but the pressure of his hand on her back eased.

"I think so." Tamara hated herself for being so weak, hated him for being so in control and ignoring her repeated pleas for Adrian. He helped her to sit up, brought her a glass of water, watched her drink it, long elegant fingers clasped in front of him. Everything about him was long and elegant. The sleek Backra of her dreams. Walking. Speaking. Real.

"You are one dream I never wanted to come true," he said cruelly, and took the glass from her hand. He wore powder-blue swim trunks and a short-sleeved white shirt open in the front and he needed a haircut and he bent over and kissed the raw patch on the end of her nose.

Then he lifted her to her feet and off them, held her up against him as effortlessly as Augie Mapes had done at Jerusha's party, and kissed her on the lips and then down her neck. Her head kept calling for Adrian, but every other traitorous, aching cell in her body responded to Backra.

34

"All I can tell you is I don't have your daughter, don't know where she is. I do have some idea of how you feel, though." They walked along the beach away from San Tomas. Tamara had practically to run to keep up with his long strides. "I've dreamed of her as I have of you, a large girl, likes to eat in the middle of the night, gives you a rough time." He spoke rapidly, as if he were more used to keeping silent. "But I don't have any evil way of transporting sleeping children here from anywhere. And I don't know any Jerusha Fistler, and . . ." He stopped suddenly, and she ran into him. He pulled her around in front of him and wouldn't let her move away. "And I'm having one hell of a time believing in you, lady."

"It's Tamara."

"Tamara. But you must be right about there being some connection between this place and Iron Mountain, or we wouldn't know each other."

"Please stop walking. I'm out of gas."

Humor etched a trace of lines around his eyes and then spread inside to take away the protective leaden quality. "Not used to the heat."

"It was snowing this morning. I came to find my child. You tell me she isn't here. Which means I'm supposed to believe she's dead."

"They do die, you know."

"She's missing! Not . . . dead." Tamara sank to a sitting position in the hot sand and stared at his knees.

" 'Least you can say the word. When was the last time you had a meal?"

"I don't know. What are you, a doctor or something?"

"Or something. But not a witch doctor like you've been treating me. Let's see, lunch is over at the Mayapan . . . if we sprint, we could just make it back to the Hotel de Sueños in time for scraps at least. Roudan's notoriously relaxed about schedules."

Tamara wasn't up to sprinting, but did manage to walk back along the beach. She recognized the unfinished church as they passed it. Just before they reached the cemetery, he guided her into a cool dark barroom and through it to a dining room with long tables. It was about half full, and the very smell of spice and tomato and other things she couldn't name almost took the last bit of starch from her legs. *What am I doing sitting down to eat with this man?*

Steaming bowls of fish stew were set before them, and brown bottles of beer. *How can I enjoy food when Adrian . . . ?* Guilt and all, Tamara ate and drank everything offered. Her grateful body sent back rounds of zipping-good feelings to equal any she'd known running. She didn't pause until they sat over coffee.

Backra, who'd managed to put away a second lunch, smiled a smile she'd never forget. "You wonder how you can still feel hunger, pleasure —anything but pain when you've lost somebody. Makes you want to punish yourself."

"She's not dead. I'd know."

"Still think I have her hidden away?"

"Maybe that was just an easy answer." The coffee was half hot sweetened milk, but still thick with flavor. It and the food were so revitalizing she began to enjoy the heat, the bright colors around her, and the man beside her. She had the urge to compare dreams with him, but there was still something guarded in his manner, as there should have been more in hers.

"Why am I a dream you wished would never come true?" she asked him.

"I'm about to embark on a new life, carefree and unattached, and you look like a little bundle of responsibility and strings."

"Gee, where have I heard that before?"

As they entered the bar, a big parrot turned upside down and wished Tamara a "Hoppy burday."

"What I really want to do," Tamara said when they were once again out on the beach, "is to search every house, run up and down the streets screaming her name. Anyway, thanks for the lunch."

"I owed it to you after, uh . . . treating you that way when we met."

"You don't look sorry about it."

"I'm not."

"We probably don't even like each other. It's just the dream-fantasy."

"That's got to be it."

"I followed you one night, when you were sleepwalking—at least I dreamed I did. And when I woke up, I'd been sleepwalking too. And a snake wound down from a vine onto your shoulders." Somehow they'd angled back to his door.

"You're lucky. That was one of the nights I was wearing pajamas."

I remember a few when you weren't.

He opened the door, and she stepped in. She noticed the boxes now. The Sahsa Airline folder on the table. "You're going somewhere? Moving?"

"This is my father's house, and that's a long story. I'm flying home tomorrow—Anchorage."

That stifling disappointment she'd felt when she stepped off the plane returned. *Over a man?* "What kind of a mother am I?"

"I don't know." He reached into a cupboard for a tube, smeared sun cream on her nose, forehead, shoulders—without asking or explaining. As she would have done for Adrian.

"Would you have time to take me into the place with the snakes?"

"If that's what you want, Tamara." He reached back into the cupboard for a spray can, and she stood docilely while he sprayed sickly-smelling bug spray all over her skin and clothes and hair. "Sand fleas have probably eaten you alive by now, but there's ticks and such in the jungle."

"Do you have to go home so soon?"

"I think it's for the best." He sprayed his front, handed her the can, and turned around for her to spray his back.

She should have returned to the Mayapan long enough to explain her absence to those she'd dragged down here, but she just followed him through San Tomas. By a different route than the dream walk, but they came to the chain-link fence and the source of the background rumble.

"This is the island generator." He pointed to the building behind the fence.

"You walked this way, feeling the fence till you could walk around it."

"In my dream I was inside your mountain."

He led the way into the jungle, and it looked even more foreign with the sharper edges of day color.

"The snake didn't hurt me," he reassured her when she paused so long he had to come back for her. "But someone else did. Did you see anybody else here?"

"No. I rushed forward to save you from the snake, and woke up in the snow."

"And I came to back at the generator with a whacked-up head. Snakes don't whack. Do you realize how this conversation would sound to anybody who wasn't us?"

"I haven't had an intelligent conversation since the day I drove into Iron Mountain. What happened to you when you were all scratched and bruised and hurt your nose?"

"I had a diving accident and decided it was time to go home. And I can't find my dad. So he must be dead." Thad explained he'd come to Mayan Cay to search for his father.

"If he's missing too, maybe he and Adrian are together somewhere."

She followed him again, and remembered that dream day on the beach when she'd first seen him. She'd followed him then too, reached out to touch his back, hadn't been sure if she really felt it or not . . . realized now she'd just done it again. This time she could feel his warmth through his shirt. This time he turned and caught her up.

They stood holding each other in the steamy place with the sun pressing down on their heads and the rank growth all around them exuding odors so dense they almost overcame the chemical smell of the bug spray. Tamara buried her face in the sandy mat of hair that formed a T on his chest, the bar stretching over his breasts and the tail extending down as she'd traced it with dream eyes the night he'd come to Miriam Kopecky's bedroom in Iron Mountain. She stood on tiptoe to kiss the dip in his throat beneath his Adam's apple, and pushed herself away, his salt still on her lips.

"Good thing I'm leaving tomorrow." He turned back along the path.

They entered the relative coolness of a shaded place, and she recognized the wall of vine even in daylight and with the blossoms closed. The scent that had so overwhelmed her the night of Jerusha's party was now a faint, muted reminder of the last time she had seen Adrian, her sleeping head on the pillow next to Vinnie's.

"Chomp down on it. Think of other things."

"You must have been very close to your father—to pick up on my feelings so fast." She looked up at him, her head cocked to one side, and sweat squeezed into the crinkles that formed in her neck.

"My son died a little over a year ago. He was twelve."

"So is Adrian. What do you think about to take your mind off your hurt for your son?"

"Once or twice I thought of you."

"Did it help?"

"Yes and no." He turned away, parted the vine to peer through.

For a moment Tamara heard a sound that reminded her of traffic on a distant highway, the roar of engines and the angry buzz of tires on pavement. Even as she concentrated on it, it faded away. Insects swarming, perhaps. This was, after all, a jungle.

Thad led her to an opening in the vine wall, next to the trunk of a palm tree.

"I thought of you sometimes even before Adrian . . . vanished. Once I visualized you riding into Iron Mountain on a horse."

He laughed. The first time she'd heard that sound. It had a raspy, husky quality, like his voice. "My legs are too long. I look silly on a horse." There was a cone-shaped hill on the other side of the wall, and a slight but refreshing breeze. A few trees angled drunkenly from the sides of the cone. Several grew on top. "This, I think, is a Mayan stela." He gestured toward a mossy rock, long and narrow, with a corner sliced off. "They used to write on them, like a book made out of stone. And that"—Thad stared up at the hill—"is, I'm guessing, the tiniest of Mayan temples or pyramids, all grown over."

Her running shoes sank into ooze, and she stepped sideways to firmer ground.

"The snake seems to have moved on. Or he's hiding in the foliage." Thad looked from the mound to her and said softly, "Even predators are sneaky when afraid, or hunting, or both."

Tamara knew they weren't talking about snakes.

The mound rose behind him, an intense jade framing his silver head. A breath of breeze nudged broad-leafed plants and separated palm fronds, changing the light-and-shade patterns that played across his body and his face, highlighting pale eyes one moment, hiding them the next.

Backra waited.

Bugs hummed on the dense air, causing a vibrating sensation in her ears. A bird shrieked some exotic message and drew an echoing reply from deep in the jungle. It was a little like Jerusha's party. But Tamara lost track of only seconds rather than minutes. She did not forget about Adrian, but she did experience a certain feebleness in her legs, a wilting of her self-control. Twinges in her lower stomach set off aching spasms like the onset of menses and lit up cravings she thought she'd forgotten the name of.

She shook her head no, but then just sort of crumbled into him when he reached for her.

35

The cool, slimy feel of the stela beneath her, the hot damp feel of Backra above. The massaging of his body against her.

And after all the cautionary words she'd flung at Adrian about this very thing, Tamara didn't even put up a flimsy resistance to his needs or hers. He was leaving tomorrow, and she was powerless. And ashamed.

Not even the fear of unknown creatures lurking in the shadows of tangled leaves and grasses or preparing to swoop down from trailing fronds and dipping branches above could dilute the drugged feeling spreading over her. Not even the thought of crawling furry insects creeping out of the weeds that choked the base of the stela to walk across her bare flesh and probe for a place to bite or sting or poison—in fact, these fears made the act all the more erotic and urgent.

She'd gone past the point of caring about anything more than the man and the moment, knowing that within minutes all the responsibilities of the adult world would return and she'd regret this act as she had few others in life.

Meanwhile Tamara Whelan savored the forbidden just like a dumb kid. His breath. The stab of sharp bone in her back as his forearm forced her to arch under him. The pressure of his entry, which sent pleasing little cramps throughout her pelvis and a shower of sensations flowing along her thighs. The press of his weight on her stomach. Even the harsh prickling on the length of her backside as carved edges in the alien rock cut through its moss cover when Backra crushed her down into it. Just the enveloping touch of him in this breathless muggy world.

Sensual memories of his naked form approaching her on Iron Mountain, the way his muscles had tensed all along his body as he'd held Dixie in much the same position in Tamara's dream floated unbidden but unhindered through her mind. And the little shock of realization that she wouldn't have to fantasize to reach orgasm because she was living her fantasy and with the man who'd haunted her dreams and in a setting exotic beyond anything she could have created.

"I don't believe you're real," Backra whispered.

Tamara wrapped her legs around him, tightened herself against him, and drew him in so deep it hurt. His release came before hers, but not long. Even as she twisted and the narcotic effect streamed through her, the image of how ridiculous they must look to an outsider invaded her pleasure. And when he withdrew, pulled her up to sit beside him, she wished she could cry.

He kissed the top of her head, stroked down her arm and along her hip, picked his shirt up off the ground, and wrapped it around her as if he understood. "It's all right."

With her eyes closed, she could shut out everything but sounds, smells, and thoughts. She could think of nothing to say to this man that wouldn't sound as ridiculous as they looked. He must think her an adolescent. And what would Adrian think if she saw them now? Tamara couldn't face any of it so she stayed hidden in his shirt and his chest and his arms.

He placed two fingers on the cavity of her navel, ran them slowly down to the reddish patch of pubic hair, let them tickle through it and then slip between her legs. She twisted to look up into his face and squeezed her thighs tight together to force him out, but only locked him in instead.

"No, I don't—"

His lips cut off her words, and his arm drove her breasts against his ribs to lock her whole body into the kiss. He spread his fingers and caused single pubic hairs to tug away and tease, and eventually pulled her across his lap until she sat astride him. When they finished this time, she did cry.

Something, perhaps it was a sound, caused her to look up. Tamara thought she saw, through tears and over Backra's naked shoulder, the shadow of a goat running along the side of the temple mound. A small figure the size of Alice. But there was no body to make the shadow.

Roudan Perdomo watched the couple. Their white skin contrasted with the depth of green surrounding them. For all their assumed superiority, these Yankees were no better than the beasts. But he watched their performance with a certain interest only partially puerile. It must be close to three years since he'd held Maria Elena in any real sense of the word.

Roudan turned back to the body on the altar. The gods of the temple had been too generous of late. After all these years of only shadows and dreams and phantoms, there was suddenly a plethora of solid gifts. All but the particular one he longed for. Not even her phantom had paid a visit in too long a while. In his dreams he couldn't find her. Had something happened to Maria Elena?

Roudan did not really believe anything so esoteric as gods had much to do with any of this, but it was a way to explain the impossible and to keep Stefano Paz and the others happy.

He spooned a solution of canned milk and thin meal into the little mouth, sliding the spoon to the back in hopes that the animal's body would swallow from reflex and habit. He'd been successful with about every third spoonful. Roudan didn't know how long he could keep the body alive while its spirit cavorted about. He didn't know how to force them back together, and couldn't reason with even the spirit of a goat. Pouring water into a plastic funnel with a slender rubber tube connected, he aimed the other end of the tube at the back of the goat's throat. The body shuddered, choked, but then swallowed the water.

Roudan hoped the two lovers on the mossy stela would not go exploring, discover the freshly dug grave he'd hastily prepared for the body whose spirit had not arrived on Mayan Cay to reunite with it.

He carried the goat body behind the stone barrier as the altar began to whir and its light to flash. He closed stone shutters as quietly as he could to keep the sounds within and away from the hearing of the interlopers outside. Perhaps she was on her way at last.

As he led her from the jungle, Thad Alexander had spoken gently but firmly about learning to live with the awful weight of the death of one's child, to expiate the guilt, to dampen the grief, and to survive. He talked to Tamara as if she were a child who'd lost a doll or a teddy bear. She'd stumbled along beside him saying nothing, too shocked and guilty at what they'd done and too amazed that a man could be so sensitive and caring—so convincing that she allowed herself to consider the possibility of Adrian's death.

She hadn't mentioned Alice's shadow, but hugged the secret to herself until she could make sense of it, speak to Russ and Agnes.

Thad said he had business in the village and pointed her way toward the Mayapan. Tamara floated along the sand street as she had in her dreams, the sense of unreality almost stronger. She'd actually made love to Backra in the jungle. A feeling of the release of things too long pent up and a certain tenderness when she walked proved the last few hours no illusion. She imagined the women taking in clothes off their underhouse clotheslines, the children playing in the streets, the man hammering a repair board on his sagging fence, knew her guilty secret. And that their shy grins were really knowing leers.

Her head felt light, airy; her legs like saggy elastic. She'd had no sleep the night before. Heat and moisture shimmered on waves of sunlight, distorting the building and people shadows on the street, making them seem other-worldly, chimerical.

She was able to slip into her cabana unnoticed. Tamara showered, changed into clean shorts and top, and fell across her bed, to dream of Adrian. An Adrian who wavered as the shadows on the street had in the heat. "Mom? Mommy!"

Stiff skin that complained when she moved told Tamara she'd had too much sun that day as she walked across the compound to the bar hut. She was still groggy from too little sleep too late, but she could appreciate the unreality of snow in the morning and moonlight through balmy air and palm fronds that night.

Dark polished tables, a black in a white coat behind the bar, and stuffed sharks with cold dead eyes leaping up the walls.

"Did you find him?" Agnes peered over a green, unhusked coconut with its top chopped off and a straw stuck in it. "What happened?"

"He doesn't have Adrian and doesn't know where she is. But he's been dreaming about Iron Mountain."

"Those two guys over there from Alabama have seen you and Adrian and Jerusha Fistler in their dreams." Russ set a coconut with a straw in front of Tamara. "I don't figure there's much chance of finding Fred or Adrian here, but there sure is something funny going on."

"I saw Alice's shadow on the island today." Tamara sipped at the rum drink with little interest. "Except there wasn't any Alice to go with the shadow."

Agnes pushed her glasses back up her nose and wiped her hands on the front of her dress as if she still wore a bibbed apron. She slid Russ a nervous look. "Can't have the shadow without the goat."

"You're just tired. Probably all kinds of goats in this damn place." But Russ returned Agnes' look.

The two men from Alabama snagged some chairs from another table and sat down uninvited. "Don Bodecker here." He said it "hee-ah." "He's Harry. We thought as long as we all been dreamin' about each other, we might get our heads together to figure out why."

Russ leaned his chair back on two legs and rested his drink on his belt buckle. He drank from a glass, not a coconut. "Sure hope you know more than we do."

"See, Don and me figured it out that when you are dreaming of someone who's asleep, they don't make any sound, and neither do you, because their mind's off traveling to dreamland." Harry wore a straw hat with a Budweiser band. Tamara watched the scar that angled up his neck and over his chin move as he talked. It looked like raw meat next to the well-done tones of his tanned face. "The mind without the body makes no sounds, and the body without the mind can't either. But when you dream about somebody who's awake, you can hear 'em because they're all together. But they can't hear you because you're not. Right, Bodecker?"

"I was planning on going home in a couple of days. But now that you are here and real and that mountain with all the tunnels in it exists, I feel like staying and getting to the bottom of this. I'd never get another decent night's sleep if I didn't. Put fifty years on me already."

"Somebody filled in those tunnels," Russ said mysteriously.

But the men from Alabama began telling stories that put that and the subject of dreams to shame. Something that rose up out of the ocean and tipped over boats, blocked out the sun. Something that Tamara couldn't believe—and she'd thought there was nothing left on earth like that.

And she couldn't see how any of it related to Adrian's disappearance. And she waited for Backra to walk through the door. The next move was his. But she listened, doggedly keeping Adrian and Backra in mind to hold on to her sanity. She hoped the stable Russ could make some sense of it all.

Unlike the lunch she'd had with Backra, Tamara's dinner seemed tasteless. Backra didn't show up. She should have organized a search for Adrian, but her strength was gone, and she went to bed hoping that reality and sanity would come with the morning and a rested head. The picture would come into focus if she could just sleep.

I haven't deserted you, honey, she promised Adrian before she dropped off.

Adrian watched the door. A fire burned in the fireplace, and its light picked out the copper in her hair. Her long lashes left shadows on her creamy cheeks, and she squealed when Gil walked in the door. Too young to tell time, she always seemed to know when he was due home. Tamara mixed his martini as he made a great thing of hanging his raincoat in the closet. Adrian waited patiently, knowing she was next.

The same comforting ritual every night. Gil winked at Tamara and feinted toward the mail but suddenly noticed the pretty, plump child and he swooped down the steps of the sunken living room to sweep her up and make her giggle and squeal some more. Tamara had a disconcerting thought: what if their daughter were not small and pretty, conventionally lovable—would he still be so delighted with her?

She looked at the drink in her hand, at the rain dripping down from the window, and back at the fire's glow on her handsome family, and couldn't understand what could have put such an ugly idea in her head.

There was ice in Iron Mountain. The snow was thin and spotty, but ice coated the trees along the creek, and weed stalks bent over with the weight. Moonbeams snapped the ice crystals to life on the giant TV antenna, but the buildings stood dark and empty.

Augie Mapes and Fred Hanley's German shepherd walked on the school playground. The dog whimpered steam into the air, and Augie knelt to stroke his coat. Tamara was surprised to realize she didn't even know the animal's name. Augie stood up and hunched his shoulders, his chin dark with beard stubble. No coyotes yipped tonight. Only the cold prairie wind made sound as the lonely figures of man and dog turned toward the house trailers and Tamara rolled over between sweat-damp sheets in the tropic night of Mayan Cay.

36

Tamara woke feeling drugged and listless. She decided to take a dip off the ladder at the end of the dock to force her senses back into working order, and dug a swimsuit out of her suitcase. She had so much to do, and no idea where to start. The thought of Adrian seemed to tear at her chest with every breath.

Grabbing a hotel towel, she slipped out without waking the snoring Agnes and came to a dead halt on the little bamboo porch. Arms folded, legs crossed at the knee, her Backra stood leaning against the trunk of a palm tree as if he'd been waiting there all night. He wore swim trunks and T-shirt.

"It is about time," Thad Alexander said. "Let's get going."

"I am *going* to do what I came here to do today, talk to people about Adrian." She knew she was blushing her embarrassment over shared memories as she walked down the little wooden steps. "I should have done it yesterday." She moved to walk past him toward the dock, but stopped at his touch.

"You're evidently going swimming. And you do have to eat breakfast. Dining room doesn't open until eight. It's only seven." He bent at the waist to pick up a cloth duffel and a plastic picnic bag by their strings with one hand. The other he slipped around her waist and led her down the beach. "I doubt if anyone's seen her except in dreams anyway."

"Now, just a darn minute!" But she didn't exactly dig in her heels. Tamara seemed to have absolutely no resistance around this man.

"A little swim and then breakfast and you'll be all juiced-up to run around accusing people of kidnapping your daughter while she slept thousands of miles away."

Tamara moved at his side, in the circle of his arm, like a tongue-tied klutz, trying to find voice for several hundred objections. Why didn't the man who'd seemed shy or at least distant in her dreams seem so now? The answer was only too obvious—she felt a twinge of the previous afternoon.

"I'd advise you not to start beating at them before you even introduce yourself, though, like you did me," Backra said, as if tuned to a similar wavelength. "Look where that got you."

She giggled without meaning to, and he looked down from his great height. "A sense of humor. And under great stress." His voice softened, his arm squeezed gently. "As a friend of mine once said, 'You're going to be all right. One of these days you're going to start over. Not everybody gets another chance.' His name was Bo. Bo didn't get another chance."

He grew quiet at that, and they walked along a beach route she'd traveled before with him, but in a dream and in a reverse course. This time she noticed the line of blackened seaweed.

Backra lifted the bags to wade around the fingerlike tree roots to enter the clearing. This time she got wet, left an impression in the water. This time they both were real.

He placed some money under a coconut husk on the steps of the cabin and pushed the outboard into the water along the dock with an outhouse on the end of it. Backra stretched a hand to her.

"Where do I begin? To ask about Adrian. Whom do I talk to?" But Tamara stepped into the boat, let him pole it out until he could lower the motor.

"When I began looking for my dad—but remember now that he was living here on Mayan Cay and disappeared from here—anyway, I started with Dixie Grosswyler, who manages the Mayapan."

"I noticed you did more than just start." But the engine came to life and he didn't hear her.

He stood with the tiller between his legs and pulled off his T-shirt, glanced quickly around the lagoon, and sighed. "No scrambled eggs this morning." He sat to steer, checked the shoreline and then the line of reef. "But she was no help, so I checked out Rafaela Paz, my dad's housekeeper, her husband—Stefano. Drew a blank. And then I talked to Roudan Perdomo, owns the hotel where we had lunch yesterday before we went into the jungle and—"

"Then who?"

"Oh, Ramael, whose boat you're sitting in. It often runs out of gas, by the way."

"Please be serious. You must know how heartsick I am about Adrian."

"Well, then I talked to everyone I met on the street, in bars, stores. They all speak English—a few of them even speak a form of it you can understand." He killed the engine, dropped the anchor, began to pull things from the duffel bag. "No answers from anyone, no clues. Even talked to Ramon Carias, the island cop. You have to listen closely to the various island lingos at least two weeks to understand him at all. Nothing. My father existed for breakfast one day. Never showed up for dinner."

"What do you think happened to him?"

"I think he drowned while swimming, although Rafaela swears both pairs of his swim trunks were still home, or he had an accident and fell into the sea or became lost in the jungle—got mired in a sinkhole. Or at his age he could easily have had a heart attack somewhere and his body just hasn't been found." Backra handed her a mask, rubber fins, and a tube with a mouthpiece. He took his own over the side with him. "Come on in. Have you back in plenty of time to play detective."

Swimming to Tamara was crawling reluctantly down a cold metal ladder into a chilly swimming pool, knowing the safety of the side was near to hand when her untrained strokes took her into deep water. Hefting herself over the side of a boat, instantly submerging herself in a sea full of suspicious creatures, and struggling to put on the fins made her wish she hadn't begun this adventure. "How can I even think of being out here with you when Adrian—"

He interrupted to explain how to breathe through the mouth with the snorkel, how to fit the mask so it wouldn't leak, rub saliva on the plastic window so it wouldn't fog over, how to relax and float in the water above the view of natural treasures, how to kick with the fins instead of stroking with the arms. "It'll seem a little strange at first, but in fifteen minutes you'll feel as at home as the fish."

Before she could make further protest, he clamped his teeth around the mouthpiece of his snorkel and did a surface dive, his fins splashing water in her face. Tamara considered trying to crawl back into the outboard, but the rim looked so far away she doubted her strength to do it without his help. Perhaps for just a little while . . . and she'd stay very close to that boat. Wishing Backra had not gone off so far, Tamara flattened out.

The sound of breakers on the reef and water sloshing at the anchored boat was magnified with her face and ears in the water. The rubber mouthpiece tasted unpleasantly of salt. The rise and fall of the cool water cushion beneath her tried to drive her against the boat. Sun warmed the backs of her legs. Tamara kicked with the fins and was surprised at how far a small effort could take her.

But the scene below made her hold her breath until she realized what she was doing, and then there wasn't enough air in the snorkel. She put her head up, removed the mouthpiece and gulped, put it back, and stretched out again.

White, yellow, red, black, purple, rust, beige, orange. Clumps of color growing out of clumps of different colors. Lacy fans that waved with the same current she did, treelike antlers of hard coral that reached up to her but were far away and untouchable when she reached back, not the inches from her fingers they appeared to be, but whole feet away.

The colors under the sun rays piercing the water were so vibrant they made the lush world above seem washed out in comparison.

For a while Tamara forgot even Adrian as schools of transparent fish —like giant guppies but with yellow streaks along their sides—swam beneath her as though they didn't mind her intrusion. Bright-colored fish nibbled on coral while tiny, darting fish nibbled on them. A fish so thin it couldn't have room for the necessary organs inspected the window in her mask as if to discover whether she had eyes.

Another world of unreality. How could there be so many?

A veritable mountain of coral humps filled with holes and crevices and a different-shaped and -colored creature in every opening. All beautiful, but some were eating the others. A regular carnival of beauty and death, and all the while the rolling motion of the sea, lifting and dropping her gently like a vast water bed. More lulling than a dream . . . dangerous! Every instinct warned her. She dropped her legs and looked up at the surface world through water droplets on her mask. Where was the boat? Panic surged over her, and she gasped in drops of salt water that waves had leaked over the top of the snorkel. Her knee hit something stinging, and she choked.

"Everything's fine. You're all right." A warm body wrapped around her from behind. Why was he always reassuring her that things were all right when they weren't?

He turned her around. The boat was there, but it seemed an eternity away. The sun was still on the water, but she was cold and suddenly tired. "Just kick with those fins. I'll stay right with you."

Backra hoisted himself into the boat and then pulled her up and over the side. "Now, little mermaid, didn't you enjoy that just a bit?"

"I did not come to this island to enjoy myself." She squealed as he applied stinging salve to her coral cuts. "Take me back to the hotel."

"Not till after breakfast. Even detectives have to eat for strength."

"My daughter's life is at stake."

"Is it?" Ash-colored eyes regarded her somberly as he started the engine, and the warm wind felt cold in her wet hair.

He did not head back for the dock with the outhouse but followed the shoreline away from the village. Tamara seethed inside but could hardly interrupt him when he began to speak of the death of his son. In a monotone, husky with an emotion that did not show on his face or even in his eyes, pitched over the noise of the engine and the boat bottom slapping the sea. In simple undramatic words that dripped pain with every monosyllable.

She knew Backra was sharing with her something he'd shared with few others. It was a shattering story, and before he dropped anchor and helped her out of the boat into waist-deep water, Tamara was crying. "I'm so sorry for—"

"Sorry is not what I'm asking you for." He lifted the picnic bag from the boat, and they waded to a strip of beach overhung with jungle and along it to a point of black coral twisting and jutting into an aquamarine Caribbean. They sat on a patch of sand behind the coral point and next to a great heap of dead palm fronds that looked as if they'd been stacked like cornstalks for an old-fashioned harvest but had collapsed instead. There was an odd marking in the sand not far from it that reminded Tamara of a television antenna, and she wondered if some wild creature could have made it. Thad poured champagne into plastic glasses, spread out a feast of hard-boiled eggs, oranges, and hunks of soggy bread.

"But you know Ricky is . . . gone. You saw his body buried. Adrian . . ."

"I know my father is dead too, and with no body to prove it. I have learned to live with the fact. As you must. I'm not trying to hurt you, Tamara."

"But what if it had been Ricky you hadn't found? Would it be so easy then? You said you hadn't seen your father in years. You'd already learned to live without him. He was old. Adrian is young. It's not the same."

"You might start with Roudan," he said when they packed up the remains of their breakfast, but she could feel his withdrawal. "My father wrote in his notes that Roudan was the key—to what, I don't know."

He was silent as he maneuvered Ramael's boat back to the dock. When they'd beached it, he kissed her in a brusque, fatherly way. He left her at the steps to her cabana with champagne bubbles in her head and walked into the cemetery.

Tamara watched as Backra stooped to feed scraps from their breakfast to the little dog who lived there.

37

Dixie was not in her office. Don and Harry had gone diving. Agnes sat in the dining room under a ceiling fan. She declared it too hot to go "traipsing" through the village asking silly questions. She didn't know where Russ was.

Tamara set off for the Hotel de Sueños, feeling she'd wasted precious hours already. Hours? It was over three weeks since she'd last seen Adrian. A sort of sick depression weighed down on her like the hot wet air she moved through. Backra was probably right. *No he's not!* Just because he'd lost his child, he wanted it to happen to her too. Misery loved company. She was disappointed that he hadn't offered to help her. Perhaps he would when he realized how determined she was.

The darkened bar was empty. She crossed to the door of the dining room, wishing the parrot a frustrated "Hoppy burday" as she passed the cage.

"Jeeroosha," the bird answered.

Tamara had entered the dining room and approached a boy carrying a stack of dirty plates before the parrot's utterance registered. She backed out to the barroom and the cage. "What did you say?"

"Hoppy burday to you, hoppy . . ." The bird righted itself, began nibbling seeds out of a whitish fruit cut in half on the floor of its cage.

"No, the other one—Jerusha."

The bird nibbled and ignored her. Tamara crawled onto a bar stool and stared at the fiery-colored feathers until she had double vision and saw two birds. She must have been mistaken, but it had sounded just like—"Jerusha," she insisted.

"Chespita," the parrot answered, and eyed her suspiciously with one eye.

"You wan' drink, lady?" A man stepped from the dining room and slipped behind the bar.

"Uh . . . no. I'm looking for a Mr. Roudan Perdomo. Is that you?"

"He takes the day off. Seferino, he's in charge today. Who is me."

"I must talk to him. Is there any way I can contact him? It's—"

"No, lady. Maybe tomorrow. You come back tomorrow, yes?"

"But there's no time to waste. . . . I must . . . Well, maybe you can help me. . . ." Tamara described Adrian and asked if he'd seen or heard of anyone who fit that description on the island. He shook his head. She could detect no sign of recognition on Seferino's face. Out in the open—spoken flat out—her questions sounded silly even to Tamara. Discouraged again, she slid off the stool and walked to the door that led to the beach.

"Jeeroosha!" said the parrot behind her.

Tamara whirled. "Mr. Seferino, do you know a woman named Jerusha?"

But the man was no longer even in the room.

She turned again and caught sight of a familiar figure in the cemetery. Russ Burnham wandered among gravestones, bending down to read inscriptions. She called him over to meet the parrot. "Russ, I heard it say the name Jerusha twice."

Russ and the bird stared at each other for long minutes, only the coins Russ jingled in his pocket making any sound. They turned away and were out on the porch before the parrot screeched derisively and said, "I hypocrite dem."

"Well, I *thought* it said 'Jerusha.' "

Russ had been wandering around the village asking if anyone had seen Fred or Adrian. "They all thought I was nuts. Couldn't understand half the answers but everybody shook their heads no while they talked. They got one policeman here, and he's on another island trying to scare up parts for his boat. Supposed to be back tomorrow or the next day."

He took her down the street and pointed out shops or stores he hadn't tried. Tamara talked to the proprietors of these and had no more luck than he'd had. "Do you think there's any way we could search the houses?"

"Don't you think you're overdoing this a little?"

She'd sensed Russ had gone along with her this far only to humor her. "You think it's hopeless, don't you?"

"I still don't get the connection between the dreams and why Fred and Adrian should be here."

"I don't know . . . it's just the only lead we have." She knocked on doors, questioned women at their washboards under houses, stopped people on the street. Most of the answers were incomprehensible. "Let's go see if Dixie's back yet. At least she speaks English."

Dixie was not in her office, but when they knocked on the door that said "Private," she opened it. Her Afro looked brushed up and trimmed for a change. She wore lipstick and eye shadow. She stood stiff and proud and looked like a different person. But the whites of her eyes were streaked with red and her voice had that nasal tone of recently shed tears. "What can I do for you?"

"Damned if I know," Russ answered.

"It's about the dreams we've had of each other and the fact that my daughter and Agnes Hanley's husband are missing and we need desperately to talk to you."

Dixie invited them in to her bed-sitting-room without much enthusiasm and remained standing after she'd motioned them to be seated. But she listened patiently to Tamara's descriptions of Fred and Adrian.

"I dreamed once of you and your girl, but I've never seen her or Mr. Hanley on the island. I'll admit the dreams are strange, but what makes you think those two should turn up here?"

"Miss Grosswyler," Tamara cut in before Russ could agree with Dixie, "have you ever heard of a woman by the name of Jerusha?"

"Well, I used to know one." Dixie sat down across from them and finally showed some interest. "But her real name was Maria Elena Esquivel."

"The same Maria Elena buried under the Virgin in the cemetery?"

"An empty sarcophagus. This old geezer came down here from the States a few years ago, married her. Took her away. Like ninety percent of the population of the third world, she'd always wanted to live in the United States."

"The geezer's name Abner Fistler?" Russ leaned forward.

"Abner . . . right. Had a cough that'd make your eyes water just to hear it. Her father was on his last leg too. He was George, the bastard of an Englishman, white as Stefano Paz, but his mom was an Esquivel. Family's died out now, except for Maria Elena. George Esquivel decided when she left she was dead. Had a mock funeral and everything. Roudan played priest and I suppose paid for the tombstone statue of the Virgin. George was dirt poor. He died two months later, and his grave isn't even marked."

"Why did she change her name to Jerusha?"

"Sometimes, when we're lucky, we get one movie a month here. Hollywood oldies with Spanish subtitles. Movie *Hawaii* had been here at least twice. Maria Elena had a flair for the dramatic, and she was taken with the Julie Andrews role of Jerusha. No TV. One movie a month, sometimes none. Some of the locals who can afford it see a movie twenty times. Whole population of Mayan Cay might total seven hundred, if you count the dogs. Anyway, she starts calling herself Jerusha. We called her Maria Elena.

"She cleaned cabanas here a year before this old guy came down to marry her. Must have been writing to each other or something. He asked for her the minute he stepped off the plane."

"He never wrote letters, never went anywhere," Russ said. "Only way he could of known her was in his dreams."

"I wonder why Roudan's parrot still says 'Jerusha,'" Tamara said.

"Roudan and Maria Elena used to have something going. The usual something, I presume. But that's most frowned upon here. Chespita was her parrot. I expected Roudan to be more broken up than he was when she left. He's never married."

Russ was filling Dixie in on Abner Fistler's death and Jerusha's state in a Cheyenne hospital when Tamara left the room with elation. Perhaps Thad's father was right about Roudan being the key to something. And his connection with Jerusha and her connections with this island ought to prove something to the doubting Backra. Although exactly what it all added up to, Tamara had no idea.

She hurried out of the compound, across the cemetery, and to Backra's house. Surely with this new information he would offer to help, believe in her quest.

Two brown children fought over his hammock. The screen door opened before she got to it. The drone of a small airplane passed above her in the still, soggy heat as a short squat woman emerged from Backra's house with a broom. Rafaela, the woman in the dream church that had no roof.

The shock of recognition on Rafaela's face was unmistakable. She raised the broom over her head. The children scattered. "Thaddeus has gone back to his home. He's escaped you, evil one."

38

"This is now the house of Lourdes Paz, wife of Aulalio, who is in heaven, and mother of his children," Rafaela said, and although she'd lowered her broom, she stood at Backra's door obviously ready to fight for it.

"He didn't even leave a message . . . or anything?" Tamara felt a numbness spreading through her. She suspected this was one shock too many. Rafaela appeared so kindly and motherly. If she'd beaten Tamara with that broom, she couldn't have been more cruel.

"He left something only for one. One thing for one who is called Tomairra."

"That's me. What is it?"

Rafaela, whose voice was so soft and look for Tamara so hard, reached inside the door for a slab of stone, the one with writing carved into it that Tamara had seen when she'd followed them into the house and Dixie had seduced Backra. It reminded her instantly of the stela in the jungle where she and Backra had seduced each other, and she had an inkling of why people commit suicide.

The stone was heavy, and she staggered as she turned back into the cemetery, where the little dog he had called "My Lady of the Rum Belly" looked at her dully. "Never pays to be somebody's lady, doggie."

The old man who'd been cutting seaweed with a machete the day before blocked her way into the Mayapan's compound; his sneer had deepened into something more dangerous. His finger traced the markings on the slab. "This does not belong to you."

"He gave it to me."

"It was not his to give."

She dropped it on the sand at his feet. "I don't want it."

"I've lost him," she said to Russ when she met him under a palm tree in the compound. She hadn't believed it when Backra said he was leaving today, and still couldn't believe he'd done it.

"Lost who?" Russ guided her to a padded lounge chair. "You look a little sick."

"Backra. He's left the island." Somehow, without putting it into coherent thought, Tamara had counted on Backra to solve all her problems. Instant savior. He was kind enough to help her find her daughter. Sensitive enough to help her finish raising her daughter, romantic enough to fulfill all her dreams, and rich enough—she'd assumed, for no reason—to help her out of a very tight financial mess now that she'd broken her first teaching contract and wasn't likely to get another in these days of dwindling job opportunities.

Of course, if she couldn't find Adrian, she wouldn't need much of one. Two island girls stepped off the porch of her cabana with brooms and plastic clothes baskets full of sheets and towels. Their laughter danced on the soft air. She could always do something like that, Tamara supposed. They didn't have to have degrees, and they seemed happy enough. *Quite a comedown from a sunken living room, though.*

"You sure do change fast. You were all steamed up about Jerusha coming from here and knowing this Roudan guy, and now—"

"Russ, do you think there's a possibility of Adrian's being alive?"

"After all this time? No, I don't. Or Fred either. I think they're both still in Iron Mountain and will probably never be found. I think it's about time you faced up to it."

"You sound like Backra."

"And it's no use running around badgering people here. They don't know anymore about this whole thing than we do."

"I guess you're right."

"But I sure would like to know *why* your girl and my night watchman are—"

"Dead."

"And who filled in all the tunnels in Iron Mountain. Went in there with a state inspector. You can walk maybe a fourth the way down in the main tunnel, and then it's limestone. Looks purer than anything we've dug in years. And if he ever reported what we saw, I never heard about it."

Tamara left him with his musings and went in to sit on her bed and stare at the wall. She couldn't even cry.

A rapping on the screen door caught her dozing sitting up. A gaily dressed man with the friendliest smile she'd ever seen stuck his head in. "Ready for da bug?" He stepped in with a canister and hose and started spraying clouds at the wood and thatch of the cone-shaped roof. "You leaf, okay? And I shoot da bug."

Tamara wandered out onto the long dock, where the water slapped with a hollow sound against the pilings below. She'd given Adrian up. But she wasn't ready to feel it yet.

When she returned to the cabana, Agnes Hanley stood surrounded by a scattered coating of bug bodies, tiny white bodies with brown heads.

"Don't make sense. Clean the place first and then spray for termites." Agnes looked hot in her gathered housedress and oxfords. The trim of her petticoat showed where the skirt had wrinkled up in back. "Don't make sense, me being here, neither. Fred's not here," she said helplessly. The circles under her glasses had darkened. "Can't even eat the food. Nothin' but fish."

Tamara felt again the extra weight of regret at her thoughtless haste in dragging this poor woman down here, holding out hope to her as a lure. Lunch was more fish, which Agnes picked at and Tamara ate without tasting.

Russ came in picking at his teeth with a toothpick and sat down beside Agnes instead of lining up at the buffet table. He grinned and slid the toothpick to the other side of his mouth. "Found a place down the street serves hamburgers."

"But you can get hamburgers at home," Tamara said. "This is fresh fish."

"Hamburger." Agnes set down her fork. "Show me."

Tamara went with them because she couldn't bring herself to sit alone with the strangers there. She and Russ left Agnes off at a little building with chipped tables in the sand and flies. They strolled on down the street, so familiar and yet strange.

"Russ, why did I come here and make everybody else come too?"

"You didn't want to give up hope. Nobody does. 'Least you get a little vacation out of it."

"I can't afford this any more than Agnes can. Broke my contract. No money. What am I going to do?"

"You can always come to Colorado with me," he said uncomfortably.

"No I can't. You'd hate it. I love fish." She laughed and he chuckled, and then he stood in the middle of the sand street and held her. "She's dead. Oh, God, Russ, she's dead."

Tamara and Russ stepped into the dark bar of the Hotel de Sueños. "Alcohol is no answer for the way I feel."

"Have a Coke, then. I'll try one of them Belican beers," he told Seferino, and found them a corner table where she could look out the window at the sea.

"You in love with this Backra guy?"

"He's gone, and I'll never see him again. And, Russ, do me a favor? Don't tell me everything's going to be all right."

The two men from Alabama sauntered in and came over to their table. "Hey, Seferino, where's Roudan?"

"He takes the day off."

"Sure is taking a lot of 'em lately. Ain't no way to run a business." They coaxed Russ into a game of darts.

"Sure do miss the Doc already," Harry said, and his dart missed the board. "Can you beat that crazy vet? After all we been through together, and he goes off without even saying good-bye."

Russ Burnham's last dart hit just outside the bull's-eye, and he leaned against the bar to give Don a turn. The parrot turned upside down and said, "Jeeroosha!"

Russ turned around and blinked. "What about Jerusha, birdie?"

Chespita squawked and fluttered her wings. A livid-green feather floated silently down, to rest on the shiny bar top.

"Doc's a loner. Probably go back to Alaska and be a hermit in the wilderness. Which—the way things have been going—ain't all that bad an idea," Don said. "I gotta be getting back too. Or I'll lose my job. Been gone too long, the way it is."

"Your uncle fires you, boy, and your daddy'll foreclose on his mortgage on that car lot," Harry said when his friend had won the game. "That turkey never played darts in his life till he came here. Now he cleans up on everybody but Roudan." He sat down with Tamara. "Not like Roudan to be gone so much. Maybe he's sick."

Russ and Don had joined them at the table in the corner when Rafaela stomped in, still angry but without her broom. She accosted Seferino. "*Donde está Stefano?*" She was so short the bar's rim came up almost to her neck, but she raised her fists to beat on it and castigated the bartender in mixed dialect.

He answered her so rapidly Tamara caught only the words "Roudan" and "*diablo*," and something about poor souls high up somewhere, and he motioned toward the ceiling.

"You guys been here long enough to catch the language?" Russ drained his second Belican. "We've been trying to talk to people all day."

"I don't know what she said, but I think he said Stefano comes when Roudan goes and she'd better clap her trap or old Stefano's going to get mad because they gotta help hungry people in the attic." Don beamed at Harry.

"You may have picked up the game ah darts, but your translatin' is pee-poor. She is pissed-off because she can't find her husband, who is sharing some kind of high-up work with Roudan. Probably taking turns knocking down coconuts from tall palm trees. And she thinks it's all *loco*—which means crazy—and that they are doing the work of the devil."

None of which made any sense to a grief-drugged Tamara until that evening when she was out pacing the water's edge in front of the cemetery with Dixie. Or rather Dixie was already there when Tamara decided she couldn't abide happier people in the bar hut or the lighted compound. Nor could she stand another minute of listening to Russ Burnham and Don Bodecker try to outdo each other in creative swearing. Tamara and Dixie had fallen in step, each quiet with her own thoughts. They shared at least one common sorrow, even if Dixie didn't know it—Backra.

Dixie stopped suddenly as a shadow figure emerged from the village street next to Backra's house and slid into the side door of the Hotel de Sueños. "Wonder what old Stefano's up to. Rafaela's hopping mad at him."

The major discussion at dinner had been the fantastic improvement in the food. "Same things are in the kitchen as always, but now Rafaela Paz is in there with them," Dixie had explained. "With Edward P. and Thad gone, she's finally consented to work for me. I don't know if she makes the sign of the cross over the stove or what, but her cooking's becoming a legend."

"Seferino said Roudan and Stefano were doing some kind of work with poor people," Tamara said now. "And that Stefano would come home when Roudan left."

"You know, I've always found those two highly suspicious. But I could never decide just why."

Stefano came out of the hotel and walked to the house next to Backra's. Even at night Tamara recognized the old man who didn't want her to have Backra's cruel parting gift.

Agnes Hanley trudged across the cemetery in her oxfords to join them. "Nothing but sand in my shoes since I got here," she complained, and then sighed and then sniffed. "Mrs. Whelan, I want to go home. I don't like this place, and Fred ain't here."

"I'll check with Sahsa for a return seat first thing in the morning." Dixie turned to Tamara. "How about you?"

"I might as well go." *I'm giving up, Adrian, baby.* "Russ probably will too. There's nothing here for us."

"May take a few days. Radio's predicting bad weather on the way." Dixie started pacing again.

"What's that?" Agnes stepped up past the empty grave of Maria Elena Esquivel and bent over. "Always did wonder what could make them funny markings in the sand."

A lizard, perhaps a foot long from its head to the end of its tapering tail, scuttled across a sandy grave and into shadow. Its narrow body left the spine and its four legs the rib shapes of the leaf-skeleton pattern that had long mystified Tamara too.

But something else still mystified her. "What kind of poor people do you suppose those two could be helping? Rafaela told Seferino that they were doing the work of the devil."

"People on Mayan Cay are relatively well-off." Dixie stared at the Hotel de Sueños. "There's real poverty on the mainland. But if I know Roudan Perdomo, he's helping Roudan Perdomo. Stefano I've always found inscrutable."

The side door opened again, and this time a tall figure stepped out. He swung a cloth sack over his shoulder, threw back his head in a wide yawn, and started toward the village.

"Roudan," Dixie whispered. "Can't believe he's leaving the bar to Seferino at night. It's their busiest time."

"Apparently off to do the work of the devil." Tamara started across the cemetery. "Let's see where he's going."

"It don't have anything to do with us," Agnes protested.

"We spent all this money to come down here. We should look into anything that seems strange."

"That'd be everything in this place." But Agnes was right behind her, and Dixie too.

Roudan moved ahead of them with a relaxed stride, apparently unworried about being followed. He headed straight for the generating plant and slipped into the jungle near the chain-link fence.

"We can't go in there." Dixie stopped. "It's full of sinkholes."

"You've lived here for years," Tamara said. "Haven't you ever been in the jungle?"

"Not very far in. Then I almost got lost."

"I've been in this way." Tamara stepped over to the break in the growth. "It's passable if you stay on the trail."

"When . . . how? You've only been here two days. Besides, it's too dark."

The moon was almost full, but it was watery rather than bright. There seemed to be a vapor between it and the earth, and the air seemed to cool even as they talked.

"Agnes, you don't happen to have that little flashlight in your purse? The one you use to find the bathroom at night?"

Careful Agnes was never without her purse, and Tamara had guessed right—never without her flashlight either. She withdrew it, handed it to Tamara. "Shouldn't we go back and get Russ?"

"There's no time. We'll lose him." Tamara hurried down the trail she'd traveled twice. Once in a dream.

<h1 style="text-align:center">39</h1>

Again the smells of the sea receded and the smell of jungle took over. She tried not to think of stinging insects, crawling things that could twine like vines in the branches overhead. The air seemed thick, and though cooling, oppressive. The flashlight was too small to do much good. The tangle of fallen palm fronds, coconut husks, and wet grasses littering their path made it difficult to move quietly or quickly.

"Do you think Roudan has some connection to your daughter or Agnes' husband?" Dixie asked behind her. "Is that why we're doing this?"

"I don't know. But you said yourself that Roudan was behaving oddly. Won't hurt to look into it." And Backra's father had claimed Roudan was the key to some mystery. Maybe it was all the same mystery. "And it was in here, Agnes, that I saw Alice's shadow."

When they came to a place where the trail was confused by several paths that could be drainage depressions, Tamara had merely to follow her nose. The sickly, exotic scent of the night-blooming cereus dictated their direction. Agnes had a squelchy shoe from stepping off the trail. She reached out to touch a blossom, and put the other hand over her mouth.

"Night-blooming cereus," Dixie said. "I think they stink. Bloom every night, close up in the day."

"Only bloom once a year in Iron Mountain," Agnes said sadly.

Tamara looked through the vine wall and saw patches of things. Of light and of dark. Pieces of a stone building she didn't remember, on stepped rises and coated with vines and jungle plants. And she thought she heard again that sound of far-off traffic, the distant engines and the angry buzz of tires.

"What's that whirring sound?" Dixie whispered. "You hear it? Like wind . . . moving through a pine branch or . . ."

"Sounds like a bunch of bugs to me," Agnes said. "Don't see that Roudan fella anywhere."

Tamara moved to another peek hole, and she could see the moss-covered stela with its corner sliced off. Embarrassment, longing, betrayal. . . . From here the temple mound merely looked like a cone-shaped hill with a few trees and lots of plants angling up its sides, and several droopy palms on top. No stone building on stepped rises.

"I vote we go back to the village." Dixie slapped at an insect buzzing her cheek. "He's got an entire jungle to lose himself in."

Agnes still peered through vines. "That hill looks something like Iron Mountain, only smaller."

A misty cloud made rings around the moon, dimmed its light even more as Tamara led her companions to the place where Backra had shown her a passageway through the vine. She avoided looking at the stela. She did notice the odd shapes along the mound that sleeping shadow weeds could make. If she were the imaginative type, she could see gargoyles and hunched lions and—

Dixie's startled yip had the effect of a gunshot in the stillness. She leaped and danced into the clearing. "Get away from there!"

Tamara played the flashlight on the ground, where the earth moved in a continuous line, angling from the vine wall out into the clearing for as far as the small light could follow it, a flow of tiny bits of jungle debris that seemed to have no end and was about four inches wide.

Dixie stripped off her sandals with a frenzy to match her dance. Tamara knelt well to the side of the tiny river to see a swarm of ants in a procession carrying the bits of leaves and grass on their heads and backs. There must have been a million of them.

"Parachute ants." Dixie brushed at her legs and skirt. Tamara took the flashlight, and jumping over the busy ants, walked to the base of the mound Backra had called a Mayan temple.

She stepped carefully around the edges of the clearing, looking for a continuation of the trail, but found nothing that wouldn't require a machete to get through. The light flashed over something at her feet, and she bent to pick it up. The flash had come from a metal hinge on the end of a bow to a pair of eyeglasses. The earth was disturbed around her, but she could find no trace of the rest of the glasses. They would definitely have to come back here in daylight.

Tamara forgot her caution and stumbled as she ran back to the two women waiting by the stela.

"Find anything, Nancy Drew?" Dixie asked dryly.

Agnes made a little choking cough and traced the flesh-colored earpiece hanging from the bow with a hesitant finger, touched the tiny transistor inset. "It's Fred's."

"Now, Agnes, lots of people wear glasses with hearing-aid devices." But a treacherous hope had ignited in Tamara too.

Thad Alexander tried to sleep sitting up in the air terminal in New Orleans. His Sahsa flight from Belize City had arrived without incident and he'd cleared customs shortly before noon, only to find his connection to Los Angeles, Seattle, and on home canceled by an airline strike.

There were many good things about being out of touch with the rest of the world, but they all ended abruptly when you tried to reenter. The motels nearby were booked. He was promised the possibility of a seat on another airline if he was present for standby anywhere from now to eternity. He waited in line for a hamburger for lunch; and steak, rare, for dinner.

Even the longed-for juicy red meat didn't do it. *Takes a while to get back into the swing*, he told himself, and found an uncomfortable plastic chair molded for humans under five-foot-five. He read a complete *New York Times* and two local papers. That took up most of the afternoon and evening. No mention of weird stuff going on in the Caribbean, just the usual hurricane watch for this time of year. The rest of the world was cracking up as per usual, but nothing like what he'd just lived through.

Eventually he found a padded chair, still plastic, which relieved the wait a little. He scanned the *Times* again, down to the tiniest of items. Nothing even going on in the Bermuda Triangle. *Well, so much for reality*. He dozed, slept, shifted, began to ache in places he hadn't known existed. And then he began to dream, but just in snatches, which was the way he slept. The dream woman, Tamara, looked at him with My Lady's limpid amber eyes—sullen now, accepting death.

"There are always hurricanes in the Caribbean this time of year," he said to the young woman in the chair next to him, who was nursing a baby, and realized he was awake but had been dreaming.

"Really?" She tried to shift herself without shifting the baby. "What do people who live there do in a hurricane?"

He looked at the exposed breast and thought of Martha Durwent and the blood streak running from her head down across her breast in the dive boat. "I don't know."

He shifted again, dozed again, woke again. The mother and the breast with the baby on it were gone. The man with a beard who sat in their place turned a page in his newspaper. "I don't know either. But how do you save the world? Have you seen this?" He slapped the paper angrily and dropped it in Thad's lap. Thad shifted, dozed.

About three o'clock in the morning Thad gave up and went in search of a coffee machine. He leaned against it, stuck in two quarters, and saw Bo Smith's expression, when he'd refused to let Thad stay inside himself, where it was safe. The coffee from these machines was always either so thin it had no taste or so thick it laid an instant coating on the inside of Thad's mouth. This cup fit the latter category, and he scraped his tongue against his teeth after every sip.

He stood at a window and watched his reflection against the night and between runway lights. The lines on his face, accentuated by the fitful sleep and the shadow-shading of uneven lighting, showed Thad what the years were doing and what they would bring.

The coffee had been one of his poorer ideas, and it hit his empty stomach like a fireball. He was soon in search of a breakfast. In the cafeteria he sat next to three men whose manner and dress pegged them as salesmen trying to make the best of a trying situation. Thad ate some pancakes he didn't want to assuage his stomach, and listened to them swap stories, laugh. He thought of his own survivor-induced relationship with Don Bodecker and Harry Rothnel.

In the men's room Thad stared at his unshaven chin and saw the dream woman of whose pain and loss he'd taken advantage, been helpless not to. He put both hands on the edge of the sink, rested his head against the mirror, and clamped his eyes shut. But he saw the gray monster swelling above a maddened ocean, life preservers from the dive boat flinging out to the ends of their rope tethers, shining an odd luminous white against a sooty sky.

He gripped the sink so hard his fingers ached, but saw the empty stretch of water where the *Ambergris* should have swung to anchor, the lone pelican diving into the water in the same area and as if the *Ambergris* had never been. Sweat prickled on his face. He smelled the cloying blossoms on the vine wall, saw Roudan Perdomo against the moonlit temple mound.

He left the terminal building to walk a concrete parking ramp in a night warm and scented with exhaust fumes. Thad had a premonition of his own death if he should return to Mayan Cay, and of the endless torment of never knowing if he didn't.

40

Neither Tamara nor Agnes could sleep that night. Russ had been off to the village bars with his new friends from Alabama when they returned from the clearing.

The morning dawned cool and cloudy, with a stiffer breeze off the sea. They had to shake Russ awake and coax him into waking Don and Harry. Tamara even talked Dixie into allowing her to cook an early breakfast for them all in the Mayapan's kitchen.

"You got us up for this?" Harry picked up the glasses' bow and set it down again.

"That little woman gets on a toot"—Russ mopped egg yolk with toast —"and you might as well give in right now, brother."

"It might be nothing, but it was too dark last night to see that much." Tamara squeezed Agnes' hand. "And it might be bad news. But three stalwart men cannot let us gals wander around in the jungle alone. Can you? Aren't you still curious?"

The three stalwarts exchanged blurry glances.

"I'm not going anywhere." Dixie poured another round of coffee. "There's weather moving in, and I've got a hotel to run. There could be flight cancellations, stranded guests. And I don't like the way the sky looks. I vote we call the whole thing off."

"This is Fred's. I'd know it anywhere." Agnes put the bow in her purse. Then she patted the purse. "I'm going in to see that place in daylight."

"Those things all look alike. Could be anybody's." But Russ Burnham looked defeated again.

Tamara couldn't budge Dixie, but within the hour had the rest straggling toward the power plant. "If it is nothing . . . at least we'll know."

My Lady shivered in the cemetery. She looked up as the door to the man's house opened, but he didn't come out to leave food for her. Instead, another came to lean on a post of the house and scan the sky, listen to the water, fold her arms above a swollen belly.

No birds in the sky this morning, no seabirds screeching arguments over fish heads and entrails at the water's edge. Waves roared against the surf. Even the water rolling against the beach foamed with anger, crept closer to the tombstones.

My Lady could smell rain, far off yet, but coming. The heaviness in the air pressed on her body and ears. She scratched at her shoulder with the toenails of a hind foot and whined softly. She glanced at the other dogs who inhabited this graveyard to see if they were getting nervous, and caught the woman with the bloated belly watching her.

Thad Alexander looked down on piles of dirty, lumpy clouds from his window seat on the 737 over the Gulf of Mexico. The sun shone up where he was, and the cloud cover which seemed to be only a matter of yards beneath the plane looked ominous, impenetrable.

When the jet did descend into them, turbulence forced the flight attendants to abandon the drink cart and belt themselves in. The plane shuddered, swooped, bucked. The captain's disembodied voice reassured the passengers in Spanish and then in heavily accented English. The disturbance lasted across Yucatán and until they broke through to the gray world beneath. Clouds left droplets on the plane's skin, shredded off the wing tip like gauzy fungus. But the landing strip at Belize International Airport was dry.

The cabdriver who raced him to the sea and the little Mayan Airways terminal shrugged off the weather as just part of life in Central America at this time of year. Only rarely did a storm center reach beyond the ring of protective cays and islands and the second-largest barrier reef in the world to pose much of a threat to the mainland. Of course, the last one that did wiped out half of Belize City and killed thousands, but that was years ago.

When they reached Mayan Airlines, all flights were canceled until further notice. A man oiled the slides on the tiny building's wooden storm shutters. Others tied down light aircraft. Thad convinced the driver to rush him to the waterfront, but the supply boat to Mayan Cay had left long ago, just as the driver had promised. He stood on the loading wharf and stared out at the almost imperceptible line where dark clouds met a dark sea.

But the sun shone bright and hot on Edward P. Alexander III and the man creature who claimed to come from the future.

"Why does she keep bobbing and fading like that?" Edward asked.

"Energy waves flaring off in all directions. How can you primitives have formed family and social structures and yet never learned to control yourselves?"

"Help me," the specter pleaded in thought like the engineer spoke, her terror almost more palpable than she was.

"Direct your will to completing yourself," the engineer, whose name was Herald, told her. "Hold all other ideas and emotions under strict command."

Blue jeans, white blouse, arms, hands, and feet in socks levitated just above fluted black coral. A plump, pretty face, a fall of coppery-brown hair fastened with a barrette. The filmy body of a tall, overweight teenager formed in front of them like a three-dimensional transparency. Edward could see foam flecks on the sea and cloudless, sun-flattened sky right through her. He thought he could even see wetness glisten on the skin beneath her phantom eyes.

She rubbed the knuckle of a forefinger across her cheek and stared at her hand, then up at Herald with an awe normally reserved for gods.

Edward knew he was dreaming, was probably asleep in the shade of his blind at that very moment and missing the best light and all sorts of iguanas, but he couldn't help but think this dream had some meaning, something important to tell him. This dreaming could be a warning that he had been premature in reaching certain conclusions in his manuscript.

The engineer claimed to belong to a race using time to transport people and goods from one place to another, a fancy new system running into trouble because the terminal for arrival and departure had to be in place early on in time, and the people alive at any historical period could mess up something called the funnel. And this engineer was sent to repair the system and became trapped "between" time.

"Your understanding of time is too limited, too surrounded by misconception and ignorance for there to be any true comprehension," he said sadly but condescendingly. "The breakthrough won't occur for centuries. But I had planned to arrive in this century at the Northern Terminal. Not here."

"This young lady mess up your funnel?"

"It's possible we collided, threw each other out of frame. The question is, why wasn't the funnel cleared upon my entry, and how did she get into it in the first place?"

"No, the question is, why are you solid and she isn't?"

"As I have said, mind and body travel the funnel separately. She's mind only, appears to be the victim of some sort of accident. It's not the first time we've had primitives caught up in the funnels. We had no idea the planet was so crawling with human life before the destruction.

The system isn't perfected. There should have been further testing, but those who would profit could not wait . . . or would not."

He thought-said all of this with the total lack of expression he'd worn on arrival, yet Edward could feel the depression washing out from him. "The one nonpolluting, nondestructive, ever-renewable source of energy —time. And immediately there's trouble."

"You can't go home? Ever?"

"No. Nor can you, old Edward. Resign yourself." The engineer paced before the fallen blind, and the apparition followed him like a puppy. "Poor primitive child. Her body must be lost in transit."

"No, it's in Iron Mountain. I saw it in bed. And I came here." She began to fade and to wail like women will.

"Control your distress. Picture this Iron Mountain for me."

Edward was irritated by the soft deference with which the engineer treated the girl, while he addressed Edward with patient scorn.

"Ah, the Northern Terminal, I should have guessed. What are you called, child?"

"Adrian."

"Adrian, at the Northern Terminal, or your Iron Mountain, there is a gleaget . . . a something shaped roughly like this and made of a metal substance." He closed his eyes briefly, and Edward received a picture in his own mind's eye.

"Never saw one that big before." Edward crawled around on his hands and knees to draw what he'd "seen" in the sand with his finger.

"Yes, that's it. What can it be? We've been troubled with interference from this gleaget, and I was to have investigated its—"

"Augie Mapes's TV antenna," the apparition exclaimed-thought, and disappeared again.

"Her disquietude is becoming intolerable." Herald actually shuddered. "Why does her imagined form carry so much excess flesh?"

"Some people eat mostly to sustain themselves, others mostly for pleasure. And some people are in constant need of pleasure."

"They consume pleasure? Your world will never replace the one I have lost, old man, but it does grow more intriguing."

Edward tried to explain the concept behind a TV antenna, but had to admit it was one he knew little about.

"It transmits nothing? Why erect a receiver that not transmit a signal as well?"

"I suspect we're working on it."

A wail from somewhere above them, and Herald comforted the girl back to earth and to her "imagined form."

"She's lost between time too?"

"Only if this is our first caught moment. If so, she'll repeat with us. According to theory, at least. If not, she'll be expelled to wander when we repeat it."

Edward felt his impatience rising to equal his curiosity. "Well, if you can travel in time, why didn't you travel back to see what the problems would be before you made all this mess for everybody?"

"Traveling in time and traveling through it are two different things. The first is a dangerous undertaking, as witness my own predicament. And we lost over ten percent of all those implanting the terminals to begin with."

In time, through time, between time. Edward decided this dream man had trouble with prepositions too. "And people's minds upset this transportation system?"

"Energy waves of all sorts. Mental energies, power generation, electrical, micro, macrordial, crescential."

Edward walked off into the bush to urinate, and wondered how the engineer managed this feat in his all-of-a-piece suit. Perhaps he'd progressed beyond the need for this graceless act. He imagined a smirk on the man's face when he returned. "Well, as long as you're here to fix things, you might stop feeling so sorry for yourself and take a look at this end of the system."

The engineer looked up from a possibly brooding contemplation of the sea. "It does need repairs to its shielding. But without contact with the Northern Terminal, it would be difficult to repair it."

"I take it that machine in the temple mound is your doing. Being caught between time doesn't mean you can't move around in space, does it?"

"No one's ever returned to tell us." He rose, his suit moving with him like skin, only better. "If she can be expelled, it's possible that I might be able to send this poor child back to her body at the Northern Terminal. But I can promise nothing—I'm only an engineer, not a krusegan."

"Some of your words don't make sense."

"A gap in your knowledge, old Edward. There are many."

"And if she doesn't get back to her body?"

"It'll die and she will wander. Better for her than being locked in here with us. With your eternal questions. I would like to see your machine, primitive. I'm curious to see if we can leave this beach. Anything will be better than this useless chatter."

41

Thad Alexander's suitcase banged against his leg and swung out to clunk into a sheet of corrugated roofing tacked onto sections of wooden packing case that formed one wall of a half-story shell house. The impact set a baby to screaming on the other side of the kludged wall.

A man sat on a crumbling step in front of a boarded-up building across the street. He had a bottle in his hand, a slouch to his shoulder blades, and a hard stare for Thad. He spit into the gutter without turning his eyes, and Thad fought the urge to glance over his shoulder when he'd put the man behind him. These streets were no place for a lone, relatively rich Yankee.

He was looking for Mingo's Bar—a legendary dive known for its food, booze, and brawls—because a dockhand told him he might find someone there dumb enough to take out a boat in the approaching weather and because he needed lunch. Mingo's was just a block off the waterfront, but he'd been told this detour was necessary because a small area of the city had been washed out in a storm years ago and never repaired.

He turned a corner and found more people lounging on the street, a few even sleeping. No sidewalk here, no paving except in neglected patches. What wasn't shacks or people or gutted buildings filled with blanket tents or chickens or goats or dogs was dirt, packed yet dusty. A poster with a picture of a local politician, one hand raised in an oratorical gesture, his mouth open in the middle of a word, blew across Thad's path, then flipped over and sailed across the street. He'd seen that poster in the airport. But without the inked-in beard, fatigue hat, and cigar that turned the man in the photograph into a near-likeness of Fidel Castro.

Two young toughs like you might see anywhere walked close behind him, one brown, the other almost white. One with a thick straight stick threaded through his bent elbows and behind his back. They smiled at him.

"You lost, mon?" The one without the stick moved up beside Thad.

"I'm looking for Mingo's Bar." Thad was almost bigger than the two of them together, but he probably wasn't as mean, or as desperate, or as at home. Sweat tickled his chest, his crotch. The wind off the sea was cool. What must this street smell like in the heat that normally prevailed here?

The boy with the stick flanked his other side and said some jibberish, hardly disturbing his smile. And then he laughed, dropped the stick, which could have made a worthy ax handle, down his back and into his hands.

Thad held his breath, tightened his hold on the handle of the suitcase, registered the lack of sympathy in the eyes of an old woman dumping something in the dirt gutter not five feet away as the boy's stick lowered to snare a turd, either human or canine. Thad and the woman watched the turd rise, its center mushed onto the end of the stick, and point to the left.

"Mingo's barrio," the kid whispered through his smile, and sure enough, there was a gate with a small sign burned into wood, and everyone on the street laughed in a crescendo that carried Thad, who walked but wished he weren't too proud to run, off the street and onto a short and narrow wooden sidewalk flanked incongruously with snow fencing about five feet high. A heavy hemp netting reached from there to a roped arch above, enclosing Thad in a world between. The laughter behind him died, the laughter ahead mixed with the clank of tableware, the mutter of many conversations mingling.

He had to duck through the doorway, sidestep to let a push broom and the man behind it pass, and then parry a dart with a bright yellow tail on its way to a ringed board. The smells of curry and beer and stale smoke overcame any that may have wafted in from the street. Thad stood still to let his eyes adjust to the dimness and the rest of his senses to the abrupt change of vibrations.

Mingo's was smaller than he'd imagined it, more orderly (at least at this early hour). Tables and chairs were all grouped in the center of the room, leaving the corners and sides free for darts. The walls were floor-to-ceiling corkboard, with dart boards ringing the room at regular intervals except for a portion of one wall reserved for the bar. Young men moved among the tables carrying plates ranged along both arms. They wore green carpenters' aprons.

When Thad sat down, one approached him with a raised eyebrow. "You want food?" He hunkered so Thad could reach the plate closest to his shoulder.

"Two dollars, B.H." The waiter lifted his arms so Thad could slip the money into one of the many pockets in his apron and take silverware wrapped in a paper napkin from another.

Juicy curried chicken, cornbread seasoned with bacon drippings, and a peculiar mixture of rice, beans, and peas in a sloppy sauce. He had the plate half-empty before beer arrived to wash it all down. For a time in that street he'd considered the possibility that he'd never eat again.

"Hey, you'll bust that skinny gut eating like that." The reporter, Ralph Weicherding, pulled out a chair across from Thad for a woman a head taller than he and took another for himself. "There's another course, you know."

Thad stared stupidly from the woman to Ralph and back again, chewing the last of the chicken. "Thought you were in Guatemala City."

"Was. They sent me back." Weicherding put his hand on his companion's light-chocolate arm. "Want you to meet Romana Guerrero, friend of mine on a short vacation from Belmopan. Honey, this is Thad Alexander, the crazy vet I told you about who chases dogs around in cemeteries."

"How do you do?" Romana's voice came honey-soft and deep. Her half-smile left a suggestion of coolness in her eyes, and polite disinterest. Too large-boned and plump for conventional prettiness, she was gorgeous by any other standard. Voice, size, bearing, and dress—she was all of a piece. Black hair pulled back in a bun, gold-loop earrings, simple white blouse over a full chest and above a dark peasant skirt—she neither wore nor needed further artifice or makeup. What did she see in Weicherding?

"Yeah, got back to find snipers horsing around in Guatemala City and the bureau sending dependents back to the States. Me they send here to cover impending storm on the cays. Wouldn't you know? First blow-up that could be news, and they kick me and family out of the country. In different directions. So Romana and I decided to have a last little fling. She used to live here before they moved the capital to Belmopan. Works in a government office."

Ralph was a small man with a large tuft of hair that stood up over his forehead and looked impossible to comb down. He always seemed interested in the tiniest of details while appearing world-weary. Thad liked him, but for no conventional reason. Nondescript-baggy might describe his clothes and body, but there was a spark in him Thad envied.

"You look terminal," Ralph said. "We saw you come in, staring like you just had another fun experience in the Metnál. Let you eat before we came over."

While Ralph and Romana enjoyed a coffee-and-chocolate-flavored pudding, Thad worked his way through another platter of the main course, leaving only the cornbread. He explained his reason for being at Mingo's.

"Hell, you don't want a boat. You'd get caught in the middle of things. Best way is by plane. Get out there in forty-five minutes, before the storm hits, if it's going to."

"I tried. Mayan's not flying. Probably wise to wait it out on the mainland now anyway. Might even be through here and gone by tomorrow."

"I gotta be out there when it hits, so I can describe all its fury in fantastic prose which some chickenshit'll reduce to two sentences anyway."

"How're you going to get a plane?"

"I'm going to bribe Roger, that's how. He's got a plane and no sense at all." Weicherding's smile grew cherubic. "Supposed to meet him here, but it looks like he's gonna pull a no-show, which is not unusual for Roger. So, children, the three of us are going to hunt him out of his drunk, sober him up, and fly into the very tooth of danger." Ralph laughed, and his irrepressible forelock bobbed like a chicken's comb.

An uncomfortable odor, a little too thick even for jungle, a little too sweet. It wafted back and forth on the wind. Tamara waited to see if anyone else would mention the smell. Everyone seemed intent upon ignoring it.

"Way I figure," Harry Rothnel said, looking up at the odd-shaped hill, "is that used to be a good deal higher, but it has gradually sunk with time, until what we are seeing now is just the topmost part of one of those Mayan pyramids like you see in Tikal or Chichén Itzá."

"But those pyramids have temples on top, and stairs going up the sides," Don said.

"Not before they were all dug out and fixed up, they didn't. Looked just like this one. All kinds of 'em still in the jungles on the mainland that haven't been excavated." Harry put his hands up to his nose and said between them, "Let's face it, folks. There's something dead around here."

Agnes Hanley gasped and looked down at the glasses' bow in her hand.

"Oh, Agnes, he didn't mean . . . Probably just some animal." But Tamara had a sinking feeling.

"Yeah, last time I smelled a smell like that was when somebody's pig got caught in a drainage pipe." Don Bodecker looked at the other men uneasily, stretched the tendons in his bull neck until his chin pointed heavenward, and relaxed them. "But I suppose we ought to look around."

"What if it's Adrian?" Tamara followed them, almost afraid to look at the ground. Russ tried to motion her back.

"It's a animal ah some kind, all right." Harry poked a stick at the ground on the far side of the clearing and held a handkerchief over his nose.

Tamara had to breathe through her mouth as she came up to a grave tortured by scavengers. Something black and white where it wasn't torn and pulpy. At first she thought it was a frigate bird, but just before she swerved her eyes from the stick swiping at a moving mass of flies and maggots, she saw a small hoof, cloven.

"Alice." She tried to block the image imprinted on her brain, knew she only drove it in deeper. Knew it would come back again and again when her guard was down. "Alice is . . . was a goat," she explained, and rushed back to the other side of the mound, where Agnes waited.

Agnes had pulled the front of her dress up over her nose, and a triangle of limp petticoat showed below. Her glasses had slid to the lump end of her nose. She looked a little like an Arabian caricature. "Is it Fred?" she asked through her dress, and it puffed out between buttons with her breath.

"No. Alice. Jerusha's goat. Alice didn't come here on a plane."

A welcome wind shifted the air, and the men crossed the clearing, all of them in a curious loose-legged gait. Russ Burnham was green-tinged. The other two gulped at the new air.

" 'Nother grave over there," Harry said in a deadened tone. "This one ain't an animal, but they sure got to it."

42

Edward P. took the engineer back along the beach toward San Tomas, the girl's imagined body bobbing and floating along behind. He knew no direct route to the pyramid. "How are you going to repair this terminal thing?"

"Simply try to shield it against outside energy waves."

"With what? Metal? Some fancy plastic?" Might as well play this dream for all it was worth before he awoke.

"Native rock has been surprisingly effective."

"That's why it's in the mound? That rock had to have been shipped here. Damn little rock on a cay."

"This was once part of a landmass, and will be again." Water ran off Herald's amazing suit. Dirt clung to it only for seconds, and couldn't seem to stain it. Wading through shallows, crawling over mangrove roots, Herald and his suit remained bandbox smooth and tidy.

The sea continued to wash, the trees to move with the wind, while the few creatures they encountered appeared locked in an absence of motion. A hermit crab stilled in the process of crawling out of one shell seemed to be reaching for the abandoned home of a larger snail. A man-o'-war bird with wings about to fold, caught in midair, as if about to land.

"Why are the creatures stilled, but not the wind and the sea? Because the wind and sea are timeless? And creatures aren't?"

"I'm astonished at your reasoning, old man. You must be well advanced for the species of your time."

"Told you, my name's Edward." He was increasingly put off with this guy's manner, a surface sophistication he'd met in some people when awake. A veneer that scratched up when rubbed. "Why astonished?"

"Because I was wondering the same question even as you asked it. Have you also noticed the weather since we left our beach, old man? Edward?"

"Cloudy, cool. On our beach, is it still sunny and hot?"

"I'm sure of it."

"And the bird, the iguanas on the exposed coral when you landed . . . or whatever, are they still moving?"

"Yes, and I suspect they are finding this world as odd as we are. Remember, this is merely a moment in time."

They came to the beach in front of the Mayapan Hotel. Dixie Grosswyler stood between the bar hut and the main building. Even at this distance and with the shapelessness of her dress, Edward could see she'd stopped in midstep. But he turned suddenly to the man behind him and pointed out to sea. "Out there, inside the reef, a boat disappeared, and one rumor has it that it reappeared for a time and was gone again. And when it reappeared, the family was still alive. They hadn't known they were gone. That machine of yours could have done that?"

"Possibly caught between time, as we are. As I said, there are mechanical malfunctions if the shielding material is removed or—"

"If someone ate scrambled eggs . . . food, sustenance, on a boat that disappeared and reappeared, where does the renewed sustenance come from if it's been consumed before the boat reappeared?"

Herald strode up into the compound to study Dixie. "Time is out of frame here. If only I could get back and tell the world."

Edward ran after him. "But the eggs . . . sustenance . . . how can it replenish? Can it replenish? Just don't wake me up yet."

Herald bent down to peer into Dixie's face, then straightened and focused on Edward. "It doesn't seem possible that sustenance once consumed could replenish just because the consumer reappears . . . yet, if the reappearance is at a point before the consumer took nourishment . . ." A crease in the perfect brow? "If the people were living before they consumed . . . would then the sustenance also exist? Because it had not yet been consumed?"

Edward danced on the sand like the phantom Adrian. "Well? Tell me. Once consumed—what?"

"I don't know, but I find that a superlative question." He circled Dixie. "This is a female. Younger than you. But older than Adrian."

"Superlative deduction." Edward couldn't hide his disappointment. "You really don't know?"

"No, but I'll work on an answer for you." Herald studied the Mayapan's buildings. "Strange form of construction."

"Tourist-gimmicky." Edward realized that he'd been aware of a noise for some time now but hadn't allowed it to sink in. It seemed to come from the bar hut. They found the source to be a group of men at the bar, their mouths pursed in a one-note song, a perpetual "owwwwww." The mixture of timbres and keys reverberated like a drawn-out death rattle.

Edward was startled by the expression of intense scorn with which the black bartender surveyed the merrymakers. But that long-expected fear finally caught up with him. And not because of young Aubrey behind the bar. He looked closely at the face of each singer; there were six of them. He turned to the lone woman in the hut. She sat at a back table. "I don't know any of these people except Aubrey. I was in here just last night, and the people were all different. I remember Dixie telling me—"

"Speak in words as you are used to, old Edward. Your thoughts are such an untrained jumble they pain my brain."

"—that most of the cabanas were empty, that she had many guests coming in over the next few days, but that this was a 'dead' week. She had about four couples, a family or two, and a single. And that all the adults were in the bar, while the kids played outside. Some of these faces should be familiar, but none of them are."

"I find something else even stranger. Look at that." Herald forgot his repugnance at touching an aging primitive and pulled Edward around one of the bar stools so he could see what Aubrey was doing with his hands.

Aubrey was pouring the contents of a bottle of Coca-Cola into a tall glass that already contained a half-inch of clear fluid which was sure to be rum. But part of the dark cola hung suspended in mid-pour between bottle and glass. "And yet the wind blows and the ocean rolls. And sound . . . these awful voices of the males here still exist. We have a mystery, Edward."

"But this can't be the same moment you say we're caught in," Edward persisted. "The people are different."

"Known theory can explain the suspended fluid. But not the movement of wind and water outside, not the presence of captured sound." Herald was definitely aspark now, even without expression. "There should be no sound. I so wish I could return and tell them."

Edward left the bar hut, passed Dixie without a glance.

Four white women played cards in the dining room. None of them had a face Edward knew. The three women in the kitchen all wore familiar island faces. But one of them was his own Rafaela. "What are you doing here? Always said you wouldn't come to Dixie unless I died."

Rafaela held a knife above a chopping block with an onion on it and stared at the floor across the worktable with a dreamy but bored expression he'd never seen before.

"Don't touch her." Herald was right behind Edward, with Adrian at his heels. "This is our moment in time. They are merely passing through. I don't know the consequences if we should disturb anything."

"Just how much do you people really know of this 'time' you're fooling around with?"

"Less than I thought, apparently. But I've learned something of time I should have known from birth. There is never enough of it." Herald almost ran from the room, calling over his shoulder, "Let us hurry to see if we can save this poor child and see more of this world before we must repeat."

43

My Lady followed the others along the trail away from the sea, falling back if the female growled warning at her, moving in closer when she dared. She'd never been this far into the trees before. She didn't want to lose sight of the others. She was a village dog, a beach dog, and this was a wild place. But My Lady had sensed even before the others that the beach would not be pleasant soon.

The male appeared to know where he was going, and the two females followed. My Lady could identify the people smell along this route. Perhaps they would come upon some who had food to leave.

There were other smells, too—on the air, drifting up off the ground, each one distinct from the others. The fear smell from the two ahead of her, and her own. The smell of the giant plants and trees looming over her and the creatures who lived hidden among them. And the faint but growing smell of death coming from far ahead.

"You sure this thing'll stay in the air for forty-five minutes?" Thad yelled over the clamor that reverberated around the cabin of the antique four-place Stinson.

Roger, one of the Mayan Airline pilots who thought he'd gotten a day off because of the weather, wrapped a long white scarf around his neck and threw both ends over his shoulders à la Snoopy. He studied Thad for a moment. "No."

The Stinson was still on the ground, but the wings sort of waved in the wind that tossed the palm fronds around like salad, as if the old craft wanted to fly like a bird instead of a plane and couldn't wait to get on with it. Outside, Ralph Weicherding was trying to drag Romana Guerrero on board. Her bun had blown out into a modified bush, her peasant skirt was wrapped around her thighs, and she outweighed Ralph.

"That lady shows good sense." Roger flicked at a gauge with the nail of a forefinger. A sticky needle moved cautiously to the right. There were a fair number of empty holes in that instrument panel, a few cut wires hanging down from behind. This was the pilot's own "recreation" plane.

Thad was half-scared and half wondering how danger could frighten him so much after the eyeball in the Metnál. He'd missed Vietnam, however narrowly, because somebody in Washington decided veterinarians were too scarce in Alaska and because Thad's name had appeared on a proposal to save wildlife in a projected refuge that had never been heard of since. Mostly, Thad treated big dogs and little cats and their winter-weary owners. He thought the eyeball had been his combat service, but it made no difference now. He'd watched his mother die, and his son, and would have expected this experience to matter less. "Hope this thing doesn't have the original engine."

"Only fifty hours since last overhaul." Roger flashed a set of Hollywood teeth. "Many bucks and new stuff put in this old baby."

"How'd Weicherding talk you into this, besides money?"

"What's besides money?" Roger stuffed some padding back into the pilot's seat. "Almost everything's fixed up but the cabin."

"It's the cabin that keeps us in here and the 'almost' that keeps this thing in the air to Mayan Cay."

"You got it."

The door opened and the UPI reporter crawled into the seat behind Thad. "She won't come. And the first wise-off on that remark wins a free broken jaw."

A crony of Roger's released the tie-downs that weren't doing much to hold the Stinson at bay, and it taxied around one of the corrugated lean-tos that served as hangars in this demented place. The nose of the plane sat up so high it filled the windshield, and the pilot had to look out the side windows to navigate. Thad stared up at the haze of whirling propeller and tried not to think about how much he wished he'd had good sense like Romana Guerrero. The Stinson picked up speed. It crabbed sideways in the wind, and he caught a glimpse of marginal runway, mercifully empty.

"Don't you have to radio for clearance or something?"

"What radio?" And pitching palms and a few houses and a choppy sea and the surface of the earth dropped out from under them. They rose in a wind-zagged course and leveled off, clearing most of the windshield of Stinson nose.

Thad turned off his stomach halfway to his throat and swiveled around to the reporter. "Didn't you say you had three kids?"

"Yeah. And a wife and a mistress and two parents and a mother-in-law. Never expected Romana to turn chickenshit like that."

The vibration of the floor massaged tingles into Thad's feet. Mist streamed along the windshield and hid the wings. Cold air rushed through gaps where the fabric fuselage met the doors. Those gaps seemed to shift shape with every buffet, every creaking.

The Stinson seemed to hit a wall of wind, rise for a second, and then fall like an elevator with a severed cable. The motion brought back the taste of curry to Thad's tongue and the plane down below the cloud ceiling. "How're we going to find one little island in all this?"

"Good question."

"Will you quit sounding like a grade-B movie?"

"Then stop feeding me lines." Roger laughed at his own joke, made a gesturing sweep over the instrument panel. "Relax. Some of these work."

They were flying no more than five hundred feet above the sea, the waves frothing below mirrored in the dingy scuds rolling across the cloud layer's underbelly. Patches of rain sheeted out the windshield vision, and Thad held his breath until things cleared.

"Weicherding tells me you were in on that big dive accident out here," Roger shouted over the noise of the Stinson that drowned out the turbulent sounds Thad knew must be orchestrating outside. "Take my mind off our little problem and tell me about it."

Ralph Weicherding had been unusually quiet until now. Thad had assumed this was because of the noise and the necessity to raise his voice so from his position behind them, and perhaps because he was still pissed-off at Romana. But the reporter leaned forward now and began telling of what he'd heard of the accident and pausing for Thad to fill in spaces, prodding him to fill out flat statements as if he was interviewing.

Thad was relieved to find the UPI reporter sweating and pale. Part of his energetic forelock had even lowered to stick to his forehead.

A blast of wind hit on Thad's side of the plane, and they flew sideways for a while. The clouds tumbled down to meet the water, and his eyes strained to see their path through the mist.

Instead he saw imagined shapes. Swirls that turned into monstrous prehistoric birds disintegrated as they swooped and met the Stinson. A colorless semi jackknifed to catch their fragile craft between the cab and the tilting trailer. A giant ship, top-heavy with sail and with a jutting bowsprit, leaped out of nowhere and surged toward them while Thad described the eyeball that had killed Bo Smith. His throat hurt from yelling, and he hoped the crazy pilot was in better shape than he was.

Roger had been putting them on about having no radio. He had a two-way with which he could communicate with anybody he could get close enough to. He explained Belize was one of the few areas left in the hemisphere that had no VOR beacons close enough to navigate by. "That's why we don't fly in heavy weather." He picked up a hand mike that had dangled to the floor by its cord. "This is the Baron . . . on unscheduled private charter . . . heading for Mayan Cay. Anybody read?"

He seemed unperturbed by the lack of an answer, continued questioning Thad about the accident. Rain pelted the Stinson, as if trying to drive it into the sea. Wind switched to the front, and they seemed to fly in place.

"That eyeball thing must have been just about due west of the island," Roger said. "I circled the British ship when she brought those oceanographers out here. That marker buoy you left is gone, by the way. Just for breaking rules, I've been altering my route to make a pass over the area." He peered out the side window, leaned across Thad to peer out his. "But of course I could see then."

"I hope we're not going anywhere near it this time."

"Well . . . as a matter of—"

"No games now, shithead," Weicherding yelled right behind Thad's ear. "You head a straight course for Mayan Cay, hear?"

They broke out of the clouds and were startled by pale, watery sunlight. A channel or canyon between cloud banks, with just a haze of cirrus above. White water spread out in a peculiar fanning motion from under the wall across from them, a wall seemingly vertical that rose out of sight, great humps and heaps piled one atop another, looking like a soiled avalanche sliced clean through the middle.

The Stinson turned up the canyon between clouds, and the haze above lent a haloed effect to the sun, almost disappearing over the western rim.

"You're not looking for that eyeball, I hope," Thad said.

"Just putting off having to chop through that thing." He nodded at the solid-looking cloud wall.

"We got to get to Mayan Cay before this storm turns ugly," Ralph reminded him.

They banked, turned, flew back up the canyon and uncomfortably low. "There's something. See it?"

"No. Listen, Baron, the deal was—"

"What kind of reporter are you? No curiosity."

The Stinson circled an area of sea that seemed like any other. There was nothing above the water but the foam of cresting waves. Roger took the little plane up and then dived it at the spot he insisted they see.

Something white or light-colored appeared for an instant, wavered beneath huge swells, only an outline and patches of its center visible between great lines of angry froth. Thad had an impression of an enormous domed building, but then it was gone.

"Just the way the light was shining on the water," Ralph pronounced.

They circled again, but this time saw nothing. The Baron leveled them out, and they bumped around on invisible air ruts until he decided to turn and aim the Stinson at the cloud wall. "Looked to me like the top of an underwater astrodome."

Thad wasn't that positive he'd seen anything more than a memory Roger was working hard to conjure. The propeller sliced into cloud, and they were alone in an opaque goo that looked like inert gray jelly but shook and hammered them until Thad could hear his teeth rattle.

"Know what they're calling this storm?" their pilot asked happily.

"You provide barf bags on this heap?" Ralph's voice vibrated with their motion, making him sound like they'd just landed on a street paved with bricks, and at breakneck speed.

"They call this one Clyde." Roger's laugh came sharp, cut off midway, and ended in a quivering growl. "How you going to work up a decent terror by a name like Clyde? I ask you."

Thad Alexander remembered his premonition of death in the airport in New Orleans. Ralph Weicherding began to gag in the seat behind. And then to swear and gag some more.

Roger the Baron hit the instrument panel in several places with the heel of his hand and started to frantically fiddle with things. "Now, where in hell are we?"

44

"I think it's Fred Hanley," Russ whispered. He looked sick, disbelieving. "There were pieces of a plaid shirt and a boot and stuff like he wore. Nobody dresses like that down here."

Tamara could think only of Adrian. It began to rain, and great broad leaves and fronds sagged even further. They gathered under protective trees, not talking, unable as yet to make any decisions. Russ and Tamara stood on either side of Agnes, each putting an arm around her. The rain washed much of the stench from the air, grew heavier, making their shelters useless, soaking into their clothes.

"What am I going to do now?" Agnes shuddered within the circle of Tamara's arm. "What am I going to do?"

Tamara had no answer for her friend, could only hug her tighter. That buzzing that had reminded Agnes of insects and Tamara of tires on far-off asphalt sounded from somewhere on the mound. And suddenly Roudan Perdomo stood above them as if he'd risen from solid earth.

He was looking at the sky, letting the rain wash over him as though to refresh himself in it, but he lowered his eyes at Russ's startled grunt. One of the other men swore.

Tamara had the weird expectation that he'd raise his arms and lightning would flash and his voice would be like thunder. That he'd invoke some god to kill them or chase them away with lightning bolts. The gloom, the rain, the violated graves. The whole creepy, sagging, dripping place. Her own intolerable pain. Roudan's uncanny materialization. All these combined to make it seem logical that something fantastic must happen. Something powerful and frightening. Even though the big black man wore sopping slacks and a silly International Harvester cap and rain streamed down his bare chest.

The separate groups moved slowly together from beneath their futile shelters to form a semicircle at the base of the mound. Tamara stood in the semicircle's center, bewildered at not remembering the steps she'd taken to get there, sensing that they should all turn and run, sure they'd made themselves a convenient target for something she didn't understand. The raindrops grew so thick they almost obscured Roudan, made him waver like the chimera shadows on the street in San Tomas on the day Backra had loved her.

"Hey, Roudan, what you doing up there?" Harry Rothnel's voice was soft with wariness. You could almost hear the "boy" on the end of the sentence. "How'd you get up there so quick?"

But it was Don who broke the half-circle, everyone standing so close they touched, and started up the mound as if determined to separate the men from the boys. The rest straggled up behind him, Tamara still expecting something outrageous, still unable to do anything but follow.

Roudan spread his arms across the mouth of a lighted hole and stared at Tamara's hair as the men tried to question him. She reached back to help Agnes up.

"Just what is going on heah?"

"There's a body down there, Perdomo."

"Jerusha," Tamara said.

The rain shifted from lukewarm to chilly, as if somebody upstairs had changed spigots. Lightning flashed, but Roudan just stood with outstretched arms, mesmerized by Tamara.

"Maria Elena," he said finally, and lowered his arms as if she'd given a password and he'd answered it. "There is only a man there now, and a dog. In my dreams I can't find her at your mountain."

"She's in a coma in a hospital. They can't wake her up." *And I killed her plant and do you have my daughter?* But she couldn't bring herself to let loose the hope again.

"Her spirit is lost, then?" He seemed to ask this question more of himself or the rain or the rising wind than of any of the sodden people clustered around him. Red streaked the whites of his eyes, and he appeared to be near exhaustion. "I did not want her to go to that place," he explained. "Why did you not listen to me, Maria Elena?"

Roudan pushed his way between Agnes and Tamara and walked down the hill, head bowed, fists clenched.

"You got some explaining to do, Perdomo." Don started after him, but Harry grabbed his arm.

"You see the look on his face? You're liable to get your clock cleaned. It's not like he can go all that far anyway."

Tamara stepped through an archway of fitted stone about four feet thick. It led to an inner room, where light flickered. The others filed in behind her.

"It's a funny place I don't like," Agnes said. "Reminds me of us going into the mine when we shouldn't have. And look what's come of that."

They stood dripping on a floor of the same cut stone as in the archway and gawked at a gleaming silver column surrounded by a diaphanous glass or plastic casing. It stood on a tiered platform. A smooth, hollowed-out place in a column resembled a shapeless and hooded figure, very tall and broad-shouldered, suggested a priest or a cloaked death figure. Candles in ornate candelabra reminded Tamara of those found on church altars. They sat atop a series of rock partitions ringing the circular room that were shoulder-high with three-foot spaces between each. Candle flames rose in narrowed tapers toward some draft from above.

"Never heard of the Mayans having anything like this." Harry's voice didn't echo, as would have seemed likely in this rock-bound, conceivably holy place. Instead it thinned out as if sucked up into the invisible ceiling like the flames on the candles. Illumination came from somewhere above the column, making the candles unnecessary.

"Your machine, Russ?" Agnes Hanley croaked.

"One just like it." His swallow sounded dry as paper. "There's one of these in Iron Mountain, Wyoming."

Don Bodecker spread his feet, crossed his arms, and proclaimed mystically, "An ancient phallic symbol . . . or statue . . . or—"

"There's nothing ancient about this thing." Harry stepped up to put his hand on the clear casing.

"Don't touch it!" Russ pulled him off the tiered platform. "I've seen one of these, I tell you. It'll send you on a trip no pill or airplane could. Everybody haul ass before this thing decides to get in gear."

Thunder crackled outside, wind and the smell of rain swept through the archway. Candle flames danced. That buzzing noise sounded more like a whir close up. It filled the silent room, while the sides of the archway floated together, shutting in the stunned group. Only Russ Burnham moved, but he was too late. He pounded on the rock, ran his fingers around the outline of a doorway no longer there.

Russ turned to stare at the thing in the middle of the room, its light glistening off the sweat beads on his face.

A doorway appeared noiselessly in the clear casing surrounding the shining column.

"Take cover!" Russ shoved Tamara behind the nearest rock partition, and she could hear the frantic scrambling of the others to obey his panic.

She tripped over something on the floor and sprawled across it, hitting the side of her head on rock. Her eyes teared. The air whined. The light on the wall not shaded by partition blinked.

"Keep your heads down," Russ ordered them all, and pushed her farther into the slightly yielding but lumpy mass she'd fallen across. "It'll suck you in if you don't."

The light blinked so rapidly now it gave her vertigo to look at the wall, and she did feel a tugging, as if the air were trying to pull her around the barricade.

"Don't anybody stand up. Don't look," Russ yelled. "Wait it out."

Whatever lay beneath Tamara was breathing on her hand. The air generally was in a chaotic swirl, but under her palm it came in slow, tickling, moist, warm exhalations—interrupted with coolness during inhalation.

Her fingers groped the contours of a human face.

She pushed away, and just in time to see the candles and the candelabrum on the next partition tip over and fly away. Russ tried to force her back down.

"Russ, there's someone here."

Although there was plenty of light in the center of the room, all was shadowed behind their barricade. Tamara could just make out the profile of a woman's face. And a lock of long hair being tugged into the light and around the edge of rock partition. It was copper-colored, like Tamara's.

45

Ramon Carias hung half out of his sidewalk-stand police station, the microphone of his radio set in one hand, the other in violent midgesture toward Stefano Paz, who stood outside. Ramon uttered an everlasting "Urrrrrrr." People on the sand streets of San Tomas appeared to be in an unusual hurry. Time had stopped them in the process of haste. Canoes and light boats were in the process of being drawn up under houses, wooden shutters in the process of becoming slammed across windows. A local store was doing a brisk still-life trade in kerosene for lamps.

The girl seemed to have settled down and become as engrossed in this momentary world as Edward P. and Herald, but she never allowed the engineer to get too far from her.

"Did time stop the moment we met on the beach?" Edward asked.

Herald peered closely at Ramon and Stefano, crossed the road to study little Yesenia Campos as she helped her mother gather oranges, spilled from a torn net grocery bag, with arrested urgency. "Time has not stopped, Edward. It is just that we are trapped in one of their moments. A moment they are living through at a normal pace."

"Well, if we repeat this moment, will there be different people here doing different things, different weather? Everything?"

"You must understand this is a situation I know only from theory, but I believe so—yes. Every time we repeat, we'll catch a different moment but not remember one experience from the last. It may depend on whether we leave the beach."

"We're repeating now, then, because Yesenia has grown some and her mother wasn't nearly so pregnant yesterday."

"But what about me? Can you send me back to my mother?" Adrian floated in front of the engineer to capture his attention.

"Is she still at the Northern Terminal?"

"Yes."

"Well, if this moment lasts for us. If this is your first time in it. If there is time. If we can find the terminal here. If your body still lives and if it is still at the Northern Terminal or your Iron Mountain . . . I will try, child, that is all I can promise."

A few tourists were out, their clothes and hair caught in a gust far stronger than the one blowing on Edward P. Again he was startled to see captured and covert glances of disdain and dislike for these visitors on the faces of a local populace he'd always thought to be warm and friendly.

"Looks about to blow up a storm. But the blowing is lighter on us than on them."

"Yes, and notice the sea." The engineer pointed to a whitecapped wave of an extreme size to be inside the reef. It broke so slowly Edward could have counted every foam ripple on its surface.

"Was it like this before, or has our movement slowed too?"

"It would be my speculation that we were so surprised to see the movement of wind and water at all, we didn't notice its rate. But I cannot be certain."

"The wind and tides can be slowed, but not stopped like people and pouring liquid. The world's always been wacky, but this dream takes the cake," Edward grumbled as he led the way past the generating plant, which made an extended burping noise. "That's the island's power generator."

"That could be a problem. Is it permanent?"

"Nothing's permanent. Next one'll probably be more powerful." He hurried on, eager to have Herald explain the machine to him before he awoke. Rain fell now in drops so sluggish they could see each one. They felt abnormally hard on his exposed face and head as Edward walked into them rather than having them falling about him as he was used to. He was almost running when he tripped on a dog in his path and knocked it on its side.

"What sort of creature—?"

"Animal, dog, canine, village stray. Hurry. This'll be no ordinary storm if the dogs are heading inland. You've got to tell me about the machine in the pyramid." Edward swerved just in time to avoid two more canines in a paralyzed slink, and he managed to warn Herald.

"Pyramid? This is not the sector for what I think of as pyramids."

"Sector . . . yes, well, I suppose the Mayan temple pyramids aren't strictly pyramids like in . . ." Edward stopped short, and again the giant was up against his back, with the see-through girl staring over his shoulder. "You have your machines in the East too? In Egypt and . . ." He could hear the fact in Herald's thoughts that he didn't know Egypt from Hades, and Edward thought of Africa, tried to visualize the shape of the continent, sensed that it didn't register either, and then formed a mental image of an Egyptian pyramid.

"Early implanters of terminals encouraged the building of natural rock structures to house the necessary equipment. And the more elaborate and mysterious, the more likely the primitives would not destroy them or remove the protective rock."

"My God, man, whole civilizations built religion and ritual around your 'nonpolluting' structures. You've polluted your own past!" Edward stomped on down the trail, truly angry and yet unable to reject the idea that due to this dream, his next book would be a sizzler. He stopped again and let the rain pelt him, instead of the reverse. "Did your people build all these protective structures, or did the people who came to worship in them or bury their kings or cut out hearts and sacrifice human beings there?"

"We merely helped. They were so primitive. Someone had to—"

"Did you cause this destruction thing you keep splitting up history with . . . by your interference? In the name of transportation?"

"There are those . . . environmentalists"—that was the closest thought Edward could comprehend, but it was mixed with the word-thought "moralists" and a sort of distrust—"who suggest this as a possibility, but I noticed expressions among as-yet-unmixed races in that tiny village we just left that would suggest other reasons. Anyone would want to blame a catastrophe of that nature elsewhere, old man."

Edward was already composing sentences for an introduction to a new book, sifting through ideas in the old that he could adapt (all that work, surely he could use some of it), when Roudan Perdomo loomed up ahead of them.

"What good will it all do if I don't remember this dream when I awake?" he absently asked the proprietor of the Hotel de Sueños, and then noticed the expression-in-progress on the stilled features.

Edward was more used to seeing the big black man grinning, joking, laughing in that high, improbable voice. But Roudan seemed not the least good-natured in this captured moment. He looked stricken, angry, grim, and on the verge of tears all at the same time. Muscles along his upper arms and chest flexed tight against his skin. Rain slid off the bill of his red-and-white cap so thickly and so slowly it appeared slightly clouded, sticky like honey.

"Don't touch him," Herald warned, and stepped around Roudan, looking him over from all angles. "Fairly respectable specimen."

"He's still young. I'm thinking he's also one of the monkey wrenches in your machine." And Edward described awaking in the jungle one night, apparently having sleepwalked. He'd found himself near the Mayan ruin, the existence of which he hadn't suspected until then. A group of villagers was filing into a lighted chamber in the hillside. "And this specimen here was standing in front of a silver column with his arms raised and reciting some kind of gibberish, and all of a sudden the ghost of a woman who used to live on this island appeared in front of him and started dancing. I figured these people'd stumbled across a machine left behind by an ancient extinct race from Atlantis."

Someone had hit him over the head from behind, and Edward P. had come to, to find Stefano Paz dragging him past the generating plant and chiding him for sleepwalking.

"Hurry, please. You've got to help me," their phantom wailed.

They left Roudan to his arrested walk and moved on. "If you're so sure your fooling around with your history causes no harm, then why are you so afraid to have us touch anyone or change anything?"

"Now that I'm here, I can see our calculations about your cultures and our effect on them have been inadequate."

"Inadequate! You plop massive stone structures down in the middle of ignorant villages and you call—"

"We had no notion of the sensitivity, advancement, and great numbers of the species before the destruction. We've always thought of you as a lower form of animal, living in caves, tribal—"

"Who managed somehow to develop such sophisticated weaponry that we could wipe out almost all trace of ourselves." Edward P. Alexander was less and less impressed with the mental powers of this future race.

"There was so little left to go by except for the legends that came down from the survivors, our ancestors, whom we think of as barbarians and don't take too seriously. And the time funnel is so new. We've only just begun to appreciate the problems and try to correct them."

They reached the screen of night-blooming cereus and walked along it to the break leading to the clearing and the mound, and an echoing roar that resonated in Edward's ears to make them tickle maddeningly. It took him a moment to realize it was a thunderclap. "If there was nothing left of us after this destruction, how'd you know about the internal-combustion engine?"

It was not until the engineer smiled at him approvingly that Edward P. realized he couldn't have spoken his last sentence aloud and been heard over the ongoing thunder, that he had instead expressed it as a thought, clear and directed perfectly.

"There were a few artifacts carefully preserved by our ancestors." The engineer looked from the broken stela to the mound. "What has happened here? The structure is overgrown and uncared-for."

"The culture you duped into maintaining these things died out centuries ago. I think there's been more than one 'destruction' on this old planet." He had to repeat that last thought three times before Herald got it. Edward had passed the age where he enjoyed the discomforts of the elements. Old bones ached like rotten teeth, and even the insides of his tickling ears felt rain-soaked. He'd been consistently amazed at the realistic detail of his dreams since arriving on this island. Now he even felt the extreme weariness all this dream walking and excitement would have in reality caused him. . . . "Could this machine of yours cause people to dream?"

"The sleeping mind floats freely and is easily picked up on the tracer waves used to transport, especially when the terminals are not well-protected." Herald started up the side of the mound, parting the rain before him, his suit shedding it like tarpaulin. "Primitives here would probably dream only of the Northern Terminal, which should not be too distressing, and then only those sleeping in a direct line with the tracer beams."

Edward sloshed along behind the phantom girl, who had faded to almost nothing in her excitement. He slipped on wet undergrowth which the engineer's suited feet gripped with no problem. So many questions. Would there be time?

46

Thad was never to know how Roger the Baron found Mayan Cay that day, not to mention its minuscule airstrip.

The Stinson lurched out of a downpour and into another, but the break was long enough for Thad to see treetops below them. The stink of Ralph Weicherding's sickness saturated the cabin's atmosphere.

"Are you sure this is Mayan Cay?" Thad yelled over the Stinson, disbelief, doubt, and terror juggling for his immediate attention.

"Well, it's something." Roger fought the wind for the wheel. "A little late for a one-eighty, friend."

He turned them around, and Thad could see nothing now, hoped they were far enough above the trees to miss them, but not so far as to lose the tiny island in the immensity of sea and storm. He'd rarely felt so helpless or so useless. They skidded sideways, sailed forward, dropped, leaped upward.

"Next time I get one of my great ideas," Ralph said, "shoot me. Okay, Baron?"

"Right. Now, watch for landfall, folks." And the Stinson turned again.

One dial in front of Thad had a straight white line meant to show the horizon and another with two arches supposed to indicate their winged vehicle. The horizon rolled alarmingly from side to side.

But once more, as if the ancient gods of Mayan Cay had decided to throw the game for the Stinson and against the storm, the passengers could see the island and its airstrip through a lift in the murk. The airstrip was clear. They weren't lined up for it, but it wasn't impossible. Roger made another pass, tried to raise the shack next to the airstrip on his radio. "What do you bet everybody's battened up and gone home to hold their roofs down?"

The break held, and the Baron fought crosswinds to head in, adjusting the flaps with an iron handle in the floor that resembled a crowbar. "Come on, Clyde, cut it out. I was only kidding."

Bucking palm trees rushed up on either side of them, and they touched down, bounced, touched down again. Thad turned to congratulate the man beside him. The busy pilot took no notice. They taxied, obviously too fast. But the Stinson was on land, and anything that could have delivered them where they were through the hell they'd survived could surely stop before it mashed them all into the schoolhouse. Thad couldn't see ahead because the plane's nose once again filled the windshield, and he was staring out his side window at layered palm-tree trunks when they parted for the one-room shack which served Mayan Cay as a terminal building.

The clearing caused a crosswind that helped to slow their speed drastically. It also weathercocked the tail around and turned the prop into the wind. The Stinson was still moving when it was shoved backward off the runway. It careened along the roughness of the shoulder enough to tip the wing on Thad's side so the wind could get under it.

The wind picked up the Stinson and slammed it against a tree. The Stinson stood upright on its tail and one wing, the prop slicing futilely at palm fronds.

"She's going to burn! Jump!" And Roger was gone.

His body had cushioned Thad, who was now left hanging by his seat strap, staring down at the ground through the pilot's open doorway. There were no shoulder straps. He had no time to think, but must have, because he'd swung his legs down over the pilot's empty seat before he released his own belt and dropped out feetfirst. He grabbed at something hanging out of the Stinson to break his fall, but it gave way with his weight and he hit hard, the pain in his ankles shooting to his knees before he fell forward onto his hands and chest.

Thad rolled over, to see Weicherding dangling headfirst out of the cabin above him, arms waving wildly, eyes and mouth making giant O's in his face. Standing and gripping the reporter's hands, he pulled with all his weight, and Ralph came down on top of him. Thad was flat on the ground again.

Ralph was off him in an instant, trying to crawl away, dragging one leg out to his side, his face screwed up as if he were crying. Thad was surprised to find the pilot lying still nearby. He grabbed Roger's ankles on his way up, pulled him bumping along behind to the far side of the airstrip, wind and panic sucking at his breath. He raced back to help Weicherding, and was halfway to him when the Stinson blew.

If the wind had not been blowing so fiercely in the other direction, the injured man would have been clothed in flame. As it was, the air was searing when Thad reached him, pulled one of Ralph's arms over his own shoulder, and rushed them both to safety.

The whole incident, from the time they had hung up in the plane against the tree, had taken seconds. But each second was so strung out by the fear that seconds couldn't possibly be time enough that Thad was convinced he'd had time to die a thousand deaths.

Dark smoke swirled off into thin curlicues, flattened into invisibility in the murk. Flame boiled and burbled up into the palm tree and hid all but a portion of one wing and the landing gear.

Thad shuddered with reaction as he helped Weicherding over to the shelter of the shack and propped him against the leeward side. Bracing into the wind, he raced back to the pilot, only to find him dead.

The man's neck was broken, his white scarf wrapped far too tightly around that neck; one end trailed back toward the Stinson on the course. Thad had hauled Roger the Baron in such haste he hadn't thought to check the man's condition. That end was badly ripped.

Thad sat dumbly beside the body, wind hurtling sea spray and sand in blistering pellets against his skin. They sizzled on the Stinson's pyre. He remembered grabbing hold of something on his free fall from the plane. It appeared Roger had already hung himself on his scarf, and Thad had pulled him down. Had there been time?

A large section of plywood sailed along the runway, never less than five feet off the ground, and turned into the jungle as if cognizant of its destination and in full control of its direction. Roger didn't blink bulging eyes when grit sprayed across his face, nor close an awful grin over his beautiful teeth. He took no notice as he and Thad and the airstrip were drenched in heavy rain.

Only Ramon Carias and two men from the village braved the elements to investigate the crash. They helped Thad carry the injured reporter to the school, where there was a minimal first-aid station. Ralph complained of pain in his head and neck as well as his hip. Thad left him on a cot in the school and headed for the Mayapan through streets emptied of all but soggy people litter swept out into the open by the wind. The people of San Tomas hid behind their shutters. Chickens in a backyard hen house squawked their alarm.

The roof of one cabana had blown off and lay scattered across the compound. Dixie had moved all her guests into the dining room, where gas lamps tried valiantly to liven up a group of very somber tourists.

"Well, look who's turned up like a bad penny," Dixie said from across the room with scorn in her tone and a look to match it.

Now, what's that all about? Thad wondered as she swept down the aisle between tables and handed him a glass of champagne.

"We're having a storm party. Won't you join us?" She put her hands on her hips and eyed the puddles he was making on the floor. "How'd you get here, swim?"

"Small plane, bad landing." Thad gulped at the champagne and wished it were brandy. "One man dead, another hurt. He's at the first-aid station. You got a physician here?"

A man in the corner groaned and stood up. The Mayapan always had M.D.'s.

"Aubrey, take Dr. Mordhurst to the school, please." Dixie turned back to Thad. "And not a scratch on you. There's no justice."

"What's the matter with you?"

"I honestly believe you don't know."

He followed her back down the aisle, where she uncorked another bottle. He didn't see any of the faces he was looking for. "Where're the boys from L.A.? And you had a Mrs. Whelan here when I left—Tamara. Has she left?"

Dixie swung around, champagne bubbles foaming out of the bottle's mouth and dripping down her fingers. "Is that why you came back?"

She refilled his glass and moved among her guests. "Five of them went off into the jungle this morning. I'm worried sick. Told them a storm was on the way, but . . . Christ, she works fast!"

"Where into the jungle?"

"Oh, there's some old hill in there, and this woman from Wyoming thought her missing husband was there because she found part of a pair of glasses like his. It's all crazy . . . Thad, where are you going?" She was right behind him when he reached the veranda. "You can't go in after them in this weather."

"Probably safer inland than it is on the beach. What're you going to do if there's a storm surge? Will you have enough warning to evacuate your guests?"

"We have storms every year, and I've never been swept off the beach yet. I can't run all these people into the jungle to get lost and catch pneumonia."

"Why? Because if they survive they'll sue the Mayapan?"

"Thad, most of them aren't in good enough shape to walk to the grocery store and back without having a heart attack. If Ramon turns on the siren, we'll head for the trees, okay? As long as you're here, come back in and help me keep the panic level—"

"Siren's down, lying across the basketball court." Maybe Dixie was right. She'd lived here for years, but . . . "I'm going to go see what's happened to the others."

"You'll get soaked."

"I'm already soaked."

47

Herald laid large perfect hands to either side of an arched-stone facing set in the side of the mound and so cunningly camouflaged by natural growth one had to stand on a level with it to see it. "Great erosion has occurred here. This should be buried."

Edward had identified remnants of an ancient temple several levels above this from the other side of the tangle of cereus vines but couldn't make them out from here. Massive stones in the facing separated down the middle, slid back into the hillside without scraping or grating, only a smooth whirring that could have been gossamer wings on air. There were no runners on the floor to account for such silence.

Inside, the wonderful machine revolved slowly. A candelabrum, with four candles whose flames were half-extinguished smoke trails entering an opening in the machine's clear caging, lay on its side, suspended on air, about five feet from the gleaming cylinder.

"Tell me, do you people and your machinery cause disappearances in the Bermuda Triangle too? And hurricanes and . . . ? Why don't you put these things deep in large mountains instead of—?"

"We do, but few are consistently inactive or undisturbed for the length of time we require. Adrian, child, I want you to stand well away from the terminal. Slip behind one of those rock shields until I can decide how to help you."

The engineer's concepts of time might be the find of Edward's century if only Edward could understand them. He'd about decided this dream was like one of those visions of old and that Edward P. Alexander was meant to prophesy to the world! "You didn't answer the Bermuda Triangle question. Hurry, I might wake up at any moment."

"Calm down, old man, excitement around that terminal could activate processes there'd be no time to explain," Herald warned sharply, and stepped over to the stone partition. "Adrian?"

He stood like a half-perfect angel, half-haloed in the light of the terminal, half-shadowed by the rock wall. "We have a problem here, Edward."

Edward noticed a tugging attraction toward the machine as he moved in the other direction to join Herald. There was a sprawl of bodies behind the first partition, and he could see more behind the next one. He could not see Adrian. "Where is she?"

"I must remove these creatures before they upset the funnel. Stand back, old man." Herald placed long, blunt fingers to either side of his head and squinted without wrinkling the skin around his eyes.

Edward watched the bodies lift one by one and levitate out of the archway and into the rain, without changing postures. They resembled store mannequins floating on invisible wires. All appeared to be tourists. "But where's the girl, Adrian?"

"There." The last mannequin had a long fall of copper hair and a thin, haggard face that looked more like fifty years old than adolescent. "It seems her body was here after all, but certainly a far different one than she remembered. Let us hope it survives."

"You moved those people about with your mind, didn't you? Could I do that?" So many questions. It was like being offered the granting of three wishes but having no time to select among hundreds of possible desires or to weigh the relative importance of each. "There's an area of ocean north and east of here called the Bermuda Triangle. Many sea- and aircraft have disappeared without trace on or over those waters. Some passengers on others have found they'd lost periods of time or that time had speeded up somehow. Directional instrumentation was fouled up as well. Could a machine like this cause these things?"

"Probably a space port. There's one not far from here, and much more powerful than an ordinary terminal." Herald pressed various areas on the wall where Edward could see nothing, and the stones whispered in from each side to fill up the arch.

"Space port? Have you discovered life on other planets? Has it discovered us?"

"Be still a moment, old Edward. I have work to do, and little to do it with." Herald laid his forehead against one of the stones of the arch. His body tensed under his magic suit.

Edward waited impatiently, trying to decide which question to demand he answer first. Had Edward begun to speak with his thoughts because of something the engineer did to him, or had he always had this ability but never concentrated on its use before?

Did those who "implanted" the terminals, and then couldn't get back to the future, did they show the Mayans or some select priests how to calculate, how to divine their magnificent calendar? Oh—and this was the most exciting of all—the stela outside. Could Herald decipher the carved language for Edward? Wouldn't Edward P. Alexander be the envy of all those dried-up scholars who'd laughed—

"Edward! No . . . control your emotions!" But Herald, the time engineer from the future, disappeared as he spoke, and so did the silvery machine . . . and the room . . . and everything else.

*   *   *

Tamara fought beneath Russ Burnham, trying to push up far enough to get a look at the person who was under her. Whoever it was, she had Adrian's hair, but the face and what she could feel of the body were far too slender. Their struggles knocked over a bowl next to the pallet on which the woman lay, spilling gritty contents onto the stone floor, and the overturned bowl began to slide past Tamara's face toward the break in the partitions. She grabbed it, sniffed it, ran a finger around its rim, and licked her finger. Sweetened cornmeal and mashed banana. "Russ, I think this is Adrian. I think Roudan's been trying to force-feed her."

He moved off her to flatten himself at her side, and had to pull a long-handled spoon and a section of clear tubing with a small plastic funnel on the end out from under him. "She'd have to have water first. Bet that's what this is for. I saw the same setup on Abner Fistler's night table the day he died."

"Choked to death, didn't he? Because Jerusha was trying to feed him when he was unconscious?"

"I thought it was the emphysema that choked him, but . . ."

Tamara lay on soaking weeds instead of the pallet. She began to slide down the side of the temple mound headfirst. She pushed herself into a sitting position. At first she thought the tortured cries were her own. But it was Agnes Hanley, crouched a few feet above, her hands over her head as if she were still behind the stone barrier. Other forms appeared through a veil of rain, in various postures of unfolding or tumbling or sliding. A patter of surprised swearing mixed with Agnes' wailing. Tamara crawled past her up the hillside on her hands and knees, rain and wind pelting her, toward one form—completely stilled and lighter in color than the others.

The woman's eyes opened as Tamara reached her, and then closed against the rain. Tamara leaned over to shield her. "Adrian?"

Wind-whipped branches and sucking mud slowed Thad's progress on the trail. Coconuts crashed in a deadly shower all around him. He almost stepped on the dog before he saw her wandering aimlessly along the path. He could feel her disorientation and fear. *My Lady?*

She allowed him to pick her up, without growling or snapping, just a shivering acceptance that reminded him of the dream woman at the temple mound. Cradling the dog in his arms, he started running, only to be brought up short by a near-miss head-on collision with Roudan Perdomo.

"Are you coming from the mound? Is she there?"

"Your woman? Yes, backra, and a crowd of others." He stood slack, reeling with the wind. "Go to her, and may you both fry in hell."

Roudan staggered past Thad and was lost in the rain.

There was indeed a crowd assembled before the temple mound, a soggy, wilted crowd. Tamara sat holding the head of a woman in a long white nightgown who lay stretched out on the stela.

But before he could reach her, Don Bodecker slid down the mound and rushed him. "Doc? God, I'm glad to see you. When did you get back? The door's gone. Harry, the Doc's here!"

"What door?"

"The door into the hill there."

The rain lightened suddenly, the wind calmed perceptibly, and the dream woman took no notice of him. She had eyes only for the form reclining on the stela.

Harry Rothnel embraced him and My Lady. "Oh, Doc, you got your doggy. Listen, we saw your daddy's machine. I'm reconsidering his stories about ancient civilizations, you better bet. Sucked my Budweiser hat right off my head. Somebody thousands of years ago is probably wearing it right now. We can't find the way back into the mound. It's so good to see you, boy. And all of a sudden we were outside. All I want now's to get back to Mobile. I can't take any more." Harry kissed Thad's cheek.

Thad had witnessed a man's death today. He'd survived a plane crash. He couldn't remember when he'd last had decent sleep. His double lunch at Mingo's had left him already. Don and Harry did not look the same when soaked by Hurricane Clyde as they did all wet in the Metnál.

The rain had almost stopped. My Lady grew restless in his arms. The temple mound looked the same, but Thad found he had no trouble believing it contained some ancient machine. He'd joined the cockeyed set his father had belonged to. "Did you see any signs my dad had been in there?"

"No. But there are graves around here, Doc. Wouldn't hurt to have the authorities in to search for him. Strangest part is, we found the persons these people came down to look for. One dead over yonder and one half-dead in this room with the machine."

Thad's dream woman didn't even seem happy to see him. "I told you she wasn't dead," she said, her look menacing. "What did you come back for, your dog?"

It was hard to believe this skeleton with skin was the same heavy girl Thad had seen in his dreams, but he supposed a mother would know. A man with short-cropped hair knelt on the other side. Thad felt along a sunken neck to find a weakened pulse. "We'd better get her to some shelter, fast."

When the man lifted her, she folded up like a bag of sticks, but she opened her eyes. "Mom?" Her voice was weak. Thad was amazed she could be conscious at all.

"Oh, baby, I'm here." Tamara Whelan walked beside them out of the clearing without a backward glance for Thad.

48

The eye of Hurricane Clyde passed seventy-five miles east of the island of Mayan Cay, turned, and slammed into Yucatán. It shattered three of the flimsy cabanas of the Mayapan Hotel, but the destruction to San Tomas generally was minimal—downed palms, roofs missing, damaged fishing boats. Some strings of lobster pots were torn loose outside the lagoon.

No storm surge washed in over the reef to smash villagers under a wall of water and carry them out to sea, as Thad had feared. "What did I tell you? Both you and the dogs were wrong," Dixie chided him. "Can't count on anything in life. Not even the worst."

"It'll never fly," Ralph Weicherding declared when Harry explained the room and the cylinder in the mound and how it tied in with Edward P. Alexander's theories of an ancient superrace.

Investigators found nothing more than a previously undiscovered ruin, probably of Mayan origin, at the mound, and no more burials in the clearing.

"The old gods are angry and won't show themselves to backras," was all they could pry from Stefano Paz.

Roudan Perdomo had simply disappeared. Thad and the boys from L.A. ganged up on Seferino Munoz and finally badgered him into admitting he'd seen the "altar" in the mound. That Roudan had promised to someday discover its secret and be able to send him and the others who wanted to go to the United States by way of it. Roudan claimed to have already sent objects to Maria Elena in the United States, and said he and Maria Elena were experimenting to secretly send people as well. The couple would soon be reunited, and rich from the fare they would charge.

Dr. Mordhurst diagnosed Adrian Whelan's condition as critical, and she and her mother were airlifted to a hospital in Miami. He and his wife flew to New Orleans with Ralph Weicherding, who'd suffered a hip injury and a crushed disc in the crash of the Stinson.

Dixie managed to coax seat space with Sahsa for her guests over the next few days, including Thad, Russ, and the boys from L.A. The Mayapan would close for repairs.

On the day after the last of her guests departed, she took some scraps from her lunch into the cemetery on the beach and laid them near Thad's stray. "Promised our erstwhile friend you wouldn't starve."

The little dog was becoming quite tame with all this spoiling, even came close enough to sniff Dixie's sandal after it had eaten. "Next thing I know, you'll be following me home. Then what'll I do?"

The hotel *would* be awfully lonesome for a while.

Sounds of hammers and power saws from every direction. It couldn't be called a flurry of activity—nothing flurried here but an occasional weather front; still, it was obvious that the village was under repairs as well as the Mayapan. Scaffolding was even going up around the church. Padre Roudales would be stunned. That church had stood unfinished since before Dixie had come to the island. All she'd been able to gather was that the villagers had started it and then lost interest. Because of the "old gods" Stefano had spoken of?

A halfhearted investigation of the temple mound was still in progress. The body of the man found there had been shipped home with his widow. Dixie knew things would quiet down now that those involved were gone. But archaeologists might well be interested in the new ruin found in the jungle. It was certainly more accessible than those lost in rain jungles on the mainland. And parties of researchers and diggers would have to eat, drink, sleep somewhere. The village was so close to the mound, it would be silly to put tents up on the mucky ground of the island's interior.

She eyed the Hotel de Sueños and wondered what were the chances of buying it up cheap. Was Roudan dead?

Dixie Grosswyler had been so lost in thought, it wasn't until she turned to leave that the jarring colors of the funeral wreath registered fully. It was shaped of gaudy orange mums, bright carmine roses, Chinese-yellow daisies—all with uniform forest-green leaves and stems, and mercifully muted with dust. This plastic monstrosity had hung from a beam of a general-merchandise store in the village for the last two years. Now it lay across the empty sarcophagus of Maria Elena Esquivel.

Epilogue

A Time to Live

1

Augie Mapes rolled up a newspaper whose headlines screamed "Mother Claims Dreams Told Her Where to Find Missing Daughter!" Then he unrolled it again for one last peek at the picture of the little schoolteacher and poor old Agnes Hanley. They looked decidedly frazzled. "Dreams Tell Widow of Location of Night Watchman's Body!"

He didn't reread the article, which hinted at "reported extraterrestrial dream machines implanted in a Wyoming mountain and a Mayan ruin." It wasn't a local paper, but one of those weekly things out of California that went in for goofy news and lawsuits and usually dwelt on the scandalous lives of movie stars or the cancer-curing powers of ground-up avocado pits.

Augie rolled up the newspaper again, smacked a recalcitrant hen on the tail feathers with it. He paused to wonder where they had buried Jerusha Fistler's wasted body. "Come on, chickies. Built you a whole new beautiful house down at my place."

He'd visited Deloris Hope the night before and learned of Jerusha's passing. The new hen house had been ready for days and was built of pilfered materials from the abandoned mining settlement. The Hanleys' dog followed him instead of chasing chickens like any other self-respecting German shepherd would have. Augie had named him D.D. for "dumb dog," but enjoyed his company in this empty place.

Suddenly D.D. yipped and tore off past him, knocking over a few grouchy chickens in his scramble, and was gone. And Jerusha the witch walked through her closed back door and floated sightlessly over the steps in the heavy coat she'd worn when Russ Burnham and Saul had dragged her unconscious from the mine. Although transparent, her face was fully fleshed and not the wizened-mummy face he'd last seen her wear in a Cheyenne hospital.

"Ghosts don't like TV!" Augie yelled at her, and raced after D.D. and the chickens, slipping on snow and ice, past windows where curled brown tentacles were all that was left of the once-lush cereus vine.

2

Adrian Whelan lay in a white room, in a bed with bars at the sides, bottles with tubes hanging upside down.

Gilbert Whelan, her father, sat by her bedside and watched her sleep. The doctors had told him she would recover, but she looked so old, so emaciated. Her cheeks were hollow, her eyes sunken in dark shadows. He couldn't believe that she'd once been forty pounds overweight or in the other nonsense her mother claimed to be true.

As for Adrian, her dreams now were not of a Caribbean island but of Big Macs and french fries, pecan pies and frosted doughnuts, banana splits with three kinds of topping, boxes of chocolates with cream fillings, and sugar-coated cereals.

Her hospital room was on the ground floor, and outside it was a walkway covered with flowering vines that fought nearby traffic for the dirty air. Tamara strolled this walkway with Thad Alexander.

"The doctors say it's delirium, Gil says she's lost her mind—she keeps babbling about a giant in a pink suit and a tall silver machine. But I saw that machine too, and I don't know what to tell her. I feel like the walking wounded myself."

"You'll never be able to explain things to her you can't explain to yourself. She's young and will get interested in other problems as she grows, be bothered by an occasional nightmare perhaps. It's us I'm worried about. We don't have the time to learn to live with our dreams that she does."

"So what do you suggest, Dr. Backra?"

"I suggest, dream woman, that we combine our dreams and our—"

"Adrian's going to be a pickle to raise. She would have been even before all this happened."

"She might not like Alaska. It can be a very cold and shut-in place most of the year. We might consider a warmer climate."

"Not tropical, not full of sand and frigate birds and heat and steam and—"

"How about a place that's a little less lonely than those we've known?" He bent to hold her and picked her up off the walkway in the process. "And maybe just a trifle steamy."

3

It was an almost automatic thing for Edward P. Alexander III to be walking along assuming his mind was concentrating on his journey and to discover instead that it was reworking an awkward sentence he'd written earlier in the day: "*The bane of science, like that of religion, is not that which it explains but all that which it ignores.*" No. Too many "*thats.*" How about: "*. . . rather that which it ignores?*" He was still stuck with the excess "that." Edward was on his way to a point of craggy coral at the very tip of one end of the island.

He arrived at last, camera and film dry, and set to reconstructing the blind he'd built several days before but which had fallen over—merely a batch of palm fronds stacked in such a way as to provide shade, hide his rather large form, and offer a suitable hole through which to poke a camera lens.

He had come to photograph an iguana.

4

In the sea off the coast of Belize in Central America, in a region known as the Metnál, a depression in the ocean floor began to move and to swell. Sand trembled for a mile around it, and a shock wave sent fish fleeing in an even wider circle, disturbed underwater currents, created new ones. Coral banks that had taken hundreds of years to build crumbled, killing countless small creatures that fed upon it, promising to starve others who had fled but could return to nothing.

The depression became a mound and remained so for several hours. The disturbances under the sea calmed. But wary sea life continued to give the area a wide berth.

The sands moved again, some particles trickled down the surface of the mound, others floated slowly upward. Dark gray patches appeared between sand ruffles now—shiny, moist-looking. Sound waves, shocking and intense, jagged toward the surface, growing silent when they broke it—but stronger. They gathered in the cloud clusters from the horizons. The clouds increased in size and darkened, while a metallic dome split the sea beneath it. Water churned around it. Even before the dome had fully emerged, a section of its roof parted and an invisible tracer reached across the heavens to guide and welcome home weary travelers of another time.

An Eastern Airlines L-1011, Flight 781, en route from San Juan to Miami and filled with human creatures who had taken thousands of years to evolve to their imperfect state, vanished in an instant.